CHAPTER ONE

IT WAS ONLY a slap, and hardly worth dying over.

But at the moment it landed against the girl's face, the Red Line subway train was rolling fast, and its clatter and rattle should have deafened the passengers to anything else. A hard slap, then. Almost brutal. And as it fell, at least two dozen heads jerked up and turned to look. At least a dozen of them were men.

It was a plump white girl in shorts and a tank top that left her belly exposed. The left side of her unfinished adolescent face glowed red where she'd been struck. A thin, brutish white man in a Boston Celtics jersey and jeans loomed above her, swaying with the roll of the car. The hand that had slapped the young woman clutched at an overhead stanchion for support.

It had only been the one slap. Not two blows, or more. Not a real beating. For ten seconds or so, no words. Then one by one, the witnesses lowered their eyes to the news headlines and video games on the screens of their smartphones.

Weldon Drake almost did the same. He had been reading *Recode* just then, an article about yet another social media startup promising to offer all the pleasures of Facebook, only this time with privacy. Such stories always amused Drake. And so he'd been on the verge of returning to the story when for no particular reason, he took a last glance at the female who'd been slapped.

There was no blood and hardly a mark. But their eyes met and for just a moment Drake saw fear, desperation, need.

spectrum

Or so it seemed to him. Even after long practice, he still found it difficult to read emotions. Mostly, he correlated facial expressions with recent events—a woman just slapped by a man might be expected to feel the emotions that Drake believed he saw. And so he trusted his perceptions. The woman was shocked by what the man had done, terrified of what he might do next, too frightened to do anything but plead with her eyes.

Drake did not care. Still, he knew that he ought to care, that Pastor Rink would expect it of him. So Drake rose to his feet. Rocking against the motion of the train, he swayed over to the couple. He had no eyes for the woman. Just the young man who'd struck her and might strike her again.

The assailant saw African skin, short-cut hair going gray, a cheap sport jacket, and even cheaper slacks. Nothing memorable except the gentle smile, with one eyebrow slightly raised. It was as if something funny had just happened or was about to.

The man in the Celtics shirt—a kid, really, not much more—turned toward him, loosed his hold on the stanchion, curled fingers into fists. "What you want?"

"Excuse me," Drake replied and pointed at the man's feet. "Couldn't help noticing. Nice shoes." The voice was a magpie chirp, and as he spoke, Drake's head cocked to one side in an attitude of wonder.

"They're just shoes," said the kid. He was a little older than the girl, but still a youth, and his face bore fading traces of last year's innocence. "What do you care?" he stuttered out.

"Just admiring the Bin 23s," said Drake. "Very nice indeed."

Drake's tastes ran to wingtips. But the kids at church had schooled him a little. He'd guarded them one night while they slept outside the Foot Locker in Downtown Crossing, dreaming of the next day's shipment of collectable kicks.

He didn't recognize the white guy's shoes. But they were clean, unscuffed, newly bought. And it seemed unlikely the young man had anything else to boast about, not even his girlfriend.

So start there, Drake decided. Get him talking so he'd turn his mind and fists away from the woman. Keep him talking till the next stop, where some new distraction might end the confrontation altogether. Or maybe

2

POWER IN THE BLOOD

HIAWATHA BRAY

ADAMANT BOOKS

Copyright © 2021 by Hiawatha Bray,
Adamant Books

First paperback edition October 2021

Book design by Kelly M. Carter

ISBN 978-0-578-94324-4 (paperback)

ISBN 9780578943251 (ebook)

www.hiawathabray.com

For Nehemiah Bray

there'd be a subway cop on the platform.

"These ain't Bin 23s," the kid grunted. His voice was hesitant, perhaps even abashed. Maybe he was embarrassed by his poverty. In any case, he was thinking about shoes now and the odd brown magpie confronting him. Not about the young girl, or about the progress of the train.

"You sure? I thought they looked just like that."

"Look, man, maybe you should just mind your own business."

"Oh, come on. I just like the shoes. What did they set you back? A couple hundred?"

"No, man, five hundred. They were on sale. Now why don't you go someplace and sit down."

"Standing room only," Drake absurdly replied. His own vacated seat remained empty as did several others besides. But Drake spoke without malice, affecting an attitude of clueless jollity. *Awfully Knowing*

The woman stared up at Drake, her tearstained face conveying wariness rather than gratitude. It was as if she hardly believed in the existence of a rescuer. No doubt she was a veteran of many such skirmishes and had already thought out the terms of an armistice. Make-up sex was part of the deal. In Drake's experience, stifled resentment made a poor aphrodisiac, but to each his own.

Drake gestured at the girlfriend. "Good of you to give this young lady your seat." In his voice there was contempt for the white man, and Drake realized at once that he'd gone wrong.

Even so, the punch took Drake by surprise. The man's fist crashed into the side of his head with the force of a thrown brick.

Drake hadn't been punched in twenty years. For a second or so the sheer novelty of it thrilled him and overwhelmed the shock and pain. But then came the surging ache of the blow and a haze that seemed to dim his vision and slow his mind, and Drake realized that he was in a fight, that no one would help, and he'd have to stand or fall.

He was still on his feet and determined to stay there. He wobbled to his full height, fending off the impact of the blow and the sway of the train. Before him, the white guy stood, hands raised in defense, but only just, as if he weren't really expecting a counterstrike. As Drake straightened out, the kid's eyes showed surprise, as if Drake had risen from the dead.

It was the white kid's best shot, Drake realized. It was the sucker punch that had ended every fight he'd ever fought. And there he was, a thirty-something deskbound journalist, still standing. Drake tasted blood between his teeth and savored it. In his madness, he half-wondered if he'd find a lightning-shaped scar on his forehead tomorrow morning. He was the boy who'd lived!

Then his head cleared, and he saw the white guy rearing back for another blow. There was no skill or martial training on display. He was young and hard, and that was all he'd ever needed against girlfriends and drunks.

Drake knew he'd been lucky; another blow like the first and the fight was over. He had to hit back, but he wasn't sure how. For years he'd punched nothing tougher than the Shift key. So he ran at the man, head down, ducking beneath his flailing right hand, and slammed him into one of the subway car's steel stanchions.

The air huffed out of the guy, and then he was squirming and thrashing, his fists pummeling against Drake's side and back, while Drake, his arms wrapped around the stanchion and his feet thrust out behind him, tried to crush the man against the metal pole.

He'd never win a fight this way, Drake realized. With the side of his head pressed against his attacker's chest, he looked out at his fellow passengers. All eyes were on them. There was alarm on a few of the faces, but most displayed a cool, appraising attitude, as if they hadn't quite decided who to root for.

Drake tried to sway the crowd. "911!" he gasped, his voice throbbing out the number as the kid pummeled his ribs. "Call 911!"

He had mixed feelings about the cry for help. There he was, a black man fighting with a white one. When the cops met the train at an upcoming stop, he couldn't count on a hero's welcome. On the other hand, his cry for the police might convince some of the passengers that he was the victim and not the assailant. There was even an outside chance that one of them might offer help.

Nobody moved.

Drake lurched forward hard, pinning the man a little tighter against the stanchion in order to get a split second of leverage. Then he slid down the man's chest and crotch and before he could react, grabbed his left leg and shoved. The man toppled full length on the floor of the car.

Drake flung himself atop the kicking, flailing man, struggling to pin down his arms. But the man continued to flail and heave, trying to buck him off. Only one thing to do: hit back. Yet Drake dreaded the idea of throwing a punch. The thought of his knuckles crashing into a human face seemed to him disgusting. But if he didn't strike soon he'd lose hold.

Remembering something he'd read somewhere, Drake cupped his hands and slapped them hard against the man's ears. The effect was remarkable. The lurching movements of the man's body degenerated into spasmodic twitches and jerks. He stopped trying to land punches and instead clutched at his head as if to keep it from splitting open.

Drake remembered where he'd read about the blow, something about the fighting methods of Israeli commandos. His next move, he recalled, was supposed to be a vicious punch to the victim's throat.

Instead, Drake sat back on his knees, gazing down on his victim. He wondered how long before the man would regain his wits and start swinging again. Could he hold him off a second time, or would he really have to hurt him? Drake realized to his surprise that he wouldn't mind doing it. Where had that come from?

Drake looked up. The girl looked on, her mouth ajar. He turned his head, glanced over his shoulder, then forward again, taking in the whole length of the car. No movement. Just silent staring. Here and there, a cell phone pressed to a rider's cheek, the caller's voice lost in the rattle of the wheels.

"Get off me!" The man flung his left hand up at Drake's face, made grazing contact. "Off me! Off me!" Like a baby brother who'd had enough of the horseplay.

Drake grabbed the arm, gripped it. "Not till you get control of yourself. No more hitting. Okay?" Drake spoke like a daycare worker addressing a hyperactive child. "Okay?"

"Okay," the man said. "Okay." He dropped his arms, ceased to struggle. His face was flushed with pain and anger, his eyes evasive. Drake knew the fight was on again the moment he let the man up. Then he felt the tug of deceleration as the train's brakes took hold. He looked up and recognized they were pulling into North Quincy Station.

"All right," said Drake. "This is your stop."

"Naw, man. Quincy Center."

"Not this time. You're getting off right here. Your girlfriend can join you or ride on. Her choice. But you're getting off this train."

The man swore at Drake, his vulgarities unleavened by wit or style. Drake just chuckled, and for a moment recalled his long-dead daddy, a man from Arkansas who knew how to curse. Everywhere you looked these days, standards had fallen.

The train braked harder now, and the pillars and billboards of North Quincy Station scrolled past the windows. On the platform stood four men in dark blue. One of them canted his head toward his left shoulder to speak into a microphone pinned to his blouse. He looked up as the car rolled past, and right into Drake's eyes.

"Cops are here," Drake said. "Looks like the MBTA is buying you dinner tonight."

The train stopped, but the doors didn't open. Nearly every passenger in Drake's car was standing, wanting out. Still, the doors remained shut.

Drake heard footsteps approaching at a slow run. He looked up to see the same cop peering in. The officer turned, waved to the driver two cars forward, bellowed, "Open 'em up!"

The car doors rolled open and the car emptied. It was just Drake now, the white kid, and his girlfriend. The four MBTA transit cops stepped through the nearest open door. One of them had his gun out but pointed at the floor, his index finger not wrapped around the trigger but properly pointed down the side of the weapon.

Drake knew what to expect. Two of the officers stepped behind him, lifted him to his feet, tugged his wrists behind his back, and applied the cuffs. Same for the white guy, which was a good sign.

"All right, what's it about?" one of the cops asked.

"It's about him assaulting his girlfriend," Drake said. "Bad enough to do it at all. But in public? No class."

"So you had to step up."

"Any gentleman would."

"Yeah. A carload of gentlemen just stepped out of this car. What were they all doing?"

"Maybe they're tourists. Me, I've been riding the Red Line for years, and I don't like seeing it contaminated with men who hit women."

The cop sighed, turned to the man. "Okay. Your turn."

"I don't know what's his problem," the man said. "I didn't do nothing. Just talking to my girlfriend. That's all. Then—bam!" He pointed to his ear. There was blood there, a thin stream of it. Drake hadn't noticed it while sitting on the man's chest. But now it was trickling down his neck, soaking into his Celtics shirt.

The cop turned to the girlfriend, arched an eyebrow. "Well?" he asked.

The girl turned her sullen gaze toward Drake, stared in silence for a few seconds. Then she turned to the cop while pointing to her boyfriend.

"Like he says," she said.

The cop turned toward Drake, displayed a wry sideways smile.

"Let's take a ride," he said, and gestured toward the door.

THE STAINLESS STEEL bench in his cell was unpadded, and Drake squirmed against it in a vain search for comfort. It wasn't the lack of a cushion that bothered him; the cell was chilled like a meat locker, and the icy metal burned his back.

Drake could not distract himself. Upon entering the Transit Police lock-up on Southampton Street, his belongings were collected, bagged, and locked away. No smartphone to help him while away the time, no reporter's notebook and pen to record a journal of the day's events. Not even a copy of that day's *Boston Record*, with his byline on page one. He especially missed the newspaper; he'd have had a bit of padding for the bench, plus the comics.

Drake didn't mind the lack of a cellmate; he might have drawn the subway guy, eager for a rematch. Still, isolation meant nobody to talk to.

So he waited for his back to warm the bench and closed his eyes to the cell and began thinking about machines. A Boeing 737 airliner, in this case. He'd been trying out some flight simulator software in his spare time. Made by a small shop in Kiev, the software promised to emulate the 737's features with hyper realistic accuracy.

Nothing, not even prayer, delivered Drake's mind from worry quite so well as the contemplation of a machine. There were times, during the divorce, when he would wander away from the newsroom and over to the big, raucous annex where the presses ran. He became a familiar sight to the stained, middle-aged pressmen who attended the great machines. Drake would usually keep to the lower level, where he'd watch the robots deliver the vast rolls of newsprint to the pressmen, who'd mount them on the giant spindles and tape them up so that the paster could attach a new roll just as the old one ran dry.

And when there were no machines at hand, he liked to meditate on the ones he'd seen or read about. Printing presses, of course, but also railroad locomotives and airplanes. He'd spent many an evening reenacting in his mind the firing procedures for a 1944 New York Central 4-8-2 steam locomotive, based on an old training document someone had posted on the Internet. Drake was pretty sure he could do it for real and from memory, if he ever got up to Canada, home to the last 4-8-2 that could still get up steam.

The arrival of the Russian software had turned his mind to airplanes. Drake pored over the user manual. Then a brief online search turned up a genuine 737 instruction manual, as well as a video in which two pilots ran the complete start-up sequence inside a real airplane.

Now Drake closed his eyes to the harsh fluorescent light and turned his back on the cold and made his way through the power-up checklist. To make it more challenging, he assumed he was parked at some benighted, backward strip—somewhere in Africa, say, with no electricity for the airplane. He'd have to cut in the plane's batteries and use them to fire up the APU, the plane's onboard generator.

So . . . windshield wipers off, hydraulics off, landing-gear lever down, engine fire switches in, test fire alarms, and switch APU to start. Now wait, like the guys in the video, until the APU's turbine was fully up to speed, and then kick in the generator bus. And that's it. A cold, dark aircraft was awake again and under its own power. A free agent now. Drake could bleed compressed air from the APU, feed it into the engines hanging off the wings, and turn them over.

Drake couldn't quite recall the engine start procedures. He wished he'd finished the manual before getting himself arrested. He might have been able to fly a complete mission—Abuja to Lagos, say—entirely in his head. A one-hour hop; Arik Air made the run three or four times a day in a 737. He'd made the trip just last year, in a window seat both ways, with nothing below but wilderness, deep green or sometimes tan. Scarcely a road, rarely a town.

And at the end of the journey, nothing. A great hollowing-out. As the taxi drew up outside the big house on Lungi Street, he saw Alicia standing at the doorway, legs apart and arms folded like a sentry. She didn't approach or gesture. She just stared. There was no wrath in it, no contempt or mockery. Mere indifference. That was all.

Drake sat there for about a minute, gazing from the cab's rear window, half-ill with rage and spoiled longing and shame. He made as if to raise the window in a gesture of dismissal, but his trembling fingers skidded off the button on the first effort. He stopped himself then, determined to give her even less than she'd given him. He turned from the window, sank back against the seat, told the driver to roll right back to the airport. He returned to Lagos on the exact same 737 and thence to an Airbus for the long ride home.

For a time, he lay on the jail cell bench, dialed in to that dark memory till the sorrow seemed near to choking him. The first nauseous wave of claustrophobia rolled in. To clear his head, Drake rolled over, so the cold of the bench could burn his right side and sting him out of one misery and into another. Then he breathed deeply and prayed for a few minutes until he grew calm.

The rattle of an unlocking door seemed to come to Drake from a great distance away. A slight sourness in the mouth confirmed that he'd dozed a little.

The guard who stood in the open doorway seemed at once wary and apathetic. "Come on," he said. "Your buddy's here."

They gave him back his belt and keys and wallet and shoelaces and smartphone, and Drake was allowed to stroll uncuffed down a corridor and toward a blank steel door. He heard a thwacking sound as he approached when the unseen guard pushed a button to unlock it. Drake gave a shove and found himself in the amber-tiled, antiseptic lobby.

There was Damon Carter, a lean six feet of black denim and black boots, his Boston Police badge on a lanyard around his neck and a pistol at his hip.

"Deacon," said Drake, "glad I didn't waste my one phone call."

"You ruined my evening. Off duty on a Friday for a change, and here I am in a jailhouse."

"I'll make it up to you, in barbecue or beer or whatever you like."

"I'll get back to you. They were fixing to cut you loose anyway. You're pretty well known in town, no criminal record, and the guy you smacked around was a proven scumbag. Nothing too serious on his sheet but enough to tip the battle of he-said-she-said in your favor."

"She said? The girl blamed me for rescuing her? After this, she's on her own."

"Wise policy, Deacon. Leave domestic violence to the professionals."

Drake nodded to Carter and together they strolled out of the station. It was about 9:45 by now, and even the long sun of summer was long gone. The two men crossed the floodlit parking lot, toward Carter's middle-aged Ford Fusion.

"As a black man in America, I'm supposed to have an intimate knowledge of jail cells and the rear seats of police cars. And yet, that was my first time."

"Was it good for you?"

"Anyway, it was brief. And I won't hate myself in the morning."

"My wife'll do it for you," said Carter. "We had reservations at the Ashmont Grill. When she sees you on Sunday, well . . ."

Carter's wife, Salome—a nurse—was a stern, astringent woman whose patients were glad to leave the hospital a day or two sooner than strictly necessary. Drake began thinking of good reasons not to attend Sunday service, then remembered it was First Sunday—all deacons on deck.

"She can take it out of my hide the next time I'm diagnosed with a serious illness," Drake said. "Now, you want to just drop me at a Red Line station? No need to take me all the way home."

"I dunno," replied Carter. "There's a Red Sox game just wrapping up, and the trains will be full of half-drunk fans. You're liable to pick a fight with the meanest one, just because he didn't give up his seat to a lady."

Drake smiled, and the two men rolled in silence toward the Southeast Expressway.

"Seriously, you all right?" asked Carter.

"He barely laid a glove on me."

"Except for that knot upside your head. Hurt much?"

"Hardly at all, to my surprise. The whole evening's been a shock. Did you know I like to fight? I didn't know. I've hardly ever done it, and I'm certainly not much good at it. And yet, it was a thrill. I could become a menace to society if I put my mind to it."

"There's a tattoo parlor on Hancock Street. Just say the word. I'm thinking *Thug Life*."

"*Thrilling* might be too strong a word. It's just that I was up for it. Never thought I could handle myself like that, but when it happened, I just did what I needed to do. And now . . . it's all right. I'm not scared or embarrassed or worried about it. Just calm and . . . I don't know. Satisfied."

"A few of these gangbangers have shot at me a couple of times and missed. It's like that. You had to handle your business and you handled it. And now you know you can. It's a good feeling, but don't let it go to your head."

"I won't go looking," said Drake. "Matter of fact, when I saw him hit that woman, I didn't care. He could have beaten her to a pulp, and it wouldn't have mattered to me. Not a bit."

Carter was silent for a bit, then replied, "So slapping that guy around was your idea of apathy."

"No, it was me trying to be a deacon. Trying to be a Christian. See, I figured out a long time ago that I don't much care about people. Never have. People matter to me when they've got something I want. Otherwise, they don't matter to me one way or the other." Drake glanced over at Carter. "Not even you."

Carter, a disciplined driver, didn't turn his eyes from the road. If he'd glanced at his passenger just then, he would not have seen much. Only blank brown eyes and a cool, indifferent face.

"So you just don't care," Carter said.

"Maybe a little, once in a while. But it happens so rarely. I saw a child in a wheelchair once, and I felt something for him. A strange, sickly feeling. I didn't even know what I'd felt until a couple of hours later. I believe it was compassion. Fascinating."

"That doesn't sound normal."

"Not at all. I'd read enough books to know that. I talked to a doctor about it. Antisocial personality disorder, he called it."

"Because it sounds nicer than calling you a sociopath."

"Yeah. He wanted to break it to me gently. Not sure why. It wouldn't have hurt my feelings."

"You do have feelings?"

"Oh, of course I do, but only for me. My health, safety, and comfort matter a lot to me. It's just that I'm indifferent about everyone else's."

"Did that include Alicia?"

Drake thought about it for a bit. "No," he said at last. "For her I felt something."

"Above or below the belt?"

"Not sure. I asked myself that question a thousand times during our marriage, and I'm still not sure."

"And what about me? Do you care about how you've messed up my evening?"

"Not in any emotional sense, no. But I know that you've done me a favor and that I owe you one. I'll repay it at the first opportunity."

"As a show of gratitude that you don't actually feel."

"Does that matter? As long as I do the grateful thing, what difference does it make how I feel about it? It's like pastor's sermon a few weeks back. Love isn't a feeling; it's a course of action."

"But that's just going through the motions," said Carter.

"It's the motions that matter, not how you feel while you make them."

"You really believe that?"

"I have no choice. If salvation depends on feelings of love and compassion, I'm headed for the ninth circle of Hell."

They drove on in silence for a time through expressway traffic that was still sluggish long after rush hour had ended. After a while, Carter asked, "Why'd you become a Christian anyway?"

"Because I'd just come very close to murdering my father."

"Very close?"

"Gun in my hand," Drake sighed. "They'd have had to dig two graves if I'd pulled that trigger. I didn't care about the old man. But I knew my life was over unless I changed.

"Right then, a verse popped into my head. From the Bible. Don't ask me which one. I've been trying to remember ever since. Could have been about Cush begetting Nimrod, for all I know. But it made me think of God and salvation. Next day I went to a church and began to pray. Been praying ever since."

"And your father?"

"Cancer got him not long after."

"And whatever it was between you, did you settle it?"

"I forgave him, if that's what you mean."

"That's what I mean. And what about *him*? He say anything to you about it?"

"Maybe. He said a lot right at the end, and most of it was pretty incoherent. But there was something in his voice as he said it. Might have been remorse. Of course, that could just be my imagination. He was pretty far gone by then. But I expect he had it on his mind. I would have, dying."

"So you can empathize with people a little bit."

"That's not empathy," said Drake. "That's common sense. I just ask myself what someone in his position might be thinking. That's all."

"So if you're smart enough, you don't need to feel for others. You can just approximate."

"It works pretty well. I've watched enough movies and read enough books to have a fair idea of what somebody is most likely to feel in a given situation. I just try to behave the same way. Usually, I get it right. It's like artificial intelligence. Computers can't really think and probably never

13

will. But if you show them millions of examples of how people behave in certain situations, you can train them to act the same way."

"But that doesn't always work, right?"

"No, it doesn't. Mainly because the computer runs across a situation it's never been trained for."

"Like that woman on the bus," said Carter, grinning. "Your brain never trained for that. You went to help her, and she turned around and got you arrested. Bet you didn't see that coming."

"Never thought about it. I was thinking about how I'd seen the same thing on a bus, years and years ago. That time I did nothing. I just looked away. This time, I was about to do the same. And then it came to me that I was a deacon this time. That meant I had to do something about it. I had no idea how she felt about being smacked around. Maybe she's used to it. Maybe it turns her on. I just knew that I represented the church at that moment, and that it would be ungodly to turn my back when a man treated a woman like that. That's the only reason I stepped in. Only reason. So I guess the whole thing was your fault."

"How's it my fault?"

"Well, to hear Pastor Rink tell it, you're the one who figured I was cut out to be a deacon."

"What?" said Carter with a surprised, snorting laugh. "So as a deacon, you get to roam the subway like Charles Bronson?"

Drake sank into the car seat, his chin against his chest. After a long pause, he replied, "I don't know. I just know that the world seems different to me now. It's like everything has changed."

It was Carter's turn to pause and think. After a few seconds he asked, "Is it being a deacon that's changing you? Or being divorced?"

"I still don't get it," said Drake. "Why me?"

"Happens to a lot of us, brother. Half of all marriages, they say."

"No, I mean why make me a deacon? I'm a divorced man. Newly divorced at that." Drake sighed, scrunched further down in the seat. "My own house is not in order."

"Nobody's putting you in charge of marriage and family ministries, that's for sure. But you're a born organizer, and a pretty good teacher as well. We've got fifty kids coming in every week studying computer science and engineering thanks to you. Some of their parents actually stick around for Bible classes. And that lecture series on smartphones and tablets packed the place out. Pastor Rink got a call from New Bethel about it. Their pastor was hopping mad—said we were trying to poach their members."

"Not a bad idea. We need some new blood."

"You're making it happen," said Carter. "And besides all that, you've got the number-one qualification for the diaconate. You show up. Every Sunday, and several times a week. Almost anytime you're asked to help out, and sometimes we don't even have to ask."

"It's either that or sit home and watch Turner Classic Movies. I love *A Fistful of Dollars*, but I've seen it fifty times."

"There's always HBO."

"Filthy."

"What about *The Wire*?"

"Brilliant. But I've seen it."

"There you go. You've run out of television, and the church has work for you to do. It's all working out perfectly. Or it was. Because now you're throwing down on total strangers in the subway and liking it."

Carter sat silent for a minute or two.

"Having second thoughts?" asked Drake.

"About you, no. About making you a deacon? Well, let's just see. No hasty decisions."

"You can't give up on me, anyway. You're invested. They wanted you to drop me from the program when Alicia left, but you wouldn't."

"Wouldn't have been fair," said Carter. "Wasn't your fault."

"Don't be too sure. I was no angel."

"She left you and moved in with somebody else."

"She wouldn't have left a good man."

"What's that mean? You beat her? You cheat on her?"

"No. I just withdrew. We lived in the same house, but that was all."

"How'd that happen? I mean, you married her, right? You must have wanted to be with her. What changed?"

"Nothing much. I think that was the problem. I was just too happy with my own company. I can sit down with a book and forget the rest of the world. That's how I lived all the years before I met Alicia. And I went back to living that way once we were married. It wasn't deliberate. Bad habits, I guess."

"Yeah, but that didn't make you a bad man."

"A bad husband, anyway. Maybe if I'd stayed single I could have become a saint. When alone, I'm pretty near perfect."

"Well, you're alone again. So you should be the perfect deacon."

CARTER PULLED OFF at Neponset, made the big looping curve onto Gallivan, then rolled across the Neponset River bridge into Quincy. He pointed into the darkness, toward an adjacent railroad bridge where a Red Line train was rolling across the waters. "Right over there," said Carter. "Right under the bridge. They found two of Whitey Bulger's victims down there. Just bones by the time the FBI dug 'em up."

Drake squirmed upright in his seat, craning to stare, though there was nothing to see. "Were you there?"

"I was on that detail, yeah. It was 2000 and I was new on the force. Easy work. No work at all, not for me. But it was kind of cool, in a morbid way. A gangster graveyard. They made that movie about it."

"Yeah," said Drake. "They shot some of it right down the street from me. They waited till the snow melted, then they put a surfboard on the balcony of an apartment building, stuck some potted palm trees and fake grass out front, and said it was Whitey's California hideout. Never saw the movie. Did I miss anything?"

"I never saw it either," said Carter.

The car swerved right onto Newport, a path through Quincy with fewer traffic lights.

"They ever going to make a movie about the gangs you deal with?" asked Drake. "Or are only white gangs cool?"

Carter laughed. "They make movies about black gangbangers too, just not as stylish. When it's white people they make it seem almost heroic. Like Michael Corleone becoming a killer, 'cause it's the only way to save his father's life."

"So those gang kids you lock up every day, you think they deserve their own version of *The Godfather*? A sweeping romantic epic about dope-slinging killers?"

"They're no worse than the Corleones," said Carter.

"True," said Drake. "I might even go see it."

Carter turned left on Furnace Brook, then right on Hancock and pulled up in front of Drake's place, a drab, gray-brick high-rise.

"First Sunday. Don't forget your communion kit," said Carter.

"Not much chance of that, not after last month. Your wife made me drive all the way back here to get it."

"She was right. You were needed. You had three shut-ins waiting on you. And it was Sister Madison's last time. She passed three days later. Think about how you'd feel today if you hadn't gone back."

"Instead, I can head upstairs and sleep the sleep of the just," said Drake with a chortle, as he swung the door open. "See you Sunday, man. And thanks for springing me."

"Thank my wife. She's the one who convinced me to come get you. I wanted to leave you there. Toughen you up a little."

"Maybe next time. I'm riding the subway a lot lately, so the opportunities for random violence are pretty much limitless."

"Well, next time you're on your own," said Carter.

"A deacon," Drake replied with mock solemnity, "is never on his own."

"True," said Carter. With a wave of his hand, he pulled away from the curb and swirled away into the night.

It was almost 11:00 when Drake unlocked his door. He noticed the familiar musty scent that had always followed him from one apartment to another—an odd amalgam of sweat, cooking smells, and clothing both dirty and clean. It was an odd smell, rather than a bad one. But Drake almost preferred the rather astringent smell of the jailhouse.

He popped open the fridge, extracted a bottle of decaf iced tea and a packet of leftover Pad Thai. The food went straight into the microwave. He'd eat that with a set of wooden chopsticks pulled from a heap of them that he'd collected in recent months. No dishes to wash; everything to go into a leftover supermarket plastic bag, then straight into the garbage chute. His latest meal would thus contribute hardly anything to the scent of the place.

There were two bedrooms. The one where he'd slept with Alicia was the best-furnished room in the house and the least used. It was dominated by a vast bed—a memory-foam mattress framed in heavy oak. Bounce on it as hard as you liked, and it never made a sound. They'd tested.

They'd bought the bed at the same time as the condo. Drake now regretted the expense, but not the bed. It slept well and carried fewer bad memories than he'd feared. So the bed would stay. But not the wall-mounted large-screen TV that faced it. Watching television in bed, one of Alicia's favorite pastimes, had always been repellent to him.

He waffled on the empty chest of drawers she'd left behind. Storage was storage; he could surely find use for those empty drawers. But some empty floor space might be even more useful to him. It would take thinking about.

One certainty, though—laundromat tomorrow, for the bed linens. They were due, and the smell rose from them.

Drake moved to the second bedroom, a little dustier, a little smellier, a raffish clutter of bookshelves and boxes with wires hanging out and going nowhere. Against one wall sat a desk and a large monitor; a large black box sat quietly huffing on the floor.

Drake pulled back the comfy swivel chair and settled in. His left hand grasped the Saitek aircraft control yoke, and his right hand fell naturally onto the throttle quadrant. Drake had dug them out recently to try out that Ukrainian flight-sim software and had been surprised by how much his fingers still remembered.

He'd been hardcore about flight sims for years. Not as serious as the fanatics who'd simulate the sixteen-hour Los Angeles–to–Melbourne run by literally setting aside sixteen hours. Still, the hobby had cost Drake hundreds of hours.

Alicia had stopped him. Too much fantasy for a grown man, she said. One time she'd put her hand on his and snatched the throttle back, and the virtual DC-3 he'd been flying nosed over toward certain doom. "I'm real," she said, her fingers warm against his, while her other hand began undoing buttons.

Now she was in Abuja, with no further objections to how he spent his time. Besides, this was work. He hadn't written about the odd little community of flight simmers in years, and it was time for a refresher. Was that guy in Milton still around, he wondered—the fellow who'd built a 747 cockpit in his garage, out of parts raided from aircraft junkyards? Surely worth a follow-up.

The microwave dinged. Drake got up, retrieved the food, settled down again in front of the computer. His hands too busy to fly, he logged into Twitch and watched as others flew simulated missions. Someone named Airbum42 was up, pushing a 737 from Denver to Dallas. Drake ate Thai noodles with crushed peanuts and watched as the simulated Rocky Mountains scrolled past.

The lump on his head was beginning to ache at last, and the rolling scenery began to nauseate him. Motion sickness—the gamer's curse. It would pass after a few days of frequent playing. He was way out of practice now, and coming that close to a concussion hadn't helped matters.

Drake decided on bed and went to brush his teeth.

THE CELL PHONE shrilled at him from the night table. Drake lurched upright, stared at the Samsung like a man who'd just suffered an intolerable insult. He fumbled for it, accidentally hit the Reject Call icon, then came fully alert at last. He checked the call log, saw it was Carter who'd dialed him. What could he want? Or maybe it was Carter's wife, unwilling to wait till Sunday to share a piece of her mind.

Drake waited thirty seconds to make sure Deacon or Mrs. Carter had hung up, then hit Redial.

"Weldon, it's Damon."

"At two a.m.?"

"Yeah, sorry. But we're needed at the church. I'm on my way. You should get there too. I'm alerting all the deacons but especially you."

"Why especially me?"

"Because she's your friend."

Right at that moment, Drake knew, and his skin chilled.

"What happened?"

"Somebody got in and attacked her. Right in the church. In the computer room."

"How is she?"

"Not good. Not good at all."

CHAPTER TWO

FROM TWO BLOCKS off, Drake saw the flash and snap of police lights and realized there'd be no place for his old Ford. He parked early and walked the rest of the way down Tremont Street, past low-rise apartment buildings and the outskirts of an old public housing project.

Reliant Baptist Church, a squat brown-brick structure that covered the best part of a city block, resembled a warehouse more than a church, except for the 150-foot steeple that towered over the south corner of the building like an afterthought. It was the work of a firm of Dallas architects, masters in the art of megachurch design, or so they'd persuaded Reliant's building committee.

The old Reliant church had been abandoned in the 1930s by a Unitarian congregation hollowed out by white flight. The pseudo-Gothic structure in red brick had too few of everything—electrical outlets, pews, parking spaces. But the Unitarians had left behind deep-colored windows of stained glass, ornate padded pews of carved oak, a bell in the steeple that had been cast by Paul Revere himself, and an Aeolian-Skinner organ with real pipes and a sound like Christmas Eve.

The old place had looked and smelled like the AME church of Drake's Chicago boyhood. But he was far from Chicago now, and Old Reliant, once so short of parking, was now itself a parking lot of black asphalt alongside the new church.

At least the Paul Revere bell still spoke at Reliant. It was seated in the new steeple, and a boxful of chips, connected to an electromagnetic hammer, awaited the order to strike. Instead of pulling a rope, an usher punched in a code. No matter: the sound was the same, and it carried for a mile or two through the Boston Sunday air.

So not everything had been lost. Besides, there was a lot more parking space, the secret weapon of evangelical churches. People pray where they can park.

The acquisition of the ministry center six years ago had helped. The former nightclub came with about thirty much-needed parking spaces. The used condoms and drug syringes were cleared away, and the first and second floors were made over into tidy, well-lighted offices and classrooms. Here trustees hashed out church budgets and eight-year-olds absorbed their Sunday School lessons.

And then came the basement—the workshop stocked with machine tools, a laser cutter, and 3-D printers; the dual computer labs equipped with high-end Alienware laptops and a smattering of costly Macs, all backed by rack-mounted servers and lashed together with Cat 6 Ethernet cable and an optical fiber link to the rest of the planet.

It had cost a quarter-million or so, money that even Pastor Rink would have found hard to raise. He hadn't had to. Boo Hendricks had come through. "God's Geek," or so he'd been dubbed by *Time* magazine. Drake had interviewed him once during a visit to Boston, aboard a restored Lockheed Constellation airliner that Hendricks had flown himself.

A rare black man who'd hit it big in tech, Darren "Boo" Hendricks was a devout believer who'd splashed out cash to dozens of churches to pay for facilities like this. "Only what we do for Christ will last," he said when asked about it. A line from a hymn. The response scandalized the secularists of Silicon Valley. The guy who'd paid $2 billion to purchase Hendricks's company said he might not have done it if he'd known.

Too late. And a little of that cash had ended up in Reliant's basement. That was Astrid country. Just about the only part of the church she'd ever visited. And now her blood was on the floor.

Astrid's bike was in the annex parking lot, where police strobes glinted off the polished chrome of the pipes. A Harley V-Rod, newish. The best thing that Astrid owned, or so she'd told him months ago, in Cambridge, that first time he'd watched her straddle it and roll away down Vassar Street.

Cops had tied yellow tape to the parking lot fence and pulled it clear across the sidewalk and wrapped it around a lamppost. A police SUV was parked on the sidewalk just inside the tape, a Kevlar-vested officer leaning against its hood.

Drake touched the tape as if to raise it, drawing a baleful glare from the cop, a muscular, florid, pockmarked man. "Back off, buddy."

"No offense," said Drake, raising both hands shoulder high. "This is my church. I'm a deacon here. I know the victim. They'll want to talk to me in there."

The cop relaxed. "They may want to talk to you, but not in there. Wait up." He turned away, hunched his left shoulder forward, and began muttering into the microphone of his portable radio, glancing back at Drake now and then to make sure of him.

Carter arrived before the conversation had ended, double-parking his Honda Pilot at the curb. He wore khakis, a church picnic T-shirt and his badge on a lanyard around his neck. The cop on the radio stood a little straighter and cocked an eyebrow at Drake's new ally.

"You with him?" the cop said, nodding Drake's way.

"This is our church," said Carter. "Where do things stand?"

"I'm just crowd control. Better if the detective fills you in."

"You been inside?"

"Yep. Messy. But she was still ticking when they slid her in the wagon, and this is Boston, so she's got a chance."

"Any idea who or how?"

"Who?" the cop scoffed. "Long gone, whoever it was. How? A long, sharp knife. One wound in the chest, way too close to the heart."

"But why . . ."

"Hey, I'm out of answers. Detective Akinyi knows you're here, and I told her you know the victim. She'll want to talk to you, all right. Stick around."

Carter nodded. "C'mon," he muttered to Drake, and they strolled over to Carter's ride, leaning on the warm hood.

"Robbery?" asked Drake after a minute or two.

"Has to be," said Carter. "Not sure what they'd rob. Not this time of night."

About the only thing at Reliant worth jacking was the Sunday offering. About forty grand a week. It came mostly in personal checks, useless to a thief. But a few thousand in cash always showed up, and the local talent wasn't averse to making a play for it. Carter had helped break up one such attempt about three years ago. Still, there was no cash on hand during the attack.

So what else? The camera gear and editing equipment in the TV studio? Pro grade stuff, but pros had no need to buy hot equipment off the black market. The big-screen TVs in the various conference rooms? Several years old, and not even smart TV sets, some of them.

There were dozens of computers, but who stole PCs these days?

Still, there was Astrid with a hole in her chest. And Astrid was a volunteer in the church's science and technology training program. The heart and soul of it, really.

A stocky black woman emerged from the annex, moving toward Drake and Carter with the rolling gait that comes from wearing a holster. She had thickly braided hair down to her shoulders, a tiny bit too much space between her front teeth, and a sullen weariness that stopped her just short of being pretty.

"You with the church?" she said, glancing at the two men.

"Yeah," said Carter. "Deacons."

"And you're on the team too, I see."

"Gang unit. Intelligence."

She held out her hand. "Precious Akinyi, Homicide."

"Heard of you," Carter said. "But we've never caught a case together."

"Sorry it had to happen like this," said Akinyi. "You know the victim?"

"Slightly." Carter nodded at Drake. "He knows her better."

Akinyi turned to Drake, her eyebrows raised, the look of a clinician running tests. She didn't offer her hand; just waited.

"I'm Weldon Drake, another deacon."

"And a friend of the victim," Akinyi said. She drew a notebook from an inner pocket, flipped a few pages. "Astrid Nelson, according to her driver's license."

"Yes. I recruited her for the program. And we did go for a drink every now and then."

"Deacons do that?"

"Sure. No rule against it."

"You say you recruited her. Is that what Baptists call it?"

"Oh, she's not a Baptist. Doesn't believe in God at all. At least, that's what she says."

"So how'd she end up bleeding out inside a Baptist church?"

"What do you mean, 'end up'?" asked Drake, his voice louder and an octave higher.

"Bad choice of words," said Akinyi. "She's at BMC by now, so she's got a good chance." She sighed, her eyes on the pavement. "Sorry, man. I'm just tired." She looked right at Drake then, with a look he hadn't expected. Her eyes were soft, patient, slightly worried. A mother's eyes.

"That's all right, officer. Long as she's okay."

"Well, anyway, what was Ms. Nelson doing here?"

"We've got a program for teaching math and science classes to neighborhood kids. Adults too. She volunteered to teach a coding class, and sometimes she helps out with our robotics club."

"She just showed up one day and volunteered to help?"

"Not quite. I sort of suggested it. Never thought she'd agree, and then she did."

"How long have you known her?"

"More than a year. She's a postdoc in computer science over at MIT. I wrote about her once. That's how we met."

"Wrote about her?" Akinyi cocked her head like a curious puppy. "You're a reporter?"

"Yes, for the *Record*."

She smiled. "Yeah, thought that name sounded familiar. You write a lot about computers and stuff like that."

"It's my beat."

"Not the cop shop. That's good." The smile faded. "You can't write about me, you know that, right? Anything you print has to come from public affairs."

"I'm off duty."

"No such thing for reporters. I shouldn't talk to you at all, except you know the victim. So you spend a lot of time over at MIT."

"I'd like to spend more. I like being around people a lot smarter than me."

"So you wrote about Astrid. Then what?"

"We'd hang out now and again and talk technology and theology. We'd end up at the Meadhall in Cambridge, tasting each other's beer."

Akinyi raised an eyebrow. So did Carter.

"Cheaper that way." Drake sighed. "Look, nothing happened. We just talked and drank beer. And then one evening about six months ago, when I mentioned the church's STEM programs, she just volunteered to help. I hardly believed it myself. I mean, she's MIT. They work those kids to death over there. But Astrid told me she wasn't going to spend her whole life staring at her own code."

"So you guys have classes at midnight on Fridays?" asked Akinyi.

"Nope. But she loves to work late. She doesn't have a key to the place, but she probably came in during video games."

"Video games?"

"Yeah, Friday is game night. Ages ten and up. Nonviolent games like Minecraft. Gives the parents a peaceful evening and the kids love it. Astrid probably came in to work on something and stuck around after everybody else left. She's done it before."

"What would she be working on?"

"No idea. Probably wouldn't understand if she told me. Fiddling with the church computer network, maybe. She's put in several upgrades for us; set up a firewall and cleaned out some malware programs. She even put in that porn filter last month. Remember, Damon?"

"Yeah, we caught a little kid looking. He was way ahead of his time— just seven years old," said Carter, shaking his head. "His mama didn't bat an eye when we told her. Haven't seen her in church since."

"You should have reported her," Akinyi said. "DCF ought to check her out."

"Didn't think of that," said Carter. "Figured she was just embarrassed."

"You're probably right," said Akinyi. "But look me up her name and address, and I'll get it checked out, just in case."

"Okay," said Carter. "Anyway, we don't know what Astrid was doing, but there was nothing unusual about her being here late at night."

"But she certainly wouldn't have left the doors unlocked," said Drake. "After nine p.m. they're automatically set to lock themselves."

"Guy broke in," said Akinyi. "Knocked out one of the panes in the door, reached in, hit the push bar, and walked right in. I see you have an alarm system, but of course it wasn't turned on."

"Astrid knew how," Drake said. "She'd have entered the code when she left."

"But you didn't trust her with a key to the place?"

"We don't want too many front door keys floating around," said Drake. "I don't have one myself. But I have keys to some of the labs and class-rooms. And I know how to set the alarm when I leave."

"So what was she doing down there?"

"Could be all kinds of things," said Drake. "We're due some software updates on the Windows machines. I'd been planning to get around to it, but Astrid could have been doing that. Or she might have been playing with the NAS box."

"NAS box?"

"Network-attached storage server, for backing up all the church's data files. I built it myself last year, out of an old PC. I like that kind of thing. Then about a month ago Astrid logged in, looked around, and busted out laughing. She's been squashing bugs ever since."

"Hard on your ego."

"Not really. I know my limitations."

"Where'd you find her?" asked Carter.

"Just inside the door of the computer lab. We'd have never found her at all if she hadn't called 911."

"Yeah, can't see in there from the front. That's deliberate, to discourage thieves. Guess it didn't work this time."

"It might have worked," said Akinyi. "At least, we don't think it was thieves. Not much sign that anything was taken. Her purse was left behind.

Credit cards and a little money. And the key to that Harley over there. I figure a thief would have taken that, yes?"

"Might not have known how to ride a bike," said Carter.

"He'd have tried anyway. It's a nice bike, worth good money. And there's the purse and the cards, and all your nice computers. Maybe two dozen, all untouched."

"And the laptop," Drake said.

"What laptop?" said Akinyi.

"Astrid's. It's Apple. A MacBook Pro."

Akinyi cocked her head. "Don't recall seeing a laptop in there. Might have missed it, but I don't think so. But why attack her and just steal that one computer? Must have been something important on there." She turned to Drake. "Probably her MIT research. You know anything about that?"

"I know just enough to write a story about it," said Drake. "That's how we met. She was presenting a paper at a computing conference. 'What to Do About Racist Software,' or something like that."

Akinyi's eyebrows rose again.

"Yeah," said Drake. "Software can be racist. At least, it can generate racist results. Astrid was researching the problem, trying to figure out how to fix it."

"But how can a piece of software be racist?"

"By accident. This Harvard computer scientist found that if you run Google searches on people with black-sounding names like Taneesha or Malik, you see ads for companies that do criminal background checks. Run the same search with white folks' names like Jessica or Cody, and you hardly ever get those ads."

"So Google knows which names sound black? What's it do, subscribe to *Essence*?"

"Google just notices what people search for. Say a lot of people who search for Taneesha also search for companies that do criminal background checks. From now on, you search Taneesha and you see more of those ads. Google's just trying to give the users what they want."

"Why would so many white people be running searches on black-sounding names?" said Akinyi.

"Who says they're white? It could be black folks looking up friends or acquaintances. Google wouldn't care either way. But it would begin to associate black-sounding names with crime." Drake chuckled. "Anyway, it let Astrid off the hook. With a name like that, she can pass for white, at least on Google."

"So what can you do about prejudiced software?"

"Astrid had a few ideas," Drake said. "It was all way too sophisticated for me to figure, but she's trying to invent programming methods that'll automatically prevent stuff like that."

"Sounds pretty impressive. But who'd try to kill her for that?"

"Exactly nobody," said Drake. "That can't be it."

"Can we get inside?" asked Carter.

"You know better," Akinyi said. "It'll be a couple of days at least."

"Don't you need us in there to confirm there's nothing missing?"

"I think we'd have noticed if anything major was gone, but you can come back in a few days and make sure. Also, I can give you the number of a good cleanup company. They specialize in this kind of thing. They get every trace. Like it never happened."

"Well, can we go see about Astrid?" asked Carter.

"You can hang out in the emergency room, but she left here unconscious, and when she wakes up we'll talk to her first. After that, it's up to the doctors."

"Okay," said Carter. "We're gonna roll, then."

Akinyi jotted down their names and numbers, then gave each of them one of her contact cards. "It's coming up Sunday," she said. "You'll have to make do with half a church."

"At the worst possible moment too," said Drake. "Gonna be a full house."

DRAKE OPTED TO ride with Carter. Climbing in, he hesitated and asked, "Wait for the pastor?"

"We could," said Carter. "He's on the way, but he lives so far out. Sister McNair's rolling too. She'll probably beat him here. Either way, they don't need us right now." He pushed the starter, and Drake was startled by a strident voice, loud on the radio. It was WBZ, the all-news station, and the announcer was belittling the previous night's late-inning collapse by the Red Sox.

"One of BZ's reporters should be pulling up any second, and TV crews right behind. Who'll catch it at the *Record*?"

"Fitzgerald, most likely. You know him."

Carter grunted.

"Didn't see him out there, but he's got to be on the way. Let's hope so. He's good."

"Yeah," said Carter. Then, after a pause, "He spelled my name right, anyway."

"Quite an accomplishment these days, believe me."

"Sad thing is, I do believe you."

Carter put it in gear, cruised up Tremont to Massachusetts Avenue, and turned right. The BMC complex loomed a couple of blocks away. The Yawkey building, all shadows and lighted windows this time of night, spanned the entire street, so that Mass Ave flowed beneath it as if through a tunnel. It was the way to Albany Street, the way of the ambulances.

Carter turned off on Harrison instead, toward the parking lot and the atrium entrance of the Menino Pavilion, the emergency room's presentable front parlor. A plump, brusque blonde woman pointed them down a corridor to the business end of the building, where a black woman, as bulky as the first but more sympathetic, took their names and directed them to the waiting area.

BMC is Boston's safety net hospital, where poor folk go when they're sick or shot or stabbed. At 4:00 a.m. on a warm summer Saturday the net was rather full. Most of the padded seats were occupied by plump, harried women and tattered men, while those too nervous to sit still prowled among the seats. Their eyes kept snapping around toward the doorway that led to the doctors, the nurses, the trauma tables, like they were waiting for the second act of a play to begin.

Drake settled into one of the chairs, its armrest tacky with some indefinable residue. His feet hadn't stuck to the floor, but he felt as if they should have. Even the cold filtered air of the place seemed tainted.

Drake shook his head and swore at himself in words better left unused by deacons. But then, deacons weren't supposed to hold themselves aloof from people like these—especially not a deacon who'd been born in a hospital just like this one.

"Too much time among the white folks," he mumbled to himself, then laughed.

"You or Astrid?" asked Carter, flopping into the adjoining seat and startling the distracted Drake.

"Me or Astrid what?"

"Overexposed to white people." Carter leaned in and whispered as he spoke; no sense annoying the dozen or so whites in the waiting room.

"Oh, just thinking out loud," said Drake, annoyed at the interruption and a little embarrassed. "Anything on Astrid?"

"The attendant's going to ask after her. Might take a while. She was here when Astrid was brought in, and going by the way the doctors acted, it didn't look good."

For no good reason, he'd taken it for granted that Astrid would survive. Carter had snatched away his ignorant optimism.

"It's the why, I can't figure," said Drake. "Who tries to bump off a computer scientist? It's not like she was working for the Iranian nuclear weapons program or something."

"You never know," said Carter. "Remember Lady al Qaeda? She went to MIT and Brandeis too. Got a PhD in neuroscience. Next thing you know she's in Afghanistan building bombs and taking potshots at the US Army."

"Astrid strike you as the jihad type?"

"Just saying, you never know with people. Nobody lives just one life."

"Yeah," said Drake. "I always knew that about Astrid. When an atheist volunteers to help out at your church, you know she's got something going on."

"Something like you, maybe," said Carter, venturing a gentle grin.

Drake chuckled. He was annoyed and the least bit flattered.

"Look, you're back on the market. You're the right color, reasonably intelligent, not too bad-looking . . ."

"Not to mention, employed," Drake interjected with a wry smile.

"See? Now factor in all the stuff you don't have—an ankle bracelet, a parole officer, or five kids by four different women. Guys like you are like Bigfoot or the Missing Link. Black women hear about them, but they hardly ever see them."

"What a load of crap," chuckled Drake. "You sound like a Tyler Perry movie. Our church is full of guys like that."

"All taken," said Carter.

"Besides, there are hundreds of guys for her at MIT. They're not all hoodie-wearing Poindexters, you know. MIT teaches them ballroom dancing, which fork to use, stuff like that. I use plastic forks most nights."

"Women don't care about that," said Carter. "Not a lot. Not when they have other reasons to care." He put away the smile, looked straight at Drake. "So you're hanging out together, drinking mead, and arguing about God, and that's it? That's all you thought it was?"

"For real," said Drake.

Carter grunted, hesitated a few seconds. "You know, there's nothing wrong with trying again. What happened with Alicia wasn't your fault."

"Well, I didn't leave fingerprints, but that doesn't make me innocent."

"Nobody's innocent. But there are degrees of responsibility. Yes, you bear some of the blame. But you didn't leave and run off with someone else."

"Hell of it is," said Drake, "I like the guy. Funny and smart as a whip. He could end up running Nigeria someday."

"You know him?"

"Oh yeah. Had him over for dinner once. He was telling us stories about Nigeria, all the political corruption. Had me howling." Drake chuckled in remembrance. "He knew which fork to use too."

"Forget about him," said Carter. "Alicia too. It's over. You need to decide your own future and quit looking back over your shoulder."

"I guess," said Drake. "But Astrid's got nothing to do with it. We're just friends. That's all."

The two men fell silent, and Drake squirmed deeper into the seat, so his feet thrust out and his torso was almost parallel with the seat cushion. It was an odd posture that hardly seemed conducive to slumber, but in a few minutes Drake had begun to snore. Carter marveled at the sight for a few minutes until his eyelids began to slump and his chin sank to his chest.

The next person Drake saw was Pastor Rink. He sat in the chair directly across from Drake, his lips moving. Something about grace and grief. For a good minute or more, Drake watched and listened, comprehending nothing. Then his weary eyes began to water and burn, and the pain confirmed his consciousness. He shrugged himself upright in the chair, glanced at a wall clock showing 5:30 a.m.

"Pastor."

"Weldon. How do you sleep like that?" A tiny smile quirked his lips.

"Not the slightest idea. How long you been here?"

"Just arrived," said Rink. "Waiting for word. Carter went to try and get an update."

"Stop at the church first?"

"Yeah, but I can't get in anyway. They got to keep the crime scene secure. Don't want to look nohow." It was Rink's beans-and-cornbread way of speaking when he was amused or annoyed, or affronted.

The voice was rich and deep, distilled in Alabama. The body was deep black, compact and muscular. Rink was the son of a Huntsville aerospace engineer, and he'd followed his father's trade for a time at the General Electric plant in Lynn, where they made engines for fighter planes. Ten years in, he'd heard the call to preach.

Rink had come to a prosperous and well-managed church, with about two hundred worshipers every Sunday, but always the same two hundred. A decade after Rink's arrival, there were well over a thousand members on the books. Not even the decay of the surrounding neighborhood and the occasional burst of criminal violence, kept the people away.

One such violent act had brought Drake to the church. It had happened six years earlier, at the very building where Astrid had been stabbed. Back then, the place had nothing to do with Reliant. Indeed, the blunt two-story brick cube had been a speakeasy during Prohibition, then a nightclub where Ella Fitzgerald and Marvin Gaye had performed, and most recently a strip club. Over the years, the church and its gaudy neighbor had maintained an uneasy peace, ruptured by police raids, street brawls, and every now and then a murder—four homicides in all.

The most recent was a drive-by that had happened about half an hour after Thursday evening choir practice. A stray round had smacked into the west entryway; had it been fired thirty minutes earlier, there might have been two corpses instead of one.

Two weeks later, the sidewalk had been rinsed clean of bloodstains, but the bullet hole was still in the entryway. Drake passed it on his way to Rink's office. He'd come not as a worshiper but as a journalist, and though the story was well off his beat, the metro desk was glad of the help.

"Four killings," the pastor said in his Alabama growl. "Four in thirty years. And that little gangbanger the other night? That's the last one. I've made up my mind. That's the last one."

Two nights after the killing, Rink and a handful of Reliant members gathered outside the church, their faces turned to the strip club. Some brought folding chairs; others dropped cushions onto the pavement and kneeled on them. Still others just stood. They carried no protest signs and chanted no slogans. Instead, led by Rink, they just prayed, from eight in the evening until four in the morning. The same thing happened the next night and the night after that, and the night after that. Rink was there most nights, though not all. Indeed, the cast of characters changed throughout the week, but the numbers scarcely varied.

Drake had come to see for himself about ten days into the protest. He spent the night, watching, talking to the church folk. He stood aloof like a proper, objective journalist, but he found himself praying under his breath from time to time.

His story about the protest made page one. The next night, a local TV truck showed up. Two nights later, it was CNN.

The club owner, a husky, latte-hued man who'd gently mocked the gathering at first, had come to regard it with dismay and a measure of awe. His receipts had dropped substantially. Two of his best titty dancers had quit on him. He'd heard from the mayor and from his mother.

When Drake arrived to interview him for a follow-up story, the man had shifted in his big leather chair, so that Drake could literally hear him squirm. "Might not be the best neighborhood for a place like this," he said. He spoke with his head turned to one side, like one of his own customers hoping to watch the show without being recognized.

A couple of weeks after that, he'd sold out and Rink had bid on the property. And a week after that, Drake walked down the aisle at Sunday morning service and asked to be accepted into the church.

That had been six years ago, and Rink had seemed to age hardly at all. Until tonight.

"I talked to the detective in charge," Rink said. "She don't know any more than me."

"Me and Damon have been trying to figure out a reason for it. We got nothing. She didn't have anything worth getting stabbed."

"How'd somebody even know to go up in there?" Rink said in a seething voice. "In a church. A church! Had to know there was nothing much in there. Even these drug fiends out here got more sense than that. In our church!"

"If she makes it," Drake said, "maybe Astrid can explain. Maybe she knew the guy. Somebody who knew she'd be there."

Rink nodded. "Old boyfriend, maybe. But was she the kind to hang around with somebody like that? I really didn't know her. She's not a member, after all. You're the one who brought her in. You think she'd have a boyfriend who'd use a knife on her?"

"Not a chance," said Drake. "A guy like that would never pass the IQ test. She gives one to just about everybody she meets. Little oddball questions. Malcolm X's real name, junk like that. Trivial stuff." Drake chuckled. "Not sure she even knows she's doing it. But that's how she checks people out. It's like she puts out a dragnet for nerds."

Rink smiled. "And she got you."

"Me? I just write about nerds."

"Oh, it goes deeper than that. Trust me."

"Much of a crowd at the church?" Drake asked, and Rink's smile faded.

"More than I'd have expected. People must be waking each other up over this. Don't blame them. Sister McNair got there ahead of me. She was wondering about Sunday. Would we have a service? I told her we need to have five or six, behind this." He shook his head. "Certainly have to rewrite my sermon. But at least there will be a service. The woman in charge—Akinyi, right? She said since the sanctuary isn't part of the crime scene it should be all right."

Drake looked up, glanced toward the entryway to the trauma ward in time to see Carter striding toward him, his face as stern as a judge's.

"She's out of surgery and resting," he said. "Decent chance she'll survive."

Rink exhaled. "Well, God is good."

"All the time," said Drake.

"All the time?" said Carter. Then he flopped into one of the waiting room chairs and fell silent.

CHAPTER THREE

IT WAS NEARLY 6:00 a.m. when Carter pulled to the curb a block away from Reliant and three blocks from Drake's car. No matter: Drake had wanted another look at the church anyhow.

The police presence had thinned a bit, though a couple of cars were still on station, and the annex doorway was still taped off. Across the street, three local TV news trucks had hoisted their microwave dishes toward the brightening sky. A preternaturally pretty correspondent from the local Fox affiliate, her face ablaze with quartz lighting, launched her live stand-up, her words inaudible over the purr of the portable generators.

Drake turned his attention toward the main church building. Its front door stood open.

"Not a crime scene," said Carter. "Lucky."

"Good chance Fitz is inside," Drake said. "Interviewing people, though I'm not sure who."

The large meeting hall on the ground floor of the church had the smell of breakfast, so Drake knew that Deacon Arthur Ralston was on the premises. Whenever he came, he cooked. Force of habit.

And handy too, for at least two dozen members were congregated in the hall. Middle-aged men, most of them, guys with early jobs who'd been out of bed anyway and heard the news as they shaved. But more than a few were retirees who lived nearby and still got around pretty good.

They sat at round tables or stood at the open half-door of the church kitchen awaiting paper platefuls of bacon, scrambled eggs, and grits. At least two of those in line were cops, large white guys made bulkier by Kevlar vests.

Fitz was on the job, sure enough, seated at one of the tables. An athletic man, clothed in plaid and denim, he had gone several days without a shave, so that the weary lines of his cheeks and chin were partly snowed under by graying hairs.

He nodded to Drake, then leaned forward to hear better as Sister Belmont, one of the older members, held forth on the outrage next door. Fitz's notepad and pen sat neglected on the table before him, the better to encourage candid talk. But his smartphone sat in the center of the table, recording every word.

Drake waved and began to move off, but Sister Belmont saw him. "You work at the paper, Deacon. You should be writing this story."

"It's a crime," said Drake. "Fitz here is the best when it comes to crime."

"Yeah, but he doesn't know us."

"He will. Just keep talking."

Sister Belmont muttered that she'd rather talk to Drake, but he started moving off.

Carter got in line for breakfast, but Drake left him there and went looking for Sarah McNair.

McNair, the pastor's most trusted aide, was a retired schoolteacher. And she knew everything—all the business of the church and all the joys and travails of its members.

He found her on the second floor, in the main church office, rooting through a file cabinet. She glanced up, offered a weary semblance of a smile. With her high cheekbones and demure mouth she might have inspired many a schoolboy crush back in the day. Even now she was a fine-looking woman, most days. Not this morning. The face was grayer, the lips dry and pale. No sleep, no makeup.

"Morning, Deacon," said McNair as she hauled a manila folder from the cabinet, dropped it on the desk, sighed, and sank into her swivel chair. "You come from the hospital?"

"Straight from there. No change. But they say she'll probably make it."

McNair sighed, shook her head. "That's good news. Praise God." Yet her face and manner seemed hardly more cheerful.

There was silence for a bit. Then, in a husky whisper, "Why? Why would anybody do that to her? And in the church too? What's gone wrong? What has happened to people?"

"Well, anybody who'd stick a knife in a helpless woman probably wouldn't mind doing it on church property."

"But that's not true. It used to be, even criminals had some respect. There wasn't much they wouldn't do. But they wouldn't have done this. Not in a church." Again, McNair sighed. "Lord have mercy."

After a few more pensive seconds, she roused herself. Picking up the manila folder, McNair withdrew a sheaf of papers.

"Insurance," she said. "Trying to figure out if we're covered for something like this. Liability, medical expenses. I don't know how exposed we are. I don't even know what they call a situation like this." She looked up at Drake, her eyes wide with alarm. "What about cleaning up? We can't ask the janitors to do something like that. You hire people, right? Specialists? Is that covered?"

"I don't know," said Drake. "But don't worry about it just now. That place will be a crime scene for days, probably. You don't have to make a move just yet."

"The pastor needs to know. He's so busy, and he's so worried. I can't put all this load on him. I've got to handle it."

She was a different McNair from the woman he'd known so long—distraught and on the edge of panic. He thought to stand near her, put his hands on her in a gesture of comfort. The thought repelled him slightly, as he knew it would. Nothing against McNair; it was Drake's lifelong unease at the prospect of physical contact with another.

It had taken him years to accustom himself to shaking someone's hand. And when the deacons of the church had inducted him with the laying on of hands, he'd felt their fingers on him and had barely resisted the urge to squirm free.

But he had resisted and remained and become a deacon. So now he had a job to do. He stepped over to McNair, laid a hand on her shoulder, looked into her fretful eyes. "Do not be afraid," he said. "Wait on the Lord. And since everyone in the church will be as confused as you, we'll all wait on Him together."

He gripped her shoulder gently, let go, then turned to leave. "Pastor was right behind us. He'll be here soon."

McNair's face, so wrought up a few seconds before, now bore a curious expression—relieved and comforted, but also slightly amused. "You didn't want to be a deacon," she said. "But I knew. I knew."

DOWNSTAIRS, FITZ HAD completed his interview and was tucking into a plate of eggs and grits. "Didn't even have to stand in line," he said through a mouthful. "Somebody just brought it over."

"Baptist hospitality," said Drake. "You eat grits in Southie?"

"All the time," said Fitz. "Cultural appropriation."

"Get anything good?"

"Enough for a first cut at it." He reached down to a black backpack at his feet, drew out a battered Dell laptop. "Gonna file something from here and then go looking for more material." He glanced up at Drake. "When you gonna file?"

"I don't do crime."

"Well, start. Otherwise, you'll be like that reporter in the Sherlock Holmes story. Murder right on his doorstep, but he's so shocked he forgets to write about it."

"I'm not in shock. It's just . . . I don't want to exploit the situation."

"Exploit? You heard the old lady. She got mad you weren't doing the interview. These people know you."

"Which is kinda the problem. Not enough distance. I can't be objective."

"Fine. Write it as a first-person opinion piece, put it online. It'll be the best-read thing on the site."

"You have a point," Drake said.

"Sure," Fitz said. "If something like this happened at Holy Trinity, all the years I been going there, I could probably get a book out of it."

Still, Drake had his doubts that the idea would pass muster with his editor, Steve Ginsburg. Steve was the mercurial type, the kind of editor who'd start out loving the idea, only to begin indulging second thoughts fifteen minutes before deadline.

"I better let Steve make the call," Drake said.

"That means giving him something to look at. So you better get busy." Fitz reached into his backpack, dragged out a reporter's notepad and a pen. "Pay me back later. Get to work."

AN HOUR LATER, equipped with a few affecting quotes from church members and his own recollections, Drake swung his Ford into an empty parking space at the *Record*, a three-story brick structure that covered a city block of costly Boston real estate. The company had needed every square foot of the space when it was erected in the late '50s. These days, the parking lot was never full, and the newsroom, even during the peak working hours of late afternoon, seemed deserted and forlorn. Even the great offset presses no longer roared as they once had, as two of the units sat idle most days, coming to life only for the still-popular Sunday paper.

At least the presses still spoke; the *Record* was that rare twenty-first century paper that was written, edited, and printed all in the same building. A journalist could still visit the pressroom, smell the ink, and watch fifteen sliced and folded copies emerge every second.

The show was nearly over. The *Record*'s new owner was selling the building, moving the newsroom to a much smaller leased space in a downtown office tower, and installing new presses in a distant suburb. It was a good call; the land was worth far more as retail space or luxury condos.

But for now, the *Record* remained. It being Saturday, the newsroom was more than usually deserted. Drake settled in at his desk, fired up the computer. While he waited for Microsoft's permission to start typing, he snatched the desk phone and punched up Ginsburg.

The phone rang twice. Then a muffled growl. "It's Saturday," said Ginsburg.

Still in bed at seven? Were the children away with their mother? "Sorry. Thought you'd be up by now."

"Weldon?" He sounded alert now, like an editor. "This is good, right? Like Google buying Facebook? It better be."

"Afraid not. Nothing really to do with our section at all. Just pitching

41

something to Metro and thought you should know."

"Metro? Not good enough for the business page?"

"It's cop stuff. Somebody I know got stabbed last night."

Silence for a few seconds, a sigh. "Man, that's bad."

"It's worse, actually. They stabbed her at church."

"Your church?" Ginsburg asked.

"That's right. She's still alive, thank God. But she's messed up pretty bad. Everybody's pretty upset about it."

"You too?"

"Me too."

"They get the guy?"

"No. Maybe when they figure out why it happened. He may or may not have swiped her laptop—not sure. But nothing else was taken, so it's like somebody had a grudge against her. Maybe an old boyfriend; I don't know. But you need a reason to stick a knife in somebody. That takes determination."

Drake fell silent for a space, and as if he were holding a haptic joystick, he sensed a nauseating vibration in his hand, the sort he might feel while trying to drive a blade through flesh.

"Need some time off?" asked Ginsburg. "Weldon?"

Drake roused himself. "I actually want to do some extra work. I'm thinking a first-person story about the church and what Astrid has done for us. That's her name. MIT postdoc. She's polished up our computer network, run a coding class for local kids, stuff like that. She's a good woman, Steve. She didn't deserve this. Neither did our church. I want to tell the story."

"You woke me up for that?" Ginsburg said, in the voice of a man who'd have flung a shoe at Drake if he wasn't a couple of suburbs away. "Are you crazy? Just start typing."

"Okay. Maybe I'll need time off later, but not now."

"Just say the word."

AN HOUR LATER, Drake's piece was well on its way. About five hundred words done. He'd planned to top out at eight hundred. A good, tight Sunday read. He'd stumbled on the correct tone too. Heartfelt, of course, but also cool and astringent. Sentiment without sentimentality. Words, not tears.

But as he tried to write of Astrid's work at the church, his fingers slowed.

He remembered watching her teach a couple weeks back. He'd wandered in on a Saturday morning, half thinking he might take the course himself.

The kids were middle school age, mostly black but a few of the local Puerto Ricans and Dominicans too. There were about fifteen of them, and most were not members of Reliant. Remembering his own boisterous youth, Drake hadn't been prepared for the sober diligence of the kids. As Astrid spoke of algorithms, the children's heads all canted to one side, their eyes all seeking the same far-off point in space. Drake did the same thing when tangled in thought; he was doing it at that moment at the keyboard, hunting for words.

On that distant Saturday, Drake had been staring at Astrid's tattoo. It was just beneath her chin, a lotus flower in black and red. She was a tall woman, nearly six feet, and while seated in the classroom he looked up at Astrid and watched the lotus flex and flutter against her dark flesh as she spoke.

"Step by step," said Astrid. "That's how everything works." She spoke with a dry, precise voice, like a girl who'd won a scholarship to the white kids' school. Dressed all in heavy denim, Astrid stepped as she spoke, her tan Lucchese boots rapping against the hardwood floor.

"Everything that happens in the world, everything you do in your life, is a series of little steps. When you're designing a piece of code, that's the way you have to think. First, what are you trying to do? Then, what are the steps you'll take to do it? Just break it down into steps. First you do one thing, then the next thing and the next thing, till you get to the end.

"There's always more than one way to do something, and some ways are better than others. In really good code, the writer always uses the fewest, simplest steps to get the job done. Get rid of any unnecessary steps and the code runs faster. And it's prettier too. Good code is always beautiful."

Astrid paused; a boy had raised his hand. "You mean, like in a video game?"

"Yep," said Astrid. "But not just the images on the screen. There's code behind those images. And if it's good code, it'll be beautiful to anybody who knows how to read it. You won't have to run the program. Just look at the lines, and see that the programmer wrote neat, simple functions, and good, clear comments to explain each step.

"Lots of code works. But perfect code—it's beautiful. Over in Cambridge they wrote the code they used to land spaceships on the moon. I've looked at some of it, and it's the most beautiful you'll ever see. It had to be beautiful because it had to be perfect. If it wasn't, three men in a billion-dollar spaceship were going to die. But they lived, and that beautiful code was the reason."

Astrid looked straight at Drake then, a wry smile on her lips. "Beauty saves, Deacon Drake."

And Drake grinned and answered, "Amen."

Do middle schoolers read Dostoevsky? Not these, and so Astrid's reference to their most recent theology debate passed right over their nappy little heads.

It was too good a memory not to use in his story, so Drake compressed the anecdote until it fit and buffed it till it shone. And then he was done. He loaded up the story with metadata to ensure the editing software would stash it in the proper cubbyhole, hit Save, then emailed himself a copy of the finished piece, for late-night triple-checking and a sure-thing backup.

It was noon by then and hardly a soul in the Saturday newsroom. Still, Drake wandered over to the cyberdesk to notify the copy editor on duty. Maybe they'd want to post his piece online ahead of the Sunday print edition.

Back at his desk, the weight of a sleepless night began to tug at Drake. He had his doubts whether to try and drive home or leave the car in the *Record* parking lot and catch the Red Line. He'd decide once the editor got back to him.

Till then, Drake popped a browser and started a random reading of news headlines. Something about a bombing in Pakistan caught his eye, but he was in no mood for such savagery. So Drake retreated to Slashdot, a digital technology news site. "News for Nerds," Slashdot styled itself, and it lived up to the name with stories about updates to the Linux software kernel and

likes the tech

innovative ways to hack <u>Texas Instruments microcontrollers.</u>

Luckily for Drake, Slashdot also featured stories he could understand—breaking news of corporate acquisitions, computer frauds, and enticing new gadgets.

He browsed through a story about an ill-starred maker of smartwatches on the brink of bankruptcy. The startup had spent $50 million of somebody else's money to learn what Drake could have told him for free—nobody really needs a smartwatch. *Better luck next time*, he mused, and nudged the mouse to reveal the next story on the page.

It wasn't what he'd expected. Not at all.

The hacker world is a relatively peaceable kingdom. Conflict was confined to online flame wars, covert digital attacks and counterattacks, and the occasional arrest of some careless try-hard who'd become a stench in the nostrils of Interpol or the FBI.

What he hadn't expected was a story about a hacker with a hole in his chest.

Famed Gray-Hatter Found Dead

**Posted by GoGimli on Saturday June 4 @10:34AM
from the rest-in-peace department**

An anonymous reader quotes a German news report:

Hamburg police are investigating the murder of Helmut Brockmann, a respected software engineer better known under his online nickname "Clinker." Brockmann was found in his apartment on Friday night by his girlfriend, the victim of <u>a knife wound to the chest</u>. The apartment had been ransacked, and the girlfriend, Christina Agnelli, said it appeared that Brockmann's laptop computer and external hard drives were missing. A spokeswoman said that the police currently have no suspects.

As Clinker, Brockmann gained fame as a "gray-hat" hacker, one who uses sometimes illicit methods to uncover flaws in computer systems, but who then uses the knowledge to help businesses and governments improve their security practices. Three years ago, his successful penetration of NATO's military computer networks made headlines

45

around the world and nearly landed Brockmann in a jail cell. Instead, NATO officials worked with Brockmann to upgrade their security policies, and Clinker became a respected and well-paid consultant, with clients in the public and private sectors.

Drake was fully awake now and alert to the odd, awful coincidence. For coincidence is all it could be. There could be no connection between Astrid and this Hamburg gray-hatter.

Besides, Brockmann's murder was probably unrelated to his online career. Hacking didn't carry a death sentence. Except perhaps that case in Mexico a few years back. A white-hat hacker named Raul Robles was gunned down while breakfasting with his father at a Guadalajara café.

The killer went uncaught, as often happens in Mexico, and the motive was undiscovered. But it was easy to guess. Robles ran a successful cybersecurity firm and loved to post YouTube videos showing off his jewelry and sports cars—and mocking his less prosperous rivals. At least one unknown member of a popular hacker forum had vowed to shoot Robles on sight.

No international conspiracy, then. Instead, the online version of Saturday night at a Mattapan bar. First disrespect, then death.

Though she was proud of her quick mind and her deep knowledge, Astrid never seemed particularly proud of herself. And she wasn't given to online boasting; the woman didn't even have a Facebook account.

A coincidence, then, and an exceptionally freaky one.

An almost-all-clear email from Metro desk revealed a few trivial tweaks to his story but nothing mortal. Nearly 1:00 p.m. Time to go. Forget the car; he'd get it sometime tomorrow, before or after church. Just now, he felt too weary to endure Boston traffic, and the Red Line subway stop was just a couple of blocks away.

On the way out the door, Drake took out his cell and phoned Carter. He answered after the first ring.

"I wake you up?" asked Drake.

"No. I'm back at the hospital. Just getting ready to leave, actually. Doctor said no visitors yet. It could still go either way."

"Not what I wanted to hear. She say anything about what happened?"

"She's not talking yet. Detective Akinyi came through, asking the same question. She's gone now."

"You know anything about her? Is she any good?"

"I've heard good things. I know she closes a lot of cases. About as good a clearance rate as anybody in the department. So I'd say there's a decent chance we'll get this guy."

"Still trying to sort out a reason."

"Not your job . . . No, wait, I guess it is your job, in a way. As long as you don't interfere with the professionals."

"Not a chance. If I find out anything it goes straight to Precious."

"You on a first-name basis now? You know she's married."

"Now's not the time, Damon."

"I know. Still, she is kind of cute, and it's not against the law to think about it. You'll just have to look elsewhere. And you probably should start looking."

"Damon, please."

"All right, skip it. I need to get some sleep anyway."

DRAKE STOOD UP for the subway ride home, despite a surplus of empty Saturday seats. That way he was sure of staying awake. He remembered the punch-up with the white kid then and chuckled. Good way to get oneself killed, but how could a decent man do nothing?

With the thought came a sense of dismay. Was that what he was now? A decent man? When had that happened? He didn't feel especially decent. No amount of playing the hero would delete the sloth and lust and arrogant folly of his life. Drake knew himself too well to believe anything that silly. He was not a decent man.

Perhaps he'd just have to settle for doing decent things, as the need arose, and hope that somehow his soul would conform to his actions. It sounded like a practical interim solution to the problem of original sin.

So he could go about the world looking for opportunities to do the decent thing. It sounded like a dreadful idea; a life of butting into other people's affairs, like that old lady at church who was forever interrupting his conversations with other members, just to offer him coffee. Her ministrations never failed to annoy him. Was he to make an eternal nuisance of himself as well?

Then it occurred to him that maybe the old lady indeed sought God's grace and favor with every offered cup. Drake decided that from now on, he'd always accept. Help a sister out.

Still, he'd rather not pester his way to a good conscience. Better to wait and see what the Lord would do. If God had some mission in mind for him, he'd recognize it when the time came and do what needed doing, God willing. He was a deacon, after all, and that was the job.

CHAPTER FOUR

ON SUNDAY MORNING the TV trucks were still there.

Drake had ridden the Red Line back to the *Record* to pick up his car. He'd parked it a couple of blocks south of the church, tucked his communion kit under his left arm to keep his hands free, and walked to Reliant to spare one close-in parking space for a senior member who didn't get around so well anymore. His path led him past the annex, still bounded with sawhorses and cop tape. He had to step into the street to evade the barrier.

Chantal Summers saw him, waved, and gave out that morning-glory grin that had gotten her the job with Channel 12. "Get over here!" she barked in a commanding voice that had no business emerging from that angular, runway-model face.

Drake knew her from his occasional visits to the TV station where they'd mic him up, dull his gleaming skin with face powder, and ask him five quick questions on some new digital gadget—never more than five. Drake wrote the questions himself, fed them to Chantal in advance. She would ask them well, her blue eyes widening with wonder, a smile at play on her coral-tinted lips. Once he'd nearly lost himself in her gaze and began to repeat the answer to question number three. Chantal had frowned, a new sight for Drake and a quarter-million TV viewers. It awakened him and saved him.

After that, she'd look at him from time to time with more attention than Drake deserved and more pity than he desired. He'd grown a little afraid of her.

But she seemed safe enough here on Tremont Street, and she might know something about Astrid, news he'd rather hear from Chantal than from a cool, indifferent hospital clerk. So Drake walked over.

"Saw your story this morning," Chantal said. "So moving." The radiant smile was there but dialed back to a sympathetic glow.

"Thanks," said Drake. "You guys ever go home?"

"We will after this. Just catching people as they go in and out. And of course I had to catch you. Five minutes on camera?"

"Make it three. They need me inside. Service starting up."

"Yeah, you're a deacon here. That like being a minister?"

"Well, they ordain you, and then you do as you're told. That's a ministry, I guess."

"Guess it'll be a tough Sunday."

"I suppose. A lot of the older members didn't know Astrid that well. She mostly ran with the younger set. Still, just having somebody knifed on church property is like sacrilege. That's bad enough. Worse if she dies."

"Not much chance of that," said Chantal. "Didn't you hear?"

"Haven't checked in yet. You got news?"

"Yeah, the hospital's saying she's out of danger."

Drake exhaled, then took a great breath of morning air, exhaled again. Across the street, he saw Sister Cabiness—a plump, middle-aged high school biology teacher—throw her head back and laugh like a nine-year-old. She must already know.

"God is good," said Drake.

"Yeah. Amen," said Chantal, nodding and grinning like a cheerleader. "I'm so happy for you. For all of you. It's such good news." Taking Drake by the arm, she tugged him over to her chosen spot on the sidewalk, rotated him toward the camera lens, flicked a thumbs-up at the cameraman. "So . . . we've all read your powerful piece about your friend Astrid Nelson in this morning's *Record*. How does it feel knowing the good news?"

IN THREE MINUTES it was over. Chantal thanked Drake, who thanked her back. A few thousand more clicks on the *Record* website, a dab more ad revenue for the company. In all, a fair trade.

And she hadn't asked about the communion kit. Just as well. Hard enough to explain the sacrament to someone on the outside looking in. But how to explain that someone like him had been granted the authority to administer it? Where did he get off carrying around a packet of wheat wafers meant to represent the body of Christ?

There was no blood in the box. Not yet. A sister at Reliant would take care of that, with a bottle of Welch's grape juice purchased the day before.

Drake crossed back over to Reliant, entered the front door and the social hall right below the nave. Breakfast was on again. He hoped Deacon Ralston had brought extra bacon. The place was as full as Christmas, with faces he hadn't seen since the holiday service. *Nothing like an attempted murder to boost attendance.*

No, that was unfair. Some people seemed to need the church most when the church needed them. There was a kind of nobility in that. Drake wondered how the impulse might be aroused in them anew every Sunday at 10:00 a.m. *Weekly stabbings?* He chuckled for the first time in two days.

HE JOGGED UP the stairs to the third-floor administrative offices and the little kitchenette where the communion kits were prepped. The place was unoccupied, but a few communion kits were already stacked on a counter, each with its owner's name labeled in Dymo tape. Drake dropped his next to Carter's. A deaconess would have it topped off by the end of the service.

He strolled back downstairs and over to the table where Sister Burke dolloped out scrambled eggs and grits. As usual, there was a choice of bacon—turkey or pork. Burke, a bespectacled fireplug of a woman, gestured with a set of tongs.

"The real thing this morning, Sister. I need the calories. And some black coffee."

"Help yourself with the coffee," she said, dumping four lavish slices of pork onto his paper plate. "Good article you wrote about that girl. I didn't know much about her. Now I wish I'd have talked to her. She's a good girl."

"Yes, she is," said Drake, pouring a full cup of hot and black.

"Better than that Alicia."

51

"Now, Sister . . ."

"Just saying. But still, she did you a favor, going off like that. Leaving you free."

"Sister Burke, I . . . Let's not, okay."

"Yeah. I'm sorry. None of my business anyway. I just want you to know, I don't blame you for what happened. Nobody blames you."

Another member strolled over, fumbling for money for the donation. "I'll take your word for it, Sister. Thanks. And don't worry about Astrid. She's in the clear, the doctors say. I'm sure she'll be back in the computer lab in a few weeks."

"I don't know. If something like that happened to me, I don't think I'd ever go back to where it happened."

"I gotta admit," said Drake, "I hadn't thought of that. Well, worry about it later. Just thank God she's okay."

Thirty or forty fellow members were clustered at tables scattered around the hall, munching and chatting. But Drake carried his plate and cup to an empty table and settled in. It was wrong of him, a deacon, to neglect the others, but a poor night's sleep made an excuse for him, justified just this once his instinct to hold himself aloof. It was First Sunday—a long communion service with visits afterward to members shut in by illness and old age. He'd have plenty of socializing before the day was out.

He gulped a mouthful of grits, slurped a little of Ralston's appalling coffee, closed his eyes, prayed a silent prayer of thanks for the food. Too greasy, too heavy. Official black people food. Perfect. He relaxed and chewed and thought of nothing. He didn't even pull out his smartphone to scan the morning's headlines. Chantal had given him all the news he'd need that day. Astrid alive and likely to recover. Drake prayed another silent prayer of thanks, exhaled, relaxed, ate.

"Can I have some coffee?"

The square-headed little boy had come alongside too quietly for Drake to notice. But there he was, his big eyes looking up into Drake's, his face playful as a skylark.

"You can have some bacon." Drake picked out a slice, held it out.

"Mama's getting some bacon already."

"She's getting coffee too."

"She won't give me any."

"Then neither will I. Your mother knows best."

Little Dante pouted a bit, though not a serious pout, and snatched the bacon. A rude gesture, but it wasn't ill-meant, and Drake let it go.

"Boy, give that bacon back." His mother, Charmaine, was hustling over, a large purse over one shoulder, a Styrofoam plateful in each hand. Drake rose to assist.

"It's all right. He's welcome to it."

"Not all right. Child got to learn manners. Give it back."

Scowling, Dante handed over the bacon, and Drake dropped it onto his plate. His mother grunted, then strolled back to get her coffee. She was the cream-and-sugar type, and Dante was too hungry to wait for her and started in on the bacon Charmaine had brought him. Drake picked up the slice from his own plate and quietly dropped it onto Dante's. The kid barely looked up. Little ingrate. His mama had a point.

Charmaine came back and settled in next to her son. It was the end of Drake's isolation. By instinct he regretted this, but not too much. Like all kids, Dante was a mobile puzzle, a Rubik's Cube that drank milk. The sub-rational desires of very young children fascinated Drake more than the transparent motives of most adults. Plus, he was a curious, active, and skeptical little boy, and cute as well.

He took after his mother, a plump woman whose head barely came up to Drake's shoulder. He'd noticed this when members had gathered at the front of the church and held hands for altar prayers. On one or two occasions, Charmaine had maneuvered next to him, taken his hand, and leaned against him closer than the pressure of the crowd required.

Served him right for buying the groceries. Last November Charmaine had run short of money after buying winter gear for Dante. Her housekeeping job didn't pay much, and Dante's father hadn't paid his cell phone bill. So Charmaine appealed to the deacon's fund. But such cash payouts were subject to a vote and at that exact moment, about an hour after Sunday service had ended, there weren't enough deacons on hand to form a quorum.

So Drake loaded Charmaine and Dante into his Ford and made for the nearest Stop & Shop. He goaded the abashed Charmaine down one aisle after another, insisting she buy whatever she and the child needed. It came to a bit over $200. Drake knew he'd get the money back from the deacons if he asked; come to think of it, he hadn't.

He'd lugged the bags into Charmaine's tidy, cramped basement apartment, accepted an offer of coffee. A mistake, he later realized. And he'd compounded the error by half an hour spent playing Super Mario Bros. with little Dante.

By chance he'd checked off all the boxes. Single, presentable, likes kids, brings home the bacon.

There was nothing wolfish or desperate about Charmaine's pursuit. Instead, it came across as steady, insistent pressure, transmitted through the lilt of her voice, the cant of her upturned head.

Charmaine was presentable enough herself, well filled out, with full lips and large, questing eyes. She'd be a welcome 3:00 a.m. armful on a January night. She'd been exactly that, for someone, about six years back. Little Dante was the proof.

Drake gave a resentful, contemptuous thought to the unknown stud who'd come and gone and discarded so much on his way out the door—a warm woman, a sweet child, a place to stand. *Men are so stupid.*

Charmaine flounced down on his left, shot him a smile. "Crowded this morning. I wasn't sure I should even come. Wasn't sure it was safe."

"No worries there," Drake said. "Cops all over the place. TV crews too. Safest church in town, this morning."

"Yeah, I realized that after a minute. Besides, it's good for Dante. He needs to be in church." She scooped up some grits, chewed a while. "But no Sunday School this morning. It's over in the annex where it happened."

"Yeah, whole building's closed."

"Why would somebody do that to her? In church too."

"Cops are working on it. Deacon Carter's on the force, you know. Gang crimes, but this doesn't look like that. Still, he knows people. They'll keep him in the loop."

"I only met Astrid once or twice, but she seemed like a nice girl. A little wild, though." Charmaine chuckled. "That motorcycle. Never get

54

me on one."

"Not a fan, myself. Too many ways to get killed in this world without seeking out more."

"Could have put that money on a down payment for a car."

"Bike like that costs as much as a car," Drake said.

"I want one like that," said Dante, grinning and chewing.

"Don't talk with food in your mouth," said Charmaine in a mild voice, more reminder than rebuke. She was usually this way with Dante, as if he were an ally as well as a son. The boy did his part; he continued his grinning and chewing, but in silence now.

"Where your mama going to ride?" asked Drake. Dialect?

Dante chewed a little faster, swallowed. "I can carry her on the back seat," he said.

"Where you gonna put the groceries?" asked a laughing Charmaine.

Dante paused, realizing he'd overlooked something. He gave a "beats-me" gesture and a grin.

"Much as that boy eats," said Charmaine.

"You all right?" Drake asked and cursed at himself as the words came.

"We're all right. Mama sent some money, so we're good."

"Well, if anything comes up, you can always call Deacon Carter." He was head of the deacon board this year, and he was married.

"I'll let you know," Charmaine said, with a warm, candid glance that left no doubt whose phone number she'd be dialing first. Drake glanced to his left; little Dante glanced up, grinned like a six-year-old ready for play. Drake turned to his plate of grits and eggs and wondered how they'd taste if Charmaine had cooked them.

IN THE NAVE of the church, a quartet of ceiling fans stirred molten air. The air conditioning had plainly failed, and the warmth of the day was mingling with the body heat of several hundred people.

There were twenty rows of cushioned pews on the main level and more in the balcony. Drake expected that nearly all of them would be full by the time the service began. At present, many members and a few visitors were meandering down the red-carpeted aisles.

Up toward the front and to the left of the nave, Robert Archer, head of the usher board, was chatting with a cluster of unfamiliar men—white guys. One of them turned his head mid-laugh. He was a medium-sized man of ruddy face and a slight paunch that a costly gray suit did nothing to hide. The mayor, Drake realized; he'd met him once or twice. His presence explained that of the other two bulky white men who scanned the room with the stolid intensity of bodyguards.

Drake considered strolling over to say hello but decided against it. Instead he kept right and walked to the front of the nave, to the pews where the deacons sat. Carter was already there, in the front row. Like Drake, he was dressed in deaconwear—a black suit with bright red tie. His head was thrown back toward the ceiling, his eyes closed. Without a word, Drake settled next to him.

"I heard the good news," he said.

Shrugging and muttering, Carter roused himself. "Yeah. Out of the woods."

"You spend the night at the hospital?"

"No point. No, I spent it at the shop, working the phone. I know a bunch of low-level lowlifes, and I tried to call them all. Only made it up to the letter E, though. I'll start in again this afternoon."

"Doesn't seem like gangbanger work."

"Not at all. But somebody might have bragged about it."

"Stupid."

"Welcome to my world. Not a lot of criminal masterminds on those streets."

"Still, robbing a church. Not much point."

"Yep. Still, people hear things. Might get lucky."

"Good of the mayor to show up."

"My boss is somewhere around here too," said Carter.

"The police commissioner? You better wake up, then. Sit up straight."

"I doubt he recognizes me. Only met him once."

"I'm practically on his Christmas card list," said Drake. "Did a story or two about police technology about a year ago. Got the grand tour."

"Well, good. You can be the one to go over there and tell him to find this guy."

"That'd be unprofessional. As a journalist, I'm supposed to keep my thumb off the scale."

"Is that what you were doing with that story you wrote about Astrid? Wouldn't call that a model of objectivity."

Drake shifted in his seat. Just over his shoulder, he caught sight of Commissioner Lang, his massive frame casting a shadow across Pastor Rink's stern face.

"Anyway, Pastor's giving him an earful right now. I don't really have much clout. He does."

"Yeah," Carter said with a chuckle. "Church ladies vote."

THE SERVICE WENT long by half an hour at least. There were words of sympathy and solidarity from the mayor, a pledge of swift justice from the police commissioner.

And there was Pastor Rink, tall in the pulpit, his amplified baritone voice conveying every modulation of outrage and sorrow, relief and rejoicing.

His usual sermons were full of scripture citations and, sometimes, massive chunks of theological jargon. But they were redeemed from tedium by his knack for the dramatic. Rink always kept something in reserve, an anecdote or observation that would turn a sermon on its head, like an optical illusion.

It came midway through this time.

"Astrid Nelson, who came to us and worked with us and taught our children so much, did what she did for our sakes," said Rink. "But not for God's sake. Because she does not believe. She's never believed."

The congregation at Drake's back, already hushed, seemed to submerge into a deeper silence at that. A couple of his fellow deacons shifted in their seats to glance at him. One of the oldest, Deacon Barkley, seemed to glower.

Drake had never told anyone. Astrid had come to teach software, not Sunday School. Now he realized it was unease that had held him back, maybe even cowardice. Drake felt as if he'd been caught in a lie.

"She told me this a few months ago. Not with arrogance. Not with pride. It was more like . . . a confession. Astrid worried that she was here under false pretenses, that there was something dishonest about her presence at the church. She had no love for a nonexistent God, but she had a real fear of . . . what? Only word I can think of is sin.

"Because you don't have to believe in God to believe in sin. Anybody who knows his own heart knows the nastiness that dwells within. The Bible tells us that the law of God is etched in every human heart, even the hearts of those who reject him. So don't have a moment's doubt that even though that girl in that hospital did not know God, she understood the condition of her own soul.

"I tried to see Astrid last night, but they told me she was in no condition to receive visitors. I was so sorry about that. I wanted so much to tell her that whatever she thought about God, that she was never, never off his mind; that she was forever and ever in his thoughts.

"And I wanted to tell her something else. I wanted her to know that we, the people of this church, would never stop loving her, supporting her, praying for her."

RINK WAS DONE not long after, and at the end of it, Drake's heart was lifted up. *It will be all right.*

He could think of a dozen reasons why things would never be all right. He acknowledged all these reasons, without pretense or illusion. And yet at that moment, none of them seemed to matter. He knew that there was far more in play than the raw hole in Astrid's chest or the cruelty of her vanished assailant or his own well-founded fears. God had something in mind here, something somehow good. Let it be worked out in His own time.

He walked through the nave, passing through the dwindling host of worshippers. Some greeted him, praised his account in the *Record.* One elderly member wrapped her arms around him and kissed his cheek.

The mayor and police commissioner were gone, the TV cameras too. Hardly anyone left except a few church members praising Pastor Rink, ushers checking the pews for misplaced purses and cell phones, and here and there a deacon. Carter was one of them. His cell phone was at his ear. On a hunch, Drake walked over to him, just as he said, "Up to it? You sure?"

Drake perched on the armrest of a pew and waited for Carter to hang up.

"The hospital?" Drake asked.

"Different hospital. Brigham and Women's. Melanie Wayne. Remember Melanie? She's getting surgery tomorrow for her back. I'll be bringing her communion. And prayer. And all the news, of course."

"Yeah, I bet all the shut-ins will want communion this Sunday. Just hope I can stay awake that long."

"How many you got?"

"Three. Brother Bartlett, and Sisters Jefferson and Walker. He's at home. The sisters are in a couple of different senior centers. I'll put a little mileage on my car today."

"Yeah. We better grab some sustenance from downstairs before it's all gone," said Carter.

"Roger that," said Drake, then groped for his phone and started speed-dialing the people on his visitation list. You never went to a shut-in member's house without calling first. Sometimes they were in no mood to receive communion, or in no condition for it, or had died the week before.

Sister Nadine Walker, a retired nurse, answered on the second ring, and Drake invited himself over. Without conscious effort, he'd shifted into deacon-speak. His often-abrupt manner became smooth and solicitous, reverent and sympathetic. Tomorrow, when he'd be interviewing the chief designer at a mobile video game company in Cambridge, he'd be jocular and a bit sarcastic. Thursday, when he'd meet with the chieftain of a billion-dollar microchip design company in Woburn, he'd be cool and distant.

For a moment he wondered what might happen if his deacon switch got stuck in the on position and he conducted every interview in the manner of his chat with Sister Walker. He might end up breaking a few more stories. Or would sources stop returning his calls?

Sister Jefferson didn't even answer the phone. Perhaps she'd managed to get out of the house, on her two new titanium knees. Good for her and for Drake's afternoon schedule. But Brother Bartlett was home and eager for news.

"Come on over," he bellowed, loud enough to sting the ear. "Nothing on TV anyway. Any chance we could use real wine?"

"Sure, if you've got some. As long as it's not Yellow Tail."

Sam Bartlett, who owned a couple of dry-cleaning shops, lived in a comfortable three-story house on Regent Street. He was a garrulous, good-natured man who'd spent much of the Cold War hovering over the North Atlantic, dropping sonar buoys and listening for Russian subs. But years of being flung from the decks of aircraft carriers had worn away at his spine. The VA hospital did what it could, but Bartlett was still laid out two or three weeks out of every year. He didn't complain much about the pain, though he took it hard that he'd never actually heard a Russian sub.

Drake left the nave and jogged upstairs to find his communion kit. Deaconess Hawthorne was ready for him and thrust it into his hands. "You going out alone?" she snapped, as if accusing Drake of something. But she meant nothing by it. Deborah Hawthorne was kindhearted, yet with a manner as daunting as a January wind.

"Yes, alone," said Drake. "Got a lot of terrain to cover."

"I can find you a deaconess to ride along."

"Not a bad idea," Drake replied. "But maybe next time. I got a lot on my mind." He took the proffered communion kit, ignoring Hawthorne's dissatisfied glare, and headed back downstairs.

For the after-service fellowship hour, the hospitality committee had made up those little mini–chicken salad sandwiches they did so well. Drake ducked into the kitchen and grabbed one from a tray destined for the social hall.

Munching as he walked, Drake headed outside, where he saw the dwindling flock of worshipers piling into the cars they'd double-parked on Tremont Street. A few gathered outside the annex, swatting at the cop tape and tossing questions at a patrolman posted just outside the door.

Drake strolled past and down the street to his car. Bartlett was closest to the church, so he was the first stop.

"WHAT KIND OF knife?" Bartlett asked.

He was a short, trim man, and his shaved head made him seem younger than he was. His skin was just about the same shade as the massive leather recliner in his living room.

Drake, perched on the sofa, looked up from his Android phone, where he'd been searching for 1 Corinthians 13.

"What kind of question is that?"

"Just wondering."

"You should have been a reporter."

"Easier on the spine, for real. But Uncle Sam had other plans for me back in 1970. And in those days, the papers weren't hiring a lot of brown people."

"And now they're hiring nobody at all. I suppose that's justice."

"Yeah, I can remember when the *Record* was almost as big as a phone book. The paperboy drop it on the porch, and the whole house shook. Now it feels like a pamphlet."

"Blame Craig Newmark."

"Who?"

"The guy who invented Craigslist. Brilliant idea, but it destroyed newspapers. The *Record* used to rake in maybe forty million a year from those little classified ads. Had a big room with two dozen people; all they did was answer the calls from people placing ads. Lord knows what all those people are doing now."

"So they looking for Astrid's boyfriend?"

"Far as I know, she didn't have a boyfriend."

"I saw her once or twice," Bartlett said. "She had a boyfriend. Or girlfriend."

"That's jumping to conclusions, isn't it?"

"Only conclusion that makes sense. She didn't have nothing worth stealing. But if she had a friend who knew where she was gonna be, no reason he couldn't have gone over there to get her."

"You have a point. But if there was somebody, I don't know anything about him."

"Cops are bound to check anyway," Bartlett said. "That's how it always works. Motive first. Find the reason, and you find the suspect."

"So I hear. But I'll leave it to the professionals. Agatha Christie books bore me."

The phone pinged and pulsed in Drake's hand. On the screen, a message flag obscured the upper portion of his Bible app. It was Deacon Carter.

"Astrid awake and talking. Heading over."

"Girl trouble?" Bartlett asked.

"Something like that. Looks like Astrid is welcoming visitors. I need to get over there."

"Will they let you in?"

"The detective in charge said she's fine with it."

"You better get going, then. Communion can wait."

"No, it can't."

Drake finished looking up the Bible passage, heaved himself off the sofa, and took up the communion kit. Setting it on the armrest of Bartlett's recliner, he flipped it open and drew out a napkin and a plastic bottle of grape juice. No time to uncork Bartlett's bottle of cheap wine.

Drake filled two thimble-sized glass cups. Then he lifted the lid from a metal container full of wheat wafers and flicked two of them onto the napkin. He took up his phone, and began to read.

"For I received from the Lord what I also passed on to you: The Lord Jesus, on the night he was betrayed, took bread, and when he had given thanks, he broke it and said, 'This is my body, which is for you; do this in remembrance of me.'"

With his left hand, Drake extended the napkin to Bartlett, who chose a wafer and placed it in his mouth. He was a chewer; Drake heard the little disk snap and crunch as it went down.

Drake put down the napkin, picked up the other wafer, and placed it on his tongue. He let it rest there; chewing the body of Christ had always seemed to him disrespectful. He sat silent for about half a minute until the bread had dissolved into mush, then swallowed.

Bartlett watched in silence, his right index finger tapping against the armrest. It was always like that with him. An impatient man.

So Drake handed him one of the two small cups.

"In the same way, after supper he took the cup, saying, 'This cup is the new covenant in my blood; do this, whenever you drink it, in remembrance of me. For whenever you eat this bread and drink this cup, you proclaim the Lord's death until he comes.'"

They drank. While the wafer had been bland and inert, the unfermented grape juice had a cloying sweetness that always startled Drake as if he'd just sipped blood.

"Amen," said Bartlett. "And get out."

CHAPTER FIVE

AS HE BRAKED for a red light at the corner of Warren and Dudley, Drake whipped out the phone again and speed-dialed Sister Nadine Walker. His apologies, but could they reschedule communion?

Her reply was cool and correct and radiated annoyance, and some sorrow. But her tone changed when Drake told her why he could not come.

The midday traffic on Melnea Cass was plentiful, even on a Sunday. But Boston is a small city, covering less than ninety square miles, so nothing is very far from anything else. It took Drake fifteen minutes to reach the Boston Medical Center. Carter met him in the lobby, still suited in black, his badge draped around his neck.

"You finish your communion visits?" asked Drake.

"Not quite. There's always tomorrow."

A security guard saw Carter's badge and waved them toward a bank of elevators. They got in and Carter pressed the button for the fifth floor.

"Detective Akinyi is in there now, talking her through it. I don't suppose she'll have a lot of energy left by the time we get there."

"She wouldn't be talking at all if she wasn't pretty tough," said Drake.

"Yeah. Biker chick."

The door pinged and opened, and Carter led the way down the ivory-colored corridor. A middle-aged woman, with an oxygen tube like a plastic mustache on her upper lip, glanced at them from her wheelchair. A couple of plump women in green smocks strode past with the detached manner of those who cope daily with other people's crises.

Drake harbored no fear of hospitals, having spent almost no time in them. But he feared what he might see in Astrid's room. There'd be no blood, no gaping wound. The doctors would have seen to that. Still, pain and fear can leave other marks.

The door to her room was cracked open, and Drake heard Detective Akinyi ask, "And you didn't know him?" Drake relaxed a little at the sound of Akinyi's voice. She sounded mature, calm, a little weary. Like a mother talking to a teenage daughter.

Carter made to open the door, but Drake touched a finger to his lips. He wanted to hear Astrid's answer, to hear her voice before seeing her face.

It came rasping out, weak and a little hoarse, and Drake strained to hear.

"Believe me," Astrid said, "I'd have remembered."

Drake smiled at Carter. Carter smiled back and pushed open the door.

He'd expected the cardiac monitor that pulsed and flickered just above her bed and the intravenous drip that fed a stream of liquid into Astrid's left arm. But he was taken aback by the massive bruise that had discolored and swollen the flesh around her right eye. The guy hadn't just stabbed her. He'd struck her in the face.

The injury that had nearly killed Astrid was invisible to him, hidden by a bandage that peeked from the top of her pale-green hospital gown. But the bruise was right there, where she'd seen it when the nurses let her have a mirror. That bruise would mock her and shame her. She'd been owned.

For a second or two, Drake savored the unfamiliar intoxicant of raw fury. Then Astrid turned her head toward the door and her two new visitors. For a moment nothing changed. And then came a warm, slow smile, tentative, as if it hurt her to smile. But whatever the pain, she accepted it and glowed at them and said, "Hey, you took your time," in a thick, rasping voice.

Drake couldn't help grinning. "No hurry. You aren't going anywhere for a while."

"So I've been told. Doctor said the left lung was involved." Which explained why Astrid spoke in short, breathy surges, with a gentle gasp every few words. "Involved, he said. Like my lung was an accomplice. Maybe I should get it a lawyer."

"No brain damage, at least."

"No more than usual."

Drake held up his communion kit. "First Sunday. Carter and me were out bringing communion to our shut-ins. You want some?"

Astrid almost frowned then, but the corners of her mouth thought better of it and twitched upward. "Not just now," she rasped. "Hurts to swallow."

"Y'all put that on hold," said Akinyi, her right hand poised over a small notebook. "I've got more questions."

"Such as?" asked Astrid.

"Well, what'd he look like?"

"Like a blur. The room was pretty dark. Most of the lights off. Standard procedure when I'm coding. Easier on the eyes."

"Coding?" asked Drake. "For the church?"

"Oh no. For me. In Computer Lab One. In the basement. I was doing maintenance. On your network. Installed some patches. Updated the anti-malware. Junk like that. Didn't take long. Then I did coding. For me."

"MIT stuff."

"Yeah. It was quiet. I was comfortable. Plugged in my Mac. Got to work."

"What time was this?" asked Detective Akinyi.

"Around ten."

"So you'd been at it for a couple of hours before the guy got in."

"Must be. A little hazy on time. Hazy on lots of things."

"Of course," Akinyi said. "Take your time."

"So anyway, door to the lab. Was open. And I heard something. Like . . . broken glass. Coming from upstairs. Grabbed my phone. Called 911. Then . . . I waited."

"You didn't confront the guy?" Akinyi asked.

"Wanted to. Hate to hide. But looking for trouble is dumb."

"So you hunkered down to wait."

"Shelter in place. Campus security calls it that. We were trained. You never know. Some kid on the MIT pistol team . . . might go nuts someday."

"So you barricaded the lab door?"

"No time. Closed and locked, though."

"But he found you."

Astrid sighed, shook her head. "Dumb. Dumb, dumb, dumb."

"Stop that," said Drake. "You did nothing wrong."

"Except I left my Mac on. I was in the back of the room. In a corner. In the dark. Safe. Then I saw my MacBook. On the desk. All lit up. He'd see. Through the glass. In the door. So I took a chance. Moved toward the desk. All I had to do. Close the lid. Go dark. Just as I got there. He saw."

"So he busted in."

"Yeah. He rattled the doorknob. Saw it was locked. Kicked it in."

The fear she'd felt then was in her face now, and Drake thought that it must hurt her bruises to grimace that way.

"And then what happened?" Akinyi asked, in a low monotone, as if she dreaded the reply.

"He came toward me. Didn't say a thing. Didn't rush. Didn't hesitate. Just walking. Hands at his sides. Pale hands. Pale face. Great big guy. White. Or Asian maybe. Not black. Definitely not."

"Then what?" Akinyi asked again. "I'm sorry, but you have to say."

"Not much to say. I grabbed a chair. Wanted to throw it at him. Never got it up. He got there first. Hit me. I think. He must have. Don't remember being hit. Don't remember anything else. Till I was here."

Astrid's eyes were streaming. Drake stepped toward the bedside table, where a box of Kleenex lay. He fluffed out a couple, smoothed them over her eyelids and cheeks. He'd never touched Astrid before and felt he was taking a liberty, but she made nothing of it.

"Let it go," Drake said. He pulled up a chair alongside the bed, settled into it, clutched at Astrid's hand. He saw Carter and Akinyi trade glances, as if they'd never seen a deacon offering comfort to a suffering woman.

It lasted a couple of minutes. Then Astrid shifted on the bed, nodded at Akinyi. "What else do you need to know?"

"We're trying to figure out why it happened," Akinyi replied. "Why would somebody want to attack you?"

"Guess we'll know. When you catch him."

"Any chance it was a boyfriend?"

"I'd have noticed. Enough light for that."

"Still, maybe we should contact anyone you're close to, just to see what he was doing that night."

"No point. I'm between entanglements."

"Any exes we should know about?"

"Back in Minnesota. None here."

Astrid didn't even glance at Drake.

"Maybe somebody you turned down?"

"Don't think so. No offers lately. I been busy." There was a wry crinkle of her unbruised right cheek, and this time a glance at Drake.

"Well." Akinyi sighed and jotted in her notepad.

"Robbery, then, I guess," said Astrid. "What else?"

"We don't see any sign that he took anything." She glanced at Drake and Carter. "By the way, we'll need you to confirm that for us. We'll let you into the building, and you can tell us if anything's gone. But we didn't notice anything missing. Computers were still there, and no other doors were forced open."

"My stuff?" Astrid asked.

"Found your purse untouched. Wallet, credit cards, key to your bike all there."

"Find my phone? My laptop?"

"Yeah, right, you had a laptop," said Akinyi. "A Mac, right? The guy must have taken that. Didn't see a phone either, so I guess that's gone."

"No sweat," Drake said to her with a half-smile. "They'll grow back."

But his attempt at a joke didn't go over. Astrid looked anxious. Not quite frightened, but worried.

"Was there anything on that laptop or the phone that was worth stealing?" Akinyi asked.

Astrid was silent for a few seconds. Then, "No." The word came out in a drawn-out hum.

Nobody spoke for a while, as if waiting for Astrid's voice to fade away. Then Akinyi said, "So what was on it?"

Astrid glanced at Drake, back at Akinyi. Her breaths came quicker now, in soft, raspy gasps. "My work. Just my work. You wouldn't understand. Nothing illegal. Just research. Formal verification. Algorithmic bias filters. Stuff like that." She glanced at Drake again. "We talked about it. You wrote about it."

"Yeah," said Drake. "I barely understood it. But I understood enough to know it's nothing that would get you hurt. So if it's about your work, you must be working on something else."

"Nothing much." Astrid stared at Drake, as if he were the only one in the room. He heard Carter's feet shuffling against the floor, Akinyi's notebook flipping shut.

"Okay," the detective said. "That's enough for now. You need your rest. I want you to lie there and think. Think about anything you missed, anything that might help us. Can you do that?"

Astrid said nothing, just nodded.

"Officer Carter, can I borrow you for a minute?" Akinyi said as she moved toward the door. Carter glanced at Akinyi, then Drake, his face showing nothing. Then both of them stepped out and the door shut.

"Alone at last," said Astrid, without a smile.

"How you feel?" asked Drake. "Really?"

"Like a punctured tire. Patch hurts like hell. Wish I didn't breathe."

"We were all so worried about you."

"Not sure why. Not a member."

"Come on. You know better."

"Yeah. Sorry."

"You should have heard Pastor's sermon. Not a dry eye in the joint."

Astrid smiled, gave out a dry, hissing chuckle.

"No, for real. I'll send you a recording."

"What'll I play it on? They stole my phone."

"We'll get you a new one. iPhone, right?"

"Yeah. I'm on AT&T."

"Okay. First, I'll hunt around more in the church. It might not have been stolen. You might have put it down someplace. I do that all the time with mine."

"I don't think so."

"Well, it never hurts to look." Drake hesitated like a man stepping onto ice. "Suppose I found it. What would I find inside?"

"You won't get inside. Not till I say so."

There was defiance in her voice. Drake had half-expected it, but it chilled him just the same.

"Well, anyway, we have to find it first," he said and saw her relax a little. "But in the meantime, why don't you tell me what you didn't tell the detective."

"I told her everything. All I remembered."

"But you didn't tell her what you've got on that computer or in your phone. What'd you leave out?"

Astrid lay silent and Drake let her think.

After a while he said, "It's got to be the laptop or the phone, or both. Common sense. Only things that were touched, except you. And you say you didn't know the guy who attacked you. I believe that. So he was after something you had. Something digital that could only be on a computer or a phone.

"Akinyi's not stupid. She'll keep at you about this till you give it up. So will I."

As he talked, Astrid had slowly shifted in the bed so that her back was almost turned toward him, and he could no longer see her face. The hospital gown exposed a patch of bare brown skin. Drake thought of how much the effort must have hurt her.

"Comfortable?" he asked.

"I'm all right." Her right hand, entubed with IV lines, was pressed against her cheek, muffling her words.

"So come on. Tell me the rest."

More silence, and then, "Not much to tell. Just some research. Spare time. Few hours a week."

"What's it about?"

"Well . . ." Astrid licked her lips. "Crime, actually."

In the silence that followed, Drake heard a nurse bustling down the corridor, a lightly laden cart rolling past the door. It was like that for maybe ten seconds.

"I just didn't think," Astrid said, her gasps coming quicker now. "I mean, we're not criminals. We didn't do anything. Just research."

"Research?"

"Yeah. Research. Into botnets. Probing them. Looking for weaknesses.

70

New ways to take them down. They're the criminals. Not us. Not us."

"I know, Astrid," Drake said. "I know."

His words seemed to calm her a little, but her breaths still came quick and her limbs twitched under the hospital sheets. "We studied stuff. So do lots of people. Universities. Security companies. Around the world. Always looking."

Drake had written often enough about botnets, vast networks of computers infected with illicit software and remotely controlled by criminal gangs. Thousands of botnets made up of thousands or even millions of otherwise law-abiding computers sitting in living rooms and business offices. Crooks used them to pump out billions of spam emails, or launch attacks on other computers, attacks strong enough to knock them off the Internet.

"So you went after some guys running one of these botnets?"

"Not the guys. No idea who they are. Don't care. Just the software. We studied it. To learn how it works. How to stop it. It's a challenge. That's why. We worked for the challenge."

"You keep saying 'we,'" Drake said. "You and who else?"

Astrid's eyes widened. "You don't think? I mean, why? What's the point? It's just a bot."

Drake squirmed in his chair, as if trying to scratch an itch. "But who's this 'we'?"

"Friends of mine," said Astrid. "Researchers. White hats. Gray hats."

"A team effort?" Drake asked.

"That's what it takes. Me, Borzoi, Clinker, Mesh. Some others."

"Clinker?" asked Drake. Above Astrid's bed, the heart monitor showed a pulse rate rising into the eighties. Drake was glad he wasn't plugged into an EKG just then.

He forced himself back into the chair, eased his grip on the armrests. "Clinker," he said, this time in a flat, disinterested voice.

"You know him?" Astrid said.

"Heard of him. Pretty well known in the security game."

"Yeah. We hung out at DefCon. Couple years back. Bot researcher. He had some cool ideas. Covert disruption of C&C. Take a bot right off the air. Bad guys wouldn't know. What hit them."

"So you guys shut down these botnets?" asked Drake.

"No. Just learning how. Big one too. One of the biggest."

"You keep in touch with your buddies, then?"

"Every day," replied Astrid, in a fretful voice. "They'll be wondering."

"Yeah," Drake said. "Look, you better get in touch. Tell them what happened."

"You're right. They need to know."

"Okay," said Drake. "How?"

"Address book. On my phone." Astrid winced then, though not from the knife wound. "Stupid. Gone. Doesn't matter. Log onto blankmail.com. Username is Snowbird."

"And the password?" asked Drake.

"Just like we talked about. That time. Remember?"

"You've never given me any passwords."

"No. That time I explained the principle. Principle of the thing. Remember? Just go hash. Right of sanctuary. Star. Easy."

"Yeah, I guess so." Drake pulled out his notebook, the kind reporters always carry, and jotted for a couple of seconds.

"You better hurry," Astrid said. "Just in case."

"Look, Astrid, chances are . . ."

"I know. But hurry."

AKINYI AND CARTER were huddled in conversation a couple of yards down the corridor. They glanced up as Drake emerged, then at each other.

"She tell you?" Akinyi asked.

It had taken no more than three seconds for Drake to open the door to Astrid's room, step out, and close it behind him. In those three seconds he'd decided what to say.

"Wasn't anything else to tell," he said.

"Or you don't know how to ask. I thought reporters were good at asking questions." There was no hostility in Akinyi's words. More like disappointment.

Drake responded in kind. "I thought so too. But then she's my first stabbing victim."

"She knows more than she's saying, that's for sure. This wasn't a random attack. And the guy took just two things—the electronics. That's what they wanted. Count on it."

"More than likely," said Drake in a noncommittal way. It made Akinyi stare at him for a second, as if she were trying to memorize his features so she could describe him later to a police sketch artist. He felt himself flushing under the scrutiny and wondered if she noticed his dark face getting even darker.

Akinyi's high-beam gaze swept away from him and toward Carter. "We better start beating the bushes for that laptop and phone."

Carter shrugged. "They might turn up. We can contact Apple. Give them her name and they'll provide the serial numbers."

"I suppose your forensics lab can find a way into the machines," said Drake, "when you get them." Not "if you get them," but "when." He figured a dose of optimism would convince Akinyi he was on her side.

"I'm more interested in their outsides," Akinyi said. "Fingerprints, fibers, dead skin. Or a good description of the trash bag who offered them for sale. Any or all of the above." She yawned, extended her arms, and tensed her body. The stretching motion pushed Akinyi's plump hips and chest against the pantsuit, a distraction just when Drake needed his wits.

"Well, I've got stuff to do," he said with a nod to Carter.

"Right," Carter replied. "First Sunday."

Drake shrugged and made for the elevators.

CHAPTER SIX

IT WAS STRAIGHT home for Drake, with not a thought for Sister Walker and her communion visit. He thought only of the secrets hidden in Astrid's emails.

An empty beer can littered the floor of the elevator. Before she'd left, Alicia had complained that the building was headed downhill. Too many apartments crammed with recent arrivals from China, nearly all of them young men. Drake had found them slovenly but well-behaved. Still, they'd frightened Alicia, who dreaded their company in the elevators. She'd urged him to move; he'd scoffed and said he was holding out for the right price.

Maybe if he'd sold he'd be in a nicer neighborhood now, with a pregnant wife for company.

The elevator pinged and Drake strode out and down the corridor to his door. In the spare bedroom, he plugged in his half-drained smartphone and woke up his dormant computer. Drake popped open a Web browser and entered blankmail.com, a Swiss company that promised ultra-secure email services, with all files stored in a country with strict privacy laws. Astrid was taking no chances.

He punched in *snowbird@blankmail.com* as her username. Now the password. He remembered Astrid's instructions. "Hash. Right of sanctuary. Star."

He typed in the # symbol, then started typing the word *sanctuary*, but with the letters transposed two keys to the right. It read as *fd,buodyi*. An ancient gimmick for creating a tough yet memorable password. Then the

74

* symbol and Enter.

Bad password. Drake grimaced, tried it again. So easy to make a typo when using the transposition trick. But the password still didn't work. Maybe he'd heard her wrong.

Then Drake chuckled and started over. This time, he typed the # sign, then *ypjku[hfd,buodyi*, and then the * symbol.

Astrid had meant what she'd said. The # symbol, immediately followed by the letters *rightofsanctuary*, transposed two places to the right, and then the * symbol. That was eighteen bewildering characters. Not a perfect defense against a determined attacker, but not bad.

It worked. The screen filled with email headers, subject lines, dates. Running his eyes down the page, Drake noted that email just twenty lines down from the top was seven months old. Astrid didn't use this account very often.

He noticed a folder on the left edge of the screen named *Silverware*. Perhaps Astrid had made it easy on herself, and now Drake, by setting up a filter to dump all her hacking-related messages in a single folder. He pointed and clicked.

Drake was rewarded with a screenful of messages. The one at the top of the stack, sent about fourteen hours earlier, bore a subject line that chilled his fingertips: *CLINKER DOWN.*

Drake clicked and read, his eyes darting across the lines too fast to absorb them all, as he scanned for the most frightful words and found them—*murdered* and *knife* and *scary.*

After a few seconds, he closed his eyes, turned away from the screen, forced himself toward calm. It took a couple of minutes. Then he returned to the message.

The FROM: field was populated by the address *gallery@blankmail. com.* No idea who that was.

More important was the stuff in the TO: field. Multiple addresses, all ending in *blankmail.com.* Snowbird was there. Astrid, of course. Then came Borzoi, Mesh, Stainless, Kirsch, and Clinker. An email to the dead. Gallery had left his own address in the field as well, sending a copy of the message to himself.

This must be a group email sent to a preset list of contacts. Likely as not,

Drake had just found the email addresses of the entire Silverware group.

Drake highlighted every address, right-clicked, and made a copy.

He opened another browser tab, logged on to the *Boston Record*'s email server, opened a blank email, and pasted in the addresses. When sending the same message to more than one person, he usually opted for the "blind carbon copy" feature, but not this time. He wanted each recipient to realize that Drake knew about the others. And he used his Record email account, hoping that a band of gray-hat hackers might respond better to an email from a journalist. Many of that sort loved publicity.

But it'd be just as well to keep his potential sources alive.

Drake returned to the Gallery email that had almost panicked him a minute earlier and took his time reading it.

Terrible news. Somebody's killed Clinker. No idea why. It's all over Slashdot. Since then I found a report in English on Deutsche Welle, and a couple of Hamburg papers that I ran through Google Translate. Not much in any of them. He was murdered with a knife. They tore up his house, took his computers.

It's probably home invaders or junkies. But we've been working on some pretty scary stuff the last few weeks and I can't help wondering if there's a connection. Probably not. But we better be careful. If you've got someplace else to stay for a day or two, I suggest you stay there. I know this sounds paranoid, but maybe we haven't been paranoid enough. So get going. And keep your ears on. If anything happens, post it to the group. Stay safe.

Not a word about what had happened to Astrid. So the Silverware squad could still take comfort in the hope that Clinker's fate was a tragic misfortune and nothing more. That sort of optimism could get a couple more of them killed.

Drake flipped back into his own outbound email window and started typing. He identified himself and told them about the attack on Astrid, the knife wound, the theft of her laptop and phone.

"No way is this coincidence," Drake wrote.

You might want to take a vacation for a few days. In the meantime, I'm in touch with Boston police. We're doing everything we can to figure this out.

If somebody is after you, telling me what you know might be your best protection. Once we publish the story, there's no point in harming you. So talk to me.

Drake made sure the message bore his sig, complete with the various ways to contact him—email, Web, Facebook, Twitter, and three different phone numbers. Then he hit Send.

Having done his duty, Drake felt free to go exploring Astrid's mailbox. It was well organized, with a multitude of subfolders. Each bore the sort of name Drake would have expected. *Tools. Samples. Reliant.* This last might well have contained lesson plans and related materials for her coding class at the church.

Still others were more personal. *Family Reunion*, for instance, and *Thanksgiving Photos 2015.* On a whim, Drake clicked this one, finding family snapshots from Minnesota. Drake glanced through a few, saw a tall, graying man with Astrid's jaw and a handsome sapling of a woman who looked at the camera with Astrid's eyes.

After a minute or two, Drake forced himself to quit. He reopened Silverware and began browsing the emails there.

THE EMAILS WENT back in time about two years, with the most recent sent about two weeks ago. A good deal of it involved the group's effort to deconstruct a piece of malware nicknamed Botch. Drake had heard of it, an aggressive little marvel that used redundant bulletproof servers in Eastern Europe as home base. Links to these servers had been hidden in the JavaScript of infected porn websites, spreading Botch to thousands of computers whose owners had come looking for MILF videos.

Botch was harmless in itself. It was merely a carrier for the true menace. Once it was on board, it signaled its masters to send along any number of hostile payloads—a keylogger to capture the user's passwords, a backdoor for bypassing the computer's security features, a stresser for running denial-of-service Internet attacks on other machines—whatever their dirty work required.

Astrid and her buddies were having the time of their lives deconstructing Botch and its various nefarious payloads, like weekend fishermen discussing their favorite lures.

Then in a message thread that had been initiated by Borzoi about three months ago, Drake saw a word that made him pause. There it was, right in the subject line: "What's up with Largent?"

Largent. Like Steve. The football player. Wide receiver for the Seattle Seahawks in the 1980s. Seven Pro Bowls. Best white guy ever to play the position, or so Drake's football-crazed father would say on Sunday afternoons.

So what was up with Largent?

"Where is it?" was the opening line of Borzoi's email. "If we're going to hit our timeline, I'll need to begin testing in the next couple days. Stainless, this is your department. Can you light a fire under Revere? Tell him we need it yesterday."

There was no Revere in the email list, so this person was an outsider. Maybe a contractor brought in to contribute a single chunk of code. Something the Silverware team needed to complete their work.

The thread ended with a simple message from Stainless. "Received and understood. Igniting blowtorch."

The crisp, sardonic tone of the message reminded Drake of his chats with Astrid. Birds of a feather.

Drake kept skimming the emails. There was much more about Botch—smarter ways to conceal it from malware detectors, the pros and cons of building in a kill switch that could deactivate the entire botnet in a matter of hours.

Astrid had said that she and her friends were working on strategies for taking down a botnet. Instead, most of the emails described ways to improve upon it. They weren't breaking Botch. They were buffing it.

Most botnet software was cobbled together by serious but undistinguished programmers who knew just enough to make nuisances of themselves. An MIT postdoc like Astrid and a few of her smarter friends could polish the code till it glowed. Like silverware.

Akinyi might need two sets of handcuffs. One for the assailant and one for the victim.

Heartsick now but persistent, Drake read on. In a message to Borzoi from Stainless, sent about six weeks ago, the word Largent appeared again.

"Here it is, everybody. Feel free to peek. Borzoi, get to work."

A notation indicated that there had been a zip file attached to the original email. Drake would probably find a copy somewhere in Astrid's files, but he saw no point in looking for it just then.

"I just ripped open my new present," wrote Borzoi. "I'm mucking around in it and what I'm seeing looks sort of familiar. Like the creator knows how we do things downtown. Looking forward to taking off the leash. Might prove juicy."

About a week later:

Turned Largent loose in the petting zoo today. Pretty bad, which is pretty good for us. I get unlimited access to every correspondent bank account. If it works like this in the wild, you could just issue the order and the money's gone. All safeguards bypassed. It covers its tracks by rewriting the logs. And it rootkits the servers. Very clean. Almost impossible to find if you're not looking, or if you are. How did code this crappy slip past QC? There's got to be at least five zero days floating around in there to make something like this work. Somebody needs to lose his job. And I guarantee somebody will.

Feel free to check my work, but I think this is the proverbial it. You guys can start welding stuff together.

Borzoi was a happy man.

Not so for Clinker. A couple of days later came a message from him headed "Second thoughts":

Guys, I'm all for getting paid. But this is dangerous. I've gone through the code and I think it's better than it ought to be. Way too good. One thing to empty out a few insured bank accounts. But this could do a lot worse. You know how many major banks run this stuff? At least half of the biggest. Somebody goes crazy with this, and it's 2008 all over again.

Steal a million and one day they stop looking for you. Steal a billion and they never stop. That's us if these people get greedy. We can still back away. Matter of fact, I think we should. I know one of the developers—we were at CMU together. One word, and it's fixed.

Borzoi, Stainless, Gallery, Kirsch—Clinker's mates replied with curses and contempt. But a couple of names were missing. Snowbird and Mesh. Not a word from either of them.

Not till further down, when Drake found an email sent directly from Mesh to Clinker. None of the other team members were copied in. Except Snowbird. Mesh must have sent her a bcc—a blind carbon copy.

Thinking about your message. You may be right. It's all fun and games until somebody loses a global economy, yes? Maybe we should shut this business down right now. I've got a career to think about and so do you.

Too bad the others disagree. But we don't really need their permission. Just ping your pal and let him straighten it out. He can say he found the bugs himself. Bet there's a bounty. So let him collect it.

If you're feeling noble, I'll understand.

About an hour later came a terse message from Snowbird: "Concur. Let's shut this down."

Drake smiled to see it. She'd come to her senses, tried to back out. Her veto of the plan had almost gotten her killed, but it also saved her. When the truth came out, Astrid would walk away.

But she'd put it off too late. Already, people were bleeding.

But what had Astrid gotten herself into? And how, and why? There was a paycheck in it, he supposed—a way to make the payments on that fancy bike.

Astrid and her crew probably figured on earning a tasty consulting fee from a bunch of black hats who knew their limitations. They'd been recruited to help them develop some serious, professional-grade malware.

A program, or a set of programs, codenamed Largent. Easier to type than *l'argent*, the French word for silver, and for money.

It was some kind of bank job, and something that would pay off big. But their employer was already big. Big enough, perhaps, to be motivated by something other than money.

Power, perhaps world-changing power. The kind any government would crave. And every government deals in violence, cultivating brutal men and giving them guns, knives, and plane tickets to Hamburg or Boston.

It was 7:00 p.m. by now, and on the other side of his window the June sky was starting to dim. For all his worry, Drake was hungry. Too late, he remembered his plans for the raw chicken in the fridge. Across the street, then, to the Foster House for beer-dipped calamari and a glass of the beer they'd been dipped in. A house specialty.

First, he checked his email. It had been an hour since Drake had pinged out a warning to the Silverware group. No responses thus far. Nor were there any new messages in Astrid's Silverware account.

It came to Drake that he had one more email to send, one he should have sent before now. He checked his online address book and located the entry for Bernard Severins, MIT professor of computer science and Astrid's faculty advisor.

Though Drake didn't know him well, he'd met Bernard Severins years before he'd known Astrid, after Severins had stood on a stage in Las Vegas and humiliated three of the nation's biggest banks.

Drake had seen the show in person. It had happened at DefCon, the big annual gathering of crackers and cybercops. Severins stood with an Android phone in his hand. He was a lean man, muscular like a cyclist, with trim black hair and a full beard, both just starting to gray a little. And he'd made a spectacle of himself by dressing like a grown-up—a crisp blue blazer, an open-collared white shirt, and tan slacks.

Severins gazed out at the thousand or so who'd come to watch.

"I need a volunteer," Severins told the crowd. "Anybody here got an account with Black Diamond Bank?" A host of hands waved at him. "Got the mobile app?" Most of the hands stayed aloft. "Mind if I borrow a hundred bucks from your account?" Most of the hands dropped away at that, amid a rustle of uneasy laughter.

"I promise I'll give it all back," Severins had said in a corn-syrup voice. "I just want to prove a point." Shading his eyes from the glare of the stage lights, he singled out one of the hands that had remained resolutely raised. "Okay, ma'am, come on up."

The woman had bounded down the aisle as if afraid of missing her chance. She wore jeans, a Red Hat Linux T-shirt, and a plump, alert face framed in lanky brown hair. She might have been a DefCon regular; a thousand miles from husband, house, and kids; up for a challenge; out for a good time.

So she stood on the stage and did what she was told, which was to open her Black Diamond banking app and log on. Meanwhile, Severins tapped away at the screen of his phone. In a minute, Severins had turned a hundred dollars of her money into his money. The volunteer laughed and squealed as her app confirmed that the money had been extracted from her account.

He told the woman to stand by—he'd need to get her contact information to send her a refund check—then called for volunteers with accounts at two other prominent banks. Two T-shirted male victims presented themselves, and one by one, Severins owned them, or rather their bank accounts.

As the laughter and cheers died away, Severins admitted he'd been a bad boy. "Standard procedure in cases like this is for me to contact the companies first and warn them to fix the flaws in their software. Well, where's the fun in that?" The audience cheered, and Severins had to shout to make himself heard. "These are banks. Three of the biggest in the country. And there are MIT freshmen who could have done what I just did. Hell, there are freshmen at Bunker Hill Community College who could do it. It's that simple. And fixing the flaw is simple too. These people were just too ignorant or too lazy or too cheap to do it. Well, if they can't be bothered to protect themselves, why should I be?"

Amid howls of admiration, Severins dropped the microphone and strode off the stage.

Not everyone at DefCon was pleased. The chief software security officer of one of the banks, there to pick up some pointers, had gotten a harder lesson than he'd bargained for. Drake tracked him down, switched his smartphone into voice record mode, and shoved it under the man's nose. He was rewarded by an almost hysterical denunciation of Severins's "unethical, almost terroristic tactics."

Statements issued by the other two banks were only slightly more civil. And Drake later learned that Severins' next meeting with the chairman of his department was both long and loud. But Severins had been right about the security problems. And the man had tenure.

Astrid had been involved on the periphery of Severins's app-cracking; she'd told Drake so later. He never knew where she found the time, or even the calories. The girl revved high, always ready for a new project. No doubt she was in the thick of Severins's research.

Besides, over beers at the Meadhall, Astrid had once hinted at a relationship with Severins that had gone well beyond the academic. She'd casually mentioned a weekend drive to Maine that she'd taken with Bart—he was "Bart" to his friends, Astrid said. He hated being called "Bernie." The envy that had pricked at Drake as she spoke had come as a bitter surprise to him.

Just now, his feelings were not relevant, but Severins's were. He owed the man an update on Astrid's condition. And there was a chance he knew something of Astrid's underground activities.

Drake didn't have Severins's cell phone number, and his office line flung the call into the voice mail system. Drake left a message, choosing cautious phrases that would not inspire panic if he hadn't heard about the attack on Astrid. Then Drake wrote up an email designed along similar lines and sent it on its way.

Drake unplugged his recharged phone, snatched up his suit jacket, and left. He drew the same elevator he'd ridden on the way up; the empty beer can was still there. Drake picked it up between thumb and forefinger, as a ratcatcher might. It felt greasy.

Over at the Foster House, Drake hit the men's room to wash away whatever had been on the can. Then he settled onto a barstool, asked for calamari and Bass Ale.

"One for the TV star," said Jerry, the barman and part owner of the place, as he pulled a pint.

Drake felt himself blush again. He hated being recognized, a foolish attitude for someone who did the occasional TV appearance. In lieu of a verbal reply, he shrugged and offered a little smile, just enough to avoid rudeness.

"Too bad about that lady at your church," said Jerry, a compact, muscular man with reddish hair and a florid face. "Police got any ideas yet?"

"Not a one." Drake was in no mood for talk, and for that reason he gazed straight at Jerry and fixed on his face an expression that he hoped would seem welcoming. He'd decided months ago, for his own soul's sake, to ease up on the misanthropy.

"Glad she's gonna be all right. God musta been watching out," said Jerry. Then, after a moment, "But a church? Man, that's wrong."

"Wrong, and strange. I have no idea why it would happen," Drake said. A split-second after the words had left his mouth, he realized that he'd just told a lie.

THE CALAMARI GONE, the beer swallowed, Drake returned home. He hadn't checked his email for an hour, not that he'd expected any. Yet there in his inbox was a reply from Severins, about fifteen minutes old.

Crazy, isn't it? I'm willing to talk, but not on the record. Please ping me back. If you're up to it, maybe we can get together tonight. I keep strange hours. I'm in Stata. Here's my cell. Phone me when you get here and I'll come let you in.

CHAPTER SEVEN

THE STATA CENTER had cost $300 million to build and looked as if it were falling down. Mission accomplished for its world-famed architect, who had once boasted that the structure resembled a party thrown by a band of drunken robots.

Drake had always liked the place, or rather the outside of it, with its angular, metallic walls that sometimes slouched, sometimes jutted above its human visitors. It was as if Optimus Prime, in the middle of transforming from one sort of machine into another, had shorted out and frozen into place.

But while the outside charmed him, Drake had never fancied finding his way through the interior, full of misshapen offices, distorted corridors, and unexpected dead ends. No matter: he didn't have to work here, and the scholars who did had brains enough to figure it out.

Walking in from Mass Ave, still a block from the main entrance, Drake whipped out his phone, dialed Severins. He might already be in the lobby, waiting. But Drake couldn't see. The front of the place was obstructed by a compound arch composed of granite blocks, with a plaque at the center of it all. It was a somber monument to the MIT cop who'd been murdered on the spot by the same terrorists who'd bombed the Boston Marathon.

"Hello?"

"I'm almost there," said Drake. "You in the lobby?"

"Right at the door." The connection broke.

So Severins had waited in the lobby. A worried man.

Severins heaved the glass door open with his left hand and extended his right. "It's been a while," the professor said. He was shorter than Drake and wiry. The beard was trimmer than Drake remembered, and his trim, graying hair seemed painted rather than combed against his skull.

"Sorry for interrupting your Sunday," said Drake.

"You're not." Severins led the way into the interior of the building, angling his way toward a bank of elevators.

"You visited her in the hospital?" Severins asked.

"Sure," Drake replied. "She seemed pretty glad to see me. She was even happier to see the police at her bedside." It was a deliberate probe, but Severins hardly reacted at all.

They elevatored up to the fifth floor, where Severins occupied a relatively spacious office overlooking Vassar Street. The place was pure function. Three of its four walls were all shelves, full of books, journals, and file folders. Not a man for wasting time at the library.

On his desk sat a couple of anonymous-looking black monoliths, and a silvery MacBook, with connections running to a KVM switch perched within easy reach of Severins's right hand, so he could run all three machines through a single keyboard, mouse, and monitor.

The monitor was huge—thirty-five inches at least—and it emitted a plum-colored glow. Judging by the icons, he was running the Ubuntu version of the Linux operating system. Severins probably had Microsoft Windows running on the other big box, and Mac OS on the laptop.

Severins gestured toward a chair. "Good of you to reach out to me. I was on the road and just got back. Saw the news. Terrible."

"Yeah, but she's okay. Or she will be."

"What was she doing in a church?"

"Didn't you know?"

Severins shook his head, and Drake told him.

"I had no idea," the professor said. "Not surprised, though. She never stopped, that one."

"Maybe that's why Astrid came to teach at the church. Her way of easing back."

"Perhaps. And at a church too. Has she found God?"

"I'm not sure she's looking. She may have just wanted to do some good for the community. But I suspect there was more to it. Almost like she was trying to atone for something."

"Atone?" Severins's eyes widened a bit. "Atone for what?"

"I was hoping you could tell me. I think she was up to something that got her into trouble."

"Something related to her work with me?"

"I doubt it," said Drake. "I'm thinking it was freelance work. But you two were pretty close. And you spoke the same language. So I thought she might have told you about it."

"We talk all the time about her research on algorithmic discrimination. That's her specialty, you know. You've even written about it." Severins's voice mellowed. He relaxed in his chair, and it seemed to Drake that if Severins had had a cigar, he'd have lit it.

"Yeah, but we both know nobody'd go after her over that. And we both know she worked on other things. I'm just asking if you know about those other things."

"I work with a dozen grad students," said Severins. "Keeping up with their research projects is difficult enough. I don't have time to track their extracurricular activities. I don't have the time, or the interest."

There was a tone of dismissal in the way Severins said it.

"Not interested, huh?" said Drake. "Well, you made time for Astrid that weekend in Maine. Somehow you squeezed that in."

Drake expected anger from Severins, or shame. Instead, one corner of his mouth quirked upward, and there was a brief puff of breath, the sound of a suppressed chuckle.

"It was just a couple of times," Severins said. "Exactly two." There was an outright smile on his face now. "You don't forget such weekends."

"Well, well," said Drake. "You're feeling proud of yourself." He allowed himself a smile of his own, as a new coldness in Severins's eyes showed that his response had hit home. "Anyway, since you guys know each other so well, maybe she's spoken to you about her hobbies."

"Hobbies? I don't think she had any."

"That's not what she said. I understand she loved to tinker with malware. Disassemble the stuff to figure out how it worked. She even had a network of buddies who shared her interests."

"Buddies?"

"Yep. Allies from the hacking community. People with nicknames like Borzoi and Stainless and Clinker."

That last name got Severins's attention, as Drake had hoped. There was that narrowing of the eyes again, but this time there seemed no anger in the professor's face. It was something more like resignation.

"Friends of yours?" asked Drake.

"We've been in touch. If you don't mind my asking, how did you come to know them?"

"Just what I read in the papers. And in Astrid's emails. She gave me the key."

Severins sighed. "That figures. Assisting the police in their enquiries, are you?"

"I just took a look for myself, to see what she'd gotten into."

"How'd you persuade her to give it up?"

"Wasn't hard. She's scared, and she's doped up on pain meds. And she needed somebody to confide in. You were out of town on business, so I got elected."

"You keep that up, you're going to make me jealous."

"You're not the type," said Drake. "Besides, Astrid didn't need to confide in you, since you already knew. About Botch and Largent. About all of it."

Severins stared at Drake in silence for a few moments. But Drake's guess—it was only a guess—had not shocked him. Severins's manner radiated guilty knowledge, but without the guilt.

At length, he smiled again, leaned back in his chair. "Yes, those names do ring a bell."

"And you know about Clinker."

"I heard the news."

"On the grapevine?"

"In a manner of speaking. I'm Stainless."

Drake had expected something like this, but not Severins's casual, candid admission. He was wordless for a few moments, mulling Severins's words and wishing all at once that he hadn't come to this meeting at night, and alone.

"So, Stainless, you're not worried about your safety? Not after what just happened to Clinker, and to Astrid?"

"I'll be fine. I'm not the one bailing on the project."

"So you don't care that Clinker's dead, or that Astrid nearly joined him?"

"That shouldn't have happened. But it did. Nothing I can do about it, unless I want to wind up the same way. Which I don't."

"Besides, you aren't having second thoughts, like Astrid and Clinker, right? Whatever's going on, you're fine with it."

"Yeah, that too."

"Why?"

"Money. Lots of it, all extracted from people with plenty to spare. They'll hardly notice when it's gone."

"You sure? Clinker seemed to think that Largent could do a lot more damage than that. It could take down major banks, maybe smash up the whole economy."

"I doubt it'll get that far. If the people we're working with start to push things to an extreme, the central banks will step in and keep things under control. Their safeguards have safeguards, you know. Defense in depth."

"Do you believe what you're saying? Do you even care?" Drake said. "A woman you slept with gets stabbed, but you've hardly mentioned her. I'm thinking the fate of Wells Fargo or Citibank matters to you even less. You going to convert your cut to gold or bitcoin or something, then ride out the disaster?"

"There won't be any disaster. I really mean that," Severins said. "Certainly not for the global economy."

Drake felt a puff of air against his neck and read it as the silent opening of the office door.

"No, any disasters associated with this matter will be of a more personal nature." said Severins, who looked up, over Drake's head, at the face of a man who'd clamped his hands on Drake's shoulders and pressed him into the chair.

Drake was scared, but not surprised. It couldn't work out any other way. That had been clear the moment Severins had admitted he was in on it. Severins had been so free with information because he knew Drake would never tell.

Drake felt the fear taper away, as resignation took its place. His future was settled now. He'd have to hurt this man who held him down, or accept his own end without a murmur. He uttered a silent prayer for strength and wisdom for the coming moments, and for mercy.

He raised his eyes to Severins then. "Like I figured. You don't care what happens to anybody. Even Astrid. Once you're finished with me, you sending this guy after her again? To finish the job?"

"Probably not," said Severins. "With any luck it won't be necessary."

"It was necessary before. What's changed?" As he spoke, Drake twisted his head a little so he could see the man's right hand on his shoulders. It was thick, with large, long fingers stained with nicotine. A smoker, and right-handed.

"She'll see what happened to her as a warning," Severins replied. "She'll keep her mouth shut."

"Maybe. She's certainly had a good scare. It might work. Or not."

"I'm willing to take the risk," said Severins.

"You really care? That's a good sign. Shows you're not too far gone. You can still back away from this, whatever it is, before you do something that can't be fixed."

Severins shook his head. "I'm not alone in this thing. And the others, well . . . the others have pretty low standards. Not much they won't do. I think I can persuade them to leave Astrid alone. But you? I think that'd be a wasted effort."

Severins raised an eyebrow, gestured at the man gripping Drake's shoulders. "You better get going," he said. And the hands shifted to Drake's armpits, hauled him upright, rotated him, aimed him at the door.

The man was strong, much stronger than Drake. More than strong enough to slide a knife into a woman's chest. The same guy? More than likely.

Drake chose to believe it, wanted to believe it because he wanted to live. The thought fed him a galvanic surge of pure rage. He'd known that he would have to hurt the man; now he wanted to.

They lurched toward the bank of elevators, Drake's left arm pinioned to his back by the silent stranger.

"What you got in mind?" asked Drake. Not a sound. He still hadn't seen the man's face, but the way he gripped his arm, Drake figured the man was about the same height as himself, though a good deal more muscular.

The elevator came and the man shoved Drake aboard, rotated him to face the doors, then reached out a thick-fingered left hand to stab at the first-floor button. Drake felt the man's breath moist against the back of his neck, and a hard, brutal object pressing against the small of his back. A gun, most likely, clipped to the thug's belt.

Drake decided at that moment that the gun belonged to him, that the killer was just carrying it for him. His only problem now was arranging the handover. The thought relaxed him, made him inquisitive.

"I don't suppose you're a grad student?" he asked. For answer, the man chuckled softly, nothing more.

"What's the matter? Grades not good enough?"

Pain lanced his shoulder as the thug yanked at his arm.

"Hey, sorry, man. No offense meant. I'm not what you'd call a genius either. I couldn't even get Matt Damon's job up in here."

Silence.

"You ever see that movie?" Drake kept the words flowing, in a bid to make the attacker feel a measure of kinship with the victim. An empathetic murderer might relax his guard and give Drake a fighting chance. At worst, he might refrain from smashing Drake's kneecaps and settle for two painless rounds to the skull.

"I don't suppose you know exactly what's going on?" Drake asked, as the elevator slowed, stopped, opened. The thug shoved him forward, turned him toward the main exit. Drake glanced through the glass doors, toward the granite of the memorial. Cops stopped by from time to time, out of respect. There were none tonight.

Still, a kidnapper familiar with the history and lore of the campus would have chosen a less obvious exit from Stata. Not local talent, then, but a muscular young import.

They turned toward Vassar Street, where here and there a few cars nestled against the curbs. Most were shabby, festooned with rust spots and sardonic bumper stickers. No doubt the property of graduate students who at that moment were burrowing away deep inside their labs. Had Drake called out to them for help and made a dash for it, they probably would never have heard his screams or the shot that would have dropped him.

The same thought came to him as they approached a newish Mercedes, an SUV with its front seat occupied by a dark silhouette. He'd long ago read that kidnapping victims should seek to befriend their assailants rather than anger them. But the same magazine articles also posited an iron rule of survival: never get in the car. Do whatever you must to stay outside, on the street. When you get in the car with someone determined to harm you, your chances of survival resemble an asymptotic curve. On the good side of zero, but only just.

So as the man inside unlocked the doors, Drake felt a moment of desperation. The thug's grip on his arm was as firm as ever. He had no hope of snatching himself away and running for it. Even if he could make a break, he'd never outrun the slugs the brutes would send after him. He'd end up dead on a Cambridge sidewalk, not far from where Officer Collier fell, but his passing would be forgotten a lot quicker. Just another street crime, featuring the least interesting of victims, a dead black guy.

If he ran, he'd die here and now. Taking a ride with the two men bought him time, and a chance to think of a way to rescue himself.

The man at his back released Drake's arm, shoved him forward.

Drake got into the car.

HE THRUST HIMSELF against the opposite door, fumbled for the latch that would let him pop out the other side. With his assailant climbing into the car, he'd be distracted for a second or two, perhaps long enough for Drake to find concealment in a pool of street shadow. But the door didn't budge; kiddie locked so it couldn't be opened from within. He'd half expected it.

The man who'd held him fast a few seconds before was visible at last, his face washed by the orange glow of the streetlights. It was a square, blunt face, high-cheekboned, Asiatic. One corner of his mouth twitched upward as if in sardonic salute to Drake for having had the presence of mind to try for the door. Then without turning his head, he slammed the door shut. The car began to move.

There were no words between the thug and the driver. Everything had been settled in advance. They'd already selected the route, the destination, the manner of Drake's death. It would be a quiet ride, and with luck, a long one. Drake settled back in his seat, drew a deep breath, closed his eyes. The nausea of dread synchronized with the swaying of the car threatened him with motion sickness. What Drake needed instead was calm, for himself and for the wary man who sat eighteen inches away. And so he sat silent, took deep breaths, and prayed in silence for a little bit. Nothing fancy or eloquent. Just the Lord's Prayer. As he prayed, he let his lips form the words, hoping the killer could see, hoping he could understand what he was seeing. The murderer had taken rides like this before, seated beside men and women who'd known they were on a one-way trip. More than once, they'd given up all hope of escape or rescue. They'd decided to make their peace with God, before the end.

Drake was just another dead man, helpless, despairing. Calling out to a God who had never before saved this man's victims and who wouldn't intervene this time either. Perhaps the sight of a praying man provided the killer with a little sadistic entertainment. Drake hoped so. He hoped the man's gaze was fixed on his face, illuminated by the passing lights, and that he failed to notice Drake's left hand creeping into his pants pocket and wrapping itself around the ballpoint pen he always carried there.

Not a knife, but sharp enough to gouge an eye or puncture a throat, if he could somehow pull it free of the plastic cap that shielded the tip. With a slow tensing of his thigh muscles, Drake pushed the pen against the car door, clamping down on the cap, then easing up just enough to allow free movement of his left hand. Little by little, his hand slipped out of the pocket, grasping the ballpoint pen but leaving behind the protective cap. He didn't pull it out all the way, not yet.

Instead, Drake opened his eyes. In front of him, he could just see the top of the driver's head. He was a big man, and Drake knew he'd stand no chance against him without a weapon. But it was the wrong time for doubt or fear. Instead he resolved on relaxation. Without a glance for the murderer with whom he shared the passenger seat, Drake gazed out of the window at the Boston night.

They were out of Cambridge now, headed south on the Southeast Expressway, back toward Quincy. For a moment, Drake wondered if the Neponset River had been selected as his final resting place. Whitey Bulger's old dumping ground. The idea amused him, bringing a welcome momentary dilution of fear.

He had to strike before they arrived. When they hauled him from the car, the two men would be alert to any resistance.

All right, then. Soon. Without making a show of it, Drake began to breathe more deeply, stoking his body with extra oxygen for the coming fight. He asked himself if there was anything more he could do to lull or distract the hoodlum at his side. Nothing came to him, and Drake felt another surge of despair. But he'd grown accustomed to despair in the past hour. Rather than unmanning him, it only fed his outrage that he should be at the mercy of a creature like this.

Drake shifted to look at the man who meant to kill him. The coarse face was turned toward Drake, the eyes heavy-lidded, the lips parted in a gentle half-smile.

Shifting his body had freed up Drake's left hand, giving him room to move. He brought his left hand out, fast, the base of the pen fixed in the palm of his hand, its shaft between his fingers, its tip aimed at the murderer's neck.

Drake thought he saw surprise in the man's face, then a look of weary contempt as the killer parried his move, swatting out with both arms to deflect Drake's makeshift weapon and take hold of his left forearm.

Now Drake was a dead man. The killer gripped and twisted, and Drake screamed at the agony in his wrist. At the sound of torment, the thug's furious face was transformed with pleasure. He grinned, delighted by his own skill and conscious for a moment of nothing else.

And in that moment, Drake struck out with his right fist and smashed it into the man's exposed throat. Now the killer's face revealed shock and rage but also terrible, choking pain. His hands fell away from Drake's left wrist to clutch at his throat, and in that moment, Drake reached into his waistband, pulled out the gun.

It felt like the nine-millimeter Beretta he'd practiced with at the gun range. Sure enough, the safety was right where he'd have expected it to be, and he snapped it off. The murderer squirmed and lurched and tried to get a hand on Drake, but he shrugged out of his grasp. In the front seat, the driver's head came around, then he leaned to his right, as if grabbing for something in the glove box.

Drake turned the gun toward the side window, fired. The boom of the shot hammered his ears; the splash of broken glass sprayed his clothing. The car swayed and lurched as the surprised driver stopped reaching for his gun and grabbed at the wheel.

Drake fired again, blowing out more of the glass. Then he swung the gun toward the front of the car and blasted the windshield just ahead of the driver. Turning to aim the gun at the backseat killer, he bellowed, "Stop this thing! Right now!"

The brakes came on, hard. He'd been expecting it and was braced. The man who'd planned to kill him and who now sprawled in misery beside him slid off the seat onto the floor.

The car veered right, halted, and Drake saw the driver reaching again. "Stop that! You want me to shoot you? Just put your hands on the wheel and sit there." The man did as he was told, and Drake unlocked his door. Then he reached through the blasted window, opened the door from outside, stepped out.

He knew the place. They were just beyond the Granite Avenue exit in Dorchester, not far from Quincy. There was no shoulder here; the driver had stopped in the right lane.

Drake heard a horn and pressed his body against the car just in time. A massive tractor and trailer missed him by a couple of feet. Its blast of displaced air tugged at his clothes and rocked the car against his back.

Drake glanced backward. It was sparse Sunday-night traffic, but he could see many more vehicles approaching, at least one of them in the right lane.

He knew he should run for it, then and there. But Drake figured that the gun had bought him some time. He raised it, pointed it at the driver, but took care to keep his index finger outside of the trigger guard. You never touch a trigger unless you're going to pull it, and all Drake wanted was a look at the driver's face.

He was leaning over again, and this time the gun was coming out of the glove box. "No!" shouted Drake, and the man let the pistol go, put his hands back on the wheel. He was another Asian man, huge, with shoulders that seemed too big for his clothes. His gleaming hair was cut short, his eyes black and unblinking, his lips compressed with hatred.

Yes, he'd recognize this man if he ever saw him again. Drake was sure of it. He'd probably wear the same expression of thwarted rage if they ever met again.

Drake looked up, saw and heard the oncoming cars. He glanced once more at the driver, turned, and ran.

CHAPTER EIGHT

HE STILL HAD his phone. He jerked it out of his jacket pocket and speed-dialed Carter.

"Come get me," he said as soon as Carter answered.

There was a moment's silence, then, "Where you at?"

"Granite Avenue. I'm crossing the Neponset River now, heading toward Gallivan. You know the McDonald's, right? Meet you there."

"Okay. I assume this is important."

"I just met the guy who stabbed Astrid."

"He tried for you too?"

"Yeah."

"So you're running."

"I think I lost them."

"More than one?"

"Two. My guess is they're not trailing me. One of them is in no condition to run."

Another pause. "What did you do to the guy?"

"Glad to tell you all about it. Just come get me. I'll find some shadows and wait. Just pull into the Mickey D parking lot and unlock a door."

"On my way."

About twenty minutes later, Carter's SUV tucked into a parking slot, flashed its headlights a couple of times. Drake emerged from the shadow of a two-story frame house on the opposite side of the street. He strolled over, slipped inside, and started talking. As he spoke, he handed over the pistol he'd used to shoot his way free.

"Tomorrow, I may wish I had this thing."

"You got a carry permit?"

"Of course not."

"Well, then. Besides, it's evidence."

"Of what? I doubt you'll be able to trace it to the guys who grabbed me. And by now they're long gone. Maybe check local hospitals for somebody with a throat injury. But I don't know how bad I hurt the guy. He might recover on his own."

"The MIT guy, then. Severins."

"My word against his. No proof I was even there."

"We still better tell Akinyi. Maybe she can think of something."

"Okay with me. In the meantime, though, I need someplace to crash."

"Yeah, going home might not be smart. They're probably parked right at your front door, waiting for you."

"It's the logical next move."

"But they don't know a thing about me," said Carter. "And I've got a couch in my basement."

Half an hour later, Drake was fluffing out a sheet and spreading it over Carter's sofa. His left arm ached where the thug had twisted it, but it felt like wrenched muscles and bruises, nothing more.

A few steps away, Salome Carter watched Drake with folded arms and an inhospitable frown. "If our kids were still at home," she said, "I wouldn't allow this. Bringing danger up in here."

From the nearby laundry room, Carter offered comfort. "No worries, baby. Nobody followed us. And it's just for one night anyway." Carter emerged with a set of towels, tossed them onto the sofa. "Besides, he's one of us."

Salome thought about it for a few seconds. She didn't quite warm to the idea, but one or two layers of ice slid away. "You hungry?" she asked.

"No, I'm good," said Drake. "Could I borrow a toothbrush, though?"

"Got one somewhere," said Salome, who shuffled upstairs to find it.

"Another thing," Drake said to Carter. "Got a laptop lying around?"

"In the dining room. I don't want to unplug it. Come on up."

"Thanks. Just want to look at something."

"What? Facebook?"

"No. Just the only evidence I've got."

It was a big laptop with a wide keyboard, and it came to life as Drake tapped the mousepad. "Windows 7? Man, you need to keep up. You're two versions behind."

"Why? It works."

"Fair point," Drake conceded. He hit the Start icon and found the default browser, Internet Explorer. Then he entered *blankmail.com*, entered Astrid's username and password.

"Username and/or password not recognized."

It was easy to make a mistake with a gnarled password like that. Drake typed it again, taking his time.

"Username and/or password not recognized."

"What you looking for?" asked Carter.

"Astrid's emails. She gave me the way in."

"And you never mentioned it? That's evidence, all right."

"Yep, and lots of it. But all of a sudden, it's not working."

"So why did you keep this to yourself?"

"To keep Astrid out of trouble. At least until I was sure she deserved to be in trouble. I was going to tell you tomorrow, anyway. I figured a few hours wouldn't matter."

"And that's why you almost wound up in a ditch." Carter shook his head.

"Be quiet a minute, will you? Got a pencil and some paper?"

Carter brought them, and Drake wrote out the password—*#ypjku[hf-d,buodyi**—that had worked before. He needed to be sure this time. It was his third try, and many security-conscious companies would lock him out after three failed attempts.

So one by one he pecked in the keystrokes, paused, tensed, and hit Enter.

"Username and/or password not recognized."

He'd made no mistakes. Not a chance.

Someone had gotten there ahead of him.

Severins. He knew Drake had seen the emails and had rushed to lock him out. Astrid must have shared the password. Why not? She'd given it to

Drake, and he'd never been as close to her as Severins.

Drake sighed, shoved back from the table. "Gone," he said.

"Perfect," said Carter.

JUST A LITTLE dawn made its way through the dusty window over the sofa, but it was enough to wake Drake. From the floor above he heard the creak and thump of human movement, and a mutter of voices. He lacked a change of clothes but showered anyway, resenting the feel of yesterday's underwear against his clean skin as he dressed. At least there was the toothbrush. Drake used it, then mounted the stairs.

In the kitchen, Salome and Damon Carter were assembling a breakfast of coffee, eggs, and toast. "You like scrambled?" asked Damon as he toiled at the stove.

"Sure."

"Sleep okay?" asked Salome, who at that moment seemed to care.

"Better than I'd have expected. I guess being scared makes a fellow sleepy."

"Then you'll sleep well tonight," said Carter. "Detectives get ferocious when you hold out on them."

"Never again. Learned my lesson. When should we go see her?"

"We're set for ten a.m. I already called her. That's why I know she's in a bad mood. Maybe by then she'll cool off a little. But you better not play any more games with her."

"No games," said Drake and dug out his phone. It was seven thirty, and his editor Ginsburg wasn't at his desk yet, maybe just crawling out of bed. Still, he'd need to know that Drake would be late, perhaps even absent for the entire day. So Drake dialed his number at the *Record* and left a voice mail, then texted Ginsburg's mobile.

"Okay, I'm free for the day. You can just drop me at Ruggles and go on about your business."

"You are my business," said Carter, as he dumped an excessive amount of scrambled eggs on a plate and set it on the kitchen table. "This is looking like something pretty big. At least it does to me, because I believe what you told me. Precious might not. And even if she does, what about Homeland Security or the Treasury Department? Will they believe you?"

"Homeland Security?" said Salome, her eyes wide with alarm. "You mean like Al-Qaeda?"

"No, I don't mean Al-Qaeda," said Drake. "No suicide vests or hijacked airplanes involved. Just a whole lot of money."

"That's just as dangerous," Salome replied, sitting down to eat.

"Agreed," said Carter. "So we've got to get this straight, and fast. I want you out of my basement."

DETECTIVE AKINYI GUIDED them to an interrogation room, a windowless, narrow space with bare, resonant walls. The detective's shouts and curses rebounded from those walls, over and over, blending and blurring until Drake had to watch Akinyi's lips to judge when one insult ended and another began.

After so much unleashed fury, her windup was something of an anticlimax. "What," she said, pausing for effect, "the hell were you thinking?"

If the goal were to terrorize Drake, it wasn't working. He'd been frightened by experts the night before. Still, Akinyi was right to be angry, so Drake replied with bowed head and downcast eyes. "No doubt about it, ma'am. I screwed up. I figured I could get to the bottom of this without getting Astrid in any more trouble. When I saw the emails and realized how deep it went, I knew I'd have to tell you. But Astrid was safe in the hospital, so I figured it would keep till Monday. Meantime, I reached out to Dr. Severins, hoping he might know something about it."

"And according to you, Severins knows all about it."

"Everything. He admitted it to me. He got me to his office and had those two thugs waiting."

"So you say. Severins has a different take on it. He doesn't know anything about it."

"You've already talked to him?"

"Detective Carter told me about him earlier this morning, when we were setting up this little meeting. I figured it wouldn't hurt to call Severins before talking to you, so I tracked down his cell number. It's right on his MIT website. Anyway, I reached him at his summer place in Barnstable. At least that's where he said he was. Claims he's been there for the past week. No idea what you're talking about."

Drake slumped in his seat. He was surprised only that Akinyi had moved so fast. Severins's denial was to be expected.

"Carter also tells me that you saw a bunch of emails about some kind of electronic bank robbery?"

"Yes, but they're all gone now. That first time I went through them, I didn't think to make copies. At the time I had no idea how serious this was."

"And now that you do understand, it's too late."

"Looks like it."

A few moments passed in silence. "That night at the church," Akinyi said, "when I first met you, I marked you down as a smart man."

Drake believed that Akinyi could see his face flush with humiliation, despite his deep brown camouflage.

"Well," said Akinyi, "I'm not an email expert, but I know how to file subpoenas. Email companies don't really delete everything right away. They keep everything backed up, usually for thirty days or so, just in case. I'll get a judge to ask nicely, and they'll hand over the files. All I need is your girlfriend's email address."

"Not a chance," said Drake.

"What's that supposed to be, chivalry? Next thing out your mouth better be that email address or you're going to jail."

Drake sighed, shrugged. "*Snowbird@blankmail.com*. And chivalry's got nothing to do with it. You'll find out when you try a subpoena. It's hopeless."

"Why not? Works with Gmail."

"Gmail is based in Silicon Valley. Blankmail is in Switzerland."

Akinyi glared at Drake in silence for about half a minute. "All you had to do was make copies. Then we'd have something to work with."

"You still do, at least a little bit. There's the gun I took from them."

"Beretta nine millimeter. Used to be standard US Army issue, but civilians like them too. I've found enough of them on the street, lying next to gangbangers."

"It might be traceable," said Carter.

"It happens sometimes," said Akinyi, without a hint of optimism.

"Well, it's somewhere to start. And besides, I remember stuff from the emails. I'll write it all down, and you can go to work on that. There's the email addresses. I remember them. And some of the stuff they talked about. They were working on a hack of something called core banking software. There weren't a lot of details, but they talked about it like it could cause a major financial crisis if somebody ever switched it on."

"What's the name of this software?"

"No idea. They didn't call it by name, not in the messages I read. One thing I remember, though. Remember Clinker—the hacker that got killed in Germany? Well, when he realized which way things were headed, he decided to pull the plug on the entire operation. So he sent a warning to the software company. Clinker was German, but he got at least part of his schooling at Carnegie Mellon University in Pittsburgh, and he went to school with a guy at the company. Again, no names, but he did use a nickname for him. Called him Soul Man. You should be able to track him down."

Akinyi flipped her legal pad to a blank page, tore it out, tossed over a lead pencil. "Write it all down."

It took only a couple of minutes. Akinyi glanced at the page, unimpressed. "That it?"

"All I can recall. But it'll give you a place to start."

"Not really. None of this means a thing to me."

"First off, I'd Google everything. The emails of the hackers, to start with. They may have used them online somewhere. Discussion forums, maybe. Anyway, when you get a hit, follow the link and see if it leads to any clues. They might post messages with more information about themselves. Or you might find the addresses of people who know them."

"You've done this before?"

"Do it all the time. It often works. Most people aren't trying to hide. These guys are different, but it's still worth a try."

"Same thing with Soul Man?"

"Right. But that's standard procedure anyway, right? Police departments keep databases of known aliases. You probably have plenty of Soul Men on file."

"Yeah, from the 1960s," said Akinyi, smirking. The closest thing to a smile he'd seen from her.

"Yeah. Maybe the guy's got an Afro. Probably won't be in your alias file. But he may be online. Somebody with connections to Carnegie Mellon and the banking industry. That gives you three variables. Find a match to all three, and you've probably got the guy."

"If you don't get him first," said Akinyi, all amusement gone.

"I plan to go looking," Drake said and forced himself to stare right back. "That's my job."

Akinyi made a huffing sound, smirked again but without amusement this time.

"Can't stop you using Google. But I can stop you from interfering. Next time you hold out on me, the cuffs are coming out. Understand?"

Her words weren't a threat. More of a plea. Please don't mess up my investigation any more than you have. Please don't get yourself killed.

Akinyi cocked her head a little, and it occurred to Drake that this woman liked him.

"Understood," he said.

"BETTER THAN I expected," said Carter on the ride down the elevator.

"Yeah," said Drake. "I half expected to end up in a cell."

"You only held back for a few hours. Forgivable." Carter tapped Drake's collarbone. "Assuming you told her everything. If she finds out you held out on her again, you'll need a lawyer. Bet on that."

"No, that's everything," Drake said as the elevator opened onto the lobby. "I'm not stupid. Not that stupid, anyway."

"But you are homeless, at least until this gets straightened out."

"Yeah. No way am I going home."

"Yep, it's back to my basement after all. Figures. I guess you can hang out here in the lobby till I get off shift. I'll tell them at the desk to look out for you."

"No, I'm going to work too. The *Record*'s got security."

"Yeah, I've seen it," said a smirking Carter. "You're lucky to be alive."

"Anyway, I sit right in the middle of the newsroom. They'd have to blast their way through six copy editors and a movie critic just to find me. They'd run out of ammo."

"Well, okay. But I'm running late."

"Not a problem. I'll Uber and put it on the *Record*'s tab. I figure this is work related."

BY NOON, DRAKE was striding through the front door of the *Record*. He rode up to the second-floor newsroom on a clanking, rumbling escalator that belonged in Macy's. It had made sense half a century ago, when a couple thousand people had worked here.

Today, as on most days, Drake rode up alone. The great hollowing of the newspaper industry had broomed away more than half of those who'd worked here a decade ago. Drake wondered why they didn't turn off the escalator and save the electricity. It might even cut down on the company's health insurance tab. Stair climbing was good exercise.

Several of Drake's colleagues looked up as he strode into the newsroom, offered praise for his Sunday piece on the stabbing. For once, Drake thought the praise was merited. Still, it made him suspicious, as though his colleagues were lying to make him feel better. A stupid thought, but he couldn't help himself.

Striding toward his editor's cubicle, Drake saw Ginsburg's gray, curly hair, just visible above a stack of documents that lined one side of his cubicle. The printed-out transcripts of congressional hearings, corporate 10-K forms, and investment analysts' reports could all be had in electronic form with a few keystrokes, but Ginsburg was a paper man. Bankers Boxes of the stuff filled the cubicle, and atop these rested the papers that Ginsburg hadn't sorted yet. Still more stacks adorned whatever portions of his desk were not occupied by keyboard, mouse, monitor, and phone. A few yards away a battered laser printer hummed and clattered. The man's consumption of paper and toner was relentless. From time to time the interns who restocked the printers would look at Ginsburg's paper pile with mingled wonder and resentment.

"Getting in this late, you might as well take the whole day," said Ginsburg, without looking up from his monitor.

"Actually, this might be the safest place for me right now."

Ginsburg still didn't look up. "What's that supposed to mean?"

"I need a minute," Drake replied.

Now Ginsburg raised his eyes. "Fish tank?"

Drake nodded. Ginsburg shoved himself upright; he wasn't much taller on his feet. Drake followed him to the empty glassed-in conference room where the editors met to plan the story budget for the print edition.

As he entered, Drake saw his article about Astrid pinned to a corkboard at the front of the room. Ginsburg gestured toward it. "Great piece," he said. "What you doing for a follow-up?"

"Trying to stay alive, for one thing."

Ginsburg cocked his head and with his prominent nose and grizzled chin, the resemblance to a puppy was almost endearing. "That's the second ominous thing you've said since you got here," he said. "What's that about?"

"It's about the two guys who tried to kill me last night. Three, if you count the professor."

Ginsburg smiled a little, as if in appreciation of Drake's joke, only to grow sober as he realized Drake wasn't joking. "You better explain."

So Drake explained. It didn't take long, and at the end, Ginsburg huffed out a lungful of air as if he'd been saving it up.

"So an MIT professor tried to have you killed."

"I don't think it was his idea. He's working for somebody else, and that somebody gave the word."

"No idea who that somebody is?"

"Not a clue. Only it's somebody with a lot of money and a long reach."

"Assuming you're right about this other guy in Hamburg being the first victim."

"Severins confirmed it."

"But that's not proof."

"Exactly. Severins denies everything, the emails have vanished, and so did the guys who tried to kill me. They might be perched outside my condo right now, waiting for me to turn up."

"Cops'll scare 'em away. This detective you talked to will check on that, if she's smart."

"She seems to be. Anyway, I'm not going back anytime soon."

"You got a place to stay? I can hide you out for a while." Ginsburg chuckled.

"No. I'm good. Somebody from church is putting me up. A fellow deacon and a cop."

"That ought to work. Of course, you're not going to be much good as a reporter. Not unless you do all your work at a desk. You're not going out on those streets alone until this whole thing is cleaned up."

"Matter of fact," said Drake, "I was thinking maybe I could help with the cleanup. I'll work my sources and report anything I find to the cops."

"I especially like that last part."

"Me too. I've learned my lesson. What I know, they'll know."

DRAKE CLEARED HIS calendar. He'd had a couple of unimportant stories on the fire, but they'd keep. For now, he wanted an explanation for the blood on the church floor and last night's brief, terrible road trip.

He'd start with Soul Man. Drake knew that he worked in a company that made core banking software, and at a fairly high level. And in his email Clinker said he'd gone to school with him at Carnegie Mellon. That gave Drake a bunch of handholds, and all he'd have to do was start climbing.

First, he punched up LinkedIn and entered Clinker's real name, Helmut Brockmann. As a gray-hatter who sold his services to legitimate clients, it figured that Brockmann would have a LinkedIn account. And so he did .

The biographical details were a perfect fit. Brockmann had done two years of undergrad work at Humboldt in Berlin. Then in 2003, he'd transferred to Carnegie Mellon in Pittsburgh, where he'd completed bachelor's and master's degrees and departed for Germany in 2005.

He'd been a private data security consultant for Siemens and Bosch as well as Philips in the Netherlands and Dell Technologies in the US. There was nothing about working for NATO, but then there wouldn't be, would there?

All right, then. Brockmann's friend Soul Man was somebody who'd attended CMU between 2003 and 2005 and now worked in banking software. He fired up LinkedIn's CMU alumni page and got the names and photos of four plausible hits—five if you counted one female graduate. A woman nicknamed Soul Man? Drake consigned her to the bottom of the list.

Drake began hunting for their phone numbers. Often a Google search got it done. Instead of trying for the corporate switchboard, just punch in the person's name and company, then add the words *phone number.*

The gimmick worked on four of the five names. Drake would have to work a little harder for the last.

One of the hits was the woman, Madhavi Chandra. She was a VP at an Atlanta company he'd never heard of. Tannheuser Software.

He called her, got dropped into voice mail. Chandra's wait-for-the-beep message was spoken in a soft, lilting voice. No trace of a Hindu accent. She'd been made in the USA of Indian components.

Drake left a brief message asking about Brockmann, then left the same message three more times at the other numbers he'd collected. To reach the fifth, a guy named Shipman, Drake called the headquarters of the company that employed him, and asked to be connected. Shipman was at his desk, but after a few questions about Brockmann it was clear he didn't remember the guy. On a whim, Drake asked about a CMU classmate nicknamed Soul Man.

"Oh, I remember her. You mean Madi Chandra. Everybody would remember Madi. Cute, for one thing. And she loved to party. What about her?"

"Not important," said Drake. "I was just told that Brockmann had a friend called Soul Man that I should talk to."

"Well, I didn't know all her friends. You better get in touch with her directly. Last I heard she was at one of our competitors, Tannheuser Software."

"Really? Their stuff any good?"

"Sucks. Compared to ours, anyway." Shipman laughed. "Tell Soul Man I said so when you talk to her, okay?"

"You have my word," said Drake.

DRAKE SPENT THE next forty minutes scouring the Web for information on Tannheuser. The name popped up time and again on banking technology sites and the online edition of *American Banker.* Its HardCoin program was like an operating system for banks, managing or monitoring every vital function. At least half the biggest US financial institutions used it, and many more overseas.

The phone rang, and a message flashed in the lower right corner of Drake's computer screen. "Caller ID Blocked."

"This is Madi Chandra. Are you Mr. Drake?"

"Yes."

"Okay, I'll make this quick. I got your message. I know about Helmut. I don't want to end up the same way."

For the past couple of hours, at his familiar desk, Drake had felt at ease again, comfortable in a comfortable world. The fear in Madi's voice broke the spell.

"Talk to me, Ms. Chandra. I can help."

"I don't see how."

Just tell the truth. After that, they'll be too busy running to come after you."

"I won't. Not like this. Not on the phone."

"Why not? These guys aren't tapping the lines?"

"How do you know? They found Clinker, no trouble. No telling what they can do. I'm getting off this line right now."

"No. Wait. You don't trust phones. Where can I meet you?"

"I'm in Atlanta."

"I'm betting there's one flight an hour from Boston. At least."

"You'd come all this way?"

"For a good story, sure."

"You can't put my name in the paper."

"I'll just listen. I won't print anything without clearing it with you, okay?"

"Let me think about it."

The line went dead.

"SHE'LL TALK TO me if I go to her," Drake said to Ginsburg.

"Maybe. Or maybe both of you end up catching a bullet."

"Not if we move fast. We meet in some public place; she tells me what she knows. I'm willing to take the chance."

"As if it was yours to take. We send you down there, we're responsible if you disappear."

"What do I do then? Just hide out in here? I can't do my job. I can't even go out to meet with sources. As long as this . . . whatever it is continues, I'm on lockdown. I might as well be in Atlanta. Probably safer anyway."

"You tell that detective about this? Akinyi?"

"Not yet. It just happened. But don't worry. I promised. Gonna write it up and send an email right before I buy an airplane ticket to Atlanta."

"I never agreed to that."

"I've got money. Besides, you asked me if I needed some time off. Well, maybe I need a day or two to get my mind right. Maybe even a week."

Ginsburg stared for a few moments. "You're gonna do it anyway." It wasn't a question.

DRAKE WROTE UP what he'd learned, including Soul Man's real name and location, and his intention to meet her. If Akinyi didn't like it, she could buy her own plane ticket.

Drake pasted all this into an email and addressed the message to Deacon Carter, who'd surely pass it on to Akinyi. Then he found a JetBlue flight leaving at 9:00 p.m. and booked a hotel as well, all on his own credit card. Maybe he could talk Ginsburg into reimbursing him if something came of the trip. In any case, he wouldn't have to crash on Carter's sofa that night.

Drake crawled beneath his desk, found the power adapter for his phone and its USB cable, and wrapped them together for travel. He undocked his *Record* laptop, found its power cable in a lower drawer, along with several of the long, thin paper notepads favored by journalists. Drake grabbed three of them and a couple of ballpoint pens. Everything went into a plastic grocery bag he'd kept handy for toting gadgets. He'd get something more substantial before boarding the plane.

Just one thing: How to get to the airport without being followed?

He glanced up, noticed that Bill Howell, who covered retail and banking, was slinging his costly leather backpack over one shoulder and moving toward the door. Drake hustled over.

"Bill, can I catch a ride?"

Howell turned his plump, pink face toward Drake, one eyebrow at a quizzical angle. Though the two men had been at the *Record* for about the same length of time, they'd rarely spoken. There was no animus between them, just no particular need to interact.

"What's up? Car break down?" Howell asked.

"Something like that."

"But you live in Quincy, right? I'm not going that way."

"Me neither. Just need a quick ride to the Red Line station. You park in the back lot, right?"

"Yeah. But the station's just a couple blocks away. I don't mind driving you, but why not walk? This got something to do with those guys after you?" Howell stifled a chuckle as he spoke, as if he hadn't believed the story anyway.

"Well, it does. I don't know if they're watching the building. Probably not. It's probably perfectly safe. But I need to get out of here without being followed. I have to make sure."

"So . . . ?"

"So I climb into your backseat and duck down, and you drive me to the Red Line. I get out and take the train to Logan."

"This is nuts," said Howell. "Like a movie."

"How'd you even know about it?" asked Drake.

"Everybody in the newsroom knows. Ginsburg brought it up in the afternoon meeting. Now it's making the rounds. Ginsburg believes you're for real, and so do maybe half the people here. The rest are wondering if you've gone nuts."

Drake felt the invisible blush again. "Look, I'm serious. I just need to know if you can help me out."

"Has it occurred to you that I might be risking my own life?"

In truth it hadn't. The thought stopped Drake short. "You're right. Never mind. I'll figure some other way."

Howell laughed out loud. "Christ, man, you should see yourself!" Howell's laughing jag continued for a few seconds, till he settled down into a chuckling grin. "You look like *The Fugitive*. Oh, don't worry about it. I just couldn't help myself. Come on. Car's out back."

"You're not scared?"

"Hell, there's nobody there. But if you want to make a desperate bid for freedom, I might as well help."

ON THE OFF chance that somebody would be watching the Red Line station nearest to the *Record*, Drake persuaded Howell to drop him one stop farther on, on the outskirts of South Boston. He hopped out of Howell's Toyota with head bowed. A train was pulling in and Drake scurried downstairs and through the doors.

Three stops later he was at Downtown Crossing. At Macy's he rounded up a backpack, underwear, socks, a khaki shirt, and trousers. Across the street at the CVS, Drake obtained razors, shaving cream and toothpaste. He placed his purchases into the backpack, along with his laptop and the charger for his smartphone. He walked about four blocks to South Station and boarded the Silver Line for the brief ride to Logan Airport.

THE ATLANTA SUBWAY was called MARTA—no doubt the letters stood for something—and it seemed to run faster than the Red Line back in Boston. The train raced northbound through evening darkness, past suburban homes, churches, malls; their shapes defined by the orange gleam of sodium lamps. After a stop called West End, the downtown skyline came into view. Sleek, modern structures he'd seen before on TV while watching the Falcons play football. Drake didn't know the names of those gleaming towers, the way he could have named the skyscrapers of Boston or New York or Chicago. But somewhere among them he'd find Chandra.

Drake had lucked into a bargain rate at the Atlanta Hilton that made it almost as cheap as a Motel 6. The AC was on high and the room was icy. The temperature matched the cool, functional décor of the place—a couple of queen-size beds with white sheets and comforters, a decent-size TV mounted on the opposite wall, a bathroom with wrapped slivers of cheap soap, a marble sink, a plastic tub, and one of those strange cloth shower curtains that wasn't quite long enough to hang down into the tub.

The room was on the ninth floor and facing north. Out the window Drake watched the light show on I-75. There was nothing else worth seeing, but Drake left the curtains open. He liked to sleep in the glow of city lights.

Drake dug his toiletries out of the backpack, stepped into the bathroom. He showered and shaved and changed into fresh underwear. He set his smartphone alarm to wake him at six, dialed the wake-up call number, and made the same arrangement with a sweet-voiced lady at the front desk.

The sheets were cool and taut against Drake's body as he lay down on the bed closest to the window. Through the undraped window he saw a great expanse of sky, but as in Boston, the city lights overwhelmed all but the brightest stars. Instead he watched aircraft coming in from the north, a column of them arrayed in stairstep fashion. One by one, they passed over the hotel and out of view. They'd continue their stately descent until they met the pavement at Hartsfield, twelve miles to the south.

Alicia had lain with him in a bed like this on their honeymoon, and at frequent intervals over the four years of their marriage. They'd hop onto the T with a change of clothes and do a weekend at the Charles Hotel in Cambridge or drive to an anonymous motor lodge in Weymouth. Anywhere they could smother their mutual discontent in a snarl of tumbled linen.

They'd coined a rule on these visits: they must never check out of a room until they'd somehow dampened or soiled every last sheet and towel in the place. They'd always found a way. First time he'd done it, as he'd headed out the door with Alicia waiting in the hallway, Drake had looked over his shoulder to see the disheveled sheets on both the room's beds, the cotton towels strewn across the floor.

He'd turned to Alicia, winked, said "Mission accomplished," and closed the door.

They'd kept that vow in two dozen hotel rooms over the four years of their marriage, joyfully at first. Later there was tedium in it, then resentment. Then came that last time.

It had been a motel in Brockton, somewhere cheap. Alicia had noticed and cursed him for it, and Drake had cursed her in turn as he pulled at her clothes, wanting nothing more at that moment than to get it done, and then he found in his rage a passion he hadn't known before. Alicia's clothes came away in shards, buttons flew like bullets, and she tore at him, ripping and slapping and shrieking in fury.

They'd cursed each other with every filthy word they knew until they were done. Drake remembered the creaking of the bed, the stale smell of the room, and the sweat that coated them both. The memory made him shudder—it had been that good.

And then Alicia spoke again, and he heard in her voice the same contempt, the same disgust. Not a tactic of passion but a frank declaration of truth. Drake replied in kind, not an automatic act of verbal payback but a devout litany of disregard for her, a recitation of every real or imagined way she had ever failed him. Alicia responded to Drake's response. It went on for an hour.

When they were done, the sweat on them had dried to nothing. They didn't pause to shower but slid their sticky bodies into their clothes. They said nothing to each other. But as Drake reached for the door, Alicia walked back to the bathroom. She dumped all the towels in the tub, drenched them in tap water, looked up at Drake, and said, "Mission accomplished."

Even now, hotels remained hateful to him, each rented bed a reminder of his great shame. Sometimes, on a reporting trip to New York or San Francisco, he'd fall back on whisky to help him sleep and forget. But this was no time to indulge himself, not when he and Astrid had come so near to death. Better to accept a few hours of bitter wakefulness and count on God to see him through.

Drake said the Lord's Prayer, then a brief prayer of his own for strength and forgiveness and good luck in the morning. And one more prayer for his worst enemy in all the world, now six thousand miles away and married to another man.

Out the window, the planes kept coming. Drake watched them and wondered where they'd come from, how many pounds of fuel were still aboard, how many hours on their engines. When sleep finally arrived, he never noticed.

CHAPTER NINE

"**I'M IN ATLANTA.** Name a time and a place."

"You really came," Chandra said.

"Told you I would," said Drake. "This is important."

"Where are you?"

"The Hilton, getting ready to check out. I need to head back as soon as we've talked."

"I didn't promise anything."

"Use your head. Talking to me is the safest move you can make."

"Unless they find out."

"They won't. Not till it's too late for them to do anything about it. And after that, you're safe. I'll just come over to your office. Or I can meet you somewhere."

"Not the office," Chandra said.

"Well, okay, then. Not the office. Pick someplace else. Someplace with lots of people."

"Public library, then. Around noon."

"Which branch?"

"The main one, downtown. Forsyth Street and Carnegie Way. There's a subway stop right next to it. Peachtree Center station. Or just get an Uber."

"Not a problem. How will I spot you?"

"You're a reporter. You must have found pictures of me online."

"Sure, but it's a library. Lots of people."

"Okay. I'm wearing a white blouse and black slacks. I'll be at the reference desk."

AFTER SO MANY years as a journalist, Drake was still a little surprised that strangers agreed to talk to him. He was slow to share his own secrets, few as they were. But approached the right way, most people will tell you almost anything. And Soul Man had the added incentive of fear.

Drake queried his smartphone for the address of the library. The readout showed a MARTA stop right across the street. No need for Uber.

He punched up Street View for a look at the place. It was a hulking, brutalist structure assembled out of misaligned concrete boxes. It resembled Boston's notorious city hall, only uglier.

It was about nine thirty, and Drake briefly toyed with the notion of dialing up room service. Then he recalled previous hotel meals and decided he'd do better on the street.

Drake checked his email, found a message from Carter: "You sure about this? Being out of Boston isn't a bad idea. But be careful. Report back anything you find out, and quick."

Drake wrote back, telling Carter about his noon meeting with Chandra at the library. "I take good notes," he said. "What I learn, you'll learn."

Drake scanned the rest of his overnight emails and found nothing of merit. He shut down the laptop and slipped it into his backpack.

THE LIBRARY WAS a long way from crowded. Still, it smelled like public libraries always do—industrial cleaning solution, the unwashed funk of homeless bodies, and the fragrance of aging paper. A few breaths and Drake felt at home.

Drake was over an hour early to the meeting. He headed over to the reference section, where he and Chandra were to meet. Even in this age of online databases, the shelves were still well stocked with thick, imposing volumes.

Drake found his way to the section on aviation and picked up *The Turbine Pilot's Flight Manual.*

Drake lifted the book and strode over to an unoccupied study table that left him with a good view of the reference area He turned to the chapter on aircraft hydraulic systems. His life had depended on them countless times, yet Drake had no idea how they worked

For half an hour he thought of nothing else but constant-displacement pumps, priority valves, and ram air turbines.

Somewhere behind him, Drake heard a whacking sound, as a dropped book landed on the floor. He glanced over his shoulder, saw a wall clock that proclaimed 11:30. Still early. Then Drake looked straight ahead. And froze. And then very slowly lowered his head to the book, studying it as if it were a lost gospel.

The woman was thirty feet away, near the main reference desk. Her dark, reddish-brown face had been turned away from Drake, but he'd seen just enough to match it up with the image on LinkedIn. Besides, she wore the promised black slacks and white blouse. Chandra. Soul Man.

She was early to the meeting as well.

But she wasn't alone. She'd been speaking to two men, white guys. One of them, in tailored jeans, dark green polo shirt, and brown leather boots, had the lanky frame of a basketballer and towered over the woman. He had short-cut brown hair, and the skin on his rumpled face was so pockmarked it seemed to be boiling. The other, in a black T-shirt, khaki slacks, and black Nikes, was of average height but muscled like a gym rat, with long, blond hair, a broad jaw, and narrow, dark eyes.

Had she hired bodyguards? Where? On Craigslist? Not likely.

Without raising his head, Drake peered up from the table. Chandra was still there, talking to the two men. He saw the tense, harried look of her face, the nervous gestures of her hands.

After a few more seconds, the two men moved. The tall one passed within ten feet of Drake, never breaking stride. They weren't even looking for him yet, he realized. Instead, he took up position behind him, his eyes no doubt fixed on Chandra.

The other man remained in Drake's field of view. He strolled to a shelf about thirty feet away from Chandra, selected a book, flipped it open. But his eyes were locked onto Chandra.

So there it was.

Chandra's old college friend Clinker had warned her about the flaws in her company's software. But Chandra had already known. She might even have placed the bugs herself. Clinker's email had notified Chandra that the scheme was as good as blown, unless Clinker was silenced—him and any of his friends who'd seen the code.

It must have taken months, perhaps even years, to plan this operation. It could end up as the biggest bank heist of all time. But only if Clinker and his pals kept their mouths shut.

And so Chandra had begun to shut them. First Clinker, then the attempt on Astrid. For all Drake knew, others in the group had also been attacked. And of course there was his own one-way ride.

The crew they'd sent to Boston wasn't the best. But Drake knew he'd gotten lucky last time. Besides, these Atlanta guys might be the first team, too smart and too tough for Drake.

The fear he'd heard in Chandra's voice had been mere amateur theatrics, good enough to get Drake on a plane for Atlanta. Good enough to put him on the spot.

But Drake's early arrival had saved him. Time to go.

He reached down with his left hand, snagged his backpack. With his right hand clutching the open book he rose from his chair, head bowed as if he was transfixed by the wondrous words he read. Slowly, he walked farther into the library, angling to his right, at an angle that would show only his back to Chandra and the two watchers. To them, he'd be just another black man in a city full of them.

He strolled between two rows of shelves, shielding himself behind the racks of thick books, then turned to sneak a glance. Chandra had taken a seat at one of the large round tables. Beyond her, Drake saw the husky man, standing, stationary and alert. Drake knew the tall one, was somewhere to the left.

He'd made it out of the trap. He could just slip out of an emergency exit—Drake saw one about forty feet to his left. Even if it set off an alarm, he'd be long gone before the goon squad could react.

Safe and free and clear. And just as ignorant as he had been when he'd climbed off the airplane at Hartsfield. A wasted trip.

But there was another option.

Drake sighed, squared his shoulders, and walked out to meet Chandra.

SHE SAW HIM emerge from the stacks and gazed right at him. It gave Drake a first clear look at the woman—the long, sharp nose; the narrow, thrusting jaw; the long, thin hands that rested on the table.

She returned Drake's gaze with a look of dismissal, the look she'd give a homeless man coming over to ask for a couple of bucks. But when Drake did not look away, when he sat down across from her, she realized. Chandra glanced left and right then, to alert the watchers. It was a bit too obvious, Drake thought, and unnecessary. By now they'd spotted him.

"Ms. Chandra?" he said.

"Yes. You're Drake? What are you doing here? We said noon."

"You got here early. Me too."

"Really? How long have you been waiting?"

"Long enough to see you set things up. One tall guy behind me to my left, another to my right."

Chandra stared. After a moment, her lower lip quivered as if she were thinking about weeping.

"So now you're going to cry over me? What about your friend Clinker? You had him killed. Lose any tears over that?"

"It wasn't like that. I just told them he knew." Chandra shook her head, her eyes downcast. "I figured if he knew, others would figure it out. I said we might have to change our plans. That's all I said."

"And then you found out what happened to him."

"Of course I found out. It was all over Slashdot."

"Well, the same thing nearly happened to a friend of mine. And to me. Matter of fact, I've got a feeling something's about to happen to me any minute now."

"I'm sorry," said Chandra. "I didn't make you come down here."

"You did a pretty good job setting the hook."

"They told me what to say to you and how to say it. They told me not

120

to ask you to come to Atlanta, because you'd get suspicious. It had to be your idea."

"And you just did as you were told."

"Of course. I've got a husband and a three-year-old daughter."

"Yeah, and a mortgage and a car note and college loans."

"Yes, I wanted the money. I still do."

"And you'll think fondly of Clinker every time you spend some of it. That's something, anyway."

"It wasn't supposed to be like that. Now, I've come too far to turn back."

"So when they told you to get me here, you knew exactly what that would mean. You know my future better than I do. You might even know where they plan to dispose of the body."

She stared at him then, shame and fear and guilt on her face, and Drake felt the lunatic urge to grasp her hand and pray with her. But the impulse passed, and anyway, there was no time. For Chandra had looked up, and was looking beyond Drake, to the two men who at that moment must be closing in on either side of him, ready to hoist him out of his seat, muffle his screams, drag him behind the shelves to an emergency exit and out into the street.

Drake had gambled that he'd have time to make a run for it. He'd figured that they wouldn't make their play inside the library, that they'd simply get a good look at him, then prepare to snatch him off the street. But they must be impatient.

Drake heard footsteps behind him, saw the dread in Chandra's eyes. "Thanks for nothing," he hissed at her, as he gathered his strength and prepared to run. But then he saw that Chandra was bewildered as well as scared.

A moment later, a hand landed on Drake's shoulder. "Deacon Drake? Been looking for you. Damon Carter says hey."

CHAPTER TEN

TO DRAKE'S LEFT, a chair scuffed back from the table, and the man lowered himself into it. A big man, like a high school linebacker gone to fat, with a round but muscular face and short black hair just going gray. An unbuttoned denim jacket, a black turtleneck, and, hanging from a lanyard around the man's neck, a badge.

The sight of him and the mention of Deacon Carter's name left Drake almost lightheaded with relief. The woman across the table glared at Drake, as if he'd been planning a murder, then stared at the detective. The newcomer stared right back. "And who might you be?" he asked, in a polite, library voice.

Without a word, Chandra surged to her feet, almost toppling her chair as she rose. One more look at the two men, she strode toward the exit.

"Antisocial, huh?" the detective said. Drake turned toward him and opened his mouth to speak, but the man touched his arm and hushed him with a glance.

Drake remembered the watchers, but almost as the thought came to him, he saw the two men walking in Chandra's wake. They paused next to the main reference desk, then sidled around it so their eyes were turned toward Drake and his new best friend. At the same moment both men looked up and directly at the man they'd come to kill. They took a good look, as if to ensure there'd be no mistake next time.

"You going after them?" asked Drake.

"For staring without a license?" the big man replied. "They repealed that law. Too bad. I'm back to arresting folks for littering. But those two didn't have a candy wrapper between them, so no luck there." The man chuckled like someone who enjoyed listening to himself.

"And you are?" asked Drake.

"Bobby Halsted, Atlanta PD," the man said, extending a meaty right hand. Drake shook it without his usual reluctance. He owed him.

"How'd you happen to be here?"

"Deacon Carter, of course. You told him what was up, and he told me. Asked me to look out for you. But before I could introduce myself I saw that you'd gotten yourself into a little situation. Happy to extract you." He fished around in a pocket, extracted a cellophane-wrapped toothpick, stripped it to bare wood. "Want one?" Halsted asked.

"No, thanks."

"Helps me think," Halsted said, then slid the toothpick between his lips. "Makes me look cool."

"That counts for a lot."

"I think so." Halsted leaned back in his chair. "So she tell you anything?"

"In words? Not much. But her actions said plenty."

"Yeah, mainly by the company she keeps. Bodyguards?"

"Kidnappers. They came for me."

"Funny. You strike me as a likable guy. What you do to make them so unhappy?"

"I just keep breathing."

"Well, you're gonna go right on doing that. Otherwise, Carter will wring my neck."

"I don't think he could get his hands around your neck."

Halsted laughed a little too loud for the library. "Don't kid yourself. He's got ways."

"How'd you two meet up?"

"Long story."

"I've got a couple hours till my flight leaves."

"It'll take more than a couple of hours. Matter of fact, you might want to change that flight."

The half-smile had never left Halsted's face, but just then there was something else there, an odd tension that Drake didn't know how to read. It roused his suspicions. After all, he'd met the man a minute before and had no idea who he was. The people he was up against would have no trouble faking police credentials. He wasn't sure how they could have found out about his friendship with Carter, but there were ways.

It all made sense. They entice him to Atlanta, set up a meet with Chandra, terrorize him with a pair of lurking thugs. Then comes Halsted, his savior, a big, friendly man with a smile, a toothpick, a badge, and a gun. Relieved at his narrow escape, Drake would practically fall into his arms. He'd go anywhere with his new protector. Without a murmur, he'd leave the library, climb into an unmarked car, and disappear.

All this passed through Drake's head in the time it took for Halsted to raise a curious eyebrow. The cop, or whomever he was, had seen the look on Drake's face too. But there was no menace in Halsted's reaction, just a look of amused understanding. He raised his left hand with palm outstretched in the gesture he might have used to calm an unruly mob. His right hand went to his hip. For an instant, Drake expected to see the muzzle of an automatic. But the hand came back gripping an iPhone, made bulky by a ruggedized MILSPEC case.

"You better call Carter," said Halsted. "Just to be safe."

Drake took the proffered phone, tapped the call icon, then Recents. Carter's name was there in Halsted's contact list. Drake tapped the entry, read the number just to make sure. It was Carter's number, sure enough. Still, just to be safe, Drake brought up the keypad and dialed the digits himself.

It took two rings.

"Bobby, what's up?"

"Not Bobby, but he's here with me."

"Glad he tracked you down."

"Not nearly as glad as I am. He got me out of a spot."

"You all right?"

"Fine now. How long you known this guy?"

"We go back a way. When you mentioned Atlanta I figured he could provide a little backup."

"So he did. And now he wants me to take a field trip."

"Yeah, I figured that too."

"Said I might miss my return flight."

"Well, miss it. It'll be worth your while."

"Changing flights costs money, you know. I'm on my own dime here."

"Don't worry about it. Bobby will get everything straight. You should go with him, hear what he has to say."

"What's it about?"

"Hard to explain over the phone. But don't worry. You're safe with Bobby. Safer than being by yourself on those streets."

"Okay. I can use a little extra security. I'll call you back in an hour, all right?"

Carter laughed. "And if you don't, what, I'm supposed to call the cops? I've already called the cops."

"Just a thought."

"Not a bad one. You're thinking like a survivor now. About time. So okay, call in an hour. Meantime just go with Bobby. You'll find it interesting."

Drake handed the phone to Halsted. He nodded, laughed, and for just a moment aimed a sharp, searching glance at Drake, as if sizing him up for a street brawl. Then he hung up.

"Ready to go?"

"Where to?"

"Not sure. We gotta make a stop first."

AS THEY LEFT the library, Drake looked for evidence of watchers. He saw nothing, but on a city street there were countless ways to watch without being seen

Halsted no doubt knew the rules of this game, but he wasn't playing. His head didn't swivel, and his eyes hardly shifted as he guided Drake to the car he'd parked against the curb, a bland gray Toyota Camry with an Atlanta Police placard resting on the dashboard.

They drove west on Interstate 20, then south on a large arterial road that ran past a golf course and a cemetery. At a three-way intersection, a friendly-looking sign proclaimed, "Welcome to Cascade Heights," and the road rolled on, lined first with small retailers and later with tidy one-story ranch homes on large, grassy lots.

He'd never been here, but Drake had heard the story of the place. Until the 1960s, Cascade Heights had been a well-off Atlanta suburb, and all white. Then black folks began moving in, and white folks began leaving.

The then-mayor of Atlanta, Ivan Allen, had tried to halt the process by erecting barriers across two roads entering the neighborhood, roads that connected Cascade Heights to nearby black neighborhoods.

It was an odd plan, as ugly and offensive as the Berlin Wall but far dumber. Did Mayor Allen figure black homebuyers were too stupid to seek out alternate routes? In any case, a federal judge ordered the barriers torn down. And sure enough, the whites of Cascade Heights had bugged out, like East Germans in 1989. Judging by the faces of the pedestrians they passed, there was hardly a white person left in Cascade Heights.

"Where we going?" asked Drake after they'd been rolling about fifteen minutes.

"Almost there," said Halsted. "Gimme a few minutes."

Halsted pulled the car in at a driveway lined with tall hedges and surmounted by a canopy of trees. He stopped the car. "Wait here," he said, then climbed out. Looking over his shoulder, Drake saw him walk toward the street. Halsted stood and watched for a couple of minutes, then came back, climbed inside, buckled his belt, and started the engine. He backed out onto the road and resumed their journey.

"Was that something you learned at the police academy?"

"Nope. Spy movies," Halsted replied. "Ever see *The Quiller Memorandum*? Old movie with George Segal and Alec Guinness? Nobody else has either. I don't understand that. Great movie."

"So what did it teach you?"

"Never let yourself be watched unless you want to be. Coming out of the library, they were watching and that was fine. We wanted them to see you under police protection. But we don't want them following us any further. So I made sure they weren't."

"So now we're back on track?"

"Yep, from here it's a straight shot."

"Where to?"

"Right where you need to be."

HALSTED STEERED THE car into another driveway, even denser and shadier than the previous one. There was the crunch of gravel, a brief passage through a veritable tunnel of greenery, and then a compact, formidable structure of gray granite with an arched doorway and double doors of oak.

"Church," said Drake. "Just what I needed."

It looked like a Gothic cathedral in miniature, the sort of church built by the hundreds a century ago in affluent neighborhoods. Funded by white worshipers, no doubt. Probably the sort who'd pleaded with that long-gone Atlanta mayor to barricade Peyton Road. Having lost that battle, they'd moved away and left their church behind, just like the Unitarians who'd abandoned Old Reliant in Boston. Many a black congregation had picked up nice church buildings that way.

Halsted walked to the door, tugged it open, and gestured.

Inside, rank after rank of dark wooden pews glowed under the soft light that flowed through tall stained-glass windows. To his right, Drake saw the sanctuary, raised high and set apart by an oak railing. To one side of the pulpit sat a massive organ console with four sets of keys, and behind the pulpit there stood rank after rank of pipes, some metal, some wood. An organ like this one would play a tune as soon as it was switched on, even if no one touched a key, for an electric bellows would shove air into the organ's wind chest and the entire church would purr with the sound of its breathing.

But just then, there was only silence, and light and a scent of dust and wood polish. Drake breathed deep and knew that Halsted had been right. This was where he needed to be.

"It's something, isn't it?" said Halsted in a hushed voice. "Well, come on." He turned left and strode toward a shadowy corridor to the right of the sanctuary. Drake followed him into the shade, and after a few steps, saw Halsted open a wooden door almost as massive as the one that protected the outside of the church. But this door was polished and unweathered. *Church Office* was written on it in Old English script applied with gold paint.

There was a reception area, a grand little room lined with dark oak bookshelves the same age as the building itself, each shielded behind glass doors. The unoccupied receptionist's desk was simple and stout, but old and of fine quality. The only twenty-first century influences were the laptop computer, a multiline phone, and a small laser printer on a table to one side of the desk.

Doors to other rooms were set in the walls to the left and right of the desk. Halsted stepped over to the left-side door and knocked twice. He hit hard too, but against the thick wood, his knocks made gentle thudding sounds, as if he'd been hitting a pillow. Without waiting for a reply, Halsted turned the knob, pushed the door wide, and went in.

It was a meeting room lined with oak paneling that rose toward an ornamental plaster ceiling. In its center stood a long, heavy table, well-polished but marked with the gentle scuffs and scars of age. Thick-limbed, straight-backed wooden chairs lined the table, six to either side and one at the head of the table, at the far end of the room.

Nobody sat at the head of the table. Indeed, most of the chairs were empty. But not all.

There were five men there, three on the left side of the table, two on the right, at the far end. All turned to look at Halsted as he pushed the door open and at Drake as Halsted ushered him into the room.

Drake felt his feet sink into soft dark-red carpeting, heard the deep silence of the room, so intense that it felt like a sound all its own. And then he heard a voice, strong, sharp, and peevish.

"About time you got here." It was from a short, plump man, gray-suited, in a white, open-collared shirt. His face was seamed and gnarled like firewood, and his close-cut hair was the color of ashes gone cold. The man half-smiled as he spoke, to soften his speech, but it was wasted effort; the impatience remained.

"You miss breakfast, Deacon Grant?" Halsted chuckled, and several of the other men joined in the gentle laughter. "You need to carry a Snickers bar, just in case, because you sure get mean when you're hungry."

Grant frowned, gazed at the table for a moment till the laughter subsided. Drake saw his shoulders rise and fall in what seemed like a shrug. Then Grant relaxed, looked directly at Drake, and smiled—a cool, appraising smile but full of sincerity. "Halsted's right. I get rude when I haven't eaten. And that's not your fault. Please forgive me."

The man named Grant rose to his feet and his four companions did the same. "We're pleased to meet you, Mr. Drake. My name is Reginald Grant. I'm a deacon here at Old Glory AME. So is Mr. Halsted, as you already know. These four gentlemen are deacons as well, but not at this church.

"Bill Harrison and Laquan Barnes are from down the road, at Stonegate Baptist in Atlanta. Meanwhile, Izell North and Marcus Lender drove in from a little farther, Haven Chapel in Nashville."

Harrison was tall and lean, in a black suit. The neck that emerged from his shirt collar was ropy with muscle. So were his arms, to judge by his handshake. Barnes, of medium height, wore a denim shirt topped by a leather jacket. He radiated a pleasant smell of old car grease, and his offered hand was sticky with waterless hand cleaner.

North and Lender were even more casually dressed. Jeans and a Tennessee Titans sweatshirt for Lender, while North wore generic khaki shirt and slacks, straight out of Walmart. The sort of stuff you wear for a five-hour drive. Nashville had to be a good 250 miles away; they'd have been on the road since 6:00 a.m. at least. There were carry-out coffee cups on the table in front of them. Perhaps they were still trying to wake up.

Seven in the room. All men, all black, all deacons. *Even me*, thought Drake.

Grant gestured to the chair at the head of the table. "For our guest, the place of honor," he said.

"Or the hot seat," said North. "Depends on your perspective."

The chair was straight-backed and uncushioned, as if designed for misery. Drake settled into it, squirmed as his back and bottom sought a position of comfort, then sat still under the gaze of the others.

"One of us is still missing, but he'll be along shortly," said Grant.

"Meanwhile, we can cover some of the preliminaries."

"Does that include the part, why I'm here?" said Drake. "Because that's my highest priority right now."

"I figured your highest priority would be staying alive," said Grant. "We can help with that. We're helping right now, by keeping you off the street. Still, I like to think that we can assist each other."

"How?"

"Oh, you'd be surprised," said Grant. "We're pretty versatile. And we get around. Even me, though not as much as I used to. I'm from Alabama, originally. Got drafted into the Korean War then went right back home to Montgomery."

Drake noted the gray hair and lined face, consulted the calendar inside his head, put two and two together. "Just in time to take part in the bus boycott. Did you get to meet Dr. King?"

Grant made a brushback gesture with one hand, like a man wafting away incense. "I barely knew him," he said. "Just well enough to save his life."

"He should have kept you on the payroll."

Grant frowned at that, but for only a moment. Then he laughed and nodded. "You talk like you write," he said. "I should have seen that coming. Anyway, I was never on the payroll. I was on duty, and I did what I had to do. I was a deacon."

"And you saved Dr. King."

"A couple of times. Not by myself. I had help."

Years ago, in Chicago, Drake had visited the 103rd floor of the Willis Tower. There was a ledge up there, with a floor of reinforced glass, extending five feet beyond the side of the building. Drake stepped out and forced himself to look straight down at the gray, deadly pavement over a thousand feet below.

That feeling was back now.

"It was the bomb on his front porch that got us involved. Up to then, we'd sat on the sidelines, not ready to make a move. Despite our resources, we knew that we wouldn't stand a chance. Not against the full weight of the United States government. And that's what we'd have been up against if we'd shown our hand back then. Hoover would have called us a bunch of communists. They'd have come for us. Now I'm about the only one left from that time. But since then we've recruited many others, including the gentlemen in this room. Some ladies too. Dozens of us scattered across the United States."

"Church deacons?"

"Pretty much all of us, yes."

"So you're part of some national organization of deacons. Kind of like the Elks or the Shriners. Dedicated to the doing of good works."

"Something like that," said Grant. "Only our idea of good works is a bit more aggressive than theirs. More ambitious too. Basically, we're in the alternate history business."

Pushing back against his growing unease, Drake allowed himself a laugh. "You mean, like those books where the Confederacy wins? I didn't take you for a nerd, Deacon Grant."

"Been reading that stuff since the army," he replied. "Back in Jim Crow days, it felt good to think about different versions of America, even the ones that would have turned out worse. It made you feel like nothing was inevitable. Which is true anyway. History doesn't run on rails. Everything depends on the choices we make and the actions we take

"Look at Dr. King in Montgomery. He wasn't at home when the bomb hit. Just his wife and daughter. But what if he'd died there? Or here's a better one: What if he'd survived, but his wife and daughter were killed? You think he'd have kept preaching nonviolence after his family got blown to pieces? Where would we stand today if Dr. King had used all his brilliance and eloquence to preach hatred and not love? The whole world would be a different place right now. Not just America. The world."

"Maybe," Drake mused. "Then again, he wouldn't have gotten too far with talk like that. Not back then. He'd have been dead in a year, and his movement too."

"More than likely. But either way, there's no letter from the Birmingham, Alabama, jail; no speech at the Lincoln Memorial; and no march across the Edmund Pettus Bridge. And without Dr. King, there's probably no civil rights laws and none of those Great Society programs that fed and clothed millions of our people and gave us a fighting chance. Without Dr.

King, maybe you're a day laborer or a street-corner hustler instead of a newspaperman. And maybe the country would be right now recovering from a second civil war."

"Maybe," said Drake. "But we can't know. We'll never know. That's why I don't do alternate history."

"Well, we do," said Grant. "Alternate history is exactly what we do. After that first close call, we intervened to protect Dr. King, and we shut down two other murder plots against him. But we've done so much more over the years. Nobody knows how close we've come to race war in this country. Could have been thousands dead. We stopped it. We've prevented miscarriages of justice that might have sent innocent men and women to death row. One time, almost by accident, we stopped an act of sabotage that could have crippled the preparations for D-Day."

Drake made a scoffing sound but grew sober when he gazed at the others. They were sitting up straighter in their chairs, leaning forward a little. There was pride in their bearing, and Drake realized that every man at this table was certain that Grant's words were true.

"Guess you don't believe it," Grant said, his eyes fixed on Drake's. "Why not? All through history, small groups of people, working behind the scenes, have changed the world. Happens all the time. Or is this the sort of thing only white folks can manage? You figure we're not up to it?" Grant grinned at that, and Drake couldn't help smiling as well.

"So that's not it. Then what's the problem?"

"Not a problem, exactly," Drake said. "But it all sounds like secret society stuff. In Chicago I used to hang out at Bughouse Square and listen to nuts on soapboxes who could conclusively prove that everything in the world was being stage-managed by the Masons or the Vatican or, God help us, the Jews. Turns out it was black folks all along. Frankly, I'm relieved."

"It's a cheerful thought, isn't it?" said a grinning Grant.

"Well, yes and no," said Drake. "If you guys have so much power, why aren't you doing a better job? The world's a mess, and our people aren't doing so well either."

"Maybe you paid too much attention to those guys at Bughouse Square. Nobody's in control, not really. Certainly not the Vatican! No, the most

Deacon ex machina

any of us can do is to exert a certain influence. We just do it quietly and behind the scenes. Sometimes we can shift events in a direction that suits us; sometimes we fail. The important thing is to make sure that our people have a hand in the affairs of this country. Our organization has achieved that goal, for well over a century."

The words sent a chill through Drake's flesh. "So it didn't begin with protecting Dr. King." *// origin story !!*

"Not at all. Our group was founded after the Civil War, in the days of Reconstruction. Our founder, well, his name would mean nothing to you. But he managed to become wealthy beyond the dreams of any black man of his time. He considered taking up his wealth and relocating to another country, like France or England. Instead he stayed home and began to build this organization. He was quite a churchman, and it seemed to him like a good idea to build his new organization around the churches, one of the few institutions of real influence that were permitted to our people. That's how it began. We call it the Diaconate. Not an original name, but accurate."

"So you're saying that you and a bunch of church deacons are rewriting the future."

"We're trying, anyway. We've had a mixed track record, of course. But that's no surprise. This isn't the Second Foundation, and I'm not Hari Seldon. Nobody can really predict the future course of human affairs, especially not with math. We're counting on prayer instead. That, and common sense, and our best possible judgment about the right time and place to make a move."

"What kind of move?" asked Drake.

"Whatever the circumstances demand," Grant replied. "Bounded of course by our best moral judgment. There are some things we just can't do."

"So that's why you guys didn't kill Hitler back in 1933"

"Oh, we thought about it," Grant said. "Or rather, our predecessors did. That was in 1936, actually. The year of the Berlin Olympics. How else to get a black guy with a gun that close to him?" Grant smiled at the memory, exposing a faceful of gleaming dentures. "A suicide mission, of course. That was the biggest objection. That and the idea of sponsoring cold-blooded murder. Either way, it didn't go down."

Jesse Owens : Hitler thought experiment

Drake took a couple of deep breaths and fell silent for a space. The others kept still as well for a few moments. After a while, Grant said, "Yeah. It got to me too when I first learned about it. It was years after the war, at a meeting a lot like this one, in Montgomery."

Drake fixed his eyes on the old man. "And of course, they didn't have Uber in those days. So it wouldn't have been so easy for you to stand up and walk out." He pushed back his chair and began to rise.

"Journalist," said North, and there was contempt in his voice. "They're watchers, not actors. Told you it was a waste of time."

"Deacon North here advised against revealing ourselves to you in the first place," said Grant. "Figured you wouldn't be interested. Now he's mad because he came all the way from Nashville, and you won't even stick around to hear us out."

"Hear you talk about plotting to murder people?" said Drake. "No thanks, I'm in enough trouble as it is, without hooking up with the Baptist edition of Al Qaeda."

At that, Grant laughed, relaxed and friendly. "Be cool, Deacon. We didn't go through with it, and that was the only time anything that extreme was even considered. We're not murderers, and we're sure not terrorists."

Drake settled down again. "So what are you?"

"Just a group of African-American churchmen who'd rather see our people take action, than wait to be acted upon."

"What kind of actions?"

"Research, mostly. Investigations. Followed now and then by interventions. The sort of interventions that might save lives if they're made early enough and in the right ways."

"Whose lives?"

"Now that," said Laquan Barnes, "is a real good question. We've been arguing about that one for the past couple of years."

"Am I my brother's keeper?" said Grant. "That's really what the fight is about."

"So it's a family squabble," said Drake. "Maybe I should just stay out of it."

"Maybe you should," said Barnes.

"It's this business with the hackers," said Grant. "Some of us feel that we ought to stay out of it. That it's out of our league."

"I never said that." As he spoke, Barnes poked at the table with the outstretched fingers of his right hand. To Drake, he seemed not quite angry. Irritated, maybe, and a little dismayed.

"There's not much that's out of our league," Barnes continued. "We've learned that from experience. It's purpose that I'm worried about. Why are we getting tangled up in something like this? It's too far from our original mandate."

"Our original mandate runs back to 1880," said Grant. "Times change. Besides, I think this fits right in with the founder's goals. A Negro church has been attacked. A Negro woman of the church was nearly murdered."

Negro. Drake was surprised to hear that archaic word. But Grant spoke it with courtly elegance, as if he loved the sound of it.

But Barnes was not impressed. "Black folks get stabbed and shot every day," he said. "We hardly ever get involved. Why this time?"

"This time, we have reason to believe that it's part of something a lot bigger, something that could damage the entire country. Maybe the world."

"The world is not our problem," said Barnes.

Grant laughed, shook his head, while Harrison, the other deacon from Stonegate Baptist, rolled his eyes upward to heaven.

"I been trying to tell him," Harrison said. "But the brother seems to believe that the US economy can collapse without hurting our people. Now that's some alternate history, right there."

The others chuckled, all but Barnes. Goaded by their laughter, his face flushed, and his dark skin grew a couple of shades darker. "All I'm saying is that this goes way beyond the sort of thing this organization was created to handle. We take on direct threats to the security and well-being of our people. Now all of a sudden, you guys want to save the world."

"And you think it's too much for us," said Harrison. "That we can't handle it. We can prevent a lynching here or a riot there, or prevent the occasional miscarriage of justice. Stuff like that we can manage. But shifting the global balance of power? That's not for us. That's for the white folks."

Barnes snorted, scowled, and shoved back from the table, preparing to rise. Harrison put a hand on his wrist. "Calm down, man. Take a breath."

"You know that's not what I meant!" Barnes was just plain angry now. In full cry, his voice was high-pitched and tremulous, not unlike Drake's own.

"Okay, okay," Harrison said. "Put it this way. First, crash the entire global banking system and millions of our people lose their jobs and their life savings. We still haven't recovered from 2008. Now imagine a financial crash two or three times worse. It'll hit the white man hard, but it'll hit our people a lot harder. That makes it our problem."

Barnes listened in silence, still tense and wary.

"Second, let's say there's a foreign country behind it all. Don't know that for sure, but given this outfit's reach and resources, it's a good way to bet. You up for another war? Because that's what this would be. An act of war. The US government would have to do something about it, probably something violent. Again, the whole country suffers. Our people suffer."

"Yes, there's harm," replied Barnes. "But it's indirect harm, and we're not even sure it's going to happen or how bad it'd be if it did. Right now, it's all fantasy. We can sit here all day speculating about threats that may never come to pass. Are we going to take on every one of them? Maybe we should go looking for those weapons of mass destruction in Iraq. The 82nd Airborne might have missed a cave or two."

Grant sighed, nodded. "Deacon Barnes makes a fair point," he said. "But our original mandate was drawn up in the years after Reconstruction, to fight the Klan. As more and more of our people migrated north, so did we. Sometimes we worked with allies, sometimes alone. Always the goal was to protect our people and plan for final victory over those who kept us down.

"And now . . . here we are." Grant smiled, shrugged. It's the twenty-first century now. Things haven't worked out entirely as I'd hoped. We don't have colonies on Mars or flying cars. But we do have black people running major cities and Fortune 500 corporations and sitting on the Supreme Court. Not too long ago, one of us lived at 1600 Pennsylvania Avenue.

"In short, the original reasons for the founding of this organization no longer exist. We Negroes are now a free people, with personal and political rights secured by law. And that changes things."

"Free?" said Barnes, "There's a half-million black men sitting in jail cells right now, millions more with criminal records so they can't get a decent job or even cast a vote. Now that's a crisis, right there. And it matters more to me than propping up Citibank."

"Only we don't tackle jobs like that," said Grant.

"Don't think we're up to it, huh?"

"Matter of fact, no. I don't," said Grant. "It's like assigning the FBI to run homeless shelters. A perfectly noble job, but not their job."

Grant shook his head, then stared at Barnes. "We investigate and intervene, and always as quietly as possible. The things that rightly bother you can't be fixed that way."

"Then what's the point of all this?" said Barnes. "Maybe we should just declare victory and go home."

"Bit early for that."

It was a soft, deep voice and it came from the doorway at the other end of the room. He wore charcoal slacks, a white shirt unbuttoned at the neck, and a navy-blue blazer. He was tall and angular, like an Abu Dhabi apartment block. He looked like a billion bucks. And he was the last person Drake had expected to see.

Reginald Grant: Old Glory Ame, Atlanta
Laquon Barnes - Silvergate Baptist

BOO KENDRICKS. GOD'S geek. The man whose wealth had helped Reliant Baptist pay for the building where Astrid had nearly died.

Boo strolled toward the head of the table, sank into a chair alongside Drake, offered a nod of greeting, first to him and then to the rest of the group.

"What'd I miss?"

The question had been intended for the others in the room and not for Drake. Just as well, because Drake was beyond speech.

"Not a lot," said Grant. "We revealed our little secret to your friend here"—he nodded toward Drake—"and then resumed our ongoing fight about the future of our organization."

"I was winning on points," said Barnes, smirking.

"I'm sure you believe that," replied Grant, "and as usual, you're wrong."

"Save it for now," Boo said and turned to Drake. "Well, what about it? You interested?"

Drake, still bewildered, played for time. "Interested? In what? I mean, they still hadn't gotten around to that part. What am I supposed to be doing?"

"Exactly what you want to do," Grant said. "You want to find out who attacked your church and your friend. We want you to find out. And we want to provide you with whatever support you'll need to get it done."

"Weapons, surveillance gear, night-vision goggles—you name it." Boo gave him a severe gaze, then broke out laughing. "Actually, we're thinking plane tickets, credit cards, spending money, a few changes of clothes. Enough to keep body and soul together. Plus whatever additional support we can provide. Which is quite a lot."

"I can imagine," said Drake. "Remind me—where do you rank on the Forbes 400?"

"High enough," said Boo. "Anyway, those *Forbes* numbers are crap."

"You richer, then? Or poorer?"

"Use your imagination. Either way, the organization can cover your hotel bills."

"Where am I going?"

"Wherever you have to go, and for as long as it takes. Within reason, of course. We expect results."

"Sounds fair," said Drake. "At this point, I'm not sure what my next move will be. There are people who worked with Astrid and know what's going on, but I'm not sure how to find them. I was counting on this woman Chandra to give me a lead. Instead, she tried to have me killed. Just like Dr. Severins back in Cambridge." Drake frowned at the memory, looked up at Boo. "You haven't got a few legbreakers on the payroll, by any chance? Them and me could pay Severins a return visit."

"Sorry," said Boo. "Vengeance is God's department. Besides, there's got to be another way. You're smart. You'll find it. Maybe get some of your colleagues at the *Record* to pitch in. This'll make a great story for whoever breaks it. But even if your editors aren't interested, we are. Take a leave of absence and we'll back you. Go after these guys. Shut down whatever it is they're trying. Shut it down."

In his several previous encounters with Boo, Drake had never heard him speak with so much fervor. He didn't sound angry, exactly. Call it determination. Boo wanted these people, and to bring them down he was willing to pay. Specifically, he was willing to pay Drake.

"Sounds appealing," Drake said. "But I'm telling you now, I'm not taking any kind of blood oath."

They all chuckled at that, even Barnes.

"Not a problem," said Boo. "But you're on probation. We don't recruit just anybody, you know. If we decide that your efforts play a material part in resolving this crisis, we'll keep you around. If not, you can go back to Boston and keep right on reviewing the latest smartphones."

Boo's voice was almost dismissive, an intentional taunt. It was an insult wasted. No way would he pass this up. There might even be a story in it, someday.

"Either way, we trust that you'll never write about us." Boo's head canted to one side, his lips quirking upward in a clairvoyant grin.

"Now that's asking a lot," said Drake. "Writing's what I do."

"Not about us. At least, not yet. Circumstances change. Maybe someday . . ."

"That's what I was afraid of," said Barnes. "You and Grant are going to mess around and turn us into—I don't know—the Ford Foundation. Just another bunch of do-gooders with deep pockets."

"Would that be so bad?" said Boo. "Suppose we reinvent ourselves, go public, even tell a few sanitized stories of our past activities? There might even be a movie in it."

"The day you do," said Barnes, in a cold, crisp voice, "is the day I walk. I signed on for a chance to take action on behalf of our people. I was recruited to fight against the violence and hatred that has held us down. Now half of us, maybe more, pretend to believe that that fight is over. Well, tell that to the families of the nine people in Charleston, South Carolina, who got shot to death in their church. Or those thugs who marched through Charlottesville and killed that woman. They're still out there, and they're getting stronger."

A handful of high school dropouts waving tiki torches aren't much of a threat," said Boo. The guys who came at Drake here can do a whole lot worse. So I say we go after them."

"And your word is law around here," said a resentful Barnes, "because you're paying the bills these days. In fact, maybe that's why you're so interested in this. Because if this bank job comes off, it could knock a zero or two off your net worth. Is that why you're getting us involved in this?"

The others murmured and made as if to defend Boo, but he waved them to silence. "The thought had crossed my mind," he said. "But I'd need a better reason than that. Remember that nothing's happened yet. Drake. I can rejigger my investment portfolio and escape the worst of it. Guys like me always can. How about you? Or your mother, Deacon Barnes? She lives on Social Security and the savings in her 401(k), right? What happens when those savings disappear? Think of all the people you know who are just like her. What will they do?"

Boo glanced around the room. "And that's why I favor getting involved. Now I know I only get one vote around here, same as anybody else. But I'm telling you now that if this gets voted down, I'll back Drake on my own. Because somebody's got to find these guys and stop them."

There was silence then, and the creaking of an old wooden chair as one of the deacons shifted his weight.

"Objections?" said Grant, and silence fell again.

"So that's it," said Boo. "We don't speak for the entire organization. But regional groups like this one are empowered to recruit provisional members. So that's what you are. Effective immediately. Your membership entitles you to every assistance we can offer—finance, research, travel, and security. Whatever you need, you've got it. We'll expect detailed expense reports, of course."

"Don't sweat that. As of now, I have no idea where to spend your money."

"Finding the other hackers, of course. You've got their emails and their nicknames. There's got to be a way to find them."

"I've put out feelers, and I'll make a few more moves. All I can do is hope at least one of them responds."

"If one of them does, get him talking. Find some way back to the people who are behind all this."

"And when I find them, what next?"

"Call the cops, of course. We'll tell you which ones. We've got friends in some of the three-letter agencies who'll know how to act on something like this."

"When you're done," said Grant, "you might get a book out of it. A few good bylines for your paper too."

In the silence that followed, Drake leaned back in his chair, closed his eyes.

"Well?" said Boo.

"I'm not sure I want your help. And I'm not sure I trust you," said Drake. "But then, one of you almost certainly saved my life today. And I won't be able to see this through on my own."

"Just one thing," said Barnes. "You already know which way I vote on this, but it's pretty clear I'm outnumbered. But get one thing clear. You don't tell anybody about us. Not one word."

Grant nodded. "I think this whole secret society thing has gone too far. But that's just me. And in any case, it's one of the rules. So I live by it. And so must you. Tell anybody about who we are and we'll just deny everything." Grant raised his eyes to Drake's and locked on. "And then any assistance from us will end, completely. You'll be on your own."

"Disavowed, huh?"

"Just like in the movies," said Barnes.

"Understood," said Drake.

Grant called the vote, but it was pro forma, with Barnes as the only no. Boo lowered his hand. "Well, that's it, then. So what's your next move?"

"Hole up someplace safe, with a phone, a computer, and Internet access. And then start hunting."

"Sounds like a plan," Boo said. "May I make a suggestion?"

CHAPTER ELEVEN

tech too

DRAKE'S RETURN TICKET to Boston went unused. Instead, at meeting's end Boo gestured him into his own ride, a hulking SUV with slick leather seats made icy by air conditioning. It was a quick ride to Peachtree Road and Boo's condominium in the Buckhead district, where Atlanta's money lived.

"I've got a few such places here and there," Boo told him. "Saves on hotel bills."

The walls were pale blue, the carpeting deep gray, and the living room of the place was bigger than Drake's whole condo. There was a bed big enough for a movie producer and a shower that might have served as a car wash.

Boo led Drake to a second bedroom that had been converted to a home office, with a stand-up desk of steel and glass, a comfy-looking high-rise chair, plenty of electrical outlets, and an Ethernet cable that dangled from a wall outlet. Without being asked, Drake unzipped his backpack and set up his laptop.

"You've got gigabit Internet in here, wired and wireless," said Boo. "Password's in the top drawer. There'll be food in the fridge as soon as you order some. I've got an open account at the Publix supermarket down the street. Just call, give my name, and they'll bring you whatever you need."

"Champagne and caviar?" asked Drake, and Boo chuckled.

"Try it and see."

"No, thanks. Just testing my limits."

"There aren't any. What you need, you get."

"I might have to hop a plane. Maybe several."

Boo took out a notepad, scribbled with a pen, and tore off a sheet of paper. "Here's Detective Halsted's number, just in case you get in trouble again. That second number and email belongs to a woman named Madeleine. You need anything, she'll see you get it."

"What can I count on her for?"

"Travel arrangements. And money, of course. Just give her your bank account information, and she'll top off your account."

"I've been meaning to update my wardrobe."

"I was hoping you'd say that. You look pitiful."

Drake couldn't help laughing. "You sound like my ex."

Boo looked on the verge of a snide reply, then thought better of it. "Anyway, get something decent. Might need to make an impression."

"On who?"

"That's for you to find out," said Drake. "This isn't a vacation. You need to spend every waking hour trying to identify the people behind this."

"No idea how I'll manage it."

"You're a reporter. Start digging. I'm paying for the shovel this time."

"Yeah, about that," said Drake. "I'm expected back at my desk."

"No. *You* expected to be back at your desk. But they'll get by without you. You told me so."

"I've got a few weeks' vacation stashed."

"Fine. Use them. Work your contacts and ours too. I told you we've got three-letter friends in Washington. I'll get Madeleine to forward you their digits.

"You got just one job. Trace these guys, and fast. I want you focused on this. Total focus. Twenty-hour days on Mountain Dew and junk food, if that's what it takes. No limits."

"Yeah, the quicker I find who's behind this and sic the cops on 'em," said Drake, "the quicker I can go home."

"Your homesickness is the least of my worries, and yours. Whatever these people are planning, it happens soon."

"How can you know that?"

"We've got a dead hacker in Hamburg and another who nearly bled out in Boston. What more do you need to know?"

"They're brutal, that's for sure. But we don't know their timetable."

"Oh yes we do," said Boo. "At least we've got a rough idea. It's the violence. That's the key."

"Proves they're in a hurry?"

"Yep. Hackers aren't killers. If somebody blows their cover they just retreat and wait for another chance or go looking for another target. Murder is stupid, and these guys aren't stupid.

"But imagine they've spent years setting this up, and they're within a week or two of setting it off. And suddenly a member of the team grows a conscience. That's years of effort wasted and a big payoff lost. Only these guys would rather commit murder than give up."

"Yeah," said Drake. "And murder on two continents, at that."

"Right. That takes resources. So we're dealing with an international gang. Or maybe a hostile government."

"None of this is making me feel any better, you know," Drake said.

"Well, you won't be taking them on personally," said Boo, "except through a keyboard. Your job is to come up with some names. Real-world human beings the FBI can locate and interrogate. You've got a few clues. Wish you had more, but that can't be helped. We need an answer, and soon. And that means that at five every morning, no later, I expect you to drag your ass out from under my three hundred-count cotton sheets, make a cup of coffee, and get to work."

WEDNESDAY MORNING, HE was up at five and at the keyboard. It was too early to work the phones, so he had a couple hours of keyboard time, enough for a hundred Google searches. But Drake favored doing things the easy way. Instead of launching a browser, he fired up a bit of freeware he'd pulled out of the SourceForge software library a couple of years ago, a search engine scraper with advanced search and copy tools.

It would take a while to track people known to him only by nicknames—Borzoi, Mesh, Gallery, and Kirsch. That, and their involvement in a bank hacking scheme, was all he knew about them. From this he needed to uncover their real names and true locations, then somehow persuade them to meet and talk.

Hardly a cakewalk, but not impossible. Hackers are creatures of habit. They hang out in the same online forums day after day and attempt the same sorts of digital crimes time after time. And once one of them has made a name for himself, he tends to stick with it.

And so Drake had a chance. At least as much of a chance as Gary Alford, the Internal Revenue Service agent who'd busted Silk Road, the notorious online marketplace that dealt in drugs, weapons, and murder.

Alford knew almost nothing about computers, but he knew how to work Google. So in 2013, he began tracking the online postings of a user who'd been among the first to mention Silk Road, a fellow with the username *altoid*. After three months' work, he found a message from 2011 in which altoid used his real-world email address. That address led straight to a Texan named Ross Ulbricht, who ended up with a life sentence.

But if Boo was right, Drake didn't have three months to find Team Silverware. Neither did he have access to NSA-grade spy tools like Palantir and Centrifuge that could cross-check billions of bits in seconds. He would have to do it one Google search at a time.

Drake said a brief prayer for success and got to work.

He started with the nicknames he'd found in the Silverware mailing list. Three of them were now known to him. Snowbird was Astrid, of course. Dr. Severins had revealed himself as Stainless, and Clinker was Helmut Brockmann, presently in an icebox at the Hamburg medical examiner's office.

That left four others—Borzoi, Kirsch, Gallery, and Mesh. Now to find them.

Drake's search-and-scrape tool would let him type in query after query and save the results from each search. Reading through that mass of mostly useless data would be the hard part. But there was no point looking for a needle until he'd first heaped up a good-size haystack.

No doubt the people he wanted would traffic in the specialized jargon of the professional hacker. They'd talk about signatures and exploits, linkers and builds, C&C and IRC. Drake made a master list with every buzzword he could think of.

His search should have included some banking terminology as well, but he didn't know any, so he settled for obvious terms like "bank" and "account."

For the next several hours, Drake fed the software every combination of search terms that came to mind. He didn't look at results but instead ordered the program to capture in full the first twenty web pages produced by each search.

Drake had a knack for losing himself in a task. So he wasn't surprised to notice that the room had grown brilliant with light from the now fully risen sun. He checked the time: 10:00 a.m. Then he right-clicked on the desktop folder where the pages were being copied. Already he'd collected about fifty megabytes. Most of it useless, to be sure, but one had to start somewhere.

Drake rose from his chair, strolled into the kitchen, peered into the empty fridge and cabinets. He should go out for something; he'd be safe enough on the streets of Buckhead to find a Starbucks. Later, he'd phone that Publix supermarket Boo had mentioned and place a full-spectrum order for groceries. Enough for a week.

But he had other calls to make. Carter first. He answered after two rings, said "Deacon," in a wary voice, then fell silent. It was as if he was making room on the telephone circuit for Drake's confusion and surprise.

But Drake just said, "Does Pastor know?"

Carter sighed. "The Diaconate? Yeah, he knows. And Pastor Burns before him. Remember Deacon Emeritus Kelly? Retired last year? He was one of us. Ever since he left us, we'd thought about a replacement. When all this happened and we saw how you handled it, we decided you were the man."

"What if I don't want to join the outfit?"

"Free country. But right now, we're the safest play you got."

"So how long have you been part of it?"

"A few years. Since then, I've assisted on a couple of operations. That's all I can tell you."

"Don't trust me yet."

"I do, actually. But we have rules. You're a provisional member, and you may not last."

"Well, Boo's giving me a tryout. He's got me holed up in a condo down here. Pretty plush, and safer than Boston. What about Astrid?"

"On the mend. They upgraded her to stable this morning. I was on the phone with her for a couple of minutes, and she sounded almost normal. Asked me to bring her a laptop. Says she hasn't gone this long without writing code since eighth grade."

"You ask her about her friends? The ones who are in with her on this?"

"Didn't get to bring it up. She said she was off for tests and treatment, then she hung up. I tried her back once and got no answer. You should take a try. If she'll talk, it could save you a whole lot of trouble."

"Yeah," said Drake. "If she talks. She's trying to decide what scares her most. Death or prison."

"So talk to her and see if something shakes loose," said Carter.

Drake said nothing for a while, until Carter broke the silence. "You mad?"

"About what?"

"The secrets. Me not saying anything."

"You weren't supposed to. And I didn't need to know, till now. So, no, I'm not mad."

"So what's your next move?"

"I've got a phone, an Internet connection, and unlimited funds."

"But where do you start looking?"

"At those email addresses I pinged on Sunday. Astrid's files may be gone, but at least I've still got those addresses. I'll work that angle as long as I can. Plus I know some people who might be able to help."

"Pretty skimpy, but I've worked plenty of cases with less."

"And did you solve them?"

"Not many. But look at the bright side. You just have to solve one."

THE NEXT CALL was to Astrid, but the phone just rang. Perhaps the ringer was turned off, or she had been wheeled out for X-rays.

So Drake gave up and dialed Ginsburg at the *Record*.

"In Atlanta, I take it," were his editor's first words. "And alive. Maybe getting out of town was the right move after all."

"I think so. And if you don't mind, I'll stay gone for a while."

"How long a while?"

"A week, maybe two. You told me I should take some if I needed it. Turns out I do."

"So this woman you went looking for, you found her?"

"Yeah. Definitely worth the trip."

"What did she have to say?"

"She didn't say a word. Neither did the guys she brought to the meeting with her."

Ginsburg was silent for a bit. "Get on a plane and get back here."

"No point. I'm in just as much danger in Boston. Maybe more. They know where I live and work back there. In Atlanta, I can keep a low profile."

"Yeah, and go broke doing it."

"I've got some money saved, enough to keep this up for a while." It wasn't a lie, really.

"What's your next move?"

"Try to find some of the other people involved in this. I just need one who's willing to talk. Then we've got a story and maybe some action from the feds. Homeland Security, I figure."

"But only if you can find the right guy and get him to talk. Do you even know where to look? Got any names and addresses?"

"Email addresses is all. I've pinged them, so they can find me, but they might be too scared to reach out."

"That, or they're dead." Ginsburg made an odd, disgruntled sound then. "Really, you want to keep this up?"

"They've tried for me twice, and they'll keep on trying. They're afraid I'll somehow track them down. I figure my only option is to do just that."

"You'll have a great story when you get back," Ginsburg mused. "If you work it right, the Record will pay for your vacation."

"It might get expensive."

148

"For you, especially. So watch your step. And bring me back something good."

[handwritten annotation: Israel Cybersurveillance Unit ? lol bd of Europeans]

NOW IT WAS time to call in backup. He decided to start with Natan Efron. He should have phoned him sooner; Efron had once told Drake over lunch that five years with Unit 8200 had cured him of the need to sleep.

Like many other veterans of Israeli signals intelligence, Efron had launched a security consulting firm. Though Drake had quoted him in stories from time to time, he was a former spy, and so Drake didn't entirely trust the man. So let him prove himself.

His phone buzzed twice and then, "Efron." The voice was a purr, the accent not quite Austrian.

"Got a minute? It's Weldon Drake from over at the *Record*."

"Hey, yeah, Weldon. Didn't recognize the number. You got a new phone or you using a burner?"

"Paranoid as ever, it seems."

"And still above ground."

"Good news for both of us, since I need a favor."

"How big?"

"Depends on how sharp you guys are. I'm looking for some people."

"My kind of people?"

"You'd fit right in."

"Well then, the possibilities are limitless. Carders? Bot herders? Flesh merchants? What?"

"Bank robbers."

"A perennial favorite. It's where the money is, after all. Boxes of it, scattered all over town in ratty-looking ATMs."

"The people I'm looking for are a lot more ambitious. They're trying to crack the core."

There was a muffled pulse of sound on the line, something between a chuckle and a snort. "Never steal anything small, eh?"

"Can it be done?"

"If you can get into the Iranian uranium centrifuges, you can get into any network on earth. But core banking code is guarded like the president and monitored like a pediatric ICU."

"But presidents get shot, and babies die."

A warm, knowing chortle came down the line. "I remember the first time we talked, you acted so knowing, so cynical. It was all a front, of course. You knew nothing. And now listen to you. You sound like a man who has heard things with his own ears and seen things with his own eyes."

"I have."

There was silence on the line. Then Efron said, "So have I."

It was more than Drake had hoped for. It took an effort of will for him to keep his voice steady. "So tell me what you've heard."

"I've said too much already," said Efron. "But I figure there's no harm done, since you've already felt the same nibbles. Yes, my team and I do a little consulting work for a couple of smaller banks. And we've also felt a few tugs on the line. Nothing too severe at this stage. Just probing. A bunch of PCs tainted with the Botch program. Of course, that's no surprise. Botch goes after desktop targets of opportunity and millions of machines have caught that particular disease. But in one case, we found that it had brought some really nasty payloads to the party. Somebody used Botch to inject some code that could reshuffle a bank's databases like a deck of cards. How much money you got in the bank?"

"I'd always welcome more."

"This code could make you a billionaire overnight or put you in debt for two billion. Just a few keystrokes. This was nasty stuff. Nasty."

"Yeah. Multiply that by every bank account in America."

"It wouldn't have to be every account. Just a few tens of millions, preferably held by midsized to big companies and individuals with high net worth. But the more the merrier. Just push a button and watch as the US economy begins to melt."

"Just the US economy?"

"You're right," said Efron. "Why be modest? A play like this could kick off a global recession."

"So you know something's going down."

"Somebody's getting ready to pull the trigger, but his knuckle isn't turning white just yet."

"Any idea when the big day arrives?"

"If I were him, I wouldn't move until I had a foothold in four or five major banks. That might take a while."

"But then you don't know how long they've been at it, and you don't know how long they've had to infect other institutions."

"Thanks for reminding me of my ignorance," said Efron. "I'll do the same for you someday."

"You worried?"

"Just enough to start contacting banks and asking them to be extra-alert," said Efron. "I told them what to look for."

"I'm more interested in who than in what."

"So you're hunting these guys?"

"Sure sounds like we're after the same people. It'll make a great story."

"No doubt. But finding Bigfoot would make a good story too. And Bigfoot won't be trying to murder you."

"What makes you say that?"

"The stabbing at your church. Your lovely, eloquent tribute to the victim—Astrid, right? She sounds delightful. And brilliant. Tell her if she ever needs a job . . ."

"There was nothing in that story about why she was attacked. I didn't know myself, at the time."

"You told me why when you called me. It was the last bit of information I needed. I'd already rooted around on the net and found out all about Astrid. I couldn't help myself. I was puzzled, same as you and the cops. Why stab her? And why break into a church to do it? Somebody wanted her bad, and I couldn't figure why.

"So I read up on her. She's a real wunderkind.

"And then I get a call from you, first time in months by the way, and you ask me to play detective for you. So I took a guess, which you've just confirmed." The chuckle again. "Please don't be angry. I think this way for a living. Can't help myself."

"So now you know. Will you help?"

"How could I resist? So what do you need?"

Drake told Efron about the Silverware group, about the seven names—the ones he recognized and the ones he didn't. He could hear the clatter of keys as Efron typed it all down.

"None of these names mean anything to me, but how much can one man know, anyway? I'll run it past my colleagues and feed it into our AI system."

"So you let computers do your thinking for you now?"

"Whenever possible. We've got some cunning little algorithms we've worked up ourselves, and all the compute power and storage that money can buy, thanks to the cloud."

"You running on Amazon AWS?"

"We went with Azure instead. You know me. I'm a born contrarian."

"I've already worked Google pretty hard. DuckDuckGo as well."

"Yeah, but these people have the good sense not to spend too much of their online time where people can see them. You've got to go trolling the deep Web and the Dark Web. And while you're more sophisticated than the average scribe, you barely know which keys to push when it comes to that stuff."

"I love the way you build a fellow up."

"Am I lying?"

"Not really," Drake conceded.

"So okay," said Efron. "Now, what do I get in return?"

"The thanks of a grateful journalist, of course. And some front-page ink when we wrap this up.

"I'm thinking a sidebar to the main story, about the legendary Israeli cyberwarrior who cracked the case."

"Should we photograph you in desert camo or a dinner jacket?"

"I look good either way."

DRAKE WROTE UP his notes, plugged them into an email, and fired it off to Efron. He made similar calls to six more of his sources, private-sector veterans of the FBI and CIA. There was even a four-letter man, a veteran of GCHQ Cheltenham. None of them were quite as quick as Efron; they knew nothing of a stabbing in Boston. But Josette Simmons, a principal at a security research firm in, of all places, Casper, Wyoming, spoke of chatter about a Botch incursion at a major bank.

"Don't mean nothing," Simmons said in a western drawl that was painted on. She was from New Jersey, for heaven's sake.

So Drake gave it back to her. "How you reckon?" Just for the hell of it, he tried to sound like he was talking around a plug of chewing tobacco.

"Target of opportunity," said Simmons. "Lots of machines catch a dose of Botch. Banks, sure, but factories, law offices, newspapers. Ain't nothing sacred."

"All the same, I'm looking to throw a rope over these varmints."

"You making fun of the way I talk?"

"Well, you're making fun of the way they talk."

"I do it with affection," she said, this time in her native Jersey Girl accent.

"Why'd you move out there anyway? Less competition?"

"More mountains. Ever been?"

"Invite me sometime. After I find these guys."

"Where have you looked so far?" Simmons asked.

"The obvious places—hacker forums and the like. Elementary stuff, and even if it works, it'll take forever."

"Have you hit Persono or one of the other data brokers?"

Drake grunted. "Not yet. Reckon I better."

"Now you're doing the cowboy thing?"

THREE MINUTES LATER, Drake logged onto Instacart and ordered a hundred dollars' worth of groceries, enough to get him through the week, with coffee at the top of the list.

Then he remembered that he had no clothes; he'd packed for a day trip. Chuckling, he launched Walmart.com and ordered up three khaki shirts, the same number of pants, as well as underwear and socks, all in the usual sizes. Boo would be displeased, but Drake didn't have time for Brooks Brothers.

He added a few more items to the order, including toiletries and a proper suitcase, all of it to be delivered the next day, Thursday.

The groceries would arrive in the next hour or so, but Drake was too hungry to wait. Instead he grabbed up the key to the place, stepped into the corridor, and took an elevator to the ground floor. As the doors opened onto the lobby, he felt a pulse of worry, a concern that one of those who hunted him might be waiting for him. But he saw nobody except a doorman who nodded him out onto Peachtree Road.

Google Maps had told Drake about a Starbucks an easy walk away. There he ordered coffee cake to go, along with the least-bitter brew on the menu. Fifteen minutes after he'd left, Drake was back at it.

Again, he called Boston Medical Center and asked for Astrid's room. Next came several rhythmic purrs and then a weary hello.

"How you doing? It's me. Drake."

"Oh, hello," said Astrid, in a voice that sounded warm and womanly, much as it had before the knife.

"You're getting better," said Drake. "I can tell."

"Yeah, everybody says that."

"It hurt much?"

"When I breathe, sure. But a lot less now. I'm eating a little more, sleeping most of the night."

"You'll get too fat for the bike, if you're not careful."

"Hey, where is my bike?"

"I don't know. Still parked where you left it, I guess. I'll ask Deacon Carter about it. Maybe he can get it moved to the police pound. Ought to be safe there."

"Looks like good riding weather."

"Yeah, Boston looked pretty good when I left. There's plenty of sun here in Atlanta too."

"Atlanta?"

"Yeah," said Drake.

"You down there on business?"

"Yeah. Your kind of business."

"I don't understand."

"Me neither. All I know for sure is that I'm as popular as you. Maybe less popular—they only tried to kill you once."

She made a sound, nothing like Drake had ever heard, and to him it sounded like fear and rage commingled. "No, you've got to be wrong. You don't matter to these guys."

"That changed when I showed up at Dr. Severins's office."

There was stillness that lasted too long, and then, "What were you doing there?"

"It was by invitation. He'd invited me over to have me murdered. I suppose it's easier that way."

"But he'd never! He wouldn't do that!"

Why wouldn't he? thought Drake. *I'm nothing to him.* Then he realized that Astrid had thought it through. If Severins had tried for Drake, he'd also been the one who had tried for her. A man she'd touched and tasted, and her life had meant nothing to him.

"You need to talk to me," said Drake. "It's our best chance. Yours and mine."

"No!" The words came out in a hiss. "All we have to do is keep our heads down. It's all going to happen soon. Then we'll be safe."

"You'll never be safe. The police will never stop looking for you, and not just the cops. You'll also be up against the world's biggest banks, what's left of them. Plus every private security company on the planet. They'll all want you, and sooner or later they'll find you."

"They'll never prove it," Astrid said.

"Keep telling yourself that. And don't forget about your friends and allies. There's nothing to stop them finishing the job."

"They'll forget about us when it's over."

"They might forget about me. I don't really know anything. But with you, it could go either way. They might let you be. Or if the heat gets too intense, they might think you'd talk to save yourself. And then they'll come for you."

She was silent for a bit, then exhaled a sigh with a sob in it. "How did I get into the middle of this?"

"I wasn't there. But I'd guess Dr. Severins had something to do with it."

"He made it sound so simple. Harmless too. Like those MIT people used to do in Vegas. Fly out there to the blackjack tables with nothing but the math in their heads and fly home rich. But we wouldn't even need to pack. Just write code."

"Well, it hasn't worked out that way, has it? Time to cut your losses."

"No."

"I know you're scared. Me too. But this is the best way for both of us."

"Definitely for you. You're not the one looking at federal prison."

"Tell them everything, and they'll make a deal."

"No." It was a different voice, the voice of a shamed and frightened child. "I can't do that. I just can't."

"Astrid? Please, girl. You'll be all right. You and me together. We'll figure it out."

"No. I'll figure it out." And the line went dead.

SO NO HELP there. She was running on pure fear now, all the old boldness drained away through the wound in her chest. Maybe in a day or two, or a week, Astrid would recover herself. She'd be safe in the hospital till then.

In any case, Drake's last hope of a shortcut was gone. He'd have to track Silverware the hard way.

He followed Simmons's lead and logged onto Persono, a data broker that kept files on every living American and many of the dead, scooped from freely available government records as well as aggressive Internet searches.

You could search by email address, so Drake punched in *borzoi@blank-mail.com*. Nothing was listed under that address. But because so many people use their email handles as all-purpose online identifiers, Persono displayed forums and social media postings by people with similar nicknames—OldBorzoi, Borzoi28, BobsBorzoi. There were about two dozen. Of course, Facebook, Twitter, and LinkedIn popped up, but more obscure networks as well, like Quora and Topix. Better yet, there were hits at a couple of the top technical forums, kHub and CodeSorz. These were social hangouts for serious programmers. Just where you'd expect to find members of the Silverware team.

Drake was just beginning to inspect the search results when the desk phone rang. The groceries were on the way up.

"Tell the man to leave them right outside the door," Drake said and hung up. He rooted around in the desk, found an envelope, scrawled "Thanks" on it, and slipped in a ten dollar bill. He opened the door, placed the envelope just outside, where the deliveryman would see it, then stepped inside again and made sure of the door locks—all of them.

He heard the ping of a distant elevator and the shuffling of footsteps on carpet. Through the door's spyhole, Drake saw the distorted fish-eye image of a man unloading two cartons from a two-wheeled dolly, then bending over to pick up the envelope. He was a wiry, young ebony kid, and he looked straight at the spyhole and waved, then grabbed the dolly and wheeled away.

Far down the corridor, the elevator bell chimed. Drake opened the door, peered out to ensure his solitude, then dragged the boxes inside.

Drake's search for Borzoi came to naught. Someone of that name had turned up at both kHub and CodeSorz. But he'd posted nothing in either place to suggest an interest in bank hacking or a connection to any other Silverware hackers. Undaunted, Drake visited each of the twenty-six other social networks that had a user with Borzoi in his name. Some visits took just thirty seconds and revealed that the user had never posted a thing. In other cases, Drake found a Borzoi who'd left a sizable digital footprint— posted comments, uploaded photos, links to favorite videos. In those cases he pored over the materials seeking any hint of an interest in hacking, legal or illegal. It took about four hours, but in the end Drake found nothing.

Midway through his search, Drake fixed dinner; a broiled salmon filet, some boiled pasta and bottled spaghetti sauce, a little broccoli. Drake ate in the living room, seated on a chocolate leather sofa, his plate resting on a cocktail table made of wood so dense and heavy that he gave up on drawing it closer to the sofa. Instead, he just leaned forward like a man about to begin a footrace.

Twenty minutes later, it was back to work and the completion of his futile search of links to Borzoi. By then it was 11:00 p.m., and Drake's concentration was beginning to fade. He undressed, showered, and climbed naked into bed.

BY FIVE THIRTY Thursday morning, Drake was at his keyboard again, fortified by scrambled eggs, wheat toast, and coffee.

He was back on Persono and checking out another of his email addresses, *Kirsch@blankmail.com*. This time it took about an hour to survey all the hits.

And then it came to him that he was doing it wrong. He didn't know Kirsch's real name. But he knew *snowbird@blankmail.com*. That was Astrid. So he should search for that address instead.

Drake went straight to CodeSorz, the hacker hangout. The site's discussion forum had a search feature; he ordered up messages posted by Snowbird. There were dozens, dating back five years. The most recent had been posted seven months before the stabbing.

Still, he had to make sure that this was his Snowbird and not some other software developer running the same nickname. That meant reading each message, searching for clues. Perhaps she'd mentioned something about Cambridge or MIT or her family back in Minneapolis, or even about her class at Reliant Baptist Church.

For two hours Drake was ears-deep in technical gabble, studded with bits of jargon that he barely remembered and had never understood.

Then in the midst of the arcana came a phrase that brought him upright. After an entire paragraph of jargon relating to the proper compilation of code, Snowbird wrote the phrase, *This seems true.*

This seems true.

More than once, in the midst of an argument about the absence of God or the best way to teach coding to ten-year-olds, Astrid would make her case and nod her head and say, "This seems true." Not "This is true," but "This seems true." Always leaving herself an out in case the facts changed or her mind changed. When she'd said it for about the fiftieth time, Drake had asked her why. "I don't know everything," was Astrid's reply.

So here she was, his Snowbird, speaking to him from a different time and place, in words Drake didn't understand. Never mind. He'd scour her messages for words he did understand, words like Stainless and Mesh.

First, Mesh. He or she had approved of Clinker's plan to warn Tannheuser that their software had been cracked. Drake downloaded all of

Snowbird's posts, then ran a simple text search—*mesh*—with wildcard commands fore and aft to make sure he got every possible variation.

And there it was, in the headers attached to eleven messages. *Meshnet88.* At last.

The messages had been sent over a five-day period, about two years ago. And they had nothing to do with bank fraud or any other crime, or so it seemed. Instead, it was about the merits of antivirus programs.

Snowbird conceded that Microsoft's free malware scanner sucked but declared it better than nothing. Mesh responded that all scanners were useless, and he'd rather rely on common sense to keep him safe. When his machines did catch a virus—and he admitted that they did—Mesh treated it as a learning experience.

It was an old debate, of mere academic interest to Drake. But then came a comment from Mesh that spurred his attention.

"We oughta know how tough this is. That time in high school we tried building a heuristic scanner? Remember how that worked out."

Snowbird had filed a reply to this message, but Drake never read it. Instead he'd flipped to LinkedIn and looked up Astrid's account there. Sure enough, she'd filled in her personal profile, including a list of schools attended.

Crosby Academy, Class of 2008. National Honor Society, Math Club, Lacrosse.

Her last stop before MIT. High school. The same school as Mesh.

He ran another LinkedIn search for 2008 graduates of Crosby Academy. Without waiting for the results, he Googled the school. Up popped an image of a great Georgian structure, the leavings of a long-dead lumber magnate, later resurrected as a private school. Astrid had come from money, and Drake had known it, but until that moment he hadn't realized how much.

And her friend Mesh, also rich. Or a scholarship student. White? In Minnesota, that was the way to bet. Male? A toss-up. But a Crosby alum? No doubt. The same graduating class, or near to it.

Drake flicked back to the LinkedIn window, where he found the names of twenty-eight Crosbyites from the class of 2008. Time to read the bios of each one, in search of a geek.

The photo of the eighth guy in looked promising. With shaggy blond hair and broad shoulders, Trace Andersen resembled a Minnesota Viking offensive guard. According to his career profile, Andersen had earned an undergraduate degree in computer science at the University of Minnesota. But unlike Astrid, he'd checked out of academia and gone to work. These days he was a regional IT manager in the St. Paul office of an insurance company called Bellarmine.

Drake looked up the phone number and dialed. The receptionist switched him to Andersen's line, which rang five times. Next came a voice mail message—not the canned variety preprogrammed into every VM system. This was Andersen's own voice—deep, resonant, a perfect match for the photograph.

Drake asked for a callback, provided his number, hung up, then redialed.

The same receptionist, but this time Drake complained that Andersen hadn't answered. Could he be connected to someone else in IT?

"What's this about?" asked the receptionist.

Drake gave his name. "Just tell him I'm a friend of Astrid."

Drake began to tune up a couple of outright lies in case the receptionist offered further resistance. There was no need. The line switched, rang, and a woman picked up.

Drake introduced himself and asked if Andersen was in the office that day.

"Nope, and good luck finding him."

"I don't understand."

"He's been gone since last Thursday. No idea why or where. He's not on vacation. And we're in the middle of a big upgrade too. If you find him, I hope you have a job for him."

"You his boss?"

"Technically, he's mine. But I've been doing his job and mine since Monday. A 'promotion in the field,' I think the army calls it."

"Got a good email for him? Or maybe his cell?"

"We don't give out that kind of information."

"At this point, how's it gonna hurt? He probably won't be working there next week anyway."

Down the line came a pause, a sigh, and Andersen's email and cell phone number.

Drake fired off an email asking for a chat. He dialed Andersen's cell, and this time got a generic nobody's-home announcement. He left a message and followed up with a text.

Maybe Trace was already on the run. Or lying at home, his mattress soaked in blood. Or maybe he was just some guy.

It hardly counted as a lead, but he'd promised to keep Detective Akinyi in the loop. And it was just possible that Akinyi could persuade a colleague in the Twin Cities to make a few inquiries.

Drake dialed her number, but Akinyi didn't answer. He told the answering machine that he'd come across something. Maybe Minneapolis could send a squad car this evening, to check on Andersen's whereabouts.

Drake kept trolling through his list of Crosby alums. It didn't take long. There were two or three other possibles in the bunch but none with quite the right look and feel. Drake ruled none of them out but chose not to invest hours on any of them just yet.

First he wanted to expand his universe a bit. Perhaps Astrid had befriended a freshman or sophomore or had been taken under a kindly senior's wing. So Drake expanded his alumni searches for three years before and after her graduation. That brought a total of 426 possible alums. How many had gone on to study computer science or had found some other way into computing? He identified 115, about a quarter of the lot—kids who fancied themselves the next Gates or Jobs or Zuckerberg. He spent the next four hours sifting the names, his labors interrupted only by a Walmart delivery driver bringing his fresh clothes.

The sun was slanting through the windows when his phone lit up and began to buzz. It was Precious.

"Where are you?"

"Somewhere safe," said Drake. "In Atlanta, actually."

"Doing what?"

"Research. Trying to track down the people behind all this."

"Why Atlanta, with everything they're pulling up here?"

"I found a few leads. And I figure the worst is over in Boston."

"You figured wrong. Your girlfriend, Astrid? She's gone."

CHAPTER TWELVE

"WHEN?"

"About two hours ago. Doctor on rounds came in and noticed the bed was empty. She wasn't in ICU anymore, so the nurses weren't paying much attention. They didn't see a thing."

"Anybody else see her leave?"

"I have, on security video. There's cameras all over this hospital, so I watched them roll out of there."

"Somebody to push the wheelchair?"

"Right. A guy. Big."

"Why wasn't there a guard on her room?"

Akinyi snorted. "You think we post armed guards on every patient?"

"Not even the ones with knife wounds?"

"We did that, we'd be doing nothing else. In the movies, assassins kill people in hospitals. In real life, not so much."

"So somebody kidnapped her right out from under you."

Silence for a moment, then Akinyi said, "It may not be that bad. We don't know she was kidnapped."

"So she just made a new friend?"

"Maybe the guy was an old friend; I don't know." Akinyi sighed. "I just mean, I've looked at the security footage. This guy is pushing her chair down the corridors, while she just sits there in the chair, apparently clothed and in her right mind. I can see her hands move, and in one video it looks like she's talking. But she wasn't calling for help. It looks to me like she was fine with the whole thing."

"You're not proceeding on that assumption, are you?"

"Of course not. We've got a bulletin out on her and the man she's with. All we can do. Unless he's kidnapped her, there's no crime here. But she was hurt bad. Doctor said she's a big risk for an infection. She's got no business out in those streets."

"Yeah, but if this guy's a friend, Astrid might be willing to take the risk. Maybe she's scared to stay in the hospital. Afraid they'll try for her again. And she's got a buddy willing to get her out, maybe hide her someplace."

Akinyi snorted. "If she's in that much trouble, she should say so. We've been begging her to tell us who we're looking for. All we've been getting is silence."

"Because she doesn't want to go to prison," said Drake. "Whatever's going down, she's in on it. She thinks you guys will handcuff her to the hospital bed."

"Not me. I don't know about any of that hacker crap. I do homicides."

"Not you, but the feds."

"They do like to make those high-tech cases," Akinyi said. "And they go for big sentences too, like they're locking up some capo in the Gambino family."

"So you can see why she's scared," said Drake. "And now she's on the run, probably with a partner in crime."

"Any idea who?"

"Another member of her hacking crew, Silverware. Right now, I'm trying to figure out who they are."

"Any luck?"

"Nothing hard yet, but I got a promising lead. Guy she went to high school with, back in Minnesota. Trace Andersen is his name." An idea came to Drake then. "Wait a second. You in front of a computer?"

"Sure," said Akinyi. "What you need?"

"Just go over to LinkedIn and run a search for this guy. First name *T-R-A-C-E*. Last name is Andersen, spelled the usual way, but with *S-E-N* at the end. No *O*. Look at the picture that pops up."

"Right. Got it." Akinyi fell silent for a good ten seconds. Then Drake heard her exhale. "All right, then," she said. "This could be the guy."

"You think so?"

"It's not a lock. Boston Medical needs to upgrade those security cameras. The video's pitiful. But there's a resemblance."

"So start looking for this guy. I can tell you he's not at his job. They haven't seen him in days. And I got no answer at what I think is his home phone."

"Okay," Akinyi said. "But where would he go now?"

"Somewhere close to home, I'm guessing. Call the Minneapolis police or maybe the Minnesota state cops."

"I'll start with the staties, let them spread the word. They probably have better databases anyhow. But there's no guarantee he's heading for Minnesota."

"The guy's a nerd. Probably never been in trouble in his life. He doesn't know how to run. So he'll go someplace familiar, maybe hide out with family or friends."

"If they're willing to hide him."

"Maybe we'll get lucky and they'll rat him out. For his own good, of course."

"Let's hope so. Meantime, get off my phone. Oh, and by the way, that's pretty decent detective work. Thanks."

Drake hung up smiling. Always good to have a friend in the cop shop.

Still, Akinyi was in Boston, over a thousand miles from Minnesota. She would have to count on the smarts and diligence of the local police, who had no stake in the outcome of her search. Akinyi could expect professional courtesy, nothing more.

But Drake wasn't lashed to his desk, and Hartsfield-Jackson International probably had two dozen flights a day to Minneapolis. Time to call Madeleine.

The phone rang twice, then came, "This is Madeleine." The voice was an astringent bark, distinct in its femininity and its ill temper. Drake decided to apply a little butter.

"How do you do, ma'am? My name is Weldon Drake, and—"

"I know who you are. Boo told me to expect you at this number. So let's not waste time. What do you need?"

Drake relaxed. Madeleine was his kind of woman. "Plane ticket to Minneapolis, ASAP. Put me on the first thing smoking. One way, economy."

"You can go first if you prefer. Boo said you get what you need."

"Economy's fine. Also, you can send me $2,000 for expenses." He read out his bank's routing number, his personal checking account number, and his email address.

"That all?"

"For now. Maybe tomorrow I'll need a phased plasma rifle in the forty-watt range, but till then—"

"I'm not in the mood, Mr. Drake."

"Right then," he said. "Get on it." He hung up.

His next move was a call to Astrid's family, though he'd have to find them first.

Astrid had spoken of her father more than once. Drake strained to recall the man's name, and then it came to him—Roland. A partner at a downtown law firm. That would make him easy to find; in Drake's experience, those guys always had web pages with email address and phone number on proud display.

Ten seconds with Google, and he had the man. The photo revealed a lean, angular face with cheeks flat and black as slate, a long neck, short-cut kinky hair without a trace of gray, an austere upward quirk of the lips that might have passed for a smile on the planet Vulcan.

Drake dialed, struck voice mail. He followed up with an email, informing Roland of the news about his daughter and requesting a face-to-face meeting on the following day.

Just as he'd dispatched the message, Drake's phone chimed out an incoming mail notice. The bank confirmed the deposit to his account. Not $2,000 but $5,000. Boo's orders, probably. Well, he might need the extra. Then a message from Expedia. Drake had been booked on Delta nonstop to Minneapolis, aisle seat, economy, 9:00 p.m.

HE WAS PACKED in thirty minutes, and five minutes after that he was rolling down Peachtree in an Uber. He let the car take him as far as the nearest subway stop. He liked trains and was uncertain about the late afternoon airport traffic.

So it was a pair of rails that delivered Drake to Hartsfield, two hours ahead of time for the evening flight. Drake made his way to Paschal's, the airport's soul food restaurant. He was tempted by the fried chicken, but he'd never had shrimp with grits, and it seemed healthier.

The savory food and a glass of Belgian ale elevated Drake's mood. Besides, after days of stasis and dread, it was good to move again, in pursuit of a specific goal. Not that it would be easy to track down Trace and Astrid, two people who did not want to be found. Maybe they were nowhere near Minneapolis. Better to hide someplace free of family, friends, and past associations. Better but tougher for two people who'd never been on the run before.

The trip was worth the plane fare, in any case. He'd visit Astrid's parents and Trace's as well, then track down a few of their old friends. Even if they hadn't seen the fugitives, they might know something.

Planes made Drake claustrophobic, so he hovered near the jetway door until everyone else had boarded, while the gate crew looked at him with ominous eyes. Then he strolled aboard, backpack in hand. It was a stretched Boeing 737, with soft blue lighting and the scent of a new Toyota. Drake's seat was near the front of the plane, on the aisle; Madeleine had chosen well.

Almost as soon as he strapped in, the airplane pushed back. Drake closed his eyes, listened to the engines spooling up, the flaps whirring out to takeoff position. In his mind, he went through the pre-taxi checklist. Parking brake, set. Throttles to idle. Elevator trim set for takeoff. Navigation and taxi lights on.

Drake had run the procedure dozens of times at home on his simulator. He reveled in the cool, unemotional rigor of aviation. In the sky there was no inconstancy, no willful folly. Not for long, anyway.

He'd read and reread a book consisting merely of transcripts, the last words of aircraft flight crews captured by the planes' black boxes in the minutes before their final, violent touchdowns. In a few rare instances, they weren't to blame. A busted rudder or a shredded turbine had finished them. But more often than not, the crews' own carelessness had brought them down. And as they'd died, they'd spoken like fools. "Sorry," one had said at the end. Another had said, "Don't do that."

At some point along the way, they'd had a chance to live. Maybe in flight school, or during refresher sessions in the simulator or as they'd studied the weather report before takeoff. Instead, they'd missed a single, crucial truth that might have saved them and their doomed passengers.

As with them, so with me, thought Drake. At this time tomorrow, he might be dead or near it, for having ignored or neglected or forgotten something.

Drake closed his eyes, recited the Our Father, prayed for a clear mind and open eyes. Then he resumed the checklist. It was preflight in the cockpit now: time to set flaps and spoilers, eyeball the engine readouts and navigation inputs, flip on the transponder. Drake neglected nothing. He counted on the flight crew to do the same.

The just shall live by faith. And the rest of us as well.

The plane lurched, turned onto the runway; the engines spooled. V1. Vr. Rotate. Positive rate. Gear up.

DRAKE AND HIS fellow travelers had the Delta terminal pretty much to themselves. It was 11:00 p.m., and most flights out of Minneapolis were long gone. So were the workers who staffed the shops, restaurants, and bars. Drake had known he would arrive too late to sample the wines at Surdyk's Flights, but he was still disappointed. Though he'd never visited the city itself, he'd often made connections at this airport and found time to visit Surdyk's for chianti and charcuterie.

This time it was straight to baggage claim, then an Uber to the Holiday Inn in the suburb of Chanhassen. Astrid had spoken of growing up around here, of swimming in its lakes. The town's name had come from the language of local Indians, but to Drake's ear it had a New England sound, more Pequot than Sioux. And it was a money sort of place, a colder, whiter version of Buckhead. So Drake had heard. But it was night and he could see nothing. Tomorrow morning, he'd take a look for himself.

The Holiday Inn was what it was, which was all that Drake needed right then. He plugged in his laptop, punched in the WiFi password provided at the desk, and logged onto his email. Roland Nelson had not responded.

Which might be a response in itself. Maybe he was out of pocket and hadn't gotten Drake's messages. But it seemed unlikely that a partner in a major firm would be that hard to reach. Or that a father whose daughter had been recently knifed would stray from the phone.

More likely, Roland Nelson had chosen not to respond. Maybe he did not care about his child. Perhaps he had no wish to speak with a journalist, even if he was also a friend. Or maybe Roland Astrid was stretched out in the family's upstairs bedroom right now. *Tyro.*

Drake mulled each of these options as he showered, brushed his teeth, phoned downstairs to arrange a 5:00 a.m. wakeup call, and tumbled into bed.

NEXT DAY, HE'D showered, shaved, and dressed by 5:30. Drake grabbed his smartphone and redialed the number for Astrid's father. Yes, it was early for a phone call, but a fearful parent would welcome the call, no matter the time.

Two rings in, Drake heard a click, then "Hello." The voice was rich and resonant.

"Roland Nelson?"

"Yes?"

"My name is Weldon Drake. I'm a deacon at Reliant Baptist Church and a friend of your daughter."

"And you're an early riser, I see," said Roland. "Commendable."

"So what's more important to you, Mr. Nelson? My sleeping habits or the whereabouts of your child?"

This time, Roland spoke with the urgency of a father. "You know where she is?"

"No idea. I'm hoping that together we can figure it out."

"Please excuse my rudeness, Mr. . . . . Drake, right? I've got a lot on my mind."

"Forget it. Nobody's at his best at this hour."

"Well, what can I do to help?"

"Not sure. I'm thinking we should get together. I can bring you up to speed, and you can tell me whatever you can."

"Face to face?"

"Better that way."

"So you're coming to Minneapolis?"

"Landed last night."

"I'm impressed. Please excuse me—I'm not a churchgoer. But is this what deacons do?"

"Not as a general rule. But I'm also a newspaper reporter, and this crime made a lot of headlines back in Boston. Everybody in town wants to know more."

"Not sure I like our family business spread up and down Commonwealth Avenue."

"Oh, you know Boston?"

"I was Harvard Law. You didn't read my CV?" Was that a tone of injured pride in his voice? Drake couldn't help grinning.

"Sorry. Missed that part. And Astrid never mentioned it."

"So you two talked a lot?"

"A good deal. I'd say we were reasonably close."

"I see," said Roland, then paused long enough to convince Drake that he didn't. "Well, let's meet. You know Minneapolis?"

"I don't but Uber does. Just give me an address."

OUTSIDE, THE DAY had broken clear but humid. Uber came through with a spotless Honda Civic, driven by a balding brown man with aquiline features—a Somali, perhaps. Without a word, the driver hustled them along a wide boulevard bounded on either side by the anonymous architecture of the suburban Midwest—office parks, warehouses, a strip mall now and then, and tracts of woodland judged unworthy of development. After a while, the car turned left onto a road called Great Plains Boulevard. They were going south now, judging by the angle of the sun. To his right, Drake saw maybe a hundred acres of gray-green water, bounded by a beach and several docks occupied by entry-level sailboats. A mile down the road, to his left, a slightly smaller lake gleamed under the early sun.

"Land of ten thousand Lakes," said Drake. The driver, who didn't need reminding of the state motto, said nothing.

The subdivision, called Premier Court, came a mile or so later. The car turned left and took a serpentine course past several massive colonial homes, each on a lot big enough for a whole colony. The Nelson house, as large as any, was gray with white trim around the windows. It was set back at least half a block from the street and fronted with a lawn like the outfield of Fenway Park. The driver rolled up the long driveway and let Drake out in front of a four-car garage that would never be occupied by a Honda Civic.

As the Uber rolled out, Drake heard the front door open. The man who stood there was dressed in a gray pinstripe suit with matching vest, a button-down Oxford shirt, a red-and-black rep tie. His wingtip shoes were made of leather that seemed to glow from within.

Roland Nelson was ready to receive visitors.

"Mr. Drake, a pleasure to meet you." Roland extended a hand. It felt dry, hard, peremptory. Not the handshake of a frightened man.

"Sorry about the circumstances," Drake replied.

Roland gestured him through the front door, through an entryway that was all vaulted ceilings and skylights. By contrast, the living room was dark with oak and brown leather furniture, and for all its expansive scale, a little claustrophobic. It was the sort of room, thought Drake, that would make a fellow happy to leave for work in the morning.

The leather of the chairs was softer than it looked; it barely squealed as Drake settled into a corner of the sofa.

"So, do you have anything for me?" asked Roland.

"I was about to ask you the same thing," Drake replied. "Granted you don't know where Astrid is, but at least you can fill me in on the most obvious question." So obvious, in fact, that Drake didn't bother asking. Astrid's father was a Harvard man, after all.

"It's a long story but easily summarized," said Roland. "We don't get along."

He spoke in a cool, dispassionate voice, as if he were lecturing a roomful of 1Ls on torts.

"I didn't get along with my father either, but I turned up for the funeral."

Roland cocked his head at that, arched an eyebrow. "My daughter is not dead."

"Somebody wanted her dead and might try again. So she got out of the hospital and went on the run. And she didn't run here. Maybe knowing why not will help us find her."

"I already know why not."

"Yes, but are you doing anything to find her?"

"I've talked to the police in Boston. I've given them everything they've asked for."

"Did they ask why she hadn't come to you?"

"Obviously. They're hardly stupid. I explained that my daughter and I aren't very close."

"So why is Astrid so unhappy with you?"

"The divorce, of course." Roland gestured to the big, dark, leathery room, as if to indicate the absence of a woman.

"Didn't know you were married."

"Twelve years. Astrid was our only child."

"You must be very proud of her."

"Indeed. But the feeling isn't mutual." Roland shrugged, stared at his hands for a few seconds. "I take responsibility, of course. My wife, Cheryl, initiated the divorce, but I'd given her cause. I'm a patent lawyer, Mr. Drake. You might not think there were so many temptations in that line of work. But it only takes one."

"And Cheryl wasn't the forgiving type."

To Drake's surprise, Roland laughed. "I didn't want her forgiveness. I wasn't sorry. Not then. Even now, any regret I feel is offset by the pleasure I found in Lucille's company. That was her name—Lucille. You know how some men seek a lover who'll give them the understanding they don't get at home? Well, my wife understood me perfectly. Lucille didn't have a clue, about patent law or anything else. But she adored me. That was enough."

"A good enough reason to break your daughter's heart?"

"If I'd known it would be that way . . . if I hadn't been so sure of getting away with it . . . I might have chosen differently. But I can't swear to that, even now."

"You and Lucille still together?"

"She's long gone. Took an administrative job at a hedge fund a couple of years ago. Last I heard, she was getting ready to marry one of the partners. She emailed me about it. Said she'd finally met a man who understood her." Roland chuckled, and Drake couldn't help smiling.

But then Drake asked, "You think Astrid would have appreciated the joke?"

Roland chuckled again, but there was little mirth in it this time. "No. She never saw the humor in the situation."

"Where's her mother now?"

"Chicago, I think. She took up with a musician who played one of her favorite bars, and now she's with him. Touring, Cheryl calls it. A bit old for a groupie, but this bass player of hers doesn't seem to mind."

"She keep in touch with Astrid?"

"I couldn't say. Neither of them talk to me much, so I'm not sure how much they talk to each other. No idea whether Astrid has figured it out yet, that her mother's a drunk and a whore. Or that my side thing with Lucille came after two years of putting up with her mother's drinking and whoring. I never talked to Astrid about her mother's behavior. Actually, I connived with Cheryl to cover it up. For the good of the child, of course. But when I made one little slip, and she found out about it, she brought it up right at the dinner table. Hit me right between the eyes with it. Astrid too."

Roland's voice, already a dark baritone, had gone raspy with suppressed rage.

"Guess by then she had the bass player going on. She just needed a reason to walk. Something to make her look less bad in Astrid's eyes. So, I got to be the monster. The girl's never forgiven me."

The two men sat silent for the better part of a minute. "You never told her your side of it? About her mother?"

"That it was all her fault, that she was an alcoholic slut? Astrid would have just hated me more."

Drake sighed. "Well, under the circumstances, I guess you don't have any idea where to find her."

"No idea."

"What about a guy named Trace Andersen? Any idea where to find him?"

Roland cocked an eyebrow. Just one, like Spock. "Name's familiar. I think he was one of Astrid's running buddies from high school. Big, hairy white guy, right?"

"The same. He was seen at the hospital with Astrid, heading out the door. She looked to be going along of her own free will. So we figure they're on the run together."

"She must have reached out to him. They had it going on back in the day. I guess maybe they still do."

"Maybe. But I don't think she reached out to him. It was the other way around. This guy Trace is nearly as much of a geek as your daughter. Runs IT at some big insurance firm downtown. Turns out that he also stayed in touch with Astrid. And she somehow roped him into this hacking crew of hers. They went to work on something that got one of the crew assaulted and one of them killed."

"Killed? Who?"

"You wouldn't know him. Another friend of Astrid's, a German living in Hamburg."

"Hamburg? But . . ." Roland's voice trailed off as he thought it through. "Two different countries? What kind of outfit is this?"

"A major criminal gang, I figure. Or worse yet, some government outfit."

"Theirs or ours?"

"I'm not that paranoid. Besides, I can't think of a reason why the US government would do something like this. But it's easy to imagine plenty of other potential players. Like every other member of the United Nations. Or any number of criminal cartels, foreign or domestic."

"Any idea who?"

"Not a clue. But for now that doesn't matter. We need to concentrate on finding Astrid, and Trace too. So you're the idea man now. You know them both. Where would they go?"

"If they're smart, they're nowhere near Minneapolis. They've got to know the cops will come here looking, and maybe the killers as well."

"That rules out your home and Trace's parents' house too. But that leaves them a whole metropolitan area to hide in. So until we come up with a better working hypothesis, let's assume they're somewhere around here."

"Fair enough," said Roland. "But I've got no idea where."

"Maybe one of them has a friend who'd let them move in for a few days. I doubt either of them has planned any further ahead than that. They're running scared, and they just need a place to crash. Especially Astrid. She's in no shape for a long road trip."

"I know a few of Astrid's friends but not all," said Roland. "And I met Trace's parents one time, at a school event. We never became close friends." He reached into an inside pocket of his jacket. "I'm pretty sure I've got their contact information here." After about twenty seconds, Roland asked for Drake's email address and forwarded the details. Drake dragged his phone out of a hip pocket, just in time to hear it ping with incoming mail. The Andersens were an easy reach—just a couple of miles away.

"They may be in the dark as well," said Drake, "but I'd better check. And of course if you hear anything . . ."

"Maybe I'll give you a call."

"Maybe?"

"Who are you, that I'm obligated to report to you about my daughter's whereabouts?"

"Look, we're on the same side here."

"That's open to dispute," said Roland. "It's moot in any case. I doubt she'd call me if I were on my deathbed, or if she were on hers."

"She nearly was."

"Like I said." Roland rose from his chair, tugged his vest till the pinstripes were in perfect alignment. "I invested a small fortune in her, you know. But I invested more than money. I taught her the habits of success. I walked out that door at seven every morning and returned at eight almost every night, and I'd be exhausted. But I always made time to review and correct her homework, and oversee every special school project, and attend every special event. Because that was my job. My duty. And I did my duty. Right down the line. Except that one time. And that was that. She'll never forgive, and she'll never forget.

"But I'm still her father. And I'm not putting her fate into your hands. You're just some guy from a newspaper who wants a front-page story and maybe a chance to get into her pants." Roland sneered. "When she's fully recovered, of course."

Drake resisted the urge to slap the man, but he checked the rising of his right hand. Roland saw it and took a half-step backward, raising his left arm to ward off a blow that never came. Drake realized with satisfaction that he'd frightened the man.

"You hear from her, I expect you to let me know."

There was little chance of that now, if there ever had been. But the words gave Drake a place to put the fury he felt. He turned and headed for the door, and Roland didn't even try to show him out.

DRAKE STRODE DOWN the driveway toward Great Plains Boulevard, punching in an Uber request as he walked. It wasn't easy; his fingers still trembled. Why? Where had that come from? Roland's father was an unpleasant piece of work but hardly worth an assault arrest. Drake knew that other people with his particular personality issue would sometimes respond to wounded pride with ferocious rage, but he never had. Was he changing? Getting worse? Or was there something healthy in his urge to hammer him?

Whatever. "Be angry, and sin not," the Bible said somewhere, and Drake figured that this time, he'd just managed to clear the bar.

Now for the Andersens. Roland had given him the parents' cell phone numbers. As he waited for his ride to arrive, Drake dialed first the father, Brandon, and then the mother, Celeste. Both calls went to voice mail. Drake introduced himself, explained his visit, and asked for callbacks.

Drake settled in the back seat, asked the driver to turn down the NPR news broadcast, and began to dial. It was about 7:30, which made it 8:30 Boston time, and Drake figured that Precious Akinyi was an early riser.

"Guess where I am?"

"Minnesota, right?" Akinyi replied. "The *Record*'s got a bigger travel budget than I thought. They're letting you play hunches."

"Yeah, but I might come up dry," said Drake, who decided to leave the Diaconate out of it. "I've been talking to friends and family. Nobody here is talking. Either they're shielding them or they really haven't been in touch. And that means my hunch was worthless and they're a thousand miles away."

"But they're not. Turns out you're on the right track."

"How can you be sure?"

"Banking records. You don't need a warrant for stuff like that. Just a subpoena."

"Sure wish I could subpoena people."

"You have my sympathy. Anyway, I started with a credit reporting agency. They told me Astrid and Trace both use Bank of America, which made my life easier. So then I subpoenaed the bank for their recent trans-actions. They came through in a couple of hours."

"And?"

"Nothing's happening with Astrid's account. But Trace has been spend-ing money and spending it in Boston."

"So it was definitely him at the hospital."

"Unless Astrid has two friends who look like Vikings. He flew in on Delta yesterday morning and checked out a rental car at the Enterprise lot. I'm still trying to get an ID on the vehicle, but given the price tag, it's not a Ford Focus. I bet it's something big and comfy where an injured woman can stretch out and sleep. A minivan or maybe a seven-seater luxury SUV."

"Makes sense."

"Next time he used the card, it was for gas at a service station on the Mass Pike, about sixty miles west. More gas about 260 miles down the road. They were in upstate New York on I-90, near a town called Her-kimer. They grabbed fast food there too. And Trace spent a couple hun-dred at a drugstore there."

"First aid stuff?"

"Had to be. He knows he'll have to clean and rebandage that wound."

He'd undress her. He'd see her. The thought angered Drake at first, the same sort of anger he'd felt in the presence of Astrid's father. But this time he felt like a fool. Trace could hardly let her die of infection.

177

"You there?" Akinyi said, and Drake realized he'd been still as a dropped call for ten or fifteen seconds.

"Weak signal," he said. "You hear me now?"

"Yeah, fine," the detective replied. "Anyway, Trace didn't stop to patch up Astrid. Next hit on the credit card comes last night from a motel at the Indiana border. A Marriott. No Motel 6 for Mr. Andersen. He needs to watch his expenses. But he's a real gentleman. He paid for two hotel rooms, not just one. This guy's starting to sound like a keeper."

"And you think she's bringing him home to meet her dad."

"Wouldn't be surprised. They ate and gassed up again just outside Chicago, then stopped again near Madison, Wisconsin. That's the last entry. Most recent, anyway. Looks like he's making a beeline for Minnesota."

"They could have flown," said Drake.

"With the shape Astrid's in? TSA would have had a lot of questions about lugging a badly injured woman through airport security. Figures he'd take his chances on the open road."

"Wish I had something more exact."

"I shouldn't even be giving you this. But I figure there's no harm in it. If you find them for us, it'll take a load off our budget. Assuming you let us know. Which you will."

"Yeah, or else." Drake smirked. "Relax. I got no reason to keep secrets here. When I know, you'll know. Then you can decide what to do about them. After all, they haven't broken any laws."

"Yeah, right."

"So, okay, which ones? Sure, something stinks, but we don't know what it is. And that makes it way early to start reaching for handcuffs."

"Yeah. For now, keeping them alive is the main thing. If I get any more precise location data, I'll send it along. You find them, keep an eye out for hostiles. If we can track them, maybe these guys can."

"I'll tell them just how trackable they are. Might scare them into doing the right thing. I figure to talk them onto a plane, back to Boston and out of harm's way."

"And right onto the front page."

"When it's safe, and not before."

DRAKE RETURNED TO his hotel room; for the moment, he had no place else to go. He needed a lead, from the Andersens, from Akinyi, or maybe from a deeper search into Trace's online messages.

In any case, he was in the right neighborhood. Trace and Astrid were headed for home, or someplace fairly close to home. But why? If they weren't trying to reach family—Astrid certainly wasn't—why not just flee to a neighborhood with no connection to their past? That would make them much more difficult to find.

Drake could imagine only one reason. He had a safe house in the vicinity, someplace secure where he could hide. After all, Trace himself had dropped out of sight after the attacks on Clinker and Astrid. He must have gone somewhere. Later, Trace decided Astrid was too vulnerable in the hospital. So he'd risked his own safety and come out of hiding to go get her. And now he was taking Astrid to his hideout.

It was just a question of figuring out where it could be. Nearby, for sure, but nearby covered a lot of terrain. How could he narrow it down?

Drake opened his laptop and logged on once more to CodeSorz, the Internet hangout where he'd discovered Trace Andersen, alias Meshnet88. This time, he punched up every public message sent to or from that handle. There were well over six hundred of them; Trace had a rather promiscuous online social life. Drake downloaded the lot and then ran a series of word searches. *Crosby*, the name of his high school, brought up one of his notes to Astrid that Drake had already seen, plus one more—a fellow alumnus seeking help with a job hunt. There was no hint of a deeper friendship, of someone who knew Trace well enough to hide him.

Drake paused, trying to think up search terms that might lead him somewhere. He tried "hide," "room," "basement," "attic," "safe." Some of the words produced no hits at all, while a few, like "room" and "safe," did make appearances, but only in irrelevant, innocent contexts.

After a while, Drake remembered the many nearby lakes. Surely there would be summer cabins along their shores. Growing up in Chicago, his father had spoken of people who owned such places on Lake Michigan and lived there during the heat of July. Drake, a city kid in full, had never understood the envy in his father's voice. Nothing was better than Chicago in the summer, it had seemed to him.

Did Astrid's family or the Andersens own such a second home? Maybe, but they'd be poor hiding places. Their hunters could search them out and lie in wait.

But what about a cabin belonging to someone else? Did either of them have a friend who owned such a place and would be willing to lend it out for a week or two?

Drake tried another search, this time with the keyword "cabin."

Nothing.

"Summer home."

Nothing again.

What else might one call such a place? Come to think of it, somebody might just call it a "place," as in, "We're going to the summer place on Lake Michigan for the Fourth of July. Care to join us?" But "place" was so generic a word that it might pop up in a hundred or more useless messages.

But not "lake." That was a very ungeneric word, rarely used except to describe a specific body of water.

And so Drake typed it in and waited. A single message came up, sent a couple of years before by somebody called Servalan. It was a throwaway line, a tiny part of a long and abstruse thread. Trace's company had just acquired a midsized life insurance company in Colorado that relied on IBM's DB2 database software; Trace's company ran Oracle. Two very different schemata, and integrating them was proving to be a nightmare.

Servalan, whoever he was, had responded to Trace's cry for help, no doubt because the two of them knew each other.

There were about two dozen messages between them, suffused with database arcana that Drake didn't begin to understand. But near the end of the thread came a parting comment from Servalan.

"Sorry I missed The Mistake on the Lake last year," he or she had written. "You always bring the best beer."

Some annual get-together of frat brothers, perhaps. Hardly helpful in any case. But Trace might say something useful in response, so Drake moved to the next message in the thread.

There he found a lot more database babble. But at the wrap-up, Trace wrote, "The Mistake? Sorry you missed it. I hope to make new errors of judgment this August. And of course I'll bring beer. Fat Tire or something decent, direct from St. Paul. It's either that or shop at Colley's. And I just can't face the horror of Bud Light."

Nothing more about a lake, then. No name, no location.

But Trace had revealed a location, after all. This "Mistake by the Lake"—no doubt some kind of party—had happened somewhere near a store called Colley's. Probably it was an all-purpose convenience store, the kind that sells string cheese and milk and generic beer.

It didn't sound like a chain store, like 7-Eleven. It was probably a stand-alone retailer. That meant there'd be only one of them in the state, or maybe the country. Would a store that small have an online presence? No reason why not.

So Drake searched and found. There was a Colley's in Stearns County, about eighty miles northwest of Minneapolis. Drake punched it up on Google Maps and switched to satellite view. The store sat about a mile from two separate bodies of water. One of them, Ebon Lake, looked to be maybe fifty or sixty acres in area, while the other, Lake Franz, was about half as big.

So Drake now knew where Trace liked to party. It was a decent bit of research, but he felt no urge to congratulate himself. There was no way to know whether Trace was even thinking of this as a hiding place. Even if he were, how could Drake hope to find him? The satellite image showed dozens of cottages, most with boat docks, fringing the two lakes. Finding the right one would be almost a matter of sheer luck. Besides, he didn't fancy the idea of wandering the general area, asking random questions or peering through windows. He didn't know how many black tourists they got in this part of the world, but Drake guessed people of color were thin on the ground.

He needed a break, maybe a better location fix from Akinyi. Until then, Drake would wait.

As there was no point in waiting hungry, he strolled down to the hotel lobby. The free breakfast buffet featured one of those make-it-yourself waffle irons. A waffle, plus bacon and eggs, was a lot more breakfast than his usual, but he expected to burn it off, sooner or later.

He'd brought along his smartphone, and out of habit, he began scanning the tech news. A husband and wife, both Chinese nationals, had been busted at San Francisco International Airport; one of them carried stolen prototypes of some new 5G radio chips. A maker of Internet-connected smoke detectors had discovered a flaw in the Z-Wave radio protocol that would let intruders set off alarms simultaneously in ten million American homes. A biased algorithm did something to hurt somebody's feelings.

Drake smiled. Astrid would get a kick out of this. With any luck she'd healed up enough to take an interest in the wider world. She might be staring at a computer screen right now, mumbling, "I told you so," and every now and then, "This seems true."

He realized that he wasn't just searching for the fugitives to prove himself to the deacons or to get a front-page story or even to forestall whatever disastrous crime they'd sought to commit.

He missed Astrid. He wanted to talk with her again. He missed her voice, warm and pensive, as she mulled some abstruse problem in network security, telling Drake about it as if he had brains enough to help. He'd try anyway, from time to time, and that would sometimes bring forth from her a brief, barking laugh, a sign that Drake had said something dumb. Drake took no offense; he knew his limitations. But Astrid would break off the laugh, as if to spare his feelings, in such a winsome way, with downcast, embarrassed eyes and the remnant of a smile. And it made Drake want to be a fool all over again.

"A child," Drake muttered aloud. "She's just a child." Then he glanced around to assure himself that no one had heard. And then he resumed his breakfast.

BACK IN HIS room, Drake kept at it. He decided to give up on word searches and instead started reading every one of Trace's messages, or at least skimming them, in hopes of running across anything that might suggest a hiding place. It was probably a waste of time, but Drake preferred to waste time doing something, anything that might offer a clue.

Even so, Drake's diligence had begun to wane by 4:00 p.m., and he was grateful when his phone rang and Detective Akinyi's number popped onto the screen.

"Got anything?" he asked.

"Sure do. A Minnesota hit. They stopped for gas at a Mobil a little west of St. Paul, about four hours ago, and at a convenience store about eighty miles northwest of there, about ninety minutes later."

"Store wouldn't happen to be named Colley's, would it?"

"Not bad. How'd you know?"

"Sheer luck, believe me."

"And does that give you a location?"

"It puts us close," said Drake, taking care to use the word us. "It puts us very close."

"How you figure?"

"There's some kind of hangout near there. He's used it before. A lake house, I think. For vacations."

"Belong to his family?"

"I don't believe so. He's not stupid enough to go someplace obvious. Must belong to a friend. Or maybe a landlord who rents it out during the summer."

"Either way, you still don't have an address."

"But I'm in the ballpark. I'll be even closer when you get an ID on their ride."

"No problem. It's a Ford Explorer, dark blue, with Massachusetts plates."

"That's what I'm talking about," said Drake, as Akinyi read out the plate number and Drake jotted it down.

"Now I just have to keep my eyes open for the right house."

"And you'll just ring the doorbell."

"Why not? There's no reason for them to be scared of me."

"I'm in their shoes, I'm scared of everybody," said Akinyi. "Maybe you better leave this to the pros. Figure out which house and let the local PD take it from there."

"These guys haven't committed a crime, remember? Why would local cops talk to them?"

"They will if I ask 'em."

"Professional courtesy," said Drake.

"Plus the chance to be in on a big-city investigation."

"Boston's not all that big."

"A lot bigger than the backwoods of Minnesota."

"Either way, I'm doing this on my own. If I need help, I'll holler."

Akinyi sighed. "Okay. You'll be all right. Probably."

DRAKE ROLLED NORTH on I-94, the falling sun at his back, his car's long shadow leading the way. He'd needed an hour to check out of the hotel, Uber to the nearest rental car office, and get on the road. Then came a half-hour crawl through Twin Cities rush hour traffic. But the worst was soon behind Drake, and the Ford Focus was doing the limit and a little more.

It would be just getting dark when he arrived, but that didn't rule out a few discreet inquiries. He'd grab a motel room first, then maybe look around before bedding down. He could begin a serious search at sunup, around 5:00 a.m.

Drake's GPS pinged, and he rolled off the interstate and onto a state highway. Seven miles on, he saw the neon sign of Colley's coming up on his right. It was a sizable store, not quite a supermarket but a good deal bigger than a 7-Eleven. The windows were full of illuminated signs for beer brands that Drake had avoided for years. In the parking lot, a battered RV, a late-model Toyota, and a Cadillac Escalade reflected the neon glow.

Drake kept going, to a motel he'd picked out before departing Chanhassen. It was a no-name independent operation, located in what looked like an old Red Roof Inn. In any case, the present management was doing a creditable job. Drake's room was clean and the WiFi worked. The soda vending machine even stocked Coke Zero. A bottle of the stuff washed down a cold Subway sandwich that Drake had purchased on his way up.

Between mouthfuls of salami, he phoned Carter and filled him in.

"You're a natural at this," Carter said.

"Luck and diligence," Drake replied.

"Like I said," Carter answered back. "So tomorrow you start looking for the car."

"Maybe tonight. I could wander around a little. Drive up and down the lake road and see what turns up."

"Better to wait till morning."

"Probably, but there's no harm in it. And I want to get this done."

"Well, keep your windows rolled up. They probably don't get a lot of black folks in that part of the world."

"I'll try not to be too obvious."

"You got everything you need?"

"The Lord has provided."

DRAKE FELT LIKE a shower. The soap was a sliver, barely adequate, but he relished the sandpapery feel of the cheap bath towel and dried himself with extra vigor. He shoved his dirty clothes into the backpack and carried it with him to the Ford. Soon he was on the road again, rolling back the way he'd come, toward Colley's.

The place was exactly as he'd imagined. Bigger than it looked from outside, it made a tolerable substitute for the Meijer's supermarket ten miles farther up the road. Here a hassled vacationer could find bacon and eggs and bread.

And beer. A whole back wall of it in massive coolers. Bud and Miller, mostly, with several vile IPA microbrews to add a touch of class. Drake thought about it for a minute, then reached into the cooler and grabbed up four six-packs of IPA. The right beer for the job, he figured.

With precarious care, he gripped two six-packs in each hand and staggered to the checkout counter. Setting them next to the cash register, he shook his hands to let blood back in, and mumbled to himself, a little too loudly, "Now, I just gotta figure out where I'm going."

The counter man, overhearing him, flashed a smile. "New around here, huh?" He was a slight, wispy-haired white man with arcane scrawls and runes tattooed down the length of each pale arm. He wore a black Captain Morgan T-shirt, the gift of some liquor distributor, no doubt.

"I'm from Minneapolis. Never been this way. Beautiful, though. All the lakes."

"Planning to fish?"

"No, man, not this trip. S'posed to be going to a party, but I lost my phone, and I don't know exactly where it is. One of these lakes, I know that. He works for the same company as me. Bellarmine Insurance."

"Bellarmine?" The word didn't sit well with the counter man, who frowned and cocked his head like a suspicious spaniel.

"You know the company?"

"No. I just know some of the people there. Bellarmine people. You're early this year."

"Early?"

"Yeah, usually it's July. Not the Fourth. Toward the end of the month. Twenty or thirty of them show up. Twenty or thirty of you."

"Well, that's gotta be a good thing, right? Lots more business for you."

"Yeah, they move the product all right. Drink anything in the cooler. In July, I start putting in supplies of Belgian ales and real German bock beer. Plenty of Scotch and bourbon too. Don't know how it tastes myself, 'cause it's too expensive for me. My regulars wouldn't touch the stuff either. But these guys buy it all."

"Well, me and Trace like our beer, but not that much. We're just hanging out for a few days."

"Trace? That your friend's name?"

"Yeah."

"Big guy, right?"

"Very."

"He was just through here a few hours ago. I was about ready to toss him out, but I changed my mind. Can't go throwing away that much money."

"Throw him out? Why?"

"No good reason, I guess. That fight last year wasn't exactly his fault. Some drunk in here, local guy, started hassling him about something, I don't remember what. Drunk threw the first punch. Those two guys tore up half the store before the county cops showed up. They did about twenty thousand worth of damage. Insurance covered about ten. So I can't afford to throw him out. I need his money."

"He never told me that story."

"Embarrassed. He came in here yesterday with his cap in his hand, talking about how sorry he was. I could see he meant it too. And then he started buying stuff. Maybe three hundred bucks worth."

"A lot of beer."

"No, not a drop. Just all the canned food and cold cuts in the place." The counter man pointed over Drake's shoulder. "Emptied that shelf over there. I still ain't finished restocking. Him and his girlfriend are settling in for a few days, that's for sure."

"Girlfriend? You saw her?"

"Nope. But he bought some girly stuff." The man lowered his voice a little. "You know. Tampons."

"Oh yeah, like that."

"Like that. Anyway, they're here. And this time, you're bringing the beer."

"Yeah. This is probably just a down payment," said Drake, gesturing at the six-packs. "But I still gotta find them."

"That's not hard. Just head down the lake road down there, just off the highway. When you get on that, just keep going about half a mile, till you get to a great, big blocky-looking thing. Looks more like an office building than a house. I think it actually belongs to the Bellarmine company. They're supposed to hold sales meetings there. Maybe they do, once in a while. But I only see 'em when it's time to party."

Drake held out his credit card. "Well, it's that time again."

IN THE DARKNESS, he almost missed the access road. But he caught sight of it just in time and made the turn.

There were no streetlamps here. Only trees that formed a green tunnel around the road. In daylight, with a brave sun filtering through the leaves, the effect might have been enchanting. But at night, the stark glow of the headlights glared off the leaves just ahead, while the terrain to left and right was still immersed in ominous darkness. Anything could be out there, just beyond the lights. Anything at all.

Drake realized he was gripping the wheel too tight. He laughed to himself and relaxed. There was nothing out here but raccoons or deer, or horny teenagers.

The road was a narrow slash of asphalt, unmarked, scrolling out into the woods. Drake had seen it soon enough to slow and make the turn. It was a narrow road, even for a Focus. If an outbound vehicle showed up, one of them would have to creep onto the bare soil on either side of the pavement and let the other ride squirt through.

For now, it seemed Drake had the road to himself. He cracked the window, listened to the swish and rustle as his car rolled past the trees, inhaled the verdant air. A good place to hide.

After about half a mile, the road rolled past a parcel of flat and treeless land. A parking area for fishermen and other casual day-trippers. Nobody there at that moment.

About a quarter mile farther on, Drake saw the house. It was as he'd been told. The place was three stories tall at least and in the form of stacked rectangles, sleek and efficient. Probably designed in the early '60s by an ex-infantryman who'd studied architecture on the GI Bill. But it was built of better materials than the typical Bauhaus structure—brown brick and warm hardwood—so, unlike many other such buildings that Drake had seen, this one had aged well.

And it was much too big for a vacation home. This was more of a corporate conference center, a place for holding sales meetings and throwing parties for prized clients. Somehow, Trace had borrowed the keys. Maybe he was entitled to them, maybe not. Either way, he must have known that no events were scheduled this week. That made it a decent place to hide, a mouse hole lined in mink.

There were no lights to suggest human habitation. All the windows showed venetian blinds, all of them shut. Still, Trace might have heard his drive-by and tried for a peek. Let him. Drake saw no point in subtlety.

He pulled into the circular driveway and onto flawless asphalt. He passed a large garage door of polished hardwood; no doubt the rented Explorer was on the other side of it.

Drake climbed out of the Focus, backpack in hand. He saw a gray and white cylinder above the door, fronted with glass. A digital video camera, probably motion-activated, probably infrared, was mounted above it, and Drake was confident that he was being watched. So he gave Trace and Astrid a good look, then leaned against the fender of his car to wait.

CHAPTER THIRTEEN

IT WASN'T LONG. There was a thwacking sound, like a heavy metal bolt being snatched. Then dead silence as the door opened.

Trace looked bigger in person, and Drake might have been intimidated. Then he saw the wariness in Trace's eyes, like someone expecting a punch to land from some unguessed direction, and noticed that the huge hands that hung limp at his side seemed to tremble a bit. Just then, he didn't seem much like the fighter who'd torn up Colley's. He was just scared.

Still, he'd opened the door. And his hands were empty. No gun, no carving knife from the kitchen, not even a clenching of fists. Astrid must have seen Drake on the security monitor and told Trace to let him in.

And so, without a word, Trace gestured Drake through the door.

He entered a shadowy foyer, carpeted in gray, with white walls and ceiling. Trace brushed past him and led the way to a living room that was vast and as cool and elegant as Copenhagen. There were stark leather sofas and stern leather armchairs and strict-looking tables of dark polished wood. An immense television hung on one wall and paintings adorned the rest. Real paintings but nothing Trace recognized. It was all Cold War stuff, abstract and distant, as if the painter had been inspired by peering through a slit in the Berlin Wall.

The far end of the room was an immense span of glass that rose the full height of the building. Translucent blinds, lowered from the ceiling, shrouded the huge window.

Drake plopped his backpack onto one of the sofas. "Now this is my idea of a hiding place," he said.

"How'd you find us?" The voice was deep and somber, and spoken at the exact resonant frequency of the room, giving Trace's words an ominous, cavernous effect.

"Legwork and guesswork," said Drake, sounding not the least bit ominous, at least to his own ears. But Trace's fretful manner hadn't changed, and so Drake figured he'd press his advantage.

"You know you're in trouble. So's Astrid. But do you know how much trouble?"

"Do you? 'Cause if you did, you'd be in Boston right now," Trace said.

"Boston? This place is a lot safer than Boston, for Astrid and for me. They tried to kill me too, you know. In Boston. Atlanta too. But in Atlanta, they knew I was coming. I didn't repeat that mistake. Just got on a plane and headed here. No advance warning to anybody."

"I didn't tell anybody either," Trace said. "So how'd you find me?"

"Like I said, legwork and guesswork, and help from a cop friend. You've been leaving breadcrumbs all the way from Boston. When I found out your company owned a conference center up here, I figured you might crash here for a night or two."

Trace sighed. "You figure the people hunting us could do the same?"

"Don't know. They don't have subpoena power, like my friend. But they might be able to pull some strings. I don't know. But that's just one more reason for you to tell me what's going on."

"If we talk, we go to prison," Trace said.

"Maybe. Maybe not." On the right side of the room, Drake noticed a staircase leading to the second floor and alongside it the stainless steel door of an elevator. "Where's Astrid?"

"She's upstairs. Resting."

"Well, let's have this conversation up there. She needs to hear this too."

Drake started toward the staircase, when a massive hand grabbed his upper arm and jerked him back. "I don't want you frightening her," Trace said.

"More than she's already frightened?"

Trace released him and led the way up the stairs to the second floor. At the top, a balcony ran the length of the house. Trace turned left, walked past two doors, tapped on the third.

"Come in."

Astrid's words were spoken in a raspy, weary voice, and though she tried for a smile, the woman who looked up at Drake from a wide white bed didn't look much better than she sounded.

She was propped up on pillows, a MacBook on her lap. She was dressed in a hospital gown, a grubby-looking one that she must have been wearing when Trace wheeled her away. Her chest was mostly covered, but Drake could see the ends of adhesive tape strips, where Trace had no doubt applied a replacement bandage. *audience*

When black folk turn pale, the skin takes on a grayish cast. Drake saw that in Astrid now and how the lotus tattoo under her chin seemed more distinct than ever. Her eyes were heavy-lidded with exhaustion and worry, and perhaps shame. Good. Maybe that shame would save them all.

"Hey, girl," said Drake. "What you doing here?"

"Figured it might be safer than that hospital."

"Not in your condition. You should be in bed for at least another week."

Astrid gave a wan smile, waved one arm. "As you see."

"I mean a hospital bed. Attentive nurses, constant monitoring, modern antibiotics. You're an infection waiting to happen."

"I'm keeping it clean. New dressing every day. Trace is good at it." Astrid nodded down at her chest. "Either way, it beats the alternative. I laid in that bed, back in the hospital, just waiting for it. Every time the door opened, I thought it might be him. Back with the knife. Now, I can think what to do next. I can breathe again."

"For a day or two, maybe. But you can't stay here long. The annual Mistake at the Lake party is just weeks away. Right, Trace?"

Trace's jaw fell. "How'd you know?"

"Homework. And if I could figure it out, so can the people who'd like to hurt you. So you need to get gone, sooner rather than later. Only I can guarantee you that your next hiding place won't be this nice. Next time it's a motel. Even the cheap ones will use up your savings soon enough. So then it'll be a homeless shelter. You'll hate that. No WiFi."

"It won't be long," Trace growled. "We only need to stay underground for a little while."

"Only till it happens," whispered Astrid.

Drake shivered to hear that. It wasn't the pain and exhaustion in her voice that alarmed him. This time, it was greed. After all that had happened to her, Astrid still thought she saw a way to get paid.

He should have seen it coming. Why else had Astrid thrown in with this lot of thieves and killers? What had he thought he was doing here? Rescuing Snow White?

Liberated from his stupidity, Drake saw with new eyes. Trace and Astrid would be fugitives, all right, but they imagined themselves as very comfortable fugitives. Maybe Trace had already worked out a way for them to score new identities. Maybe they were counting on enough money to support them for the rest of their days. Millions, then.

"So you're still expecting a cut of the profits," Drake said. "Your friends, whoever they are, will rake in billions when this deal goes down, so they can afford to toss you a couple million, just as a tip. But why should they bother? Easier for them to simply disappear."

"Not all of them can," said Trace.

Drake saw it at once. "You mean Dr. Severins, back at MIT. Yeah. He's got a wife. He's got kids. He's even got tenure. So you can blackmail him. You keep silent, he pays you out of his cut."

"Something like that."

"Not bad. You get paid, and you get payback. Only he deserves worse. He tried to have you killed."

"Less than optimal, I admit. But it leaves us all alive, and free," Astrid said, sighing. "Lately, I've learned to settle."

"He might go for it," said Drake. "For old time's sake. You two used to be tight. As tight as it gets. What did you think? He'd leave his wife and family for you?"

"I'm not stupid," said Astrid. "Well, not that stupid. It was just . . . he treated me like an equal. With everybody else, it was always like I was some kind of superior being. Not a person just like them. It was, like, the ladies at church. They were nice and sweet, but they looked at me sometimes like I was an alien.

"But Bart, I could talk to him straight. I'd tell him about some algorithm I'd finally figured out, and I'd quote the code to him. Most people wouldn't have a clue, not even other coders. Bart would just nod and answer back in Python or C Plus Plus, like he was ordering off a menu.

"I don't know if I loved him or not. All I know is, he knew my heart."

Trace glared at Astrid. "You told *me* that, once."

"Yeah, in high school," she said. "I meant it too. But we're both different now. We're older."

"Yeah," said Trace, "and you're smarter. You're all MIT and shit. I'm just another Golden Gopher with an undergraduate degree."

Astrid hung her head. "I never thought of you like that. You must know that. I wouldn't have come with you if I thought like that."

Trace said nothing, probably because he wanted to believe.

So Drake talked instead. "Whatever you know about Severins, it won't be enough to save you. Even if he's willing to pay you off, he's working for people who don't take chances. That means they keep coming, against both of you. And me too, probably."

Astrid raised her eyes. "Why would they come for you?"

"They already have, twice. I told you about the first time, with Severins. Later, they tried again, in Atlanta."

"What were you doing in Atlanta?" Astrid asked.

"Walking into a trap. But I got lucky. Still, they might try again. Or they might not. It's an open question in my case. They know if I really had anything on them, it'd be on the front page by now. So they might let me keep breathing. Or not."

Astrid sighed, a sound like coarse sandpaper on wood. She glanced up at Trace. "Maybe we better, baby."

Trace shook his head. "We go to the cops and we're ruined. It's a felony. I'll never hold down a decent job again."

"Don't sell yourself short," Drake said. "Plenty of convicted hackers are pulling down six figures as freelance security consultants."

"Yeah, after they're paroled. I can't go to jail. I can't make it there."

"Big guy like you? You'd make out. Besides, it probably won't come to jail. If this thing is as big as it seems to be, the banks will be pretty forgiving if you get them off the hook. You might just get probation."

"And a felony record," said Astrid.

"About a quarter of all black people have felony records," said Drake. "So you won't get to vote in the next election. There are worse fates. You guys keep this up and you'll find out."

The three were silent for a while. Then Trace cleared his throat. "Assuming we were interested," he said, with the deliberate air of a man in a minefield, "how exactly would this work?"

"I know people in the Boston Police Department, so we could go to them first. But this is mainly a federal matter, so you'd be doing most of your talking to the FBI, and maybe the Treasury Department. The big thing is timing. They'll want to know when this thing is going down, and the quickest way to stop it. You tell them that, and you get a lot of credit. Especially since the crime hasn't happened yet."

"I have mixed feelings about that," said Trace. "I'm curious."

"About what?" asked Drake.

"Whether we succeeded," said Trace. "People like us, it's not just the money. It's the challenge. We went after maybe the hardest targets in the world. Astrid pinged me eighteen months ago. I've been working eighteen-hour days ever since. Eight hours at the insurance company and the rest on this. Hacking at database code, looking for the best way to exploit those zero-days.

"And that's just me. Everybody else in Silverware worked just as hard. They were smuggling malware into the various bank networks or writing a payload to pump out the cash so nobody'd notice. Every piece of it has to work just right, or all that effort goes to waste." Trace sighed, smiled a little. "Even now, after everything that's happened, I kind of hope they pull it off. Even if we never see a penny. 'Cause that way, we'll know."

"Pride of authorship," said Drake. "I understand that. But I never wrote anything that got somebody killed."

Trace hung his head at that, and when Drake looked to Astrid, she wouldn't meet his gaze.

"Not to mention smashing the US economy, maybe the whole world's."

"They'd be crazy to carry it that far," said Astrid.

"Why? They'd have plenty of money. And these aren't the kind of people who care about anybody else. Especially if it's some rogue government. Iran, maybe, or North Korea. Maybe even Russia."

As he spoke the names of the nations, Drake watched Trace and Astrid for any hint of reaction. He saw none.

"You telling me that you don't know who you're working for?"

"Bart said it was safer if I didn't know."

"Yeah. He did a fine job looking out for you."

"It didn't have to be like this!" Astrid snapped. "If I'd just talked Clinker out of sending that warning . . . if I hadn't encouraged him . . ."

"Getting out of this business was the smartest move of your life. Only trouble is you went about it all wrong. You should have contacted the FBI. They'd have protected you, and you'd have walked. Not so sure about your boyfriend Severins, but he wasn't much of a catch after all."

Astrid averted her eyes. "Worst part is, I got so many other people involved in this. Trace and Clinker and the rest. I recruited them."

Drake saw Astrid's lips begin to tremble, as if she were holding back some great misery.

"You're not responsible," Drake said. "They were all grownups. They made their own choices."

"That's right," said Trace. "When you came to me with the plan, I knew it was crossing a line. I just didn't care. I wanted the challenge, and the money. So I said yes. Nobody put a gun to my head." He chuckled and added, "Not yet, anyway."

"What's your part in this?" Drake asked him.

"My specialty," said Trace, "was databases. Not core banking software, but the databases that hold all the banks' financial data. See, these guys didn't just want to steal money. They also want to wreck all the back-end databases. Great way to cover their tracks."

Drake nodded. "I get it. If you can screw up the databases, they won't even be sure how much money they've lost, or from which accounts. But it's not like nobody ever thought of this before. The really big banks use really good security practices, at least when it comes to their core banking systems. They even have regular security war games, run by the government."

"Of course. America has Quantum Dawn and the Hamiltons. The British government runs one called Resilient Shield. There's at least one a year, and that's not counting all the tests these banks run on their own. So they prepare. They prepare really hard."

"Only not hard enough," said Drake.

"Afraid not." A smile played at the corners of Trace's mouth, and Drake noticed that Astrid too seemed a little more cheerful. Perhaps they were savoring the joy of being smarter than the other fellow. "So this involves some of those zero-day exploits you wrote about."

"Several of them," said Trace. "I found a couple of them myself. Took the better part of a year, but I found them. And when I put it together with work from some other members of the team, I had a program that could do some major damage."

"Largent?" asked Drake.

"That's what we called it. French for *silver*, you know. And for *money*."

"Of course, Trace. I didn't figure you guys were football fans."

After a befuddled moment, Trace continued. "Anyway, Largent lets us get between the bank and SWIFT. That's the global network that handles bank-to-bank money transfers. Trillions move across SWIFT every day.

"See, at this level, money is motor oil. It lubricates just about everything in the world. Without it, the whole world seizes up. But we only need to divert a little. A billion here, a billion there.

"Not easy, though. SWIFT already had tough security, but then after that Bangladeshi scam in 2016, it got downright merciless."

"No doubt," said Drake. He remembered the case—probably the worst bank hack ever. The bad guys had cracked SWIFT with help from someone on the inside. They'd tried for a billion dollars and had almost gotten it, except for a misspelled word in one of their fraudulent money transfer commands. A guy at Deutsche Bank spotted it, and the game was up. Even so, they'd gotten away with about $50 million and were still in the wind.

"They sure made our lives harder," said Trace. "But that's okay. Made it more of an adventure."

"A lot more exciting than the insurance business?"

"Yeah. A real challenge. And not just getting our hands on the money.

Figuring out how to wreck their databases was even tougher."

"But these guys are fanatical about backups," said Drake. "There are copies and copies of copies. You know about Sheltered Harbor, right?"

Trace said nothing, just gazed at Drake with contemptuous eyes.

"Yeah, of course you do," sighed Drake. "It's been in the papers. I almost wrote about it myself, but my boss said it was boring. Me, I think it's kind of cool. Biggest fault-tolerant RAID system ever built. Every major bank distributes copies of its data among the other big banks. To break Sheltered Harbor, you'd have to crash pretty much every major bank in the world."

"It's hard, all right, but not impossible. Not even close. We've trained Largent to infect the entire Sheltered Harbor system."

"Is that even possible?"

"We've found a way. There's this company in Atlanta called Tannheuser that makes the core software for most of the world's biggest banks. Well, there's something wrong with it. Something really wrong. It's about the worst zero-day bug I've ever seen. Largent takes advantage of that. It can sneak into any of the banks' databases and quietly scramble the data. Forget about recovering it. Once Largent gets an hour or two to work, it's game over."

"You're proud of it."

"I admire its purity," said Trace, chuckling. "I wasn't as smart as Astrid. Definitely not MIT material. But I'm pretty good with databases. And I'm persistent. Sometimes, that's all it takes."

"So Astrid roped you in."

"Yeah. Said she was onto a good thing, something really daring. First time I'd heard from her in three or four years. She didn't want to discuss the plan through my corporate email, but she found me on CodeSorz, because of my old warname."

"Meshnet88."

Trace's eyes widened. "Wow. You really did do your homework. Anyway, she reached out to me." Trace fell silent for a few seconds. "It was like my world lit up. Back in the day, her and me . . . well, we were friends. Okay, friends with benefits. But for me, the friendship was the part that mattered. Women really do grow on trees. At least, they did for me. I'm okay-looking and I make decent money, so all I needed was Tinder. Anyway, that's what I thought, till Astrid's email showed up."

Astrid said nothing. But Drake could see a vein pulsing in her neck, and the vibration reached all the way to the lotus tattoo, so that he saw a slight throbbing in its left edge.

"So we swapped emails and then she told me to switch to Blankmail for better security. I knew something was up, but I didn't hesitate. We started communicating that way and on Telegram, that secure instant message system. Later we talked on burner phones."

"When I found out what she wanted, well, I was a little insulted for a minute. Like she was only after me for my brain."

"But you got over it," Drake said.

Trace smiled. "Yeah. Then I calmed down and listened."

"And she talked you into a life of crime," said Drake. "She's pretty persuasive."

"She didn't have to try all that hard," said Trace. "Back in the day, we'd cracked a few systems now and then. Just for giggles, you know. But it was still illegal. But Astrid and Dr. Severins, now they were into something really big.

"Then I found out they'd been recruited themselves. A guy who calls himself Epiphany."

"Really? He's got a high opinion of himself."

"Maybe he lives up to it," said Trace. "I dunno. Severins said he doesn't know or care who he is. Some guy who reached out to him after he gave a presentation at DefCon. You remember? The time he owned about three or four major banks?"

"I was there. He put on quite a show. Video got a couple million hits on YouTube."

"Epiphany must have seen it. The guy sent him a letter. Right to his office, via snail mail. Old-fashioned, but it left no traces. Promised him a stack of money to work on the project."

Drake turned to Astrid. "Did they pay him to recruit you?"

"Not directly," she said. "But he told them that he'd need a team for a job that big. They would have known that anyhow. So they provided some up-front cash and promised a big payday whenever the deal went down."

"You believed that?"

"I had my doubts, sure. But the up-front money was good. About fifty thousand so far. Even if we never saw any cash on the back side, we were doing okay. And why not more? If Largent scores a billion or more, Epiphany has no reason to cheat us."

"Except that he's a greedy thief who doesn't mind having people murdered."

"Yeah," said Astrid, with a thick, rheumy chuckle. "Except for that."

"So then one of you recruited the other members of Silverware, right?"

"That's how it was," said Astrid. "Together we parsed out the tasks we'd have to complete. Then I went hunting the underground for people with the correct blend of skills. I suppose you could call me the personnel director."

"And you did a fine job. Rounded up quite a team. Borzoi, Gallery, Kirsch, and Mesh here." Drake paused, gazing into Astrid's eyes. "And Clinker."

"Yeah," Astrid said. "Clinker."

"How'd you recruit him?"

"At DefCon, a few years back. He did a presentation. Persistent attacks on hard targets."

"Yeah, I remember. He got a lot of ink for that."

"It took him about a year, he told me. But it was a hobby for him. He had a full-time job in network security in Hamburg."

"Smart enough to crack into a Pentagon network in his spare time. I see why you recruited him."

"I wish I'd forgotten his name." Astrid shut her eyes, shook her head.

"Too late now," Drake said. "But not too late to do right."

Drake saw her eyes open, saw something like resolve in her expression. Trace saw it too.

"Hold up," Trace said. "We don't want to rush into anything. That's how we got into this mess."

"Telling the cops is the only way you get out of it," Drake said.

"Maybe," said Trace. "Maybe not. We need to think about it."

Drake chuckled. "Take your time. You've only got a band of murderers on your trail, with limitless resources and at least as much brains as me. And I found you. But maybe I got lucky. Maybe you've got nothing to worry about after all."

Trace said nothing for a bit, then, "I've got to change her bandages."

Drake felt a flush of outrage on his skin at the thought of this man touching her, undressing her. He hoped neither would notice. In a level voice he said, "You got any first aid training?"

"A little," Trace said. "Boy Scout. Never made Eagle." There was true regret in his voice.

"Okay," Drake said. "I'll leave you to it. Anything in the fridge?"

THE KITCHEN WAS even bigger than the one in Boo's Atlanta condo, which was to be expected. The place was used for large corporate gatherings, after all, and so required something on the scale of a full-fledged restaurant.

Whoever had employed it last had left it as clean as a surgical suite at Dana-Farber. Drake popped the door of a vast silvery refrigerator and found convenience-store food. Two gallon jugs of Poland Spring water. Vacuum-packed American cheese. A pound's worth of butter sticks. Pre-cut Oscar Mayer cold cuts. Three packages of bacon and four dozen eggs. Half a gallon of two percent milk. And four loaves of Wonder Bread.

On a shelf nearby were dry cereals—raisin bran, Wheaties, Cheerios. A cylinder of Quaker Oats, but no grits. Four cans of tuna. A box of Domino sugar. A box of Bisquick. Two kinds of Starbucks coffee, with and without caffeine.

In short, the makings. Anybody could put together a few tolerable meals out of this.

Massive aluminum saucepans and skillets in various diameters hung from steel hooks above a central workstation. It was about midnight, but to Drake, it was never too late for breakfast. He plucked down a midsized skillet, grabbed bacon from the fridge, and got to work.

Three-quarters of an hour later, he rode up the elevator to the second level, a large tray in hand. There was bacon, scrambled eggs, and hand-made Bisquick biscuits, along with a pot of decaf.

Drake squatted next to the door, set the tray on the floor, then stood erect and knocked.

"Room service," he called, but heard nothing except, just maybe, the rustle of bedsheets.

"Hello?" called Drake. "Breakfast is served."

Through the door, Trace replied, "We're..... . we're not ready. Can you just leave it outside?"

"Sure," said Drake. For a moment he paused, listening for any sort of sound. Then guilt got the better of his curiosity. He skipped the elevator and trudged downstairs. Settling himself on the vast leather sofa, he pulled out his phone.

Carter answered in two rings. "You find them?"

"We just had a long talk."

"They gonna come back?"

"They're discussing it behind closed doors. They're scared of jail time."

"What jail time?" Carter scoffed. "They haven't done anything yet. Might get probation, at worst."

"That's what I've told them, and it had an effect. Anyway, it might have. But believe it or not, they still think they can get paid behind all this."

"That's crazy talk. These guys don't need them anymore. They'll kill them before they pay them. And if they take any stolen money, they can forget probation."

"That's why I'm thinking they'll come around. Anyway, I'm going to stand by right here till they decide."

"So where is *here*?" said Carter.

"Don't know the exact address. It's a corporate retreat that belongs to Bellarmine Insurance, the company this guy Trace works for. It sits next to Ebon Lake. That's E-B-O-N. Punch it up on Google Maps. You might even see the house. It's a big one."

Carter fell silent, and Drake heard the clatter of keys.

"Got the lake," Carter said after about a minute. "Pretty. Bring your swim trunks?"

"Slipped my mind."

"Don't see any houses here. Can't. Too many trees. But here and there you can see boat docks sticking out into the water."

"This place has one," said Drake. "A big one."

"Okay, I may be looking at it now, but there's no way for me to tell."

"It won't matter anyway. Not till I bring them back."

"And if they won't come back?"

"I'll stick to them till they do," said Drake. "But I think I can bring them around. They're not cut out to be fugitives. I proved that by finding them. I think the lesson's sinking in, and we'll be on a plane back to Boston this time tomorrow."

Drake hung up, then called Detective Akinyi to update her as well.

"You're paying for their plane tickets and everything," she said when he finished. "Wish I had your expense account."

"Unusual circumstances," Drake said. "I'll call you from the airport, and you can pick us up. Please don't arrive in a squad car. Don't want to freak them out."

"Like I care," said Akinyi. "They're your friends, not mine. I'm just trying to close cases here."

"And these two should be able to help, if we don't scare the crap out of them."

"Fair enough," Akinyi said. "I'll come in my own car. Just got it. A BMW."

Drake grinned to hear the tone of pride in her voice. "A ride like that, you just want an excuse to show it off."

"Yeah," said a laughing Akinyi. "When you getting in?"

"Don't know yet. But when I know, you'll know."

Next came a call to Madeleine. "I'm going to need three one-way rides from Minneapolis to Boston. Seats with extra legroom, if you can swing it. One of us will want to stretch out a little."

"How soon?"

"I don't know yet. Still waiting to hear from some people. What are my options?"

Madeleine was silent for a time, while her keyboard clicked and smacked. "Next flight with three seats aboard leaves tomorrow at 11:30 a.m."

"Not sure if we'll be ready by then."

"But if you are, you'll want to get out of town quick, right?"

"Yeah."

"Right. I'm placing the order. Look for confirmation in your email."

NOTHING TO DO now but wait for a decision from the two love-birds. *Ex-lovebirds*, Drake reminded himself, but the thought didn't cheer him. Astrid, it seemed, was rather free with her affection. There was Trace, then Severins, and how many others beside? Maybe Drake might have made headway with her. Instead, he'd chosen to keep a safe, deaconly distance. *Just as well*, Drake thought.

He hadn't eaten any of the food he'd prepared. He strolled back to the kitchen, collected bacon, eggs. and biscuits onto a plate and nuked it for thirty seconds in a microwave big enough for a suckling pig. The decaf coffee he'd made was barely warm, but Drake didn't mind it that way.

He lugged it all back to the sofa and set the food on a cocktail table. There was a remote control lying there. An iPad, actually, stuffed with custom software for controlling all the household lighting and security systems. But all Drake wanted was some television. He found the on-off icon, then made his way to Netflix and punched up *The Twilight Zone*. He'd seen every episode about thirty times, so he knew he was in for something good.

Drake was in the mood for silliness, so he picked "Showdown with Rance McGrew," an episode about a TV actor who plays the toughest lawman west of the Mississippi, who's challenged to a gunfight by the ghost of Jesse James. It was drivel, but it always made him laugh.

So Drake chuckled as he consumed the late-night breakfast and when he was done eating, settled back to watch the rest of the show. Almost to his surprise, Drake found himself fading out. It was nearly two, after all, and it had been a long day. He took up the remote control tablet, switched off the set. His eyes swept the glass surface of the table till he found what he'd expected to find, the master control for the first-floor lights. With a stroke of Drake's finger, all was dark.

Drake placed the tablet on the low table before him. Hauling his legs onto the sofa, he surrendered himself to sleep.

THE SOUND THAT roused Drake came and went, too fast for identification. He knew only that it was short and sharp and out of place. It was a noise from outside, where nobody ought to be.

Drake rolled off the sofa and began to crawl toward the staircase. It was to his right and forward, toward the waterfront side of the house, and as Drake crawled, he drew closer to the vast window, assembled from large panes of glass mounted in steel frames that rose row upon row to the full height of the building. On the bottom right side, the glass was interrupted by a dense wooden door that opened onto the large yard and the lakefront. But through the slitted blinds of the window, Drake could see movement. It was hardly visible, but a dark shape was silhouetted by the light of the lake house on the opposite shore. There was someone at the window, doing something. Studying the lock of the adjoining door, perhaps. Or maybe deciding on the best way to smash in.

Time's up, thought Drake. *They're here.*

CHAPTER FOURTEEN

A CHILL OF fear prickled Drake's skin. Then, to his surprise, it faded. He felt calm, almost stoic. He was tense, but not out of dread. It was more like anticipation.

He paused at the base of the stairs, said a quick prayer, then began to drag himself up. The adjoining elevator soon shielded him from anyone who might be peering through the window, so Drake crouched on the balls of his feet, raced up the stairs, walked to the bedroom occupied by Trace and Astrid.

He reached for the knob and gave it a slight turn. It rolled underneath his hand; unlocked. For a moment, Drake felt an irrational hesitation to intrude upon them. Then he came to his senses, swung the door open, and nudged it shut behind him.

"Wake up," he hissed in a voice as loud as he thought safe. There was no reaction.

"Come on, you guys. Wake up. We got problems."

In the darkness he heard a rustle of sheets, a sleep-addled croak. "What's going on?" It was Astrid. "What are you doing here?"

"Astrid, wake him up. They found us. They're out there."

"What?" Astrid's voice was just short of a shriek. The sound must have alerted Trace at last.

"What's going on?" he mumbled. Just like Astrid. Soon they'd be completing each other's sentences.

"Somebody's trying to get in. We gotta go."

"Go." Trace's voice was stupid with sleep.

"Wake up! There's no time."

"Here?" Trace rumbled. "You say somebody's here?" Drake heard his feet hit the floor, heard him fumble with a piece of furniture. Maybe a night table.

"We don't want lights," said Drake. "We gotta go."

From across the room he heard Trace breathing deep, like a man getting ready to run or to fight.

"If they're smart, they'll have both doors covered," said Drake. "Is there another way out of here?"

"Basement. There's a corridor down there. Leads under the building and out to the jetty."

"Jetty?" said Drake, feeling stupid.

"A dock for boats."

"Are there boats?"

"I've never seen any."

"Doesn't matter," said Drake. "If we can get to that dock, it puts us behind them. We can sneak into the woods and hide out for the night. They'll never find us."

"Might work," said Trace.

"Astrid, can you move?" asked Drake.

"As far as I need to," she said. Drake heard the weary rasp of her voice and doubted. Still, the three of them would have to try.

"Which way to the basement?"

"Stairwell," Trace replied. "Back of the house." Drake heard rustling and knew the man was pulling on a shirt and pants. Which meant he'd been lying there with Astrid, skin to skin, collecting her warmth. And she collecting his.

Even in their peril, Drake was distracted by anger and envy for a moment. "Astrid, you decent?"

"Does it matter?" The chuckle in her voice cheered Drake. Maybe the girl was up for this after all.

"Okay. Trace, help her stand." Drake heard shufflings and rustlings and bedsprings decompressing. "Everybody ready?"

"Let's go," said Trace.

Drake crouched, tugged the door. It swung open on silent hinges. He paused on the threshold, his eyes and ears alert.

He heard a soft, clinking sound just above the threshold of hearing. The sound of two champagne glasses brought together in a New Year's Day toast. Or the sound of a skilled burglar laying waste to a pane of glass in the lakeside door, making an opening just big enough for his hand to reach the lock.

Time to move.

"Quiet as you can," said Drake. He stepped through the doorway, turning left toward the front of the house and the stairwell leading to the basement. Astrid and Trace trailed him.

The railing that surrounded the second level balcony provided them with some cover, but Drake squatted for a little more concealment from anyone below who might look up.

Just then, he heard the clack of a lock being opened. He heard a gentle sound of movement and fancied he even smelled something of the lake. They were in.

The door closed and a light came on.. The flashlight beam was brilliant white, pitiless, darting about the great open space of the first floor.

The three fugitives froze. They'd be seen now, for sure, if the searcher only looked up. Hope lay in movement through that far door.

In the backwash of new light, Drake looked behind him. Astrid was hunched over too, but it was no stratagem. Pain and exhaustion had hollowed out the woman. She rested her hand on Drake's right shoulder, and he could feel it tremble.

Just beyond her stood Trace. He was pressed against the wall like a cornered man. But he stood straight, barely glancing at their escape route.

Drake saw the first upward flicker of the searching light just then, and some of its backscatter showed him something in Trace's right hand, the thing he'd been groping for back in the bedroom. A chef's knife, the blade eight inches long at least.

Trace turned his face to Drake and there was rage and focus in it. "Keep moving," he said. "I'm right behind you."

Drake moved on with slow, cautious steps, each bringing them a little closer to the door. Astrid, her hand still on his shoulder, hobbled along behind. Drake could hear her breathing, a wheezing, raspy sound. He took three more steps and the sound from Astrid grew into a rheumy growl. Two steps more, and the hand on his back shook with new urgency. Drake turned, saw Astrid's eyes shut tight with effort, her right hand held tight against her mouth. At the last fatal moment, she lifted her left hand away, placed it atop her right hand. The muscles in her arms flexed as she squeezed down on her mouth as if trying to smother herself.

Astrid failed. Despite the muffling effort of fingers and palms, the cough came, deep and guttural and fatal.

Light leaped upward and caught all three of them.

"They're on the move!" someone shouted, a high tenor voice with an unfamiliar accent.

"Pin 'em down!" came another deeper voice.

Over his shoulder, Drake heard Trace's voice bellowing down at the killer. He wasn't sure of the words. A curse, perhaps. He had no leisure to process the sound, for at that moment he grabbed Astrid's hand and hurled himself at the stairwell door.

It was an emergency door with a locking bar that opened to his weight. He shoved Astrid into the stairwell beyond and slammed the door behind him just as a gun fired somewhere behind them.

Still, Drake waited, hoping the door would slam open under Trace's weight. He gave it five seconds or so, knowing that if it took any longer, it wouldn't be Trace coming through.

Then Drake nudged Astrid. "Down. Quick as you can."

Two flights below, another door opened outward into a long black corridor. No light here at all. But Drake remembered the smartphone in his pocket. He pulled it out and lit it up.

The corridor was lined with cartons, disused furniture, other odds and ends. He took hold of Astrid's hand and guided them down the corridor, as fast as he dared. Behind him, Astrid coughed again, a thick cough, hoarse and contaminated.

The corridor behind them was submerged in utter darkness. There were no flickering lights, no sounds of pursuit. Drake and Astrid pressed on, and their footfalls and their hard breathing echoed against bare concrete. Their journey must be nearing an end, for they'd covered the length of the lake house and a good deal farther.

Ahead, Drake's light bounced off a bare concrete wall. In a moment of dismay, Drake supposed that the tunnel had come to a dead end. But just to the left of the bare wall stood another door. The way out. Drake was careful to shut off his phone's flashlight and darken its touchscreen before trying to open it.

The door was stiff from disuse and opened with a fearful groan. But at this distance from the house, there was little chance the sound had been heard. Drake and Astrid emerged into the silence of the boathouse.

The far end of the building was open to the night, and light from the house on the opposite shore gave just enough illumination to reveal the look of the place. It was rectangular, with the same sleek, postwar style as the big house, with walls of dark polished wood, and a large dock in the center of the floor, big enough to hold a mid-sized cabin cruiser or several rowboats.

But there were no boats in the dock or tied to the jetty that extended about thirty feet from the right of the structure and out into the lake. Not that Drake cared. In a boat, he and Astrid would be slow and noisy, easy prey for a gunman with careful aim.

Far better to find a back door to the boathouse, then drift into the nearby trees. They would never find him and Astrid in the darkness.

Drake put an arm around Astrid to steady her, then moved toward a rear door that would put them on the lawn of the lake house. From there, a fif-teen-yard dash would take them into the trees on the right side of the house.

Drake grasped the doorknob, then halted. Leaving Astrid next to the door, he moved to his right, to a set of windows mounted in the rear wall. He knew that a sudden movement might catch the eyes of a watcher, and so he took his time putting his face to the glass.

All Drake saw was a lawn made gray by the near-darkness, surmount-ed by the darker gray bulk of the large house. He scanned the area a couple of times, intent on spotting any unnatural movement. It was safe. There was nothing.

And then, there was something. A flash of light, from a source near the house, some fifty or sixty feet away. A cold, white torch, wielded by someone with no thought of concealing his presence. The cone of light darted and wavered and after a moment, began to sweep toward the boathouse.

Drake ducked, cursed. He glanced up at the window and saw the wood of the outer frame still glowing. The searcher had locked in on the boathouse. As Drake watched, the light grew more intense, as the man holding the flashlight drew closer.

They were trapped. If they dashed toward the woods they'd be dead within ten steps. If they reentered the basement tunnel, the second gunman might well be waiting for them.

Drake felt the weight of Astrid's body leaning against him, heard her ragged breathing. Her last reserves of strength were nearly gone.

So Drake scooped her up in his arms and carried her toward the open end of the boathouse, as quickly and quietly as he could manage. He saw a rising glow of light against the roof, realized it was light coming in from the rear window, where the man with his flashlight and his gun had drawn closer.

They were out of the open front end of the boathouse now. The building extended out from the shore, and beside the jetty on which they now stood, there was nothing but water. He could perhaps splash his way back to shore and into the trees, but not without revealing himself and Astrid. Drake knew he could run no farther.

But perhaps he and Astrid could hide.

Drake lowered Astrid to the dock. Then he climbed down into the water. As he'd hoped, it was only about four feet deep so close to the shoreline. Once in the water, he reached up for Astrid, dragged her across the dock and into his arms. As he moved, he heard the sound of a door being forced open, caught a glimpse of blazing light. Then he stood Astrid upright against one of the jetty's thick wooden pilings and held her there through the pressure of his own body against hers.

Astrid's body was spent. Her jaw hung slack and a drool of saliva trickled from her bottom lip. But her eyes were open and alert, skeptical and calculating. Just as they had been when they'd sat around the Meadhall and she'd explained to him why travel between the stars was impossible, and the existence of God was improbable.

Only right now she'd be thinking of Trace, of how he'd come out of hiding to save her, how he'd stayed behind in the house to protect her, how he'd given his life to buy her and Drake a little wasted time.

Drake heard the footfalls of the searcher, walking through the boathouse and out onto the jetty, passing over the spot that hid them to the very end of the structure. Perhaps he was staring out into the lake, his eyes scanning the surface for a fleeing boat that wasn't there.

And so the man retraced his steps, a steady, purposeful tread that grew louder as the man neared the hiding place. He strode over Drake's head, went a few steps farther. And then he stopped. And from up above him, Drake heard a gentle laugh, the sort that might have come from someone reading the cartoons in the latest edition of the New Yorker.

And that was that. The man had found them. Had their bodies stirred up some telltale ripples? Or had Drake splashed some drops of liquid on the jetty at the spot where he'd climbed into the lake? He'd have all eternity to think about it, starting now.

Drake was just beginning to wonder how the man would come for him when the first gunshot smashed through the wood of the jetty and ripped down the side of his right arm.

To his own surprise, Drake did not scream. But Astrid did, a gravelly, croaking sound, weary and sick. The sound took the heart right out of Drake, because he knew that the man had heard it too. Perhaps he'd climb into the water for them. Or maybe he'd finish them without getting his feet wet, by continuing to fire his pistol down through the jetty.

Either way, it was over.

Drake's right arm was numb now and useless to him. But with his left he clutched at the piling, pressing himself hard against Astrid as if he could in that way shield her from the bullets sure to come blasting down from above. Her body was cool and limp against his, and Drake saw that the wound in her chest was under water now, an open invitation to parasites and bacteria. He began to fret about the inevitable infection, then remembered that the cure for both their injuries was just a few moments away.

He looked down into Astrid's face and saw she'd been looking at his wound. Her eyes rose to his, fearful and ashamed. All her fault, she must have been thinking, and she'd have been right.

Drake didn't care. At this moment, there was no room in his heart for blame. There was only compassion and sorrow and leaden weariness. And at last the rise of a searing, flaming pain in his arm.

His state was miserable, and he knew that he could not endure it any longer and that he wouldn't have to. And so his heart leaped with something not too far from joy when a gun barked above him, once and then again. All over soon. Soon.

He felt no new pain, no smashing impact, and Astrid's glazing eyes had not gone blank. *Try again, you fool.* But instead of another shot, there was a hefty, sullen thud just above his head. Drake looked up but saw no sign of a new hole through the planking above his head. Instead, he felt a warm liquid dribbling onto the crown of his head and trickling down his back.

And there were new footsteps on the jetty now, slow and hesitant, as if the feet were struggling for a grip. The feet thudded farther down the little pier, beyond the place where Drake and Astrid had hidden themselves. Then there were scuffling sounds and a solid thump. And then two feet appeared over the edge of the jetty.

After a moment, the newcomer spoke—a familiar dark, resonant voice. "Astrid? Astrid? You down there?"

It was Trace. Somehow it was Trace.

"Down here," Drake called. "I got Astrid. But she's bad. And I'm shot."

"Me too," came Trace's voice. "Doesn't hurt all that much."

"Mine either," said Drake. "Just numb. Where did you get a gun?"

"From the other guy," said Trace. "He never saw my knife. He was busy shooting me, I guess." His voice grew faint and fragile.

Two men dead, then. And the right two men, at that. Trace was a hero, in Drake's eyes, though it might not seem that way to the inevitable police.

In any case, it was all up to Drake now. He was the least injured of them, the only one who could call for help.

The shore was about twenty yards away. He tried his wounded arm, and the numbness was replaced with a searing rip of pain. Drake didn't care. The arm still worked after a fashion, and that was all that mattered.

He embraced Astrid with both arms and willed his legs to move. The two of them emerged from beneath the jetty, the weight of the lake dragging at their bodies as they moved. Drake's legs felt strong at first, but halfway to shore, his energy began to lag. Blood loss, he supposed, as well as the strain of hauling Astrid's body and as his own.

Then he noticed that the water was growing shallow. And then he felt the kicking, thrusting movements of Astrid's legs, in rhythm with his own. She wanted dry land and clean bandages as much as Drake did. It was good to have her on his team.

They made the shore at last, and Drake dragged Astrid onto the scruffy, weedy soil at the brink. He laid her on her back, turned to look back at the jetty. Right above their hiding place lay a heap of dark clothing, a pale hand emerging from one sleeve.

A few feet farther away, he saw Trace, a shadow seated on the edge of the jetty. As Drake watched, Trace's body folded in on itself, as if deflating, before he fell backward onto the deck.

CHAPTER FIFTEEN

DRAKE REENTERED THE house through the lakeside door, fumbling through the inner darkness toward the kitchen, where a wall phone waited for him.

The first call went to 911, of course. Trace might still have a chance, and Astrid needed rest and antibiotics without delay. It came to Drake that he needed much the same treatment, and he marveled at how little attention he'd paid to himself over the past hour. He might be setting some sort of record. A personal best. Drake chuckled at the folly of it. Then he noticed the slow, steady trickle of gore sliding down his arm, dripping from his fingers.

Drake found the inner door leading to the garage and went looking for something that might help. He found it in about a minute—a partly used roll of duct tape. He managed to get the roll started, and using his left hand and teeth, he wrapped the fibrous, sticky tape around his wounded arm. Soon, the bleeding was stopped, or at least slowed.

Back to the phone, then. Carter picked up at once, and Drake told the tale.

At the end, Carter whistled. "This is bad. I should have known something like this could happen. I should have kept you out of it."

"Spare me. These guys already tried to kill me twice. You knew what could happen."

"I'm sorry."

"Get over it. I thought we had time. That was my mistake. The issue's closed. Change the subject."

A sigh came down the line. "Okay. What's next?"

"Get hold of Detective Akinyi for me and tell her what's what. I'll drop her name to the local cops when they get here, so they can hook up."

"I guess I can tell the deacons 'mission accomplished'?" Carter asked.

"Give them an update, sure. But this isn't over yet."

"Sure it is. Astrid's got to talk to the cops now. Her boyfriend too, if he can," said Carter. "From there on it'll be up to the FBI to roll up the rest of the operation."

"Sure, if they know enough to nail the people who made it all happen. I don't think they do. Astrid and Trace were middle management. Astrid can point you at Severins over at MIT, but it doesn't sound like she's got hard proof against him."

"Subpoena his phone records, then," said Carter. "That's easy."

"But he'd be too smart to use his own phone. A burner, probably. Maybe several of them. And that means another dead end."

"I suppose Akinyi could put Severins under surveillance," said Carter, "but he'll be expecting that."

From outside, Drake heard the wail of approaching sirens. "Cops are rolling up. Paramedics as well, I hope."

"You tell them there were shots fired?"

"Of course. We needed them here fast."

"So okay. You're a black man in a houseful of bleeding bodies, in a very white part of the world. Conduct yourself accordingly."

"Will do."

Drake hung up. He picked up a kitchen towel, walked to the front door, and unlocked it. Then he flung it open, shielding himself behind the swinging door as it opened, so that he could not be seen standing in the opening.

Brilliant light washed through the open door, illuminating the entire ground floor. Drake looked behind him into the interior space, and for the first time saw the other dead man, a big guy who'd been felled partway up the stairs by Trace's knife. Deacons attend many funerals, the bodies neat and clean, composed for sleep, with no sign of what had taken them. But the reason for this man's repose was sticking out of his neck, right above the breastbone, and the man's teeth, bared in pain or fear, were slimed with his own blood.

Could the cops see this through the doorway? More than likely. And so Drake was in no hurry to reveal himself. Instead he extended his left hand with the towel in it just beyond the edge of the doorway, waving it to make clear that the hand held only a towel.

"I'm unarmed," Drake yelled. "We've got people hurt in here."

"Show us your other hand!" It was a woman's voice and despite an adrenal harshness it sounded resolute and confident. Not the voice of a woman who was likely to shoot an unarmed suspect by mistake.

Drake slowly extended the other hand. "There you go. See? Now. I'm going to slowly step into the doorway, put my hands behind my head, turn around and walk backward out the door. Okay?"

Drake did as he'd promised, ignoring the pain from his wounded arm. As he cleared the door, two cops, both white, approached from either side. They grabbed his arms and hustled him over to a Ford Explorer bearing the badge of the Minnesota State Patrol. One of the two officers, a tall, thin man, nudged him against the side of the vehicle and gave him a thorough frisking while the other cop watched. She was rather short and her Smokey the Bear tan shirt was bulked out with too many hamburgers and a Kevlar vest. Maybe the same officer who'd called to him through the door. If his blackness took them aback they kept it to themselves.

Instead of cuffing him, they led Drake through the floodlight glare. Two EMT trucks were posted there. He'd said multiple victims, and they'd believed him. A medic stepped forward reaching for his duct-taped arm but Drake waved them away with his good hand. "Out at the boathouse. Two people shot. Another one's got an old stab wound to the chest. She's on the ground across from the jetty. And there's one in the house," he said. "They're all worse off than me."

Two of the medics grabbed large plastic cases and large flashlights and sprinted for the house, while two others unloaded a stretcher and followed at a slower pace. It was just Drake and the two cops now.

The nameplate on the female one read Salerno. She asked, "So where you from?"

"Boston."

"And how'd you happen to be way out here?"

"Looking for a friend of mine. She's from Boston too. Minneapolis, originally, but she moved east a while back."

"You find her?"

"She's the one with the stab wound."

"Did you stab her?"

"No."

"You shoot anybody?"

"No."

"Who did the shooting?"

"You'll find one in the house and one on the jetty. Trace stabbed one and shot the other. All I did was hide."

"You still got shot."

"Guy found me," said Drake.

"Mind if we check your hands for gunshot residue?"

"By all means."

"Got any ID?"

"Wallet's in my back pocket. Feel free."

The male officer's name tag read Barnes. He reached into Drake's pocket for his sodden wallet, flipped it open, and rifled through cards and papers. After a minute or so, he plucked one card from the mix. "*Boston Record*? You a journalist?"

"That's right."

"Got yourself quite a story here."

"Page One, guaranteed."

"So what happened?" asked Barnes.

"I don't mind telling you, but I suggest you get hold of someone at the FBI. They're going to want to hear this too."

"Nearest FBI office is Minneapolis," said Barnes. "They'll be a while, and we'd rather not wait. We'll talk on the way to the hospital."

THE HOSPITAL AT St. Cloud, about twenty miles southeast of Ebon Lake, looked like the real deal even by Boston standards. They rolled out a wheelchair for him, insisted that he use it. He settled into the seat and let himself be wheeled into the trauma center where a nurse swabbed Drake's hands, using a gunshot residue detection kit provided by Salerno.

Drake had ridden in the state police Explorer with Salerno and Barnes. The EMTs had told him that his injury, gaudy as it was, didn't rate an ambulance.

Astrid was exhausted, and the hole in her chest had come open once more. The techs would spend the ride keeping her warm and fending off septic shock with antibiotics.

Trace was worst of all. He'd left half his blood on the jetty. As for the intruders, both were dead. One by kitchen knife, one by gunshot. Trace had been thorough.

Drake had pulled no triggers, but for the rest of his life he'd be associated with a double killing. Maybe a third if Trace didn't recover. From that day on, the story would be the first thing his friends and colleagues would consider as they looked at him, the secret wonder behind the eyes of his fellow worshippers at Reliant.

Drake had spent years learning to measure the emotional radiation thrown off by those around him—the annoyance in an editor's eyes, the fear and worry on the face of a church member stricken with cancer. But now everyone who knew him would henceforth regard him as the survivor, the one who'd come *this* close. That would change everything. How long would it take him to recalibrate, to learn to say the right things when they gave him that lucky-to-be-alive look?

He saw the look in Salerno's eyes, and decided he'd better begin practicing right now.

"It's unfortunate. I never wanted anybody to die. Not even those two. But Trace, he saved our lives. You should give him some kind of medal."

"Maybe when we find out who he killed," Salerno said. "You got any idea who they are?"

"Never got a good look at them, thanks to Trace."

"They're in a fridge downstairs, if you want to."

"If you think it'll help."

Drake was wheeled into a basement room, midsized, with tiled floor and walls, and a stainless steel table with a drain in it. Embedded in one wall was the sort of walk-in refrigerator found in the kitchens of large restaurants. A couple of waiting attendants opened this refrigerator, and through its doorway, Drake saw shelves mounted against the walls, all but two of them empty.

He and the two police waited outside while a couple of attendants shoved a gurney into the cooler. They listened in silence to the scufflings and fumblings of the move, until the attendants emerged, their gurney now burdened with a zippered plastic sack. They moved near the stainless steel table, and someone flipped on the overhead lights while one of the attendants began unzipping the bag, and Drake rose from the wheelchair to get a good look.

The face was broad, muscular; the hair blond, and the dark, sullen eyes remained half-open, even though the man who'd once used those eyes was long gone.

Drake had seen the man before, but not at the lake house. "He was in Atlanta. Waiting for me at the library."

"Yeah, you mentioned that," said Officer Barnes. "So he's one of the guys who tried to kidnap you?" Barnes said.

"Not just kidnap. I think that's pretty clear by now."

"Zip him up, and bring us the other guy," Barnes said to one of the attendants, then turned to Drake. "Maybe his partner's over there in the icebox."

Drake nodded and swallowed the urge to say, *I hope so.*

A couple of minutes later, he got his wish. The second corpse was the tall, pockmarked man from Atlanta, brought by Chandra to the rendezvous to capture and kill Drake.

"They look pretty tough," said Salerno.

"I got lucky," Drake said. "When they moved on me, I ducked out an emergency door and ran into the subway. Lost them in the crowd."

Drake hated to lie. It was a concession to the other guy, an admission that he was strong enough to make you distort reality. And yet when the need arose, Drake was a cheerful and competent liar. In this case, the lie was far more plausible than the truth—his rescue by a secret society of church deacons.

Drake had told the cops everything he knew about everything else. His story, coupled with the recent bloodshed, ought to stir the relevant authorities to action. But would they be quick enough? Boo Hendricks's reasoning was as persuasive as ever. Whatever was going to happen was bound to happen soon. The police would investigate the killings in Minnesota and the attempted murder in Boston, but it might take months. Far too long.

"If we're done here," said Drake, "I believe the doctor said something about spending the night under observation."

Salerno grunted. "Yeah, we'll be keeping you under observation all right."

Ominous words, but Drake offered a cheerful reply. "Sure. Plus I need a phone. Left mine back at the house, and I've got to book a flight back to Boston."

"Better rethink your travel plans," said Barnes. "Detectives'll have plenty of questions for you, and you said something about FBI."

"Sure," replied Drake. "Set it up. I'll talk to you all day tomorrow. Give you a signed, sworn statement. And then I'll be moving on."

"You're a material witness," said Barnes.

"I'm a cooperating witness," said Drake.

Salerno grunted again.

"Just give me a phone, okay? I'm entitled."

"When you get to your room," said Barnes.

THEY WHEELED DRAKE to a sterile, egg-colored room, with a window that glowed orange from the lights of the hospital's parking lot. In the bathroom, Drake stripped off his grubby clothes, still damp at the seams from the lake water. He felt too filthy to sleep, and despite his wounded arm, he chanced a quick shower, washing himself with one hand and keeping the bandaged arm as dry as possible. There was one of those ridiculous hospital gowns for him to wear. But it was clean and dry.

There was a whiteboard opposite the bed, where nurses jotted patient notes; nothing about him yet. Above it a wall clock declared it was 3:00 a.m.

A nurse brought him pills—a worthless extra-strength Tylenol for pain and some antibiotics, which might prove equally worthless in the era of drug-resistant bacteria. Still, better than nothing.

A drab landline phone sat on an end table. Again, better than nothing.

Ginsburg answered on the third ring. "There are twenty-four hours in a day," he mumbled. "Why this one?"

"Because I'm about to go under for about eight hours, and I'll need a lawyer when I wake up."

"Who'd you kill?"

"Nobody. But I was there when it happened."

Ginsburg was silent for a few seconds.

"Anybody you know?"

"No, but I'd seen them before."

"Them?"

"Two dead. And they're liable to have company. The guy who killed them is barely hanging on. It could have been worse. And it almost was."

"Where'd all this happen?"

"At a place called Ebon Lake, a hundred miles or so northwest of Minneapolis."

"I thought you were in Atlanta."

"Just chasing the story."

"You writing it up?"

"Can't file anything just now, unless you're up for a libel suit. I think I know what's going on, but I can't prove it. But I'm writing up as much as I can. Anyway, I will be. I need some sleep first. And a new laptop. And some feeling in my right hand."

"You're hurt?"

"It's minor. But they had to stitch me up, and some local anesthetic was involved."

"This just gets better," said Ginsburg.

"I sure hope so," said Drake. "That's your department. Can you hook me up with a lawyer?"

"In Minnesota? I suppose so. The *Record*'s law firm has offices nation-wide, so it shouldn't be a problem. Unless you committed a crime. Then you're on your own."

"Nothing like that. I'm a material witness, and the state cops are think-ing about holding me."

"So cooperate. Tell them everything."

"I have been, but they're still looking at me funny. Hard to blame them, under the circumstances. But I'm hoping an attorney can lay it out for them. I'll swear out a complete statement of what happened and promise to show up for any subsequent proceedings. With the paper's law firm backing me up, they'll go for it."

"We're not going to cover for you if you're lying."

"Wouldn't expect you to."

Ginsburg paused, sighed. "Okay. I'll have it worked out by the time you wake up. Gimme a phone number."

Drake read it off. "But try not to use it, okay? I'm hoping to be unconscious till late morning at least. I'll ping you as soon as I'm alert. Meanwhile, see if there's anything about this on the wires. You can at least get that up on the *Record* website."

"Good idea. But we'd rather have your take."

"Better to start with something more objective. Maybe I can feed you some color later."

"Works for me," Ginsburg said. "Any idea when you'll get back?"

"Day after tomorrow, at the latest. I got business in Cambridge."

TO BED, THEN, without another thought about the dead men or Trace or even Astrid. Drake stretched out, closed his eyes, and disappeared.

He awoke at noon, his wounded arm splayed over the edge of the bed. Drake recited his morning prayer and added special thanks to the nurses for not waking him with tests and pills.

A pair of Minnesota State Patrol troopers were lurking outside his room, badge lanyards dangling against heavily muscled chests. They turned ominous eyes on Drake as he emerged from his room, and Drake could see that their surprised brains were just beginning to run the where-do-you-think-you're-going subroutine. But then they saw Drake walk right past the door on the right, the one that led out of the ward. Instead, he bore left, past the nurses' station, and the cops followed in silence. At the end of the corridor, Drake turned left again, kept going, then left again, all the way around the ward. He did this four more times, each time with a little more vigor. He'd begun with a shuffle and finished with confident strides.

The cops had long since lost interest and returned to their posts near Drake's door, still within visual range of the exit just in case. Still, they smiled and waved on his third pass and paid him almost no mind when he reentered his room.

Drake turned around, peered back at the cops. "Almost forgot," he said. "Any idea when the FBI shows up?"

"S'posed to be on the way," replied one of the officers. "That's all I know."

Drake nodded, returned to the room.

Drake's attorney showed up first. He was a grizzled, dowdy white guy dressed in rumpled gray and armed with a leather briefcase of fine quality but scuffed and tattered. Just the sort Drake needed, a long-timer who didn't care how he looked, to cops or clients.

He entered Drake's room alone, looked him over for a moment, reached out to shake Drake's uninjured left hand. "Name's Rick Stallworth," he said. "Your boss sent me over. What do you need?"

"A ticket out of here," Drake replied. "I'm a material witness, and I'm afraid they'll want to hold me."

"Any reason why they should?"

"None of my doing. I'm happy to cooperate with the investigation. I just need to get out of here today."

Stallworth nodded. "Want to swear out a statement?"

"Just what I had in mind."

"I'll make the arrangements."

AN FBI SPECIAL agent put in an appearance about half an hour later, a living cliché in black suit and blue tie. Asian, though. Not white. Time marches on.

Drake stepped out of his room, plopped into a wheelchair in the corridor, and watched the special agent huddling with Stallworth and the state patrol police. After a while, they called over a nurse. Not long after, Stall-

223

worth walked over.

"All set. They're getting us a room."

It took about half an hour more to set up, in a doctors' conference room just outside the ward entrance. Stallworth had brought along a small video camera and tripod. So had the FBI man. After they were both switched on, Drake raised his right hand, swore to God and the video lenses that he'd tell the truth, and then began telling the truth.

An hour later an attendant wheeled Drake out of the conference room and back into the ward. A plump, blonde woman at the nurses' station was just setting down her telephone.

"I'll be on my way soon, but I'd like to look in on my friends," said Drake. "Any chance?"

The plump one waved to a colleague, a tall, starchy-looking woman with forbidding eyes. This nurse replied that Astrid was unconscious and not to be roused.

"Fair enough," said Drake. "Maybe just a glimpse goodbye."

Astrid's lips were bigger than he'd remembered, the flesh puffy and covered with a scaly film of dried-out skin and saliva. The intravenous tube connected to her left arm was fed by three bags of fluid. The big one held sterile salt water, while the others were smaller, cloudier. Both contained names ending in *-mycin*. Antibiotics, Drake reckoned. Yet apart from the lips and the tubes and the total freakish stillness of her, Astrid seemed in pretty good shape.

Not so with Trace. He lay two floors below Astrid's, a tube down his throat, the lids of his half-open eyes twitching and squinting as if he were watching something awful. Not likely; one of the ICU nurses told Drake that Trace saw and felt nothing—and likely never would again.

The man who had brought Trace and Astrid to this place would be having a miserable day as well. Severins would probably know by now that Astrid had survived and his hired killers had not. If so, he'd know that Astrid now had every reason to tell her tale and that her words would throw a searchlight on her former mentor. Severins would be scared and eager for a way out.

Perhaps Drake could oblige him.

IT WAS 4:00 P.M. when a nurse handed him a paper sack of pain-killers and antibiotics and turned him loose. Before departing, Drake made one more call, this time to Madeleine. She answered on the second ring—was the woman always on duty?

Drake asked after late one-way flights from Minneapolis to Boston, and Madeleine offered him something on Southwest at 9:00 p.m. "Book it," said Drake, "and email me a reservation."

"I've done this before," she said, surly as ever.

Drake's clothes were stiff, filthy, and dappled here and there with blood. The taxi driver who'd pulled up outside the hospital gave him a doubtful look. But Drake had expected it and handed the man a fifty, first thing.

The cab ran Drake back to the house on Ebon Lake. There was yellow tape on the door and a marked Ford Explorer in the driveway just behind Drake's rental car. He walked over to the state trooper to ask about his stuff. The uncertain cop reached for his radio, then switched to a cell phone.

In a few minutes they'd worked it out. "Everything inside is crime scene," the officer said. "If you left it there it stays there. The car's okay, though. It's been sprayed and sampled. It's clean. No reason to hold it. Got the keys?"

Drake dangled a fob with a rental tag.

"All yours, sir."

TWENTY MINUTES LATER, Drake reached his motel. He paid for another night, but stayed just long enough to shower and don clean clothes from his backpack.

Next stop was a pharmacy, to get bandages and disinfectant for his arm. At the hospital, a doctor had predicted a decent recovery if he kept the wound clean. He could even expect to carry a lifelong memento of the encounter—a grim and stylish scar that would do him no harm with the ladies. "Beats the daylights out of a tattoo," the winking doctor said. "Or so I hear."

Drake cleared airport security by 7:00 p.m., two hours before takeoff. He snuggled into a booth at Surdyk's Flights and ordered appetizers and wine. He spread a garlic-laden tapenade on an oval of fresh bread, forked a little prosciutto on top, took a sip of chianti, and began to think.

On the drive to the airport Drake had punched radio buttons till he'd come across a news-talk station. The bloody doings at Ebon Lake were on heavy rotation. Though the story contained few details, the reporters had managed to learn something about two survivors, male and female, Minnesota natives, high school classmates. One, the male, was in a coma; the woman was in serious shape but expected to recover. There was talk of a third unidentified person involved in the affair, but this lucky fellow had been treated and released and wasn't considered a suspect.

In all, good news. Trace might yet survive and Astrid surely would. Better yet, the publicity made it more certain that she'd now be left alone. And he as well, probably. With Astrid expected to give up her secrets, there was no point in targeting a mere journalist.

So only one problem remained—stopping the attack. Because it was still going to happen. These people had gone too far to back away.

So they'd do the deed, and soon. If enough major banks were infected, it could be 2008 all over again. A worldwide recession. Not as spectacular as a jumbo jet slamming into a skyscraper but just as harmful.

Financial crime experts from the FBI and Treasury would soon be in touch with every bank in the world running Tannhauser's software, warning them to look out. How long before they'd put that message on the wire? A day, maybe two? Then that's all the time there was to keep whatever was happening from happening.

ON AN IMPULSE, he picked up the phone, called Madeleine.

"What now?"

"I could do with some cash," Drake said. "About ten thousand."

"Why not make it a million?" she drawled.

"Can I?"

"Not without a reason."

Drake told her what the money was for, and Madeleine was quiet for several seconds. Then she said, "Hmmm. Interesting. Maybe I better make a withdrawal myself. While there's time."

"So the ten thousand is no problem?"

"I'll make it twenty-five. If you're right, better to have a cushion."

"If you say so."

"I can have it couriered. Tell me where."

"My place in Boston." He gave her the address and hung up.

With nobody out to get him, Drake's condo was safe once more. Anyway, that was the theory, and he'd soon put it to the test.

HIS PHONE BUZZED. It was Efron. Just as well. Drake could use a little Israeli intelligence right now.

"Where have you been?" Efron sounded like a man on a treadmill. "I've called ten times."

"Long story," said Drake. "What's up? You sound excited."

"More like scared," said Efron. "It's started."

CHAPTER SIXTEEN

"When?" Drake asked.

"Sometime in the past day or so."

"Really? I haven't heard about any big financial panic."

"They're keeping it quiet. Besides, nothing's missing yet. Whoever's behind it, they haven't stolen a dime."

"Then what do you mean, it's started?"

"Remember how they'd want to wreck the bank's databases? Well, to make a proper job of it, they'd also have to destroy the backups, to make sure the data couldn't be easily reconstructed. That's just what's happening."

"Where?"

"A bank called Florida Central. Never heard of it, but it's a pretty good size. Assets of forty billion. Anyway, for reasons unknown to me, someone at the bank was rooting around in the digital archives. Research for some regulatory compliance matter, probably. But whatever the cause, thank God for it."

"Why? What did he find?"

"She, actually. Anyway, she discovered major corruption in the databases. Some records scrambled, others destroyed. All random. No rhyme, no reason. But thousands of accounts are affected. They may never be able to get them sorted out."

"Terrible."

"Yes, but not fatal. Anyway, it's not supposed to be. You know about Sheltered Harbor?"

"I've heard of it. Distributed offsite backup, guaranteed secure. Only it's not, right?"

"Right. This woman reported the problem, then punched up the Sheltered Harbor system to restore the damaged data. Only it was damaged too. It was in worse shape than the primary archive."

For the first time in hours, Drake felt the pain in his ripped arm, along with a sullen weariness beyond the reach of sleep. He'd failed.

"The worst has happened," he said to Efron.

"It's started to happen," Efron replied. "But on the other hand, there's no money missing yet. So there's still time. The folks at Treasury have set up a war room in Washington and another in Tampa. They've been rehearsing scenarios like this for the last ten years. They've got a playbook ready to go, and they can call a few audibles if they need to." Far from sounding hopeless or frustrated, Efron was as cheerful as a farm boy on a deer hunt.

"It won't be enough," said Drake.

"You don't know that. Those guys are good. There's a decent chance they'll contain it now that they've got a head start."

Drake's gloom lifted. Efron might be right. "Maybe this is just some kind of test run, aimed at making sure their attack will work."

"I figure the same," said Efron. "They could have screwed around with the archives for days before anybody noticed. It was just bad luck that the victim caught them at it."

"If you're right, there's still time to limit the damage."

"Not a lot of time. They wouldn't even try this unless their system was virtually complete. Now they know it works. They must also know that there's a chance they've been detected. But the banks can't have figured out how to fend off the attack, not this quickly. So the attackers have a few more days to make their move. And so do you."

That caught Drake by surprise. "Me?"

"You're tracking them, right?" Efron chuckled. "Quite an adventure. I envy you."

"Well, there's a nice front-page story in it."

"And payback for your lady friend."

Drake chuckled. "Payback's for morons. I wouldn't walk across the street for revenge."

"But you would get on a plane," said Efron "But I'll stop teasing you. It's rude. And you're busy. What's next?"

"Going to talk to Astrid's professor at MIT. He's in on it. Maybe there's still time to change his mind."

"Appeal to his better nature?" said Efron. "Or his patriotism, maybe? Good luck."

"You figure it's foreign action?"

"Probably. Either way, this professor has gone too far and risked too much to have a change of heart."

"You could be right, but what else can I try?"

"How about fear?"

A FEW MINUTES LATER, Drake broke the connection. His neglected prosciutto had gone dry and stiff, but it was still prosciutto. Drake applied more tapenade to his bread, added the cured ham, munched some more, sipped at his wine. Then he dialed his phone.

Carter picked up at once. "What you need?"

"A stingray or something like it. You got one lying around, and somebody who knows how to use it?"

"No, man. Not a chance." His voice was reluctant, abashed, like a man reluctant to fail a friend. "Those things are under lock and key. And you gotta have a warrant. Plus, I'd have to get somebody to run it for you. That's just not going to happen."

"In Atlanta Boo told me he knows people. You know, the kind with a very particular set of skills."

Carter was quiet for a bit. "Current or former?" he said at last.

"They better be current if they're going to get me a stingray. And I need one fast."

"Where and when?" said Carter, his tone more upbeat now that he was off the hook.

"Cambridge, tomorrow."

"Let me get hold of him and see what he says."

"You got a little time," said Drake. "I'm getting on a plane. Back in Boston around one a.m. Can you have something for me by morning?"

"That's up to Boo and his connections. He'll want more details on how we plan to use this thing."

"And I'll have them once I know he can get me what I need."

"Can you tell me what it's for?"

"Same thing you guys use it for."

"Us guys have to get a court order."

"A recent development. You used to just use 'em whenever you felt like it."

"It was pretty handy," said Carter, a trace of nostalgia in his voice. "All you had to do was ask the captain. Sometimes you didn't even ask. You just borrowed a technician's van and went to work. Not anymore."

"Damn ACLU," said Drake.

"Yeah," said a laughing Carter. "They ruin everything."

IT WAS A night flight like any other. Drake wedged himself into a middle seat of the cramped, musty plane and willed himself to sleep. It was usually a futile effort but not this time. The slam of the landing gear against the runway awakened him.

An Uber brought Drake back to Quincy. He got out two blocks from the condo, slung his backpack across his shoulders, and started walking, his head down despite the darkness. Quincy's streets were well enough lighted to reveal his face to any residual watchers. Drake expected none, but he'd lost nothing so far by being cautious. As he approached the entrance, he glanced at nearby cars but saw no signs they were occupied. A look at the glassed-in lobby proved nobody was lurking there. Still, Drake kept right on walking, just in case he'd missed something. A block beyond his home, he turned and trudged back, again eyeing the cars, but this time feeling foolish, like a child caught pretending to be a secret agent. At last, he stepped into the lobby, unlocked the door, called for an elevator, and rode it up.

The door of his apartment was intact. No smashed lock, no cop tape. Could they be waiting inside? If so, they could murder him after he'd used the bathroom.

Inside, all was as he'd left it. He stripped, used the toilet, and took a shower, not caring how damp the bandages got. Then he sat naked at the kitchen table, and armed with a steak knife, he cut the bandages away. The bullet gash, held tight by stitches, was ugly enough, but it didn't hurt much. That changed when Drake scrubbed it with cotton pads soaked with a cleaning solution. The disinfectant sting mixed with the rasping ache of torn flesh, and the ensuing ten minutes were a misery. But he got it done just the same, then rewrapped the site in gauze pads and surgical tape. The result was crude but sanitary. Drake finished up by finding the meds he'd obtained at the hospital. One ibuprofen for pain, one Cipro to fend off infection.

The nurse who'd done up his wound urged him to see his doctor in Boston. It was good advice, and Drake planned to take it one of these days.

But for now, he flopped naked onto his familiar bed. It still seemed to smell like Alicia. Impossible after so long, but the idea warmed Drake's moist skin. As he drifted off, he wondered what she would have made of his new scar.

HE WAS UP by ten thirty. There'd been no break-in during the night, further confirmation that Drake was in the clear. Severins and his masters no longer cared if he lived or died. *Just like Alicia*, Drake thought, but without bitterness.

Morning prayers first. Thanks for a safe night, along with a plea for the healing of Astrid and Trace. And of course, for time and skill enough to track down the people pulling the strings.

Drake prayed as he always did, without the fervor he often saw in his fellow deacons. He prayed because he believed, not because he cared. God made sense to him, and so he would strive to recognize God's plan for his life and to follow it. But the love of God or the fear of God or the wrath of God were mere abstractions. Drake preferred the promptings of duty.

The thought reminded him that he still worked for a newspaper. Over coffee, Drake fired up his new laptop and started typing up everything that had happened since Astrid was assaulted. He wrote without nuance or eloquence. He just wanted to get it all down while it was still clear in his head. He figured he'd email a copy to Ginsburg, just to prove he hadn't been loafing.

As he typed, he waited for Carter. His fellow deacon would call, of course. But his answer would likely be no.

It was no easy thing to lay hands on a stingray and with good reason. The machine could automatically intercept any cell phone call placed within a mile or two of the device and record the source, destination, and duration of each call.

But a stingray didn't capture the actual conversation, so police figured they didn't need a wiretap warrant to use it. For years, police departments just plugged them in, turned them on, and awaited the results.

It was different now. The highest court in Massachusetts had ruled that real-time cell phone tracing required a warrant. Not likely, then, that Carter could casually borrow one.

Still, he shut his mind against refusal. This was the only play left to him.

By twelve thirty, Drake was still typing and hoping. He picked up his phone once or twice, just to confirm that the ringer was turned on, that no text messages had arrived, that the battery was charged. None of it had mattered. The phone had stayed silent.

And then it came to life. An incoming call, from Carter. It barely rang once.

"Well?" asked Drake.

"You got it. Don't ask who or how. But there's a woman who'll do the work. You just need to tell her where to meet you and exactly what you're looking for."

"I got that."

"I hope you know how sensitive this is."

"Sensitive as in illegal."

"Totally."

"But nobody needs to know. God knows I'll never tell. And the information will never be used in court. Heck, I'm not even a cop. It's probably legal when I do it."

"Your . . . assistant has a day job where she wears a badge."

"And which three-letter agency did Boo borrow her from? FBI? ATF? NSA?"

"You'll never know. Just think of her as LEO and leave it at that."

"LEO?"

"Come on. Law Enforcement Officer. I thought you worked for a news-paper."

"Yeah, well, I'm not in the muscle end of the business. So how do I reach her?"

"Write this down." Carter read off a number, and Drake consigned it to a scrap of paper. "Call her and set up a meeting. She's waiting for you. And you better hurry. This is a one-time offer. You do this today or never."

THE VOICE ON the other end sounded white and middle-aged, raspy with hard use and ill-temper.

"My name?" she replied to Drake's first question. "What you gonna do? Write it down?"

"Okay," said Drake. "Dumb question." He decided not to seem even weaker by offering an apology.

"And don't tell me your name either. Too much information. I already know everything about you that I need to know. All I want from you is who and when and where."

"You know the Stata Center at MIT?"

"I can find it."

"I'll meet you there. It's a pretty busy neighborhood. You'll be in a ve-hicle?"

"I'll take the T."

"What about your equipment?"

"It'll take the T too."

"I thought you needed a van."

"Used to. Not anymore. These days, it's man-portable. Kinda heavy, but I've been hitting the gym."

"How will I know you?"

"I told you. I've been hitting the gym. Besides, I'll know you."

"Have we met?"

"Hardly. But I looked you up. You're moderately famous, at least on Google. Lots of photos. I'll spot you."

"Fair enough."

"So what am I looking for?"

"I'll know when I see it."

It amounted to an admission that he was desperate, like a gambler down to his last card, and Drake was ashamed of having said it. But then he heard the woman say, "That's always the way, isn't it? See you at three."

IF THERE'D BEEN another angry boyfriend on the Red Line, smacking around another helpless girlfriend, she'd have been on her own that day. Drake had other worries.

Was he too late? The biggest bank heist in history had already begun, and there might be no way of stopping it. This train ride and the visit to MIT might be a total waste of time.

Especially if Severins wasn't there. He was generally in his office this time of day, or so said his personal page on the university's website. A helpful admin in his department confirmed that he'd shown up for work that morning, but he might depart at any time. Perhaps he already had.

The Red Line, immune to Boston's choking traffic, was the quickest way to get there. In silence, Drake prayed for more speed.

HE ARRIVED AT Kendall-MIT half an hour later. Above ground, the air was as hot and thick as it had been down in the tunnel. He walked down Main and took a diagonal sidewalk that cut behind the biomedical laboratories of the Broad Institute and through a vast expanse of lawn.

He was about five hundred feet from the entrance to Stata when he felt, rather than heard, the sound of breathing close to his left ear.

"And about time too," she said in the same smoky voice. Drake turned and saw. She was as compact as a punctuation mark, with pale, much-wrinkled skin and the face of a whippet. Her jeans were scuffed and faded but intact, and her T-shirt advertised a candy bar. *Snickers*, it said, but he doubted there were any to be had from her.

"Keep walking," she told him. So the two of them strolled past the Stata main entrance and down Vassar Street.

"What's the range on that thing?" asked Drake.

"A mile or more depending on conditions," she replied. "You'll get everything."

"And you'll help with the analysis." It hadn't been posed as a question. Drake would need assistance in understanding the collected data.

"I don't know what you're looking for," she said.

"Same kind of stuff you look for every day. Nothing extreme, believe me."

"That means getting in touch with some phone companies."

"You know exactly which people to call. Bet you even go to their kids' birthday parties."

"I have, actually." She even snickered.

"So okay. It's three twenty-five. Start monitoring at around three thirty, and keep it going for, say, an hour. If it hasn't worked by then, it never will."

DRAKE LEFT HER, reversed course, and walked back to the front entrance of Stata, past the monument to the MIT policeman murdered by a couple of Islamist fanatics. He half-expected a couple of would-be murderers waiting for him. But that was foolishness. If they wanted him he'd already be in a dumpster or a ditch. Besides, he wasn't expected.

Still, Drake decided against the potential entrapment of the elevators and took the stairs. Severins's office door was wide open, and the man sat at the giant monitor, much as he had the night he'd commanded Drake's death. He didn't see Drake at first; no doubt the man's ability to shut out distractions had gotten him where he was today.

Drake didn't knock or greet but strolled right in and flopped into a chair. Severins looked up, and the shock on his face made Drake feel better than he had in days.

"We need to talk," Drake said. "Actually, you need to talk. Unless you're planning to spend the rest of your life in a federal prison."

He watched as Severins shut his mouth, smoothed his brow. Severins wasn't trying to pretend he hadn't been surprised. He was just taking command of himself, getting set for what came next. When Severins spoke, his voice was as placid as the waters of Ebon Lake.

"Not sure I understand you," the professor said. "Please explain."

"Your girlfriend is alive and well and talking. Your name has come up. Several times."

"Close the door," Severins said.

"I'd just as soon keep it open. Rather not be behind closed doors with you."

Severins shrugged, his hands in his lap. But the right hand was tapping against his thigh, a constant, rapid flutter of the fingers.

"My only wonder," said Drake, "is that she didn't open up before now. Afraid of prison, I guess. But there are worse fates. Your people convinced her of that."

"Convinced her? I don't understand."

"The bloodbath in Minnesota. You didn't know? Maybe the people you work for don't always keep you in the loop. By the way, how'd you know Astrid had checked out of the hospital? You bring her flowers? Or did you just phone once in a while to check up on her?"

Severins said nothing.

"Whatever," said Drake. "Anyway, you called your pals to warn them. Maybe you figured they'd move up the timeline on whatever it was they're trying. But they did more than that. They showed a lot more concern for her than you ever did. They went looking for Astrid. And they found her. So did I. Turns out I wasn't much help. It took an old boyfriend of hers to save Astrid. He saved us both. Made a mess doing it, but that's not my problem.

"So anyway, your friends tried for Astrid again. And they failed. But they died trying. And that's given Astrid a whole new perspective on things. Now she knows just how serious you people are about shutting her up. And she knows that her only defense is to not shut up. So she's telling the whole story to the FBI."

As he spoke, Drake saw the white man flush red. Message received.

Despite his evident dismay, the professor spoke in a calm voice. "I'm not responsible for whatever fables she's telling you. I'm sure they're lively enough. Astrid was maybe my most imaginative student. That's what I saw in her. Imagination. Not intelligence. For brains, she was only in the middle rank."

If the insult was supposed to anger Drake, it failed. "Granted, she wasn't as smart as you," he replied. "You knew enough to realize that this isn't the kind of deal you can walk away from."

Severins made a slight nod of the head, said not a word. Drake realized he really was smart. Smart enough, at least, to have guessed that Drake had switched on his phone's voice recorder and was capturing every word. And so Severins's words were as substantial as fog. The man said nothing that might incriminate him. He denied nothing, confirmed nothing. He had absorbed the surprise of seeing Drake and his dismay at the thought of Astrid giving evidence. He was as calm as the night he'd handed Drake over to his death.

"So you're still tight with your bosses, whoever they are. That'll bring you comfort in your old age, as you sit in a Supermax cell. This time tomorrow, you'll be talking to the FBI. Or you could start talking to me right now."

"What do you mean?" It was a harmless, noncommittal answer, as expected.

"Same pitch I tried to make Astrid," Drake said. "You can still get out from under. Tell your side of it to me. We'll get it in the *Record*. The publicity ought to buy you some security."

Severins chuckled. "I'm not in any danger, Mr. Drake."

"Given the mess you've created here in the US, I can't imagine your employers are pleased with you. Here's your chance to get clear of them."

Severins said nothing. But his face bore the stolid immobility of the committed. This was a man who'd dismissed all fear, all doubt. He had made up his mind.

"I'm busy, Mr. Drake. Anything else?"

Drake wanted out too. He was weary, sore, and angry. He wanted new bandages for his wounded arm and a full night's sleep. Besides, there was nothing more to say. It was Severins's turn to start talking, and the sooner Drake left, the sooner he'd begin.

So Drake rose, reached into his shirt pocket, withdrew a business card, and laid it with a soft snap onto Severins's desk. "Okay. But you change your mind, just reach out."

Without one word more, Drake walked out, found the staircase, headed down. On the way, he took out his smartphone, stopped the useless audio recorder, and checked the time. It was 3:38. The clock was running.

Outside, he found the listener in a large green park behind the building. She didn't have her laptop out, pecking in software commands. She wasn't gazing into the screen of her smartphone. In fact, she appeared to be doing nothing at all. She just lay on the lawn, her eyes closed, her head resting on her backpack.

"I left him at 3:38 p.m. I checked."

"Good."

"You getting good signal?"

The woman looked as if she'd been insulted. "Getting too many signals," she said. "This'll take a while. We'll be in touch." She opened her eyes, stared up at him. "Do us both a favor now, okay? Keep walking. I don't want to be seen with you."

For a foolish moment, Drake was offended. Then he came to his senses, grinned, and moved away without another word.

HE SAW NO point in making for the *Record* building. Too many questions would be asked, and he wasn't ready to give answers. So it was back to Quincy and a dinner of calamari and beer at the Foster House, before returning to his apartment.

It would take hours to get an answer from the stingray woman, and Drake considered spending the time in flight. He hadn't touched the Saitek joystick and throttle in a long time. A simple, simulated mission might do him good. The Logan-to-LaGuardia shuttle, perhaps, in a vintage Delta Airlines 727 trijet.

The last of the '27s had been retired years ago, for good cause. The plane was noisy, the barely insulated cockpit was icy at altitude, and with one engine too many, it guzzled fuel. But pilots had always loved the 727. It was fast and nimble yet flew so well at low speed you could land it on a postage stamp.

Drake relished an hour running touch-and-goes on LaGuardia Runway 31, perhaps with an easterly thirty-knot crosswind to keep him honest. But then he felt himself yawning and came to his senses. He needed sleep, not relaxation. It was 7:00 p.m., an odd time to go to bed. But if he were lucky, the next few days would be exhausting.

He rolled into bed, waiting for the chime of his phone. For a long time he heard nothing.

WHEN THE SOUND finally came, the room was dead black. Drake rolled out of bed, lifted the phone from the nightstand. It was 4:15 a.m., a better rest than he'd hoped for.

"You find anything?"

"You tell me," the listener rasped. "I sent you an email with my results. Didn't you see it?"

"Asleep," Drake said. "Don't you ever?"

"Not on a job."

"I admire your diligence. So okay, maybe you can give me a hint."

"I listened for ninety minutes, picked up about five dozen outgoing calls. Tracked the IMSIs for each phone. Nearly all of them had names attached. Sent you the list. You can tell me if your guy is among them. Six of the outgoing calls were made from burners. No idea who was making the calls. Those six may be your best bet."

"You got the numbers they called?"

"And the locations of the phones. It's possible to spoof call destination so that's another roll of the dice. But this whole thing's been a fishing expedition."

"Start to finish. I'll reply to your email, let you know if I got a bite."

"Don't bother. It's a one-time address. I'll never use it again. Or this phone either."

"I hope the guy I'm tracking isn't as cautious as you."

The woman chuckled. "Nobody is."

The line went dead.

DRAKE WOKE HIS dormant PC and logged into his personal email account. An inbound mail from a throwaway address included a sizable attached file, formatted as a spreadsheet.

Drake brought the file on board his local machine, launched Microsoft Excel. The first column was full of hash marks because the data field was too wide to fit. Drake enlarged the column and saw the lengthy alphanumeric strings. IMSI numbers. Not important in themselves. He widened the next column and saw a list of names, the owners of these phones. There was also a listing of the times the calls were placed.

Next came columns of information about the destination of each call—the phone numbers, along with whatever other data could be had. With landlines, IMSI was replaced by something better—the name and address of the person or business on the other end. When the call had gone to another cell phone there was sometimes a name associated with the account, but several were anonymous.

As for the location of the person being called, there was no exact address given. Instead, Drake saw a set of latitude and longitude numbers. Presumably the coordinates of the cell tower that had handled the call.

Drake scanned the caller names and found exactly what he'd expected. Severins was not to be found there. If he even owned a traceable phone, he hadn't used it during this ninety-minute stretch.

So if he called at all, it had been on a landline or on a burner phone. If it were a landline, Boo might have enough residual juice to get a look at the calling records, but it would be a heavy lift. Besides, if Severins had sense enough to avoid using his cell phone he'd avoid his office phone as well. So it was a burner or nothing.

Of the six burner calls, two were placed within fifteen minutes of Drake's visit to Severins. One was a call to the Legal Sea Food restaurant in Kendall Square, a couple of blocks away. No good. The other had gone to another burner. There was an IMSI, the number of the phone, and map coordinates.

Drake copied the latitude and longitude, then launched Google Maps and pasted in the numbers. The call had traveled about three hundred miles, to a spot in upstate New York. Binghamton.

It was light outside now, about 5:30 a.m. But Carter was an early riser, so Drake dialed the number.

"Anything?"

"Plenty. Whoever she was, that lady knew her stuff. She scooped up dozens of calls, most of them innocent. Maybe all of them."

"Any burners?"

"Several. One of them dialed out at three fifty p.m., not long after I left. The call lasted a good twenty minutes."

"To who?"

"No idea. Another burner. But the call terminated at a cell tower in Binghamton, New York. Rod Serling's hometown."

Carter chuckled. "So our guy was calling the *Twilight Zone*?"

"Might as well be if we can't narrow it down any better than this. I was thinking you could help. Hang on a sec." Drake's hands flickered over his keyboard, a dance that terminated with a decisive mouse click. "There. I just sent you the details on this particular call, including the phone number at the receiving end, in Binghamton. I want the phone records for this guy. Matter of fact, I want it for both guys. I mean, that's just one more subpoena, right?"

"Shouldn't be a problem. And it's related to an ongoing investigation so I don't think I'd be stepping too far out of line. What are you looking for?"

"Every incoming and outgoing call for the last, say, thirty days or so."

"Yeah. You might see some familiar names and faces."

"Exactly."

"I'll get on it. Might take half a day."

"Make it quicker. We're short on time."

OUT OF INSPIRATION, Drake forced himself out of the apartment and into the stairwell, where he trudged to the ground floor, then walked all the way up the building's sixteen stories, then down again, then up again, then down, then back up to his place on the eighth floor. He was sodden and breathless at the end of it.

Inside, he stripped naked, stepped out onto the balcony to cool, then showered and dressed.

There were eggs and a sealed package of smoked sausage in the fridge, grits in the pantry. It took Drake about fifteen minutes to slice and simmer and scramble himself a breakfast. He punched up CNN and stocked up on news as he ate. There was nothing about the collapse of a major bank. Perhaps the feds were hushing up the Florida crisis. Or perhaps it simply hadn't bubbled up to the consciousness of the editors at the *New York Times* or the AP or the *Wall Street Journal*, the agenda-setters who decided for the rest of America what was news.

They'd have a change of heart soon enough if the attack proved as bad as Drake expected.

Drake decided not to wait for word from Carter. He grabbed his phone, dialed Madeleine.

"I need Boston to Binghamton, New York," he said. "What are my options?"

"It'll take a few minutes."

"Fine," said Drake. "Call me back when you've got something."

Drake cut the connection, then sat there staring at the wall, breathing slowly, building up his nerve. He had the outline of a plan in his mind, an unlikely plan that might barely work but could easily be the end of him. And yet Drake couldn't come up with anything better.

And so he took up the phone again and called Efron.

"I need something," Drake said, "and I'm not even sure it exists."

As Drake explained, Efron was silent for half a minute, then gave out a deep, thrumming chuckle. "Oh yes," he said. "It exists. In Israel, we've got school kids who can do it."

"Good. How quick can you get me one?"

"How quick can you drive to Waltham?"

"I've got other things on my plate. How about you send a courier? I'll pick up the tab."

"Oh no," said Efron. "I've got this. Consider it a contribution to the war effort."

AT ONE O'CLOCK, the phone rang. Carter. At last.

"Got something for me?"

"I might have everything." There was good cheer in Carter's voice, and more. Exaltation. "That number in Binghamton? This isn't the first time it's reached out to Cambridge. I found three other calls to that number."

"It's our guy."

"I'd bet that way. Especially given the timing."

"Timing?"

"First call was June second."

Drake was silent for a time. "Am I missing something?"

"Quite a bit. When did they hit Astrid at the church?"

"Of course. June fourth. Two days later."

"And that guy in Germany?"

"Yeah, Brockmann. They got to him on June fourth too."

"So Severins sees the email thread, realizes that his allies are getting cold feet. He calls this guy in Binghamton, and within twenty-four hours, people are dying."

"Lemme guess. The second call came two days later. Right before I visited Severins."

"To arrange a proper greeting when you showed up."

"And the third was after Astrid went missing."

"Yep."

The mathematics of coincidence. Add three of them together, and you've got no coincidence at all.

"Any other calls?"

"One more, to Atlanta."

"I'm thinking a chat with Soul Man at Tannheuser Software."

"Yeah, fits the pattern."

"So who's answering the phone in Binghamton? Got any ideas?"

"Yeah, a pretty good one. All the calls hit the same cell tower, which just happens to be on the outskirts of an industrial park. Lots of low-rise buildings, warehouses mostly, but a few offices for rent.

"I reached out to the management company that runs the place. They've got a pretty interesting tenant there, an outfit called Cleft Consulting. Owner is a guy named Trower, Mason Trower. I ran the name and location through some legal databases, and his name popped up. Nothing criminal. A civil lawsuit, filed about five years ago against IBM Corp., claiming age discrimination. Settled out of court."

"Any juicy details in the court filings?"

"I'd say so. Before he was laid off, Trower was working on banking software. The lawsuit says his specialty was security. Claims he was assigned to harden a system called Sheltered Harbor. Some special system for backing up the bank's databases."

Drake was fully awake now. "I know what it means," he said.

"In the lawsuit, Trower said he was the guy who made it work. Claims IBM milked him dry, patented his best ideas, then right-sized him right out the door."

"There's a lot of that going around."

"IBM said different, of course. But the settlement's sealed. We'll never know who's lying. Either way, Trower ends up on the street. A fifty-seven-year-old software engineer who's probably never worn a hoodie in his life. Take him a while to find a new job, I'm thinking. And the settlement money from IBM wouldn't last him forever."

"So he becomes a consultant," said Drake. "That's what they all do."

"Consultants," Carter said. "We get 'em up in here sometimes, advising us on policing techniques. They put on a good show. But they hardly ever give you anything useful."

"It's useful to them. They get paid, right?"

"Yeah, and right now business is good. I talked to Trower's landlord. He's not sure what Cleft Consulting does, but they do it all night. Fair number of cars parked outside, twenty-four hours a day. Tell you something else. Landlord said the guy was there on a short-term lease, but he still paid to have Verizon come down the street and drop some fiber on him. Said he needed a really fast connection to satisfy his clients."

"That's a hint," said Drake. "So's the part about the short-term lease."

"Bet on it. Turns out the lease expires in a couple of weeks."

"God's way of telling us that this is about to go down."

"Like the *Titanic*," said Carter. "So our next move is . . . what?"

"You go back to rounding up gangbangers. Me, I'm off to Binghamton."

"Hold up a minute. Every time these two guys get on the phone together, something bad happens. For all you know, Severins ordered up another hit on you. Maybe it's time to lay low."

"Not likely. It's too late to gain anything by killing me. I told him the story's filed and ready to run, so there's no point."

"You really about to run a story?"

"Not quite yet. But next time you check your email, you'll find my notes. I take very good notes. Lots of detail."

"If they're that good, just hand them off to me and the FBI. You can step back now. You've done your part."

"And how long will it take the FBI to spin up an investigation? How long before they take steps?"

"A day or two."

"And we don't have that long. Whatever is happening has already started."

"Even if you're right, you can't do anything to stop it."

"I don't know. Maybe not. Maybe I'll think of something. Either way, they're getting stopped. I won't let this happen."

"It's a big step up the food chain. Long before you got close to this guy, they were trying to kill you. What do you think they'll do if you show up on his doorstep?"

"I suppose they'll try harder. Frankly, I haven't decided what to do. I just know I'm going to do something."

"But why do anything? You're lucky to be alive. Why not let it go?"

"You're asking me that? You're the one who recruited me."

"Not for this. Not for what you're doing now."

"What is that supposed to mean? These guys are about to commit the biggest bank heist in history. They nearly murdered a friend of mine. They nearly murdered me. They just about killed a brave guy who saved my life and Astrid's. And they desecrated my church. They desecrated my church. And I'm doing something about it. I'm doing something about all of it. I thought that's what you wanted me to do. If it's not, you can take your money and your plane tickets and your three-letter friends and fuck off. I got this."

Drake fell silent after this, and for a time, neither he nor Carter spoke. After a while, Carter sighed. "Yeah. Point taken. There's a bright side, though. Looks like this whole sociopath thing of yours is in remission. You don't just want revenge for yourself. You want it for Astrid too, and even for Trace. That's a big boost in empathy. You been taking pills or something?"

"No, man," said Drake. "All natural."

"Good," said Carter. Then, "So you still going?"

"On the next thing smoking."

CHAPTER SEVENTEEN

DRAKE WAS SEATED in the back of the plane, until a shame-faced flight attendant asked with needless humility if he wouldn't mind riding up nearer to the cockpit.

"Weight and balance issues," the young man said.

It was that kind of airplane, a Canada-built twinjet with sixty seats, fewer than half of them occupied.

Drake assured the attendant that he didn't mind a bit. The attendant, by way of apology, grabbed his backpack from the overhead and led the way to a seat just ahead of the left wing. The seats up here were spaced farther apart for more leg room. A definite upgrade.

Not long after, the plane was pushed back from the gate. It was a complex trip. First to Philadelphia, then Ithaca, then fifty miles by rented car to Binghamton, a town too small to rate its own airport.

The courier dispatched by Efron had delivered an envelope that was now tucked inside Drake's backpack. Now Drake must make a delivery of his own and place the contents of the envelope where they would do the most good.

If Efron was right, the attack on Florida Central Bank was a trial run. But by now the timetable for the main event would have been shoved as far forward as the criminals dared. Maybe even tonight.

The police were in the loop now, but they might not be ready to make a move for days or weeks. Not nearly soon enough.

But Drake wasn't bound by niceties like probable cause or judicial review. There was nothing to stop him but death, or the fear of it. And though Drake still felt that fear, the feeling no longer dismayed him. It was like a mild headache now, painful but irrelevant. All his life, Drake had felt indifferent to the fate of others. Now he'd lost interest in his own.

The realization worried Drake, and he offered up a prayer. Then he snuggled back into his seat for a nap. It might be the last good rest in some time.

HE AWOKE UPON touchdown in Philadelphia, where he spread himself across a row of seats at the gate for his connecting flight and dozed again.

It was sheer good luck that a gate attendant spotted him just before closing the jetway door. She jarred Drake awake, and he staggered onto the plane and into a seat. It was a turboprop this time, and the hum of the props knocked Drake out one more time as the plane turned toward Ithaca.

The plane touched down at 8:00 p.m., and Drake hustled over to the Avis lot and grabbed a Toyota Corolla, tossing his backpack into the trunk. He was feeling fresh, and there was little traffic. His destination, Cleft Consulting, was an hour away down a two-lane highway that wended past ranch-style homes and wooded hills, or so his preliminary research had told him. Just now there was virtually nothing to see.

He had an hour to think and to plan, but such things were beyond Drake. He was about to do something dangerous and illegal, and having had little experience in such matters, he didn't know what to plan for.

But Drake knew he'd need tools, the sort you couldn't carry onto an airplane without hard looks and tough questions from TSA. So he launched Google Maps on his phone and found the address of a home improvement store, about seven miles southwest of the airport.

It was a cavernous place, brilliant with fluorescent light. The air smelled of paint and plastic and fresh-cut wood, and the blue-clad workers who staffed the place surprised Drake by their delight at seeing him. One of them, a short middle-aged woman with stiff, blonde hair, guided Drake from aisle to aisle as he sought out the tools for the job—a rubber mallet, a short crowbar, duct tape, work gloves.

The bright, clean efficiency of the place, the sweet, fresh smell, the kind attention of the clerk all elevated Drake's spirits. It was hard to believe that anything too awful could happen in a world occupied by such a place as this.

Drake's good cheer lasted long enough to carry him out of the store's parking lot and onto the state highway. The sun was long gone now, and he rolled south into darkness.

Now at last, he was ready, and the thought banished Drake's recent optimism. But there was no doubt in him either.

His toolkit was complete. And he'd copied all his notes to Dropbox, with share links to Ginsburg at the *Record*, to Carter, and even to Madeleine and Boo Hendricks. He'd written up everything he knew about the Largent affair—the attack on Astrid, the attempt on his life in Atlanta, the confessions of Astrid and Trace, the bloody showdown at a Minnesota lake. And his impending visit to Cleft.

It wasn't the whole truth, to be sure, for there wasn't a word about the deacons. The document would therefore raise questions for its more thoughtful readers. For example, how had Drake managed to escape the Atlanta trap? He couldn't tell the truth about that, and he wouldn't put a lie in the *Record*. And how had he tracked the conspirators to an obscure industrial park in upstate New York?

Good questions, the sort he'd ask himself if writing a story about all this. Drake had to hope that nobody would ask them, at least not until he'd been proven right. At that point, the questions would probably never be asked. With suspects in hand, who would care?

In any case, the document left a trail for others to follow. The story wouldn't go cold, whatever became of him.

Beyond that, there was too much Drake did not know. The layout of the place, for instance, and how many people were there. In the absence of such information, he'd have to be on site before deciding on his best move.

Drake had no access to a gun and was glad of it. He might reach for it in fear or anger, and then somebody would die. He would, most probably. He'd have to rely on the nonlethal gadgets he'd brought along and on his native ability to improvise. These were all the help he had.

At that thought, he began to pray, a vague, wordless prayer that took up the final ten miles of the journey. Because Drake knew from hard experience that he wasn't ready for this.

Then we're stupid and we'll die. The line from an old film came to him, and the recollection that the character who'd said it in the movie really did die.

Lucky for Drake that this was not a film. If there was anything to the faith he had embraced, then he had to believe that he was under God's care and would receive grace to do right when the time came.

It seemed to Drake such an absurd idea that he embraced it all the harder. He felt his confidence surging within him and began to wonder if this might be the way some men became fanatics, out of a desire to feel all the time what Drake was feeling just then.

Perhaps it was the faith of a sociopath, a man so attuned to self and so indifferent to others that he supposed his earthly affairs merited personal attention from the Lord of the Universe.

Yet the gospels held this very absurdity at their core. Either it was true or it was not. It seemed as good a time as any to find out.

THE GPS ALERTED him to his destination about thirty seconds before he saw the sign—Cayuga Industrial Park—in crisp white letters against a green background.

Drake turned left into the driveway, dark with tree shadow. Soon enough, it curved into a large blacktopped parking lot adjacent to several low-rise structures. None was more than three stories high, and their brick walls glowed amber under bright sodium lights.

An industrial park like any other. A spare, unglamorous place where the rents are cheap and the neighbors mind their business. Drake had visited dozens over the years, and he almost always got lost. There were no signs on the buildings, no clue about their occupants. Just big white numbers painted on the corner nearest the parking lot—*1, 2, 3, 4, 5, 6.*

Drake stopped the car, glanced left. As he'd expected, a large sign bore a tenant directory. Cleft Consulting occupied Building 5, perhaps five hundred feet farther in. The lights down there showed a smattering of parked cars, the only vehicles to be seen in the whole lot.

Drake killed his headlights and rolled into a parking slot near Building 1, choosing a spot out of sight of anyone in Building 5 who might be looking. He climbed out, backpack in hand, and began walking toward the rear of Building 1. As he'd hoped, a service road ran behind it, with loading dock and a trash dumpster. The left side of the road tailed off into a shadowland of brush and trees. A fellow might move back and forth in there, his presence revealed only by the noise of his thrashing.

Instead, Drake clung to the right side of the road, close to Building 1, where he could move fast and quietly, and a narrow slash of shadow offered a little concealment. Building 1 showed a few windows at the first and second floors, as well as a couple at basement. Every window was dark.

There was a wide expanse of illuminated pavement between Buildings 3 and 5. Drake doubted that anyone was watching, but he ducked into the greenery on the left side of the service road and made his way through the leafy darkness. The ground behind the buildings sloped upward, as if the office park had been built in a valley. As he walked, he rose higher and higher so that he now looked down at the parking lot from an elevation of eight or ten feet. He liked the view, and so he kept going through the woods, guided by the lights of the lot.

Soon he had Building 5 ahead on his right. Drake paused while still parallel with Building 3, an angle that showed him Building 5's front door and seven cars in the parking lot. A mundane sampling of Toyotas, Hondas, and Hyundais, unusual only for being there at such an hour.

No telling how many people were inside; too many, for sure. Drake needed to depopulate the place. Or failing that, he needed to distract the occupants.

He thought a minute, then pulled out his cell phone. There was a decent enough signal here, making it easy for him to install an SMS app. That done, he punched up the cellular edition of Microsoft Excel and examined the spreadsheet of phone calls captured by the stingray. He'd already highlighted the entry he wanted, the one from Severins's burner to Trower's. Swapping apps, Drake began punching the two numbers into the SMS app he'd just installed.

It was a spoofer, a seedy but legal gimmick that would make a text message seem to come from a different phone than the one that had dispatched it. This message would appear to come from the burner phone that Severins had used to call Trower right after Drake's visit.

After confirming he'd entered the correct numbers, Drake paused to think. What message should he send? Something terse—the words of a surprised and frightened man, words that would inspire panic in the guilty-minded.

After a few seconds, he smiled to himself, then began tapping the screen. Just three words, *feds here scatter.* All in lowercase from a man with no time for the shift key.

It might not work. Trower might be too busy to notice the incoming text, or maybe he'd realize this one was a spoof; for all Drake knew, the two men might have a prearranged panic signal made up of meaningless words like *strawberry letter 23.* Or maybe he'd make a callback to Severins to confirm the message. No—not at all likely. Whoever Trower was, stupidity would have no place in his character. And phoning a criminal confederate just captured by the police would be an act of profound stupidity.

Besides, even if Trower realized the text hadn't come from Severins, it would still convey the same message . . . You're busted.

How would Trower respond? No way to know. Drake hit Send, offered a silent prayer as his message went its way, then settled in to wait.

He'd figured on half an hour before he'd give up and think of something else. But it never came to that.

Within fifteen minutes, Drake saw the building's lobby doors swing open. Two men came out, stocky men wearing black windbreakers, black slacks, black shoes. Their pale faces gleamed under the orange light. Another man emerged from behind them, a white man with even whiter hair, dressed in a plaid shirt, jeans and walking boots. While the first two men gazed back and forth, leaning forward a little as if preparing to leap at someone, the white-haired man strode back and forth, peering into the surrounding darkness. He shaded his eyes from the sodium glare with a hand held over his eyes, like a Comanche scout from a John Ford western.

The man was looking for the police who might at that moment be surrounding the place. The police who weren't there.

Was it Trower? Whoever it was, he was scared. It showed in his quick, nervous steps, the rapid motions of his head as he scanned the tree line for threats. The men in black, for their part, moved nothing but their heads. They were searching too, and with no more success than the white-haired man. But these two knew how. Their heads moved in sync, each of them moving at the same moment after having spent exactly the same several seconds gazing at a sector. And even at a hundred yards distance, Drake could see that their fields of vision rarely overlapped. Each man inspected his own separate zone, for maximum coverage in minimum time.

Drake's heart sank as he saw it. These people, or at least two of them, knew what they were doing. Former police or more likely former soldiers, people accustomed to standing watches on hostile land. If he somehow managed to get inside Building 5, those were the people he'd find waiting for him.

But he'd find at least two fewer of them if he entered now.

Drake got to his feet, as quietly as he could and careful not to rustle any nearby branches.

In the parking lot, he saw the white-haired man talking to one of the black-jacketed professionals. To his surprise, Drake could hear some of the words, driven over the distance by anger and fear.

"Not me!" the white-haired man shouted. "You do what you want, but when they get here, I'm not gonna be here!"

The man turned and began walking toward one of the parked cars, a drab and weary old Camry.

He never made it.

CHAPTER EIGHTEEN

THE BLACK-JACKETED target of the old man's wrath didn't reply in kind; he hardly reacted at all. Instead, he glanced at the other muscular man and nodded.

His partner stepped in front of the man in plaid and did something with
his hands. He did it fast, whatever it was, so that Drake did not see the nature of it, only the result. The plaid man staggered, slumped, dropped into
the waiting arms of his assailant.

Drake saw no blood, no wounds. There was no way to tell whether the
man was dead or just stunned.

The big man in black squatted, tossed the limp old man over his shoulder, turned, and walked back toward the building. In the doorway, Drake
could make out two other faces, grizzled and pale. They stepped back and
out of sight, as the man carried his victim inside. His partner soon followed, and the door closed.

Had Drake's text caused that? Perhaps.

But how soon would the effect of Drake's text wear off? For the next
few minutes the remaining crew would probably get a motivational speech,
something about the virtues of courage and persistence. And about the
ugly consequences of attempted desertion.

They'd all be gathered in one place to hear this lecture. And sure enough,
Drake saw the lights go on between the slits of venetian blinds covering a
large window at the front of the building, not too far from the door. Probably a conference room for all-hands meetings.

For the next few minutes at least, everyone would be in that room.

Drake began moving again, tracking through the trees alongside the rear of Building 5, eyeing the exterior, looking for the right spot. He saw it near the far corner of the structure, just above the pavement. It was a narrow window, connecting to the basement.

Perhaps he could pry it open with the crowbar? No time. He needed something quicker.

Drake threw aside caution, scrambled out of the trees, across the pavement and over to the window. There was shadow here, enough to shield him from casual watchers. But there'd been nothing casual about the men in black. He'd need speed and silence to make this work.

Drake opened his bag and took out some duct tape. He was dismayed by the sharp tearing noise it made coming off the roll. Through gritted teeth, he carried on, applying tape to the window glass in overlapping strips. The job was done in under a minute.

Time for more noise. Drake put back the tape and extracted the mallet, its heavy striking surface made of thick white rubber. About as quiet as a hammer could be.

But would it be quiet enough? It would depend on how things stood inside with the hacking crew, and the enforcers. What were they doing now? Still with the pep talk? Or had the enforcers merely ordered their terrorized captives back to work?

It didn't matter. Drake was committed. He'd get his answers on the inside.

He hauled his arm back and gave a single vicious blow to the upper right corner of the window. It crushed under the impact. There was only a slight rattle of shattered glass, thanks to the duct tape, but the muffled thud of the hammer would have alerted anyone within ten yards.

No help for it. Drake struck three more times, hard, until he felt the entire window cave and slump. The duct-taped remnants fell away from the frame and into the blankness of the un-illuminated room.

Drake donned a pair of work gloves. He tossed the hammer through the opening, then the bag. Drake used his gloved hands to remove the last few shards of glass from the frame, then climbed through. His footfalls resounded off concrete and cinderblock. The dim light from the window confirmed that the room was empty.

Drake put away the work gloves, found the door, turned the knob, eased it open.

Ahead lay a corridor that seemed to run the length of the building. A narrow corridor, its cinderblock walls and buffed concrete floor were lit by dim incandescent bulbs mounted every ten feet. It was congested in places by stacks of cardboard boxes bearing familiar brand names—Dell, HP, Cisco. Equipment for their data center.

The nearest door, on his left, had a panic bar for unlocking, and a red EXIT sign just above it. The way up.

Drake looked to the door, tested the outer knob. As he'd expected it was set to lock. He reached back into the bag, grabbed the duct tape, and tore off a strip to block the latch and keep it from springing back into the doorframe. His way out.

Drake approached the emergency exit, glanced through its narrow window, and saw what he'd expected to see—a stairwell going up toward the first floor. He pressed the panic bar. No fire alarm sounded, and he passed in, let the door close behind him. Then up the stairs to the first floor.

He'd feared that the door might have been locked against him, but it wasn't. It swung in, and Drake peered around the corner and toward the front of the building.

Nobody was in sight. But from down the corridor, Drake heard the barely audible sounds of speech. The words sounded deep, resonant, a little weary. The voice was attenuated by distance, and so Drake could hear only a few distinct words, uttered with extra force. "Almost there," he heard the speaker say. "Almost there."

The corridor was more brightly lit and floored with cheap commercial carpet. About ten feet down and to his right, Drake saw an open doorway. Over the muffled sounds of speech, he could hear the purr of small cooling fans.

Drake inhaled, held it, stepped through the door. He was fully exposed and the worst of it was waiting for the door to quietly swing closed behind him. As soon as it had, Drake sprinted across the corridor and into the room.

It was a generic sort of room of middling size. In the center sat six unoccupied desks, facing each other to form a central work area, where each man seated at one of the desks could see his colleagues at a glance. A bundle of data cables rose from the opening at the center of the gathered desks and were gathered into a cable tray that ran along the ceiling. The cables led to a pair of black steel equipment racks that stood along the left wall. The racks were full of gear, sheathed in anonymous black. Servers, quite a few of them, and probably virtualized, to give ten machines the power of a hundred or more.

Command and control.

Upon each desk sat two flat monitors, along with a keyboard, a mouse, and a laptop plugged into a docking station. Nothing more, not even scraps of paper.

He glanced at the monitors on the nearest desk, expecting to recognize nothing. Instead, amid the smattering of open windows, he spotted a mIRC client, the same software he'd often used in pre-Facebook days for live chats with fellow aviation gamers. The program connected to Internet Relay Chat, an archaic method for sending text messages, but one with global reach. No doubt the malware under Trower's command was sending status reports via IRC and dialing in from time to time for further instructions.

So the commands that would begin the bank assault would be transmitted from here, maybe right over that keyboard. Some commands had already been sent to the bank in Florida. And now they were preparing to launch the next phase, whatever that was. Or perhaps he was too late and the cash was already flowing.

From down the corridor came more muffled voices and rising above them all a brisk, shrill bark. "Enough of all this! You finish this! Right now!"

No more time. The crew would be stepping into the corridor at any moment. Whatever Drake could do to stop them must be done in just a few seconds. And that left him a single option. Efron's option.

Reaching into his pocket, he withdrew the USB key that Efron had sent to him via messenger. He pulled back the plastic cover that sheathed the metal plug. With his left hand, he felt the back of the laptop on the desk facing him until his fingers identified an empty rectangle cut into the plastic. Then with his right hand, he inserted the key.

He gazed down at the screen, waiting to see if something would happen. And nothing did.

Just what he'd been told to expect. But then, it might mean that the hackers had deactivated their USB ports, to prevent just this kind of attack. The prudent thing to do. But they had no reason to guard against an inside job, and so Drake was gambling that they hadn't. If he were wrong, a lot of money was going to end up in the wrong hands, and a lot of major banks would be driven to the brink of collapse.

If that happened, Drake would read all about it in the papers. Or not at all, if he didn't get out of here.

He turned back to the doorway, poked out his head, glanced down the corridor, and saw the end of all his luck and all his hope.

About ten feet away stood the white-haired man in the plaid shirt, the man who'd been a limp heap of flesh minutes earlier. His face was pale and bruised, and he leaned against the wall trembling and gasping. At the sight of Drake, his eyes widened and his lips drew back in a silent shout. What was in his eyes? Fright? Rage?

The face of the black-jacketed man behind the white-haired man showed no such ambiguity as he strode down the corridor toward Drake. There was surprise on the man's broad Asiatic face, but only for a moment, because this was a man who'd been trained to expect surprises. Now his face showed nothing but a solemn concentration as he closed the distance between himself and Drake.

Outside, in the trees, Drake had not been able to see exactly what had been done to the white man, to make him fall so limp, so fast. Now he saw.

CHAPTER NINETEEN

DRAKE NEVER LOST consciousness. Instead, it was a loss of agency, an instantaneous disabling of arms and legs and will. And in exchange for his loss, a deep, abysmal pain. If Drake had been able, he'd have screamed.

He fell into the big man's arms, just as his previous victim had done and felt his feet dragging down the corridor and toward the conference room. His head was buried in his assailant's chest, half-smothering him. The little air he got came with the musky smell of the man's body and clothing. An animal smell, nauseating.

Drake felt himself falling backward then, unable to save himself from impact with the floor, but it didn't come to that. Instead, he landed in a chair that rolled and swiveled beneath him.

Harsh fluorescent light lent a slight bluish cast to the room, which was painted in the usual corporate beige, except where whiteboards covered one long wall. As Drake felt himself regaining control of his muscles, he moved his right arm and nudged the edge of a conference table. His hand felt for it and touched thick, polished wood. Arrayed around it were more chairs like his own, a couple of them occupied. They were white men, and not a year less than fifty. There was defiance in their faces as they glared back at him. And something more. They also seemed whipped. Scared.

To one side of the table, others stood, gazing down at him. Three more white men, including the bruised one who'd been worked over in the parking lot. And then there were the two muscular black-clad men. Chinese perhaps, or Korean. One was a little shorter than the other, with an indented scar along his left cheek that looked as if the flesh beneath had been torn out.

The battered white man looked like Drake felt, his body swaying like a man who'd had too many. He reached out toward an empty chair, then paused to glance at one of the big black-clad men. That one gave a small, precise nod, and the old man pulled the chair around to face Drake, then fell into it about as gracefully as Drake had.

His curiosity overcoming his pain, Drake managed to gasp out, "You . . . Trower?"

The man nodded. The bruise on his face was a big one, purpling his skin from cheekbone to lip, and so it must have hurt the old man to smirk at him, as he was doing now. "Message was from you, right?" he said.

Drake just nodded.

"No cops?" the man said.

Drake inhaled hard, focused on moving his jaw and lips. "Not yet," he said. "Coming, though. They know I'm here. Just a matter of time."

The scarred black-clad man strode forward and slapped Drake hard. "Who you tell?" he bellowed. "Who you tell?"

When his head stopped ringing, Drake looked at the man. There was no sign of rage. The hard blow and the loud yell were tactics meant to jolt him into compliance. As blood drooled from his lips, Drake felt a certain respect for the man. A professional.

"I told a friend of mine, back in Boston."

"He'll call police." It was a blunt statement of fact, not a question.

"He'll call police. Missing persons report. I'm missing."

The scarred man nodded. "So why are you here?" he asked. "Why not just send the police?"

"Not enough evidence," Drake said.

"Still not enough evidence, then. You got nothing. And we got you."

"They'll come anyway. Looking for me."

The interrogator turned to his partner. Without a word, he raised an eyebrow.

The other, taller man in black shook his head. "Doesn't matter," he said, in the same clotted accent. "Local cops. Just sidearms. We can handle it."

These people were willing to tangle with the police, perhaps even kill them. They'd meet them outside, lure them in, then make them disappear.

Which would be crazy. The cops would soon be missed and more would come. It would buy them no more than an additional hour. It would only make sense if they'd already pushed the button. Largent must be at work even now, extracting billions from bank after bank. How much more could they steal with an extra hour?

And afterward, they'd run. At least the two Asian guys would run. They might have other plans for the others, and for him.

Drake had no chance against the two huge men. Even if he'd had a pistol in his pocket, he wouldn't have liked the odds. So there was nothing to do except sit back and wait for the cavalry. If the cops were smart, they wouldn't press the issue. They'd accept the claim that Drake was not inside, then back off and call for reinforcements. If not, they'd end up in a heap.

"Come on," the interrogator barked, then turned to the wounded white man and said, "You too."

Drake found he could stand, after a fashion. He shambled a few steps, then looked up, waiting to be told where to go.

"You know the way," said the interrogator. Back to the control room.

Drake staggered out into the hallway, with Trower close behind. Leaning against the wall for support, he felt his shirt scuffing against the cinderblock as he walked. When he reached the open doorway, Drake nearly lost his balance and toppled onto the floor of the room, but he caught himself just in time, stumbled in, and flopped into a straight-backed chair next to the rackful of servers. He looked up to see the rest of the party following. Trower made an effort at dignity as he settled into the foremost of the swivel chairs at the six-sided desk.

The pain was easing, and a tingling began in his arms and legs. Drake flexed them a little, feeling his limbs once again responding to his commands. A few more minutes and he'd be able to move with something like his former dexterity. He'd scamper if the chance arose. But not through a door still clotted with aging white guys and cool, brutish Asians.

Drake watched as the other five middle-aged men filtered over to their desks. All of them stared at Trower like members of an orchestra awaiting the signal to begin.

It came not from Trower, but from the interrogator. "Back to work. Quickly."

Heads bowed, keys clicked. Drake stared at the interrogator and saw something more than cool professionalism. There was arrogance as well. He was not perfect.

The Asian stepped out into the hallway, and Drake saw him beckon to his partner. A private huddle. Perhaps a conference on the best strategy for handling the cops or maybe on the easiest way to dispose of a roomful of inconvenient Americans.

Whatever the reason for their departure, it bought a little time, and an opportunity to hold a conference of his own. Drake gestured to Trower. "Chinese? Japanese? Koreans?" he whispered.

"Koreans, actually," Trower said. "North Koreans."

Drake sighed, shrugged. "Figures. And today's the day you pull the trigger."

"It's been pulled," said Trower. "We've got a list of banks, and we'll be hitting them all over the next two hours." He glanced at the monitor behind him. "I'm tracking our withdrawals. Here you go: Montrose Bank—that's a big regional out of Colorado—$850 million gone, and the archival records scrambled to cover our traces. There's another half-billion out of South Side Bank in Chicago. And Duerson Bank in Kentucky is checking in. We scored a hundred million from that one.

"Can you imagine the looks on their faces as they watch the cash draining away? Can you imagine? It's a masterpiece."

It must have hurt Trower to do it, but his lips rolled into a proud smile.

"And here you were getting ready to make a run for it," said Drake.

Trower's face fell. "Maybe I did panic a little bit."

"Not panic. Good sense. They're coming."

"Just one more hour, and we'll have more money than Microsoft."

"And you'll never spend a dime of it in peace."

Trower frowned at that, but his eyes grew hard. "I'll take that chance."

"Yeah, now that you have to. Your friends made up your mind for you."

"Yeah, well, you're right about that. I woulda been gone. I can't be doing any time. Not at my age. So I panicked. I'm okay now. Nothing's broken." He looked at his lap for a few seconds, breathed hard. "Back in the day, I coulda kicked that guy's ass. Now look at me."

"You'll look worse in two hours," Drake said. "When they've got all the money transferred to Pyongyang or wherever. What do you think they'll do with you then?"

"Pay us our cut," said Trower. "A fat cut. Five percent. Doesn't sound like much till you ask, what's five percent of five billion?" The smile was back, but it seemed hollow.

"Bullets are cheaper, and knives are cheaper yet. These guys like knives."

"No reason to kill us," whispered Trower. "We'd never tell the cops."

"Not till you're arrested. Then comes the immunity offer. Give us the ringleader and you'll walk. One of you would take that deal, probably all of you. They know it. So you die. Tonight."

Trower's eyes flinched downward. He rotated his chair back toward his monitors, began sliding the mouse with precise little movements. But as Drake watched, the motions of his mouse hand became larger, his clicks at the button more aggressive. Drake knew the signs; he reacted much the same way whenever a familiar computer failed him.

Trower looked up and over the top of his monitor for a couple of seconds. Drake saw the side of his jaw move as if to speak, but before anything emerged, another of the white men spoke. From where Drake sat, he could see the man's furrowed brow and staring eyes. "Mason, what's up with this?" the man said. "I'm getting nothing."

"Me either," said another of the men. "I was sending the go-code to Citibank but then it all just locked up."

They were smart men, all of them, and so they had the wit to keep down their voices. So they didn't shout. Instead, their mutters and whispers were jacked up an octave or more as concern turned to panic.

Drake was the least frightened man in the room at that moment. The others gaped at their computer screens like men seeing the end of everything.

"The cops are coming, all right," said Drake. "But not soon enough. My way is quicker."

Trower turned to him, furious now. "What did you do?"

Drake gestured to Trower's laptop. "Feel around in the back. You'll see."

Trower's fingers began a panicked scrabbling around the perimeter of his machine, freezing when they felt the nubby USB key that Drake had planted a few minutes before. Trower jerked it out, held it up. "What is this?"

"I have no idea," said Drake. "Got it from a friend of mine. Israeli. I'm not absolutely sure, but I've always suspected he worked on Stuxnet. You know—the software that crippled the Iranian nuclear centrifuges?" Drake smiled to see the dismay on Trower's face. "Yeah, you know."

"How do we clean it up?"

"No idea. I told him what I needed; he said, here you go. I do know it's in there somewhere, trashing all your files. Not just on that one machine, either. Whole network."

"He's right," hissed one of Trower's buddies. "I'm locked up here. Getting nothing."

The other four white men groaned, muttered, and swore, smacking at their keyboards. One by one, they slumped backward into their chairs, looking old, sick, scared.

"You know you're a dead man now, right?" said Trower.

"Yeah, more or less," said Drake. "Almost made it out, though."

"How?"

"Same way I came in. Busted basement window. While you were getting slapped around. But now, we're leaving through the front door, in sacks probably."

Drake's shrug melded into a shudder. He knew what was coming, and while he'd tamed his dread of the long darkness, he was helpless against the thought of the physical savagery to come. It was a bad thing to die. But to see his flesh tear and feel his bones shatter—this was the king of terrors.

He gave himself over to it and turned his full face to the horror. He felt his limbs tremble, his bowels liquefy. Tears stained his face.

And then he looked over at Trower, saw the man staring back in fear and wonder. And laughed. He couldn't help it. The look on his face! Trower was that stupid. He'd expected to live through this.

So had Astrid and Trace. He'd half expected to survive himself.

But then he remembered that they were all still alive. Maybe stupidity was stronger than death, after all. The fear fell away as the laughter rose within him, emerging in barking guffaws that bounced off the cinderblock walls of the room and out into the corridor.

The noise of it brought the two killers back. They stood in the room's fluorescent glare, and Drake saw surprise on their faces.

In a moment, Trower would explain the joke. A minute or so after that, Drake would be dead.

For a second, no more, Drake wondered what it would feel like. Then he focused, took a deep breath, and got ready.

CHAPTER TWENTY

"WHAT'S SO FUNNY?" asked Drake's interrogator.

Drake kept laughing. The blow to his torso a few minutes earlier had made breathing a chore, so he found it impossible to talk and laugh at the same time. And he had little to say in any case. Instead he just kept chortling, his head bowed forward, and gestured toward Trower.

The interrogator turned his gaze upon the white man. "Well?"

Trower held up the USB key. "We're screwed."

"What's that?"

"Poisonware." Trower nodded toward Drake. "He brought it."

"And you let him plug it in?" the Korean asked in a voice that simmered.

"Of course not. We found it in here. It's why he sneaked in. To plant it."

"What did it do?"

"Dunno. Just—everything's locked up. It's ignoring all our commands. We've lost control of the botnet. I can't even send an email."

There was silence for a moment. Then the interrogator turned his eyes upon Drake.

"Fix it. Now."

And that was how it began.

Drake replied the only way he could, that he had no means of repairing the damage. He added that he wouldn't help them even if he knew how. There was a certain pleasure in the act of bold defiance. Besides, Drake knew his insolence would not make matters worse. Nothing could make matters worse.

The short, scarred Korean nodded to his partner. The taller man walked around behind Drake's chair, grabbed his arms and hauled them back, pinning Drake to the chair. Then the scarred one took out a small, rather elegant knife. Drake had seen the type before. To give himself something to do, he goaded his memory, trying to recall the name of such a blade. A poniard? A dagger? What did they call those things?

The Korean used his free hand to grasp the front of Drake's shirt and rip it away, exposing Drake's chest. The Korean gazed down at him with appraisal in his eyes, like a man at a meatpacking plant eyeing the first carcass of the day. Then he reached forward, toward Drake's left armpit. Drake felt the knife tip dragging across his skin, to a point where his shoulder joint lay beneath his flesh. The knife paused.

The scarred face loomed a few inches away. At this range, Drake could see the man's calm had begun to fray. He saw sweat beginning to collect on his brow and the blood flushing up to the man's face.

Inches from Drake's face, the Korean said in nearly a whisper, "You fix this."

Drake said nothing. But he squirmed in his seat, as if trying to shove his left shoulder away from the knife and right through the back of the chair. It was wasted effort; the tall one held him fast.

So now there was nothing to do but what he did. Drake looked into the eyes of his tormentor, shook his head in refusal, and waited for the consequences.

He didn't know what the man did, only that it made the world disappear for an eternal time, to be replaced with a pearl-gray landscape of agony. Drake screamed, too loud, and the noise resounded off the cinderblock walls and tormented his ears, his personal contribution to his own misery.

It lasted forever, only it didn't, and the ending of it was the worst of all. It meant there was more.

"You fix this!" There was no cool reserve in the interrogator's voice. Not anymore. Now it was all rage and, yes, fear. What awaited him in Pyongyang if he returned with empty hands? The thought made Drake smile, just a small upward quirk of the lips, all he could manage just then. But at the sight of it, the Korean made an incoherent snarling sound and went back to work with the knife. Other shoulder this time.

There was more and more. The knife went in at different spots, and Drake felt his chest and torso dampen. The moisture was thick and heavy, and it crusted over, so that it cracked against his skin with each indrawn gasp of agony.

Yet as bad as it was, Drake could feel that the wounds were causing him no permanent harm. And however grim his thoughts were as he suffered, he was still able to think. The torturer wanted him miserable but still rational. He held out hope that Drake could still somehow fix all this. That Drake could save him from the consequences of failure.

So they were both doomed, then. There was justice in that, and the thought warmed him.

At last, he heard the Korean bark, "All right, then. Your choice." Drake could barely see straight by then, but he felt himself hoisted out of the chair and hauled toward the door. The massive Korean who'd held him fast during the torture was dragging him out of the room and down the corridor.

His head down, Drake saw nothing but grubby carpet as he was hauled along. From his recollection of the place, he knew they were headed toward the rear of the building. He realized their destination when he felt himself slammed against the panic bar that unlocked the rear stairway. The door sprang back under his weight. Drake fell through, fell down half a flight of steps, and came to rest on an intermediate landing. The silent Korean caught up with him there and completed Drake's journey to the basement with a shove from his booted foot.

He was nothing to them now, a sack of garbage, and without a word, they each grabbed an arm and dragged him to the door opening onto the basement. They hauled him toward the front of the building now, past cartons of computer gear, past reels of Ethernet wire, and past the room where Drake had made his entry, on and on, until surely they were about to run out of corridor. They dropped Drake to the floor and one of them fiddled with clinking keys, then unlocked a door.

Drake was being dragged again, across the threshold and into a room lit by fluorescent fixtures to a painful blue. It was just bare space. Cinderblock walls and a concrete floor. The brilliant blue illumination lent neither charm nor cheer; rather, it enhanced the ugliness of the last room

Drake would ever see.

He lay on the cold concrete floor in silence, looking up at his captors. At a gesture from the interrogator, the other stepped into the corridor. He came back about half a minute later pushing two office chairs on wheels. He rolled the chairs into the room and closed the door behind him. Then the two men grabbed Drake underneath his shoulders and hoisted him into one of the chairs.

The interrogator seated himself in the other chair, spun it toward his buddy. He muttered a few words, and the other big man left, no doubt off to terrorize the elderly men upstairs. The interrogator knew he did not need any more help handling Drake, after all.

The man spun around and rolled his chair toward Drake, putting them face to face. He seemed calm once again and spoke in a slow, placid, almost friendly voice.

"Hurts bad," he said. "I know. And I can do worse. Much worse. Believe me."

Drake nodded.

"But first I want to offer the easy way."

"Yeah. Always my preferred option," said Drake. "Definitely."

"So what you do is, you go back up there and override what you have done."

"And then you kill me."

"Maybe not. No need once we have the money."

"I can identify you."

"I'll be long gone."

"And your American friends upstairs? They'll talk."

"I doubt it," the interrogator said. "We pay them very well."

"Sure you will," said Drake. "You'll probably pay them off right in this very room." He looked around. "Yeah. No windows, nice thick walls. Nobody'll know a thing till the landlord comes around and notices the smell."

"Nobody's going to die here," the interrogator said, his voice stern now. "Not unless it's you."

"Yeah," said Drake. "You'll certainly outlive me, for a day or two anyway. New York to Pyongyang is a long trip. You go through Beijing, right?

So go in style. Get a first class seat and order big meals, because for the rest of your life you'll be eating grass."

It was a pointless provocation, but it struck home. The interrogator nodded. "Bad for me, yes. I might not survive it. That's why I don't care what happens to you. Live or die. We make a deal, we both benefit. I let you walk, maybe even give you money."

"Money?"

"Just petty cash. For expenses. At least $300,000. All yours."

"You really that desperate."

"Not about me." The big man sighed. "Look, you not stupid. You never get this far if you were. So I'm not gonna lie. If this thing goes bad, I'm in trouble. Real trouble."

"Looking at a demotion, huh?"

"Not about me. My wife. My child. That's how it works there. They know I can just keep running. They never find me. But there's a man outside my house every day. Once this goes bad, they go to work on my family."

"Big mistake, being a family man in your line of work."

"Only kind they use for such jobs. Family at home means we always come back."

"Then go back and save your family. Take the responsibility yourself."

"You know how they would kill me?" the big man said. "Might take weeks. Months. And not just me. They would still kill my whole family. Just to make an example. I fail, they die."

At that moment, Drake realized how little he had changed. All the prayers, the reading of scripture, the diligent performance of his diaconal duties had fooled everyone who knew him, maybe even Deacon Carter. But as he looked at the fearful face of his torturer and contemplated the terrible future of his far-off wife and child, Drake couldn't have cared less.

There was only room in Drake's heart for his own pain, his own fear, his own certainty that he was about to die in this barren room.

"So you see," the interrogator said, "you and I can help each other. Just give me what I want."

The man pleading with Drake for his life and that of his family would be cutting Drake's throat when he learned the truth. And that was all Drake had

271

left now. The truth, and the end. He said one last silent prayer and sighed.

"Same answer as always," he said. "I can't make it stop. Nobody can make it stop. So it's over. For all of us."

All fear and sorrow dropped from the interrogator's face then. He'd made up his mind. With a swift step he walked over to the chair, wrapped his left hand around Drake's mouth, drew his head back. Bluish light glinted off the blade upraised above his throat. And then the light vanished.

CHAPTER TWENTY-ONE

THE UTTER DARKNESS blinded and startled the killer, and Drake felt his grip loosen. In that instant, he kicked against the floor, spinning the chair that held him from the Korean's grasp. A moment after that, he rolled out of the chair and onto the floor, invisible in the absolute black.

Drake heard the Korean grunt and blurt out a word or two, something sharp and bitter. And a moment after that, Drake heard gunshots from the building above. The massacre had begun.

He had no idea what had happened to the lights. Maybe a side effect of the malware he'd fed to the computer network or maybe deliberate sabotage by Trower and his crew looking for a way out. Or maybe a drunk driver had taken down a power pole by sheer coincidence.

In any case it was the only chance Drake was going to get. He heard the killer rustling and thrusting through the room, checking the corners, hunting him down. He'd be listening for movement and waiting for the sound of the opening door, gun out, ready to fire.

Drake had hardly moved since rolling off the chair and had a fair idea where to find the door. As quietly as he could manage, he crawled toward the exit. He pressed his bare and bloodied chest against the cold concrete, and each forward thrust aroused the pain in half a dozen cruel, cunning wounds. But in silence Drake thrust on.

Just to his left he heard his captor flailing, but nearer, coming up on his left. Drake angled his crawl a little to the right to buy himself some space but kept moving toward the wall.

He hit it, felt cold cinderblock and nothing else. No door. It lay to the left or right. Surely left. But that was the way toward his pursuer. So Drake moved right till he felt himself in a corner. At once he crawled backward, pressing against the right-side wall of the room, then slid about five feet to the left and lay dead still.

As he'd thought, the Korean was also feeling for that corner. He was trying to be silent, but Drake heard his footfalls as he reached the same corner Drake had visited a few seconds before. Now the Korean too was pressed against the right wall and sliding backward into the room. Drake heard his shoes on the concrete about one foot from his head.

Drake waited until the Korean had walked a few more steps behind him. Then he drew himself up onto his feet and silently walked back toward the wall. He was there in a moment and began sliding left. Three steps carried him to the door. The way out.

There'd be noise, and a light in the corridor to show his silhouette. An interior door opening onto a corridor would open inward. Could he fling himself through the door before taking a bullet? Unlikely.

An option came to mind. One option only, and a dismal one, but it was all he had.

Drake stood on one foot and silently removed one of his shoes. He reared back and with all his strength flung it backward into the room.

If the shoe had somehow struck the Korean, it would have revealed Drake's position, and that would have ended it. Instead, Drake heard the big black Nike thud against the far wall. Half a second later, he flung the door open.

He winced in anticipation of the smashing impact of a bullet as he turned right, but no gunfire came. Just the footfalls of a man in instant pursuit.

The only light in the corridor came from the exit signs over the front and back stairwells, barely enough to navigate through an obstacle course of computer cartons. But Drake knew where he was going.

The stack of empty boxes lined against the corridor wall would have offered no protection against gunfire, even if they'd been full of computers. But Drake swatted at them as he ran, knocking a few into his pursuer's path. A couple of extra seconds was all he could hope for, but perhaps all he needed.

Head ducked low, he scrambled toward the door he'd taped open. He couldn't see it, due to the dark and to the stack of server boxes just outside it. But if Drake couldn't see it, his pursuer might miss it as well.

Drake flung himself against it and nearly fell into the room. His scrabbling fingers found the ends of the duct tape, ripped it away. He shoved hard against the door to lock it behind him.

And he could not, because the full bulk of the Korean slammed against him, hurling Drake backward into the room.

There was nothing now but death. Drake could lie there and wait for it or meet it halfway.

His hands and feet scrabbled on the slick concrete floor, desperate for a chance to stand. The move pushed Drake back toward the smashed-out window. In the dim wash of light that streamed in, he saw the huge man looming above him, motionless, poised to strike.

Drake felt something then, under his right hand. It was slick and flexible and it crunched a little as his weight came down upon it.

Drake knew what it was and he grabbed for its edge. His right hand missed its grip at first, but then he caught hold of it, swung it like a shield in front of him, and grasped the other edge of it in his left hand. Now his back was against the wall, and with his legs Drake pressed back against the cinderblock and shoved himself to his feet.

He was just in time to see a massive fist stroking like a piston for the side of his head. He did the only thing he could do and raised the sheet of duct tape in front of his face, gripping it tight, never minding the trivial pain as its lining of shattered glass ate into his fingers.

Drake's improvised shield deflected the blow and it landed on his upper skull. The violence of it whited out his brain, just for a moment, and after that every movement seemed to come in discrete steps, like a movie running through a projector frame by frame.

He heard the killer's breath huffing out as his fist hit the glass, then a little yelp of surprise and pain. And then Drake felt himself wrapping the taped-up glass around the man's arm, holding it tight, twisting and wrenching it against his flesh, grinding the glass into him. The man bellowed, flung his arm out, and cast Drake back to the floor.

And then the man began to dance, or so it seemed to Drake. He held his right arm out in front of him and grasped it with his left. Little gasps and groans came from him, as did the barking curse he'd uttered just a few seconds before. For just that moment, he'd forgotten about the man he'd come to kill.

The glass had hurt him bad enough to slow him down, but he was still standing. In seconds he'd finish the job.

Then Drake saw his hammer, the heavy rubber-headed mallet he'd used to break the glass. He scooped it from the floor and in the same motion brought it around to slam into the side of the man's head.

The Korean groaned, dropped to his knees. *Still too tall*, thought Drake. He swung again, harder. The man toppled onto his face.

Upstairs, Drake heard a confusion of voices and mixed in among them a long, bitter wail. Then through the shattered window he saw against the outer landscape the backscattered light from red and blue strobes.

THERE WERE TWO police SUVs out there and four officers crouched behind them, their pistols ready. All four looked up as Drake emerged from the rear of the building and jogged toward them. At the sight of the bloodied man, the officers' hands trained their guns toward the threat. Drake slowed his steps, raised his hands high above his head, flailing the fingers.

"Inside!" he shouted. "Hurry! He's killing them. Killing them . . ."

The cops let him draw nearer, till he was behind the small arc formed by the two police cars. But their guns never wavered till Drake was behind cover. Then came the command, "Down! Face down!"

It was just the thing Drake longed for—a little rest. So he complied without a murmur, sprawling his arms and legs wide, relishing the cool of the asphalt pavement against his naked chest. The policeman who cuffed him wasn't gentle about it, but he'd expected no less. They were welcome just the same. He'd had enough.

"Your name Drake?" The words came from a different officer a little farther away. Perhaps the man in charge.

"That's me," he replied. "ID in my back pocket."

"Okay," the voice said. "Keep him cuffed, but sit him up."

That's exactly backward, thought Drake, who'd have been glad to lie there all day if they'd just unbind him.

The officer who'd cuffed him was gentle about helping Drake to rest his back against one of the cars. He must have decided that it pays to be courteous, especially when the person you're manhandling might be somebody who mattered.

The cop in charge was a tall, stocky white man, wearing sergeants' stripes and the uniform of the New York State Police.

"We got a call from Boston, said someone named Drake was being held against his will."

"Glad to meet you. Look, something bad's going on in there. You're going to need an ambulance, maybe several. And the FBI. Don't go charging in, though. There's a guy with a gun. Two of them, come to think of it. Big guys. Asian. I left one lying in the basement. He'll be out of it for a while, but not long. The other one's—I don't know which room, but he's in there somewhere."

"Somebody meeting that description took a couple shots at us as we pulled up, ducked back inside," the officer said

"You better get to him quick. They were holding other people, six of them. Before you arrived, I heard gunshots."

The commander got on his radio to call for more units, while his partner went to the rear hatch and pulled out a short-barreled Armalite. He whistled through his teeth to the other pair who stood near the second car.

"Active shooter!" he shouted. "One of you hold this guy. The other, on me!"

There was a moment of disputation between the other pair, each no doubt arguing for the honor of walking into a shooting gallery. But it was settled in seconds, and Drake found himself in the company of a thin, gray-haired officer. While his partner went into the trunk for his rifle, the officer came over to Drake, looking serious and competent but also a little shamefaced.

"I figure, let the kid go in," he said, as if Drake had asked for an explanation. "I've kicked plenty of doors in my time. The thrill is gone."

Drake just shrugged.

The cop's buddies chambered rounds and stacked up outside the door. The sergeant's arm knifed forward and the three men disappeared inside.

The last cop gestured to Drake, opened the back door of his SUV. "Get in," he said.

Drake had no objection. He climbed inside. A moment later, the cop drew his weapon, pointed at the pavement, his finger off the trigger.

DRAKE HEARD MORE gunshots, seven or eight at least. The other Korean making a last stand, Drake figured.

The old cop who guarded him raised his weapon, leaned toward the open doorway, but made no move to enter. Minutes passed with no more shots, and the policeman lowered his guard.

Drake watched the door for a bit, then sighed, closed his eyes to rest. As he so often did, he thought of aircraft, their power and elegance and rigor. At any given moment there were thousands of them in the air, and just then Drake would have liked to be on any given one of them. Even Lagos to Abuja, one more time. Maybe if he'd shown up on Alicia's doorstep like this, wounded and bleeding in an honorable cause, she'd have thought twice about him. Not taken him back, maybe. Too late for that. But she might have thought about it for a minute or two. She might have at least considered the possibility that she'd written him off too soon.

It was a pleasant fantasy, though impractical. How would he get aboard the plane? Nobody would fly him anywhere in his present condition. He'd have to get cleaned up, get a little first aid. Maybe a night's sleep and a morning's good breakfast. There were good diners in upstate New York. He'd find one. Buckwheat pancakes if he was lucky. Not many places served them these days. Yes. Buckwheat pancakes and scrambled eggs.

The clunking sound seemed to come from a block away. But it was right by his ear—the sound of the SUV's door opening. Hands reached in and nudged him.

"You all right?"

"Huh? Oh. Fine. Just fell asleep."

The old cop helped Drake out of the vehicle, stood him upright, turned him around, and removed the cuffs.

"All clear," he said. "No more shooters. But it's a mess. Three dead. Another one's shot but alive. Four others okay. Locked themselves in a room. Shooter was trying to get at them when we showed up."

It was welcome news. With so many surviving conspirators, the FBI would stitch this up quick. Soon Drake could start typing. Three or four days at least on the front page.

All of them would talk, of course. Was Trower still among them? He'd surely have a good story to tell. Or was he one of the three who'd died?

"So just one hostage lost?" he asked.

"Yeah, and another wounded. Our guys neutralized the shooter, then they swept the building. Found another Chinese guy dead in the basement."

CHAPTER TWENTY-TWO

THE AFTERNOON ANCHOR on CNN affected his most solemn tone as he described the crisis at four of the nation's major banks. It was as if the stolen money—$8 billion at least—had come from the man's personal account.

Drake lay back in his hospital bed, judging the performance. That's all it was, surely. The man on the screen must have felt what all journalists feel while covering hurricanes, earthquakes, or terrorist attacks. Yes, there was a generic sort of regret for the unfortunate victims. But mainly, he'd feel himself fortunate to be on deck when the disaster struck.

For Drake, who'd been in the midst of it, it might have meant a Pulitzer or some such, under different circumstances. But not now. He was out of it now.

He wondered at how little he cared. Perhaps his illness was getting worse. Perhaps he was becoming indifferent not only to the needs and desires of others but also to his own.

Or maybe he was still numb. There'd been drugs, of course, administered in the emergency room to hold him still for the inevitable stitching-up. But his emptiness went well beyond the pharmacological.

The interrogator was dead, and Drake had killed him. That had not been the plan. Drake had only wanted to escape. His blows had only been intended to stun him and buy Drake time to race out the door and seek invisibility in the woods.

In fact, the blows hadn't killed the Korean, or so said one of the EMTs who'd arrived not long after Drake's escape. The man bled to death, an artery carved open by a bit of broken glass. It was a manageable wound. The Korean could have stopped the bleeding himself without too much trouble. But then Drake clubbed him into unconsciousness and left him there to bleed out.

He'd killed a man by accident. And the man's wife and child now faced a slow and ugly death.

And yet, for Drake, there was no horror. None at the thought of the deaths of innocents, none at the thought of the blood on his own hands as he'd shoved another man into the pit. For his victims, Drake felt nothing at all.

Years ago, after a savage dispute with Alicia, he'd realized that her love had failed to change him. There was lust in him, more than enough. And there was pride, the urge to possess a woman of such charm and beauty. He'd interpreted these feelings as love and thanked God that he had at last received a heart of flesh.

But that night he'd known the truth. His heart was the same as ever. Alicia, who'd been deceived at first by his playacting, had seen the truth soon enough, and fled from him. The way she'd left had made people put the blame on her. But Drake knew better.

Ever since that time, Drake had renewed his experiments in compassion and mercy, his stumbling efforts to do right for the right reasons. There'd been prayer and study of scripture and the performance of good works— dishing up meals at the food pantry, a stint tutoring convicts. Noble deeds that had gotten Drake nominated for the diaconate.

That it was all sham and fakery was obvious to Drake, but when he tried to say as much to Pastor Rink, he wasn't having any. What mattered, the pastor said, was what you do, not how you feel.

Well, now Drake had taken a life, and maybe a couple more. That's what he'd done. And how did he feel? Right now, he felt like lunch. And he felt like eating it alone.

THE FBI TURNED up by late afternoon. It had taken that long to round up the special agent who'd interviewed Drake back in Minnesota.

The nuisance of having to travel from middle-of-nowhere Minnesota to back-of-beyond New York State seemed to trouble the man not one bit. For now he was working the biggest case of his career.

As before, Drake told him not quite everything. He'd found his way to Trower's data center not through an illegal phone intercept, but through an anonymous source he'd been cultivating. Drake refused to say any more and the special agent didn't press. After all, he had no reason to care. As for the assistance of the deacons' group, he said not one word.

But Drake did speak about Efron and his poisoned USB drive. The man would revel in the free publicity, and in any event he'd earned it.

And Drake admitted to breaking into the building and planting the drive. Crimes, both of them. Somehow, he doubted there'd be the slightest interest in prosecuting him for having saved the US banking system.

The FBI agent was the chatty sort, so Drake learned as much as he revealed. The hacker team in Binghamton had quite a backstory, it seemed.

Trower was among the dead; apparently he'd led the abortive attempt to escape the building, complete with the short-circuiting of the electrical system, a move that had saved Drake's life and several others too.

Trower was a bold man, an army veteran who'd ridden a tank into the great showdown at 73 Easting during the First Gulf War. He came home, earned a degree in network systems, and worked for twenty years at the data security unit of IBM, only to get washed out during one of that company's occasional downsizings, along with several friends, some of them guys even older than Trower, all of them convinced they'd been dumped because of the respectable paychecks that came with their seniority.

Talking it over with his unemployed colleagues, Trower realized that he wasn't the only one of them who felt cheated. And further conversations revealed a willingness to share their misery, while finding a new way to make a living.

Thus was born Smoothbore, a black-hat operation specializing in financial hacks. In the past five years, Smoothbore had managed to lift about $20 million through unauthorized bank transfers and credit card fraud. They generally worked on their own account but weren't averse to hiring out their skills to larger criminal syndicates. So when an unknown party named Stainless got in touch and offered a hundred thousand dollars in up-front money for a plan to hit some bank, Trower was willing to listen. And when the hundred thousand in bitcoin showed up in Trower's digital wallet, Smoothbore went to work.

Stainless was, of course, Severins. It would be good to know how he'd been recruited. And since the FBI had detained him as he was about to board a nonstop to Beijing, they'd wring the truth out of him soon enough.

Later that evening, Drake dialed Carter.

"About time. I knew you were alive, but that was all. Local cops didn't say much."

"I expect that's the FBI's doing."

"Yeah, but they told me about the fatalities."

"I don't know what to tell you. It wasn't supposed to happen. I just wanted to get out of there."

Carter was silent for a long time.

"You did that?"

"Just one of them. It was an accident."

"Oh man. I didn't know."

"Not proud of it," said Drake. "Not ashamed, either. Like I told you, I'm not in the habit of caring."

"Sounds to me like you do. You sound miserable."

"Only because I don't want to be a killer. It's not a good thing to be, is it?"

"No, it isn't."

"You ever kill anybody?"

"Not even close. I've been lucky."

"Yes, you have been."

A DAY LATER, Drake strode out of the hospital in Binghamton, with a few new scars. The police had impounded his rental car, but they returned it readily enough. It had been searched, but everything was still in place, including the laptop he'd tucked under the rear seat. Drake climbed aboard and drove back to the Ithaca airport. Two hours later, he was in Boston again.

An Uber got him to Boston Medical. There was a uniformed cop outside the room who glanced at Drake's ID, then at his face. He nodded and let him pass.

Astrid's eyes were closed, and under the harsh overhead light, the skin of her face seemed gray, autumnal. Even the lotus tattoo beneath her chin had faded. Her arms were skeletal, as if someone had poked a hole and drained all the muscle out.

One of her nurses had warned him. An infection from the Minnesota lake was riding her hard and draining her strength. But Drake hadn't expected this. He stood silent, doubtful about rousing her. He decided to give her peace and turned to leave.

"Weldon?" She spoke his Christian name in a dusty croak.

"Right here. Thought you were out."

"In and out. Comes and goes."

"Yeah. Nurse says you're pretty sick. But nothing they can't fix. Give it a couple of weeks."

"Time enough to find a lawyer."

"I suppose," said Drake. "I don't know how that works."

"Me neither, but I'm learning all kinds of things."

"We'll figure it out." He thought to suggest a chat with her father; he was an attorney, after all. But he thought better of it. "I'll help any way I can."

"Thanks," said Astrid. "But I'll manage." For all the weakness of her voice, the words sounded decisive. Final.

"What about Trace? How's he making out?"

"He's not," said Astrid. "He's in Minneapolis. Near his family. Still hasn't woke up. Maybe he never will. Lost too much blood." She sighed. "Trying to save me."

"To save us," said Drake. "We both owe him. Anything I can do?"

"You a doctor now?" said Astrid. Her lips quirked upward in a parody of the old, skeptical smile. "Let it go, Weldon. Let it all go. Forget about us. You have my permission."

It was as if Drake had once more been dashed into that cold Minnesota lake. "Forget about you? Why would I do that?"

"You will, soon enough," said Astrid. "It's who you are. You think I

284

don't know? You're pretty good. But you're not that good."

Drake had no words for his dismay.

"MIT is full of people like you. Men and women. Lots of brains, not much heart. They can simulate empathy and compassion, so they won't die horny and alone. You're no different, except you've also got that religion of yours. You think it's a sin not to care, but you can't help it. You're born that way."

"People change." Drake spoke just above a whisper.

"Not enough."

Drake didn't have much to say after that, so he sat in silence and waited. In time, he heard Astrid's breathing grow deep and regular. In silence, he rose and departed.

THE RED LINE brought him home. There Drake picked up his Ford and drove it back to the *Record*. The rear parking lot was nearly full, but Drake wedged his way in.

Near the door sat the usual stack of US Mail tubs. Drake grabbed a stack and lugged them toward his desk. There he settled into his chair, booted up his computer, and began purging files, even wiping the contents of his shared network folder. He backed up his emails, address book, and calendar, stashed the file into his personal Dropbox account. Everything else that mattered was already there, so his work was soon done.

After that, Drake began sorting the contents of his desk into the mail tubs. He'd been at the task for nearly half an hour before Steve Ginsburg appeared. "What the hell you doing? Why aren't you typing?"

"No welcome home?" said Drake.

"You know you're welcome. Especially with the story you've got to tell."

"No," said Drake. "It's a story I've got to not tell."

"Not tell? These guys made war on the country, broke two or three banks, and killed a bunch of people. And you were in the middle of it."

"Right in the middle of it." Drake picked up a Lucite cube representing some long-forgotten journalism award. He considered tossing it but decided it might matter to him someday. So it fell into one of the tubs.

"It's pure Pulitzer. Front pages for at least a week. National TV interviews. You're about to become a star."

"Not going to happen, Steve. Sorry."

Ginsburg opened his mouth to reply. But his eyes were fixed on Drake's face, and something he saw there made him shut up. Instead he stood silent for about half a minute, watching Drake pack.

"So you're leaving." It wasn't a question.

"I can't stay. I'm a journalist. I'm supposed to tell the story. That's my job. And this story I can't tell." Drake shut a now-empty desk drawer, shoving it a little too hard so that it made a tympanic boom. "I can't write about the people who helped me or the laws I broke. And I'm never going to write about the man I killed."

Drake had heard of white people going pale. For the first time in his life, he saw it happen.

There was an unoccupied desk nearby. Ginsburg grabbed its chair, dragged it over, fell into it.

"I didn't know."

"Yeah. The cops are being stingy with details, which is fine with me. You I owe, so I'm giving you a heads-up. Please keep it to yourself. I know it'll come out eventually. But not now and not here."

"Self-defense, right?"

"If it wasn't, I'd be in a cage. As it is, they think I'm some kind of hero. Maybe so. But I don't want to be that kind of hero."

"You feel bad. That makes you a decent person."

"I don't feel bad. The man had it coming, and I gave it to him. Not on purpose, but he's just as dead. And I couldn't care less."

Drake sighed, leaned back in his chair. "That's the kind of hero I turned out to be," he said.

"You feel guilty about that?"

"No. I don't feel guilty. But I am guilty." Drake finished emptying out the top drawer. He shrugged, smiled. "None of this is your problem, of course. You've just got to get a paper out the door. But that paper is supposed to report the truth, and I'm in no position to tell the truth. Under those circumstances, having me on staff would put us both in an impossible bind. So I'm out."

Ginsburg had no words for a while. He just shook his head and watched Drake pack. At last, he asked, "What will you do?"

"Freelance, I figure. Or pick a different career altogether. I've got a little money saved and a few ideas."

"Dying industry anyway," said Ginsburg, his eyes fixed on the scruffy carpet.

"Just keep typing. Man is born to trouble, and we'll always want to read about it—our own or somebody else's. And you've got a great Boston story to chase. You want to get to the bottom of what happened, put somebody good on it. Fitz would be my choice. Best crime reporter in town. But when you send him to talk to me, don't be surprised if all he gets is 'no comment.'"

THE NEXT FEW of days, Drake stuck close to home, eating and sleeping. He discovered a new capacity for sleep, and a man who'd hopped out of bed after six hours now flopped onto his living room sofa at 7:00 p.m. and didn't come around until noon the next day.

Evenings, he flipped on the TV, looking for something. On Tuesday, he tried and failed for the fourth time to develop an interest in a TV show about a hoodie-wearing hacker. There was too little about his efforts to raid the ultrasecure network of a global corporation and far too much about the hacker's vacuous, drug-addled private life. No doubt the writers were trying to make the fellow seem more interesting. But self-pity and substance abuse seemed to Drake two of mankind's dullest pursuits.

After a while, Drake gave up and went flying. He launched his 737 simulator, the one from Ukraine, and began working up a proper flight plan, Boston to Denver, because he felt like mountains. He found a nice one ready-made at Simbrief.com and uploaded it directly into the sim. Drake marched step by step through the preflight and taxi checklists, then touched a microphone button and called for pushback clearance. A make-believe ground controller—an actual person running an ATC sim—came through with permission and taxi instructions, and Drake began a leisurely progress toward Runway 27 Left.

This was more like it. The big dual monitors showed everything: the sky, the twinkling waters of Boston Harbor, the constant takeoffs and landings of other aircraft, each under the active control of another Internet-connected human. The surround-sound speakers filled Drake's ears with the hum and purr of an active cockpit, with radio calls to and from a dozen other aircraft.

Within three minutes, Drake had no thought for his wounds, his losses, or his sins. There was nothing now but the keening engines, the glory of Boston Harbor falling away beneath him, the great, grand left turn that took him over land and brought the nose of the aircraft around toward the hazy glow of the west.

Then Drake heard a noise he hadn't heard in a long time. A soft trilling sound that came from just beyond the bedroom door. At first he thought it was from the flight sim. Perhaps a warning that he'd neglected to tuck in flaps or a reminder to shut down the APU. He was beginning to scan the instrument readings in his simulated cockpit when he remembered the true source of the sound. Drake slapped the space bar to freeze the simulation, then walked out of the bedroom and over to the intercom.

He barely remembered how to use the thing, so rarely had he entertained visitors. But the first move was simple enough. He pressed the button marked Talk.

"Yeah?"

"It's me." Carter's voice.

"You bring beer?"

"Something else."

"Hang on."

Buzzing him in was harder to figure out, but in thirty seconds or so, it came to him. Drake held down the button for a good long while, just in case. Then he strolled to his front door, unlocked it, left it ajar. He strolled back to the bedroom and hit the space bar.

Drake wondered for a moment if he should putter around the kitchen for a bit, trying to assemble some sort of refreshment tray for his guest. Drake had seen such things done in TV shows and movies, and by his ex-wife, so he knew the right moves. But it would have been no more than that. He remembered how Alicia would invite people over from time to time, her genuine pleasure at preparing food and drink for her guests. Her guests, not his.

Drake was confident he could have put on a convincing show. He'd played so many roles over the past few weeks: journalist, deacon, rescuer, killer. He could carry off the part of the gracious host. But as he steeled himself to smile, it occurred to him that there wasn't a thing in the house. No drinks. No snacks. Just a couple packages of frozen chicken.

Drake smiled and relaxed. The performance was canceled. He spent the next couple of minutes watching the simulated landscape of upstate New York rolling beneath his digital aircraft.

Though the door was partway open, Carter was polite enough to knock. Drake froze the sim once more, rose from his chair, walked to his front door.

Carter hadn't knocked. It was Boo Hendricks who stood in the doorway, with Carter just behind him.

"Brought a guest," Carter said.

"Hoped you wouldn't mind," said Boo.

Drake threw the door wide, ushered them in.

"I wasn't expecting to receive guests," he said. "No eats, no drinks. I could order out for something."

"Forget it," said Boo. "I know you've been busy. Just wanted to look in on you. Make sure you're okay."

"Healing," said Drake. "Give me a week before I hit the weight room."

"I suppose you'll be spending a lot of time with the FBI."

"Yeah, I'll be chatting with them again next week."

"We'd appreciate it if you could keep the deacons' organization out of it."

"Well, not completely out of it," said Carter. "If you're asked about funding and support for your little adventure, tell them it came out of the deacons' fund at Reliant. It's true, technically speaking. And the church has the right to spend that money however it sees fit."

Boo nodded. "It's the larger organization I'm thinking about. It's been under the radar for over a century, and we'd just as soon keep it that way."

"I get that," replied Drake. "That's one reason I won't be writing this story for the *Record*. Matter of fact, I won't be writing anything for them."

"What, they promote you to editor?" Carter grinned as he said it.

"No. I'm out."

Carter stared. "You quit?"

"The job just doesn't fit anymore," said Drake. "It's like, I've crossed a line."

"The death," said Boo.

"A nice way to put it," said Drake. "Makes it sound like natural causes. But I was the cause."

"And you did nothing wrong," said Carter. "It was him or you."

"Now tell me something I don't know. I was there, remember?"

"Yeah," said Boo, and sighed. "It didn't sit well with some of the others."

"Second thoughts about inducting me?"

"A few, yes. Deacon Grant—you remember him?—he said that this killing might be a sign from God, a sign that you don't belong among us. He's afraid that you are a man of wrath."

Drake was taken aback by his own reaction—the surprise, the hurt.

"I didn't act in anger. I acted to save myself. And I never intended his death." Drake realized that he sounded plaintive. He was pleading.

"I know," said Boo. "And I went to bat for you. So did Barnes and Harrison, by the way. We see how you carried this through. All the way. No limit. When somebody like that comes along, you don't turn him away."

Drake sighed, relaxed. "I can't even tell you why. I just know I had to keep going."

"For your friend," said Carter. "For Astrid. That's why."

"I'm not so sure."

"Because you're heartless, right?" said Carter. "Sure. Suit yourself. But for whatever reason, you got the job done. So you're in."

"Thank you." At that moment, it was all Drake could think to say.

"Meanwhile, I understand you're out of a job," said Hendricks. "How long you planning to stay unemployed? I can find something for you, no problem. Here in Boston or anywhere you want."

"Oh, I'm not going anywhere," said Drake. "I have responsibilities at Reliant. I'm a deacon, you know."

There wasn't much to say after that. Boo chatted up this idea he'd been working on, a software project that just might bring in his next billion. Drake listened, smiled, brought forth a few encouraging words. Boo seemed satisfied with his performance, but Carter knew him better. He stuck out his hand, said he would have to be in court in the morning.

The door closed behind them; their steps receded down the hallway. Drake returned to the spare bedroom, to the monitor screen where a simulated airliner waited for him in a simulated sky.

Drake seated himself, reached for the joystick. Then, spurred by a memory, he took up his cell phone instead. The number came up after a quick search. Sister Nadine Walker, member of Reliant for forty years, trapped by a shattered hip, hungry for a word of blessing. He'd been bringing Sister Walker a communion wafer when a phone call from Carter diverted him to Astrid's hospital bed. Drake had forgotten Sister Walker since, his duties neglected in a welter of blood and fear.

And lack of heart. Just then Drake saw himself as plainly as Astrid had at their final meeting. But she hadn't condemned him. And Drake decided that he would be at least as merciful to himself. He had to start somewhere.

So he prayed over the phone for forgiveness, and for a deacon's heart. And then he dialed.

ABOUT THE AUTHOR

Hiawatha Bray is an award-winning technology reporter and columnist for the Boston Globe. He's the author of "You Are Here," a history of modern navigation.

Bray is also a deacon at Peoples Baptist Church of Boston, one of the nation's oldest African-American congregations.

Born in Chicago, he lives in the suburbs of Boston with his wife and three children.

Mariush - 32fu040 Kindle...

Boo Kendricks -
Robert F smith
Vision Equity Partners ?
- referred to by first
name - Beyond

- Totally scrutiny
- African American
- Tech Reporter
- from Chicago

- on the spectrum

- grew up poor

- Tried to kill father?
- Divorced?

- familiarity w/ Africa
- Fascinated w/ pilot training software
- Church deacon

- overlap w/
WSJ is Reporter

Names of Public real ?

|| Does to care)

Isaac Asimov - Foundation

|| 1890 - Klim - models?

Personal
priority

Dr Sevrus ?
Cassandra ?

CPSIA information can be obtained
at www.ICGtesting.com
Printed in the USA
BVHW080331260921
617490BV00008B/108

9 780578 943244